CELESTIAL SPHERES BOOK #1

FYR

LISA BORNE GRAVES

AUTHORS 4 AUTHORS PUBLISHING
Marysville, WA, USA

Published by Authors 4 Authors Publishing
1214 6th St
Marysville, WA 98270
www.authors4authorspublishing.com

Library of Congress Control Number: 2019943577

E-book ISBN: 978-1-64477-021-4
Paperback ISBN: 978-1-64477-022-1
Audiobook ISBN: 978-1-64477-023-8

Edited by Brandi Spencer
Copyedited by Renee Frey and Brandi Spencer

Front cover labradorite illustration ©2019 Matthew Graves. All rights reserved. Design and layout by Brandi Spencer.

Authors 4 Authors Publishing branding is set in Bavire. Titles, headings, and map are set in Mr Darcy. Handwriting is set in URW Chancery. All other text is set in Garamond.

FYR

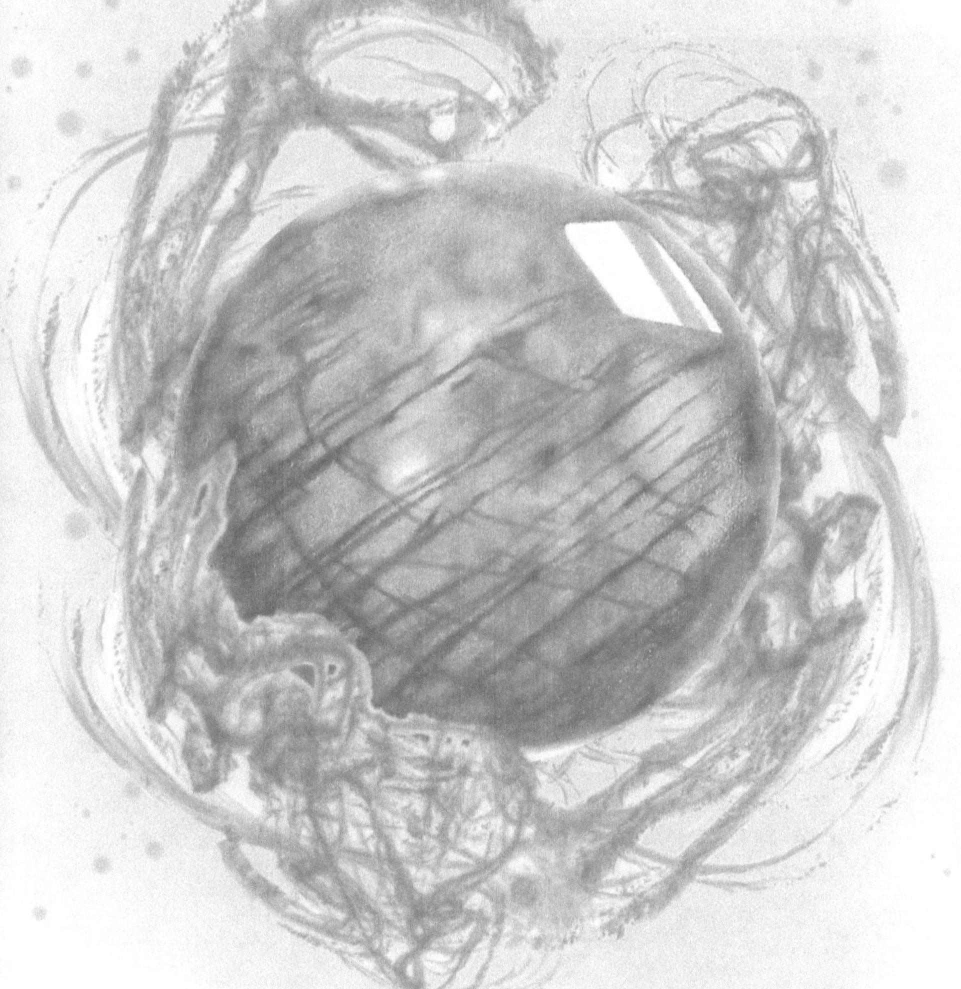

LISA BORNE GRAVES

Authors 4 Authors Content Rating

This title has been rated 17+, appropriate for older teens and adults, and contains:

- frequent intense kissing
- moderate implied sex
- intense violence
- domestic violence
- moderate positive and negative alcohol use
- moderate language

Please, keep the following in mind when using our rating system:

1. A content rating is not a measure of quality.

Great stories can be found for every audience. One book with many content warnings and another with none at all may be of equal depth and sophistication. Our ratings can work both ways: to avoid content or to find it.

2. Ratings are merely a tool.

For our young adult (YA) and children's titles, age ratings are generalized suggestions. For parents, our descriptive ratings can help you make informed decisions, but at the end of the day, only you know what kinds of content are appropriate for your individual child. This is why we provide details in addition to the general age rating.

For more information on our rating system, please, visit our Content Guide at: www.authors4authorspublishing.com/books/ratings

Dedication

To my husband, for all the laughter, support, endless optimism, and productive "painting-writing parties" that made this book possible.

Works by Lisa Borne Graves

Celestial Spheres

Fyr
Draca
Bladesung

The Immortal Transcripts

Quiver
Fever
Shudder (February 2023)

Stand-alone Titles

Apidae
"Dare"

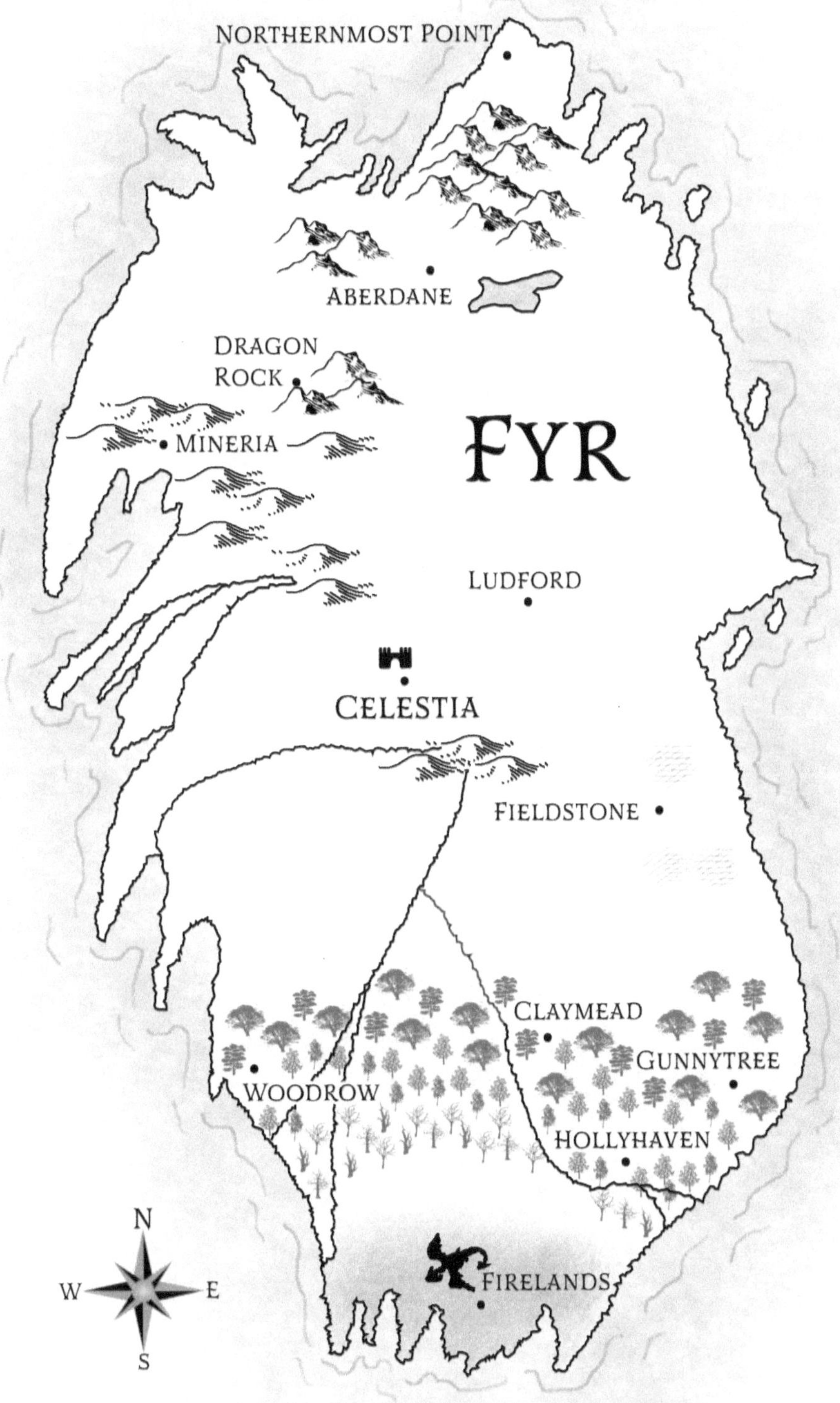

NORTHERNMOST POINT
ABERDANE
DRAGON ROCK
MINERIA
FYR
LUDFORD
CELESTIA
FIELDSTONE
CLAYMEAD
GUNNYTREE
WOODROW
HOLLYHAVEN
FIRELANDS
N
W
E
S

TABLE OF CONTENTS

TABLE OF CONTENTS

PROLOGUE

Ruby hurried through the market at a brisk pace, as if busy instead of running for her life in a full-out sprint. She didn't want them to realize she knew she was being followed. She pulled the hood tighter around her neck, hoping to obscure her face and lose them in the crowd. Fate was on her side, for her cloak and dress fit in pretty well at this historical-seeming playground—or some type of educational environment—where a lot of people were dressed as if it were long ago for these earthlings. The guests, or students, were dressed differently than the staff, the boys and girls similarly favoring the durable leggings they called skinny jeans.

Her eyes scanned the crowd, looking for the girl whose light she could sense. Ruby didn't know who this girl was, nor why she was in the Earth sphere, but she knew this girl was one of her kind since intense light magic pulsated within her. It was the only beacon of magic Ruby could see for miles, the powerless humans of this sphere having such dull, toneless appearances. After she had found the girl yesterday, she planned to meet her and impart all her knowledge, explain her plight, and give her the stone. Early this morning, Ruby realized that her enemies had found her. She imparted all of her wisdom and power into the stone, a dangerous move because if her pursuers got ahold of the stone, they'd have the power to either destroy or save her people. She knew enough about them to know which choice they would make. It was imperative for Ruby to get the stone to this girl without them seeing the transfer.

Ruby rounded the corner and saw the power emanating from the girl. She looked just like a normal teenage Earth girl, dressed in those skinny jeans and a light jacket, her black hair half fastened back as if it wouldn't stay put, her skin tone darker than Ruby's. She was with her friends, chatting away, yet she would become someone much more vital. Ruby slowed down and meandered over until she was right next to her. Ironically, the girl was browsing a stand of gemstones and jewelry as if she innately sensed the magic within the power stones. This could work. Her enemies would think she tossed the stone in these baskets and have to search for ages.

Wasting no time, she slipped the stone unobserved into the girl's shoulder bag and leaned forward to examine the stones for sale. Even the stones in this realm were weaker than in her world. The girl moved on and away while Ruby lingered at the stand a bit longer.

Soon, the kids were being rounded up and put on buses. She stayed long enough to watch the girl get on the bus and for it to pull away. She sighed with relief as she saw the distance between the stone and her enemies growing. She just hoped it all worked out, that the girl found the stone and that her family found the girl. As a firebrander, Ruby could read the future in flames. The visions had shown her this was the right path, the only path, but no firebrander could foresee a future that stretched beyond her lifetime, and the flames showed nothing past this moment. Ruby knew what that meant as well, so there was no point in prolonging the inevitable. She walked away from the fairgrounds, toward the woods, her steps more confident than her mind. Her enemies would never let her rest until they had the stone and her powers. And as soon as they found out she had cast them all into the stone and given it away, they would kill her, because their kind took no mercy, no prisoners, and they knew that no matter how much torture she was subjected to, she would never betray her people.

LABRADORITE

Toury was utterly exhausted after the school's field trip to the Renaissance Faire and was almost falling asleep on the bus ride home. She was such a history nerd that she had loved every minute of it, feeling as if she had stepped into one of those historical romance novels her mother read and had no clue Toury borrowed. She could easily imagine herself a damsel in distress, her hero—no, that wouldn't do. Toury was no helpless maiden. She would save the hero instead.

"That was a bore," Jenny said.

"Absolutely," Amanda agreed.

Toury kept her mouth shut and stared out the window. She had to hide her love of reading and history, for one never exposed such weaknesses as a love of learning to her friends. Her friends. She called them that, but she didn't really fit in with them. They didn't fit in either, being too rebellious, awkward, dorky, or just not athletic or beautiful. Toury, not having a place, fell in line with them. Looking around at the five of them, she admitted it was a motley crew that was pretty far down the social ladder. It was one without loyalty, ready to throw each other to the wolves if it meant surviving the high school social war front. She had never felt like she belonged in her entire life—at school, with other kids, even her family—so this town and school were no different. It was only temporary. Her father was in the Coast Guard, and they moved every couple of years or so. She preferred it that way, for when she hated a school, they'd move soon enough.

When they arrived back at the school, Jenny and Amanda climbed into Jenny's beat-up Honda Civic, along with Tad, Will, and Fiona. They ignored her, except Will.

"Can we squeeze Toury in?" he asked.

Jenny looked at her without much sympathy. "I'm sorry, not getting a ticket for overloading the car."

"It's fine." Toury shrugged. She was used to walking home because riding the bus as a senior was rough. She'd rather walk the mile home.

Will gave her a pitying smile but then was laughing a second later as Jenny sped off. She had a feeling Jenny didn't like her and only put up with her because of Will. And Will only liked Toury because he thought she was pretty. Some start to the school year. Maybe she would welcome a mid-year move, despite graduating in eight months.

School was only a bit worse than home, so she enjoyed a purposely prolonged walk. Toury sighed, bolstering herself, and trudged through the front door of her house. Her mother and father were standing in the kitchen, arguing again. They were headed for a divorce. The negative energy evoked by their fights weighed heavily on her, the thick tension smothering her when she entered the house. It could only be better for all of them if they split. She wasn't sure which one to live with. Neither of them, if she had a choice. Maybe she would emancipate herself. She was seventeen after all. She didn't think she could wait another ten months, until her eighteenth birthday, to be free of them.

"Toury," her father said, nodding to at least acknowledge her. It was a rare occurrence for him to note her existence.

Her mother simply glared at her father still, lips pursed and arms crossed for battle. She didn't even give Toury a glance.

"Dad," she said, returning the nod. She grabbed a soda can out of the fridge, noticing her presence wasn't wanted, for they stopped arguing once she walked in.

"Toury, could you please go upstairs?" her mother commanded more than asked, still not looking at her.

She rolled her eyes at them and left the room. "I can still hear your bickering up there," she muttered as she stomped up the steps, well-knowing she was acting like a petulant child. Well, if they were going to act immature, so would she. For added effect, she slammed her bedroom door. They must be bickering about her. They never cared otherwise about her overhearing their daily spats. Whatever they could find fault with, they would, and then they'd argue about it until it ended in broken vases and cars screeching out of the drive.

Toury threw herself on the bed in a huff and stared at the ceiling, contemplating. She couldn't figure out why her parents were still together, or even why they had adopted her in the first place, except her mother alluded to her being thrust upon them. By whom was the mystery. Toury's last name didn't match theirs. When she'd inquired at the tender age of five, she was bluntly told she was adopted, and her birth parents' stipulation was Toury had to keep her "weird" names so "she would know her place in the universe." She was stuck with Tourmaline Hematite and ridiculed beyond belief for it. Not to mention her eyes. She had gray eyes—not an interesting blue-gray, but a solid steel gray. Freaky eyes. Her own gaze sometimes weirded her out in the mirror, and if she was unnerved by herself, it only meant other people most likely thought worse.

Her parents always thought she was odd, and they never wanted her. And she never wanted them. As a child, it hurt, as all she wanted was someone's love. This desire for love faded with the realization she may never get it, and she grew strong, shying away from affection, friends, and boys. She didn't need them because dreaming about things that couldn't come true only broke her, and depending on others only disappointed her when they broke promises. She was safer in her bubble. Except her parents' raised voices burst her bubble and attacked her solitude, throwing barbs at the emotional fortress she was enclosed in, threatening to break her again.

Yes, she'd had enough. She would get herself out of here, emancipated. She would need a lawyer then. She leaned over and went into her purse to grab her phone to look one up when her fingers brushed up against something cold and smooth. She pulled it out and examined it. A stone, a completely perfect sphere about the size of a jawbreaker, lay in the palm of her hand. It was blue for the most part but had reds, browns, and yellows swirled through it. It looked kind of like a tiny Earth.

She felt it spark in her hand. Toury dropped it on the bed. It had to be one of the precious stones that held a small static charge. It must've fallen into her bag at the Renaissance Faire. Or maybe one of her so-called friends thought it would be funny to make her shoplift without knowing it. But wouldn't they have called her out and gotten her in trouble if that were the case?

Then she noticed the red, brown, and yellow swirls on the sphere were churning and moving about. Great, now she was seeing things. Toury rubbed her eyes. That didn't work because the color swirled faster like a little storm inside the tiny orb now. It was beginning to glow brighter and pulsate molten orange like a beacon was heating up at its core. She had the urge to pick up the piece of labradorite again. Wait a minute. How did she know what kind of stone it was? She had never heard that term before in her life.

She dumped her purse out and sifted through the contents, locating her phone. At least there weren't any more freaky stones in there. Her emancipation plan on hold, she typed labradorite into her phone. It gave her an igneous rock definition, so she was right. She gulped and clicked on the first website that talked about the stone's meaning and uses. It held magic? Used by healers and sorcerers and such? That was folklore, fairy tales, not reality. She shook off the thought and kept searching.

She clicked on website after website, but nothing said anything about the stone glowing like a flame was inside of it or its pattern moving. She was apprehensive, and it didn't help that the voices downstairs were shouting so loud, she could hardly focus on what she was reading.

The voices were reaching an alarming crescendo, her mom saying, "I don't want her! You take her!"

Followed by her dad saying, "Me? I'll be out to sea for long spans of time. You know I can't!"

Great, just as she thought. They were splitting up, and neither parent wanted her. Even more pressing than her dreadful future was this freaky stone glowing brighter as if beckoning her to touch it. She was terrified but truly felt as if the stone were drawing her in somehow.

Toury had enough of it all. She dropped her phone on the bed and impulsively grabbed the stone. The stone was scorching hot, burning her hand, but when she tried to drop it, the smooth rock was stuck as if it had fused, melded to her palm. Then a static pain radiated up her arm and shot through her entire body, making her shake uncontrollably. Her teeth chattered, and her hair stood on end. This was exactly what she imagined it must feel like to be struck by lightning, and the pain seemed never-ending. But at last, she fell back onto her bed, her ceiling fading away and her eyes drooping closed. She was so tired.

A girl's voice she didn't recognize whispered to her in the darkness: "The darkness is coming. We need your light. Come home."

Then there was nothing but the darkness that the voice foretold.

2
A MISSIVE

"Why are you sitting in your room, moping?" Princess Mary challenged. Alex's sister leaned on the doorframe of his bedroom in an inelegant slouch their mother would censure her for if the queen were present.

"I'm not." He realized his defensive tone betrayed him. He liked to tell himself it was merely deep thinking on important issues, but even he knew that was a lie. There were many reasons for his brooding.

"What bothers you today? The threat of the necromancers, your curse, the Magicians' Guild strike, the famine in the east, Father's ailing health, or the disappearing nobles?" Mary chided as if these things were trivial. She was teasing him, as always, and trying to make light of bad situations.

It did force him to give her a small grin. The truth was, at the age of seventeen, he might have to take over and rule the land. All this weighed heavily on his princely mind, but what bothered him most, a worry that rendered more anxiety than all the turmoil of his land put together, was a very different and perplexing issue.

"You're forgetting the largest worry of them all," he pointed out. "Marriage."

Mary's smile faded, and she walked into his room, making a "harrumph" type of sound as she joined him at his table that looked out over the orchard. Mary was expected to marry soon too, but the harassment had only begun for her recently since she was two years younger.

Ball after ball, soiree after soiree, pushy noblewomen shoved their daughters under his nose. Two years thus far of this pressure. His father said to marry for beauty; his advisors, for magical powers to enhance the strength of his future children; and his mother, for love. So far, no beautiful, powerful, noble girl had swayed him or honestly sparked any interest.

What should have been paramount to him, instead of worrying about who he'd get shackled to, was solving the quandary about how to lift the necromancer's curse that had been placed upon him as an infant. It was a simple curse but impossible to lift, one that allowed negative energy to weaken or influence him. It was dangerous, so dangerous, some were protesting his future reign in favor of his spitfire sister. But Mary was young and reckless. And there was the problem of her disinterest in ruling and her abhorrence for politics.

"I don't see why I have to marry. You're the future ruler." Mary sulked. They were trying to marry her off at the tender age of fifteen, but she wouldn't have any of the suitors, and it didn't seem the suitors would have her either. She was not the court's ideal example of genteel or passive, and definitely not obedient. Their mother was hell-bent on sending her to Madame Mage's Finishing School—a one year program that promised to turn out powerful, beautiful women and a list of suitors—in hopes she would "settle down into a woman."

"Anyway," Mary said. "Mother sent me to fetch you. We have company."

"Which guy or gal is it this time? Mother's always playing matchmaker."

"I didn't ask. Don't abandon me. Please, come down," Mary whined, which made him feel guilty and annoyed simultaneously.

His mother's request was really an order, so he straightened himself up, threw on his medallion, which was the equivalent to Mary's circlet, and then offered his sister his arm as they left his rooms.

When he entered his mother's drawing room, he wanted to bolt immediately because of one girl in the room: Justine Citrine. He bowed and kissed her hand as expected. Her amber eyes examined him through thick blackened lashes. Her bright yellow hair was splayed up on top of her head in intricate curls, and her corset was so tight, he wondered how she breathed at all, but it did nicely display her ample bosom. In short, she was the belle of the court, one of the prettiest and most talented sorceress debutantes, and she made witty conversation, showing a well-turned-out mind. The problem was, she just didn't tickle his fancy.

"Are you excited about the Citrine Centennial Ball?" Justine asked him. It was a big deal for her, marking the hundred years since her family's rise to nobility. It was difficult for him to feign interest since many noble families dated back much further. Alex's family was royalty dating back to the unwritten times, thousands upon thousands of years ago when dragons had breathed men—his ancestors—into being. And now the royal family had dwindled down to him, his sister, and his cousins, Henry and the now missing Ruby, to forge the new generation of Sapphirians, hence the obsession with them marrying as soon as they came of age.

"I have much more pressing concerns than yet another party, but I am looking forward to some frivolity," he said. Yes, he was being curt, but he was tired of faking politeness when it came to Justine. The girl lapped up compliments like a fat cat offered cream, so he learned to avoid bestowing any. There was more that bothered him about her—her conceit, her superficiality (the dyed hair, false lashes, and makeup were overkill)—and then there was something else that irked him that was difficult to describe. There was this feeling of negativity lingering under the surface of her shallow package, as if her core was rotten.

His mother gave him a look of censure, and his sister choked back a laugh, hiding it in a cough.

He remained standing, refusing to get stuck in the room any longer than he had to. His valet-bodyguard David would save him soon enough with some "important" missive that was either an old or fabricated message.

"Of course." Justine smiled, but her eyes bored into him with restrained anger. "You have many important things to do. A kingdom cannot run itself, after all."

Counterfeit to the core. He'd prefer she take it in stride and have a witty comeback, but what could he expect? He was Prince Sapphirian. Offending him could be viewed as treason and, if severe, was punishable by burning at the stake. Part of that scenario pleased him, which made him feel a little guilty.

She was just like the rest of the debutantes. They were too simple and fake. Some were intelligent, of course, but they were taught that a woman was to act inferior and pleasing. That didn't sit right with him. Girls should have some spine, some pluck. He admired his mother's strength, how she helped his father rule in her subtle way. Or girls should be like his sister, Mary, who wouldn't let him get away with anything. These were the only real relationships he had, the only real women in his life. To imagine he'd find a woman out there who would be as strong or spirited as his mother and sister was pointless. He ought to resign himself to a marriage of convenience with the debutante who irked him the least. But not yet and definitely not Justine.

"No, a kingdom cannot run itself, such a wise observation," his sister said in a seemingly sincere tone. Only he and his mother knew well enough she was mocking Justine.

"But one should at times let his troubles go, no? One night of frivolity, as you say, now and then can cleanse one, don't you think?" Justine added, trying desperately to control the conversation.

Now he understood her family's rise in power and favor. Like a pet, she was trained to say only what was appropriate and agreeable. His parents preferred these sycophants while he abhorred them. Mary's rolling of her eyes told him she had similar thoughts to his at the moment.

"Yes, of course," his mother responded, then gave him a pointed look because he didn't answer. He couldn't help it. He didn't have time for silly girls. "I try to tell him that he doesn't need to be so serious all the time," his mother continued. This was true. He rarely had time for fun, and the curse made a heavy, unhappy feeling weigh him down most of the time, like plodding through life with a set of armor always pressing down on him.

There was a tap at the door, and his valet-bodyguard David walked in. Alex could jump for joy. "An important message for you, Your Highness." David handed a scroll to Alex. His mother sighed in annoyance, knowing the typical parlor trick he used to get him away from company.

He looked at the wax seal and noted the symbol of a book pressed in it. It was from Tobias Firebrand, one of the best cunning-folk seers out there, a commoner with extraordinary soothsaying abilities.

It was no phony or old correspondence, but a new message David was delivering. Alex opened the missive quickly and looked at the short message. *Prince Sapphirian, I have information concerning your cousin. Please come at your earliest convenience.*

He must've gone pale, for his mother's concerned voice inquired whom the letter was from. This was classified information, so he simply handed it to his sister, who was closest, as he excused himself and his sister from the Citrines' company with all the politeness society demanded. The least he could do was spare Mary from dealing with Justine. His mother took the missive from Mary and read it.

Alex heard his mother's intake of breath, and she handed it back to him with an equal measure of concern and hope in her light brown eyes. Alex burned the scroll into nothing but ash in his hands by conjuring fire with merely the thought of it. Descendants of dragons—all Sapphirians—held strong ties to fire magic, of course. Then he tossed the ashes into the grate of the fireplace. Justine's face was hard set, and her brow scrunched in what seemed like frustration. Most likely, it was about not being included in the conversation or Alex fleeing her presence. He couldn't care less how she felt.

He and Mary fled the room and headed to the stables. His guards and retinue were already joining them. David must've been informed of the urgency when the letter was delivered.

"Do you think she's alive?" his sister asked.

"There's only one way to find out." Alex was afraid of what he might find out. He had so much hope in Ruby, who had foreseen a savior, someone who would break his curse. She had vanished before she could have another vision of it. "If she is okay, she may just have the possible solution to all our problems."

"Yes, Brother, your problems, not mine. I'm being shipped off to Madame Mage's. Mother will see me married before the year ends."

"And me as well." He sighed. "All right, most of our problems will be solved." He had to admit his parents had been pretty patient, not forcing his hand when it came to being wedded, but they might force it once he turned eighteen.

He kissed his sister's cheek and hopped up on his horse. Mary was annoyed to be left behind if her crossed arms and bold glare were anything to judge by. The curse was his burden to bear, not hers, and he couldn't have her snooping around as he tried to figure out this savior situation. He could trust no one, not even Mary.

3
FYR

Toury woke up to a bright blue sky with puffy white clouds and a warm breeze tickling her arms. As her mind tried to figure out how she had fallen asleep, outside of all places, something prodded her side. She turned to her right to see a young boy holding a stick and poking her with it.

"Are you dead?" he asked.

"Of course not!" She pushed the stick away with her hand. Her left hand clutched something. She peered at her palm and saw the stone. She remembered holding it, light, pain, and sleep, and a voice saying some nonsense about light, dark, and home.

"Why are you wearing men's clothes, and why do they look weird?" the boy candidly inquired. She examined her attire, which was still the purple scoop neck T-shirt, jeans, and sneakers she'd worn all day. She sat up and looked around but only saw endless fields and a steep hill. Then she directed her gaze to the boy's expression: screwed up like he was thinking hard and coming up with nothing. He wore breeches, boots, and a loose white shirt as if he were from a long time ago, and he was filthy. Dirt was smudged on his face, and his hands were caked in mud. One hand still held the stick, and the other had a wooden pail filled with what looked like mushrooms hooked on his wrist.

"Am I at the Renaissance Faire?" she asked. She was confused, disoriented.

"What kind of fair is that?" He looked at her as if she had sprouted another head.

"Very funny. Who put you up to this?"

"I dunno what you mean." He took a hesitant step back, his mouth slightly parted and eyes widening.

"Are you frightened of me?" She suddenly felt bad. This didn't seem like a joke anymore, or this kid was the best child actor she'd ever seen.

"I'm not scared of you, but that's scary." He pointed at the stone.

"Yeah, it is," she said under her breath. She stood up and slipped the stone into her pocket and dusted herself off. First thing, she had to figure out where she was. "Okay, so where am I?" Toury asked, deciding to play along with whatever this joke or game was. She would not get frightened, and she would not be too gullible.

"In a field," the boy responded.

Right, so she was not going to get home easily with these results. "I see that. Something a little more helpful, like a town, street, you know, city name nearby."

"Ludford is the town right over this hill. The capital of Fyr, you know, Celestia, is only a half day's journey on foot. If you got the funds for it, you can hire a carriage or a horse and get there much faster."

Ludford sounded familiar; she had no idea why or how. And where on Earth was a place called Fyr, or Celestia for that matter? "A horse? What about a taxi or a car? Don't your parents have a car?"

"I don't know what those things are. Who are you?" the boy asked, scratching his head. He had never heard of a car? Either this was a really well-played joke, or she had lost her mind. But somewhere deep down, she knew it wasn't some prank. The idea of the horse and carriage for travel seemed normal to her, but she had never ridden in one before. It wasn't like she frequented Amish country. Why were things vaguely familiar or, at least, easy to accept when she should be freaking out? Had the stone fried her brain?

"I'm Tourmaline Hematite, but I go by Toury. And I think I'm very lost."

He let out a whistle and then grinned. "Why didn't you say so, Lady Tourmaline?" The little urchin bowed to her.

"Are you mocking me?" she asked, stunned by his behavior.

"Not at all," he rushed out. "You must've knocked your head some, or maybe you were attacked—and your clothes stolen—but you're a noble. We bow to all nobles."

"How do you know I'm a noble?"

"All nobles have stone names." He gave her that crazy-person stare again.

Hematite was a stone, as well as Tourmaline. She had looked up her name's meaning once to see why her parents would give her such a weird one. Being named after stones seemed strange at the time, but now there was a supposed reason behind it, according to this kid. This was getting weirder. She would not freak out. She would stay strong and cool. There had to be a logical explanation for all of this.

"Okay. Can you help me get home?"

"Of course. I'm supposed to be gathering mushrooms, but if I bring home some Sapphirians, my ma won't fuss."

"Sapphirians are money, huh?" She just checked with the boy because her mind already somehow knew that. She could envision the round gold coins with a man's face on them, the more expensive ones with tiny gemstones set inside. "As you can see, I have nothing on me."

"Your family will."

He began walking, and she followed. She thought of her bickering, unloving parents who had just verbally admitted that they didn't want her. "I don't think they have any of that kind of money," she said. More likely, they wouldn't pay for her return even if they did. But they might not be here, so she was confused as to whom the boy was talking about.

"The only Hematite in Ludford is Lady Edwina, and she's a spinster—although Ma says I shouldn't say that because it's rude. Anyway, she has no family, until you showed up, I guess, and oodles of money. She'll reward me."

Her real family? Conflicting emotions of dread and excitement warred inside her. Meeting her biological family could be amazing or horrific, but either way, it would be life changing.

"I'm not sure. I don't actually know her."

"A Hematite is a Hematite. By law, she must take you in."

They crested the hill, heading for Ludford, she supposed. Once she reached the top, she looked down into a valley of old thatch-roof and tile homes, feeling as if she had just walked into a Renaissance landscape painting. She eagerly walked down the hill, her trepidation fading under the more powerful emotion of curiosity. The history buff in her marveled at the scene. As they walked closer, she noted horse-drawn carriages and carts and people on horseback. The boy had not been joking. Not one car was in sight. She had this overwhelming feeling of nostalgia as if this were home, but she had never been here before. It was as if a part of her understood everything, but it was buried in the back of her mind, and she couldn't access the details beforehand. It was as if she remembered things after seeing them.

Instead of walking into the village area, the boy led her toward the outskirts of town.

"Best we take the long way with you dressed like that." He looked her over again. "There are some nasty men by the mines and downtown. Seen them rough some girls up. Ma says she'll box my ears if I become one of them. I don't know why I'd wanna be like them, anyway."

"You would never," Toury found herself saying. "You are like a noble knight saving a lady. I know you'll grow into a great man one day."

The boy beamed up at her. Then his face shifted into crinkled brows and a frown. "What's a knight?"

So she didn't seem to be in the past. The boy awaited an answer.

"I read about them in a book. Knights are the best chivalric heroes who spend their lives saving people."

The huge grin returned to his face, and there was a hop to his step after that. Toury turned her attention to the village they bypassed and took in everything like a sponge. The people were dressed in old fashioned clothing, which looked a little bit like the Renaissance, but a bit more like the eighteenth or nineteenth century. Women wore hooded cloaks over dresses with rich embroidery, reminding her of Renaissance paintings, and yet they had plunging necklines exposing cleavage, suggesting corsets of later times. The men favored breeches—these weren't those big puffy ones, though, but slimmer like shortened trousers of the Regency era. They all seemed to wear tall boots, doublets with or without jerkins, and cloaks. Oddly, no one sported a hat, but a couple women sported snoods, which reminded her of hairnets her former school's cafeteria ladies wore but fancier and more stylish.

She wasn't as savvy when it came to architecture, but it appeared the same with a mixture of thatch-roofs, brick, stone, Tudor trimming—it was a hodgepodge of history. This place seemed timeless. She felt as if she were on a movie set, but the dramaturg responsible for historical authenticity was clueless. But here, she was the ignorant one. She saw a sizeable castle or fort on the outskirts. The boy must've followed her gaze, for he explained, "The Sapphirian Emerald Fort. The King's mad sister lives there, along with Lord Emerald, Lord Henry, and Lady Ruby. 'Cept she's gone missing, the rumor has it. Heard my ma whispering to her friends about it."

The royal family, the Sapphirians, she realized, ruled this land. This wasn't make-believe or a joke anymore. This felt so real. And Ruby? Chills went up her spine at the name, although she couldn't figure out why.

"What's your name?" she asked the boy as they headed to a large Victorian-looking mansion with bay windows but a tiled roof and Tudor woodwork on the outside.

"Duric," the boy said.

"Duric what?" she asked.

"What do you mean Duric what? I'm just Duric. People like me don't get last names until we get a profession. I'm just Duric of Ludford."

"I see. Why do I get a stone name then?"

"Because you're a noble, silly." He shook his head at her. "You have oodles of magic in you."

"Magic?" Her stomach flopped in nervousness at the idea. Surely, the boy was fibbing.

"You really hit your head hard, didn't you?"

"Yes, I must've," she agreed, not confident enough to tell the truth of how she got to this place. "Indulge me." She rubbed her temples to calm herself and to try to make sense of whatever she could.

"Okay," the boy began with a tentative voice. "Your lot is made up of sorcerer blood. Me, the cunning folk as they call us, I'm just magician blood. We can do this and that with magic, see snippets of things, do a few tricks, but your lot can do it all."

The boy was vague, but she was almost at the threshold of information overload, and her head was about to explode. She was afraid to ask any more questions. Nor did she want to admit to the boy that she knew nothing of sorcery or magic. On top of that, she didn't want to believe any of this was real. She wasn't magical or a noble, but she had to hide that fact from little Duric because she needed to play along with this charade in order to get home.

They approached a large house, and the boy knocked on the door. Toury braced herself. Now that she was faced with the reality of meeting a long-lost relative, her dread surpassed her excitement. Family was not something she associated with kindness, loyalty, love, or anything remotely positive. She had a terrible feeling about this, but there was no turning back, and she needed to get home.

4
A FLAME

Tobias Firebrand was a cunning folk per se, but the rumors suggested he was a baseborn son of the nobility. He was the best firebrander—reader of fire—in the kingdom, which made it obvious he unofficially belonged to someone in the royal family, but no one had claimed him. At one time, Alex had had many great-great uncles, a few of whom had womanized and never settled down. Without a father's acknowledgment or the Sapphirian eye color, Tobias would never be included as a Sapphirian. As an old man in his early sixties, it was likely his parents had taken that information with them to the grave. Being baseborn did not allow him to rise above head firebrander of the Magicians' Guild—well, he was until the strike.

"How goes the strike?" Alex didn't beat around the bush. No one ever accused Alex of being anything but direct.

"Your Highness, the terms have not yet been met by the Sorcerers' Guild. Any way you could speak to your father to hasten it? More nobles will go missing if we cannot work together to solve this."

"I know. I have tried. I will try again. The king speaks nothing of the strike to me, but I have an inkling the sorcerers are holding out, feeling the magicians are the ones responsible. You have news of Ruby?" Alex pressed toward the subject of more interest to him.

"Yes," the man said wearily. "That's why I called you here. She wasn't taken."

"What do you mean?"

"She ran away." The old man said, staring into a flickering flame that danced in a small pot on his table.

"To where?"

"One of the other spheres." The man did not expand.

"Which one?"

"This cannot leave this room. I trust no one save yourself, Your Highness..." he raised his hand to stop Alex's interruption. "I do not even trust your father in this. There are so many secrets being kept, so much negativity and darkness all around. I politely disagree with you, Your Highness. I fear there are necromancers among us starting this tiff between our guilds and fueling the strike. By the way, I have made you another amulet to try to ward off that."

He walked away and fished into a drawer. Alex shuddered when the man's back was turned. Necromancers among them in positions of power, maybe in the very court of sycophants his father trusted? He was astonished by the news. His father was insistent necromancers were magician born, and since Alex only heard of nobles vanishing, he had believed it. How naive to think his father knew best. Alex was beginning to fear that this was becoming the most deep-rooted and threatening conspiracy in Fyr's history, and his father was in denial, happy to blame common folk because it better suited his worldview. As of late, Alex was beginning to question his father's ability to rule. The astonishment quickly gave way to anger and resolve. He would not let them win. No one would make him weak, vulnerable. He had fought the darkness for so long, and he would continue to fight it. And as much as it hurt his ego, he would seek out this savior Ruby discovered and employ his help. He was the prince, and by the god of fire and goddess of light, he would not let them destroy what was to be his kingdom one day. He would work around his father to do so.

By the time Tobias turned around, Alex had composed himself and said, "Another one?" He had let the man try many innocuous cures over the years, but nothing seemed to work.

"This one is made of black tourmaline, pure stones. It will prevent outside evil from overtaking you," Tobias told him. The man chose his words wisely. Nothing could stop the dark curse inside him, but protecting him from any additional evil might just be key in keeping him safe. Without question, Alex slipped it over his wrist and hid it under his sleeve, thanking the man. A feeling of the burden being lifted slightly overcame him—the power stones doing their work.

"There was more I couldn't write in your note, Prince Sapphirian. Lady Ruby Sapphirian visited me three days ago."

"That was the day she went missing! Why didn't you tell me?" Alex felt the fire build up in him. He had to suppress it and push it down. It would do no good to unleash his rage and accidentally burn the only man he trusted, who had helped him at every turn since he was a little boy. Back then, Tobias had been his firebranding tutor. He was the one who taught Alex how to control the dragon's fire inherent in all Sapphirians. Unfortunately, all that fire-conjuring power was directly tied to his emotions. Betrayal and rage bashed around inside him, and he pulled back the emotion through a deep, controlled breath.

"I'm sorry," Tobias begged. "She pleaded for me to keep it secret. I told her I would have to tell you, Your Highness. She cast a fire oath on me."

Alex sank into the chair in realization. The fire receded, but he hung onto it with his mind to keep the curse back, the two always battling over his autonomy. He sighed. No one could break a fire oath, or they'd be consumed by flames from the inside out. The only thing that allowed a fire oath to be broken was the death of the person who had cast it. If Tobias could now speak of it, his cousin Ruby was dead.

"I'm so sorry," Tobias said sadly, sitting down at the little wooden table across from him. He patted Alex's hand.

Alex pulled his hand away, pressing down his sadness. Grief was for later; retribution was for now. He would not show weakness. "She came for knowledge? Help?"

The man nodded. "There was no good in the flames, nothing. She would be taken by this unknown enemy and her power stripped from her, and that power would be used to destroy all that we know. All of Fyr would be lost. So she made the rash choice to run. She asked for a labradorite sphere, and I gave her one. Then she cast the oath so I could not tell."

"Labradorite? So she went to the Earth sphere? We must go and find the stone. Who knows what she put into it, and who has it now? If the necromancers get ahold of it..." Alex stood up, ready to run into a battle in a foreign world by himself if it meant he could save his people.

"Please, sit," the old man said. "This leads to the matter of the savior we discussed."

Alex had completely forgotten about the savior when hearing about Ruby. It was his only fault, his father had told him on many occasions; he thought of others and not himself. He must learn to think about himself. A selfish king is a living king, after all.

"I think the savior has come into being, has developed his or her powers suddenly," Tobias said.

"What does that have to do with Ruby?"

"Ruby was extremely powerful, Your Highness, so much so that if we could have lifted your curse, you two could have worked together to save the land from darkness."

"But now she is dead." Alex slumped back in his chair, feeling defeated at every turn. He would mourn the loss of Ruby later, but his father had instilled in him that a ruler does not show emotion. He had struggled with controlling his emotions as a child, but he had adapted to understand that public and private lives were two existences he would live separately for the rest of his life.

"I cannot see what happened. You have exceptional fire reading abilities, Your Highness. Perhaps, together, we can see what Ruby did with that stone. I think you are right. She most likely did more than use it to transport to Earth. If she gave that stone to someone and transferred powers or information through it, that person could very well be our savior."

Alex motioned for him to proceed. The man fed the flame in the branding bowl and chanted. Alex leaned forward and grasped Tobias's hand. He stared into the fire, willing his magic to rise out over the milky blackness of the negativity curse and to spread down his arm and flow to Tobias' hand.

The flames instantly leaped high and wide, and inside them, they saw the outline of a scene in vivid detail as if it were painted by fire, light, and shadows. The contours of the flames showed a troubled Ruby, frightened by shadows following her. She chanted and placed her hand on the stone, and a surge of light came out and went into the stone, making sparks in the fire they were watching. They saw her in a market, slipping a stone into a bag, but could not see whose bag it was; then she was in the woods, being consumed by shadows. The flames went back down into a small flicker, the vision of the recent past over.

"The necromancers killed her," Alex said. "They want the power to take over this sphere. Can they actually succeed?"

Tobias mopped his balding head. "Yes, they can. Labradorite is an effective power holder. Ruby may have transferred everything into it. With the power naturally in that stone and Ruby's power, whoever has this stone can destroy or save our world."

Alex blew out a heavy breath. "Why would she do this?"

"Ruby must've thought it better than letting them take the power from her. She seemed to have a plan and found someone of our kind on Earth. I don't know who. Since your birth, well, since the curse was placed upon you, nobles have disappeared. We have found a lot of them through visions; most have died, but we didn't know how. Ruby's vision—perhaps because it happened in the Earth sphere—is the first to point to the necromancers and the fact some nobles who vanished are still alive. They may be in the Earth sphere or another one completely."

Alex blew out an overwhelmed breath. Finding the stone would be nearly impossible.

"As long as the necromancers do not know where the stone is, we may be safe. If Ruby was smart, she most likely enchanted it with blood and power magic as a protective measure. The right blood would then be needed to unlock it, the right powers to absorb her strength and knowledge. Most likely, she used the strongest magic—her own blood."

"So only a Sapphirian can unlock it?"

"Yes, but not absorb it. Fire burns fire. She would need someone descended from light. Someone who could absorb her power and knowledge and, in a sense, save us all."

It all hit Alex suddenly as the pieces clicked together in his mind. "So Ruby created the savior? Surely, the person who has this knowledge to destroy the darkness can lift my curse, particularly if he has light magic."

"Unknowingly, I believe Ruby's done all this. I think she was trying to pass on information and keep the power out of the necromancer's hands."

"How much labradorite do you have left?"

"Until the miners' load arrives, only four."

"Then I will send you with two of my most trusted guards to the Earth sphere to look for this savior and stone. Take the fourth stone to bring the savior back. I will need to unlock the stone for him." Then he added, "And no one is to know about this. It is a covert operation."

"Yes, Your Highness. May I make another suggestion?"

Alex nodded.

"Have any other men you trust scour the lands as well. It is possible the labradorite transported someone back to our sphere since Ruby did not return. It can usually hold a couple charges for the round trip."

Alex nodded and paid the man a hundred Sapphirians, which he tried to deny, but Alex left them regardless, to pay for the stones. The money was only a small part of what he wished he could do for the man.

Nothing sat right with him. Alex was not a patient person. He wanted the savior in his care, safe, and his kingdom protected. Defending Fyr meant banishing this curse foremost, and the fact that it felt self-centered rubbed him the wrong way. But it wasn't selfish if he was curing himself to save his people.

5
SPHERE

The door creaked open, and a grim old man greeted Toury and Duric. He said nothing but, "Yes?" as if they were rude for even knocking. Toury, not sure what to say, looked to the boy. Duric straightened himself up as if he were mimicking a gentleman's rigid posture and tilted his nose up in the air, looking decidedly snooty. Although this was no laughing situation, Toury stifled a bubbling giggle.

"Please, sir. This lady would like an audience with Lady Edwina Hematite."

"Lady?" The man sneered, barely giving her a glance. Part of her wanted to punch him in the face, but that wouldn't make a good impression on her long-lost relative. "And who shall I say is paying a call?"

"Lady Tourmaline Hematite at your service," she said, and for some reason, she curtsied. She had never done so in her life, but her body just told her to do it. Strange, that.

The man, who she realized was a butler, measured her up with his probing eyes. Taking in her outfit, he tried to disguise a disgusted face since her clothes were strange—scandalous according to Duric—in this land. When his eyes locked on hers, the disgust transformed into a look of surprise. Despite his reservations, he opened the door and escorted them inside to a sitting room.

She sat down, but Duric looked at his dirty trousers and remained standing, holding his wooden bucket. He whistled a tune she was not familiar with as they waited. After five minutes according to the grandfather clock, but what felt like an eternity, the door opened, and in stepped a middle-aged woman who had a prim appearance and a protruding nose. Aside from the nose, she could've been attractive in her youth. She had wheat blonde hair, a slim figure, and—now Toury understood the butler's behavior—the same startlingly gray eyes.

The woman looked her up and down with a severe, probing stare, noting the eyes as well. Then she looked at the boy.

Finally, after the uncomfortable evaluation, she spoke. "Who is he?"

"Duric of Ludford, my lady. I assisted your kin to your doorway. She was lost and confused."

"Then what are you still doing here?" she asked the boy in a strict tone that reminded Toury of her least favorite elementary school teacher, Miss Heany.

"He expects a reward for his troubles. I took him away from his work, and he may be in trouble for it." Toury explained.

The woman stared at her with a bitter expression and then called her butler, Harold, to give the boy five Sapphirians for his troubles and to send him on his way, and then she ordered tea. Duric looked pleased with the amount and followed the butler out.

Her aunt, wordless, stared at her for an uncomfortably long time; the only sound in the room was the beat of the pendulum swaying in the grandfather clock.

"Thank you," Toury said to break the silence.

The woman sat down. "You sure look like a Hematite and a Tourmaline, but I'll have to check that. Where have you been, and how did you get here?"

She did not at all want to confide in this woman, but she was family. If Toury could not confide in her, then whom? She had no one she could rely on in this strange place, and she had to find her way home again.

"I lived in a place near Philadelphia, you know, Pennsylvania?"

The woman looked at her blankly.

"The United States?"

No response.

"North America, you know, Earth." She added the last word sardonically.

At her last word, the woman had a quick intake of breath. "You were on the Earth sphere?"

Toury never heard it called that before but nodded.

"Now I know where my wayward brother went."

"Brother?"

"Baron Aschen Hematite, my brother and, obviously, your father. There were no more Hematites left but us. I don't suppose you have siblings? A brother maybe? Would be nice to see the name carry on. Where is my brother? Is he alive? Did he bring you back to this sphere?"

"Can you slow down, please," Toury begged. "I'm utterly lost. I have no idea about my real parents. I was adopted. I just want to get home. I'm lost. And I have no idea about spheres. And you said I looked like a Tourmaline too?"

"Your mother," she said with disdain. "The Duchess Emilia Tourmaline. They eloped, vanished, and angered the royal family. She uprooted my brother's life completely. You have her hair, figure, and coloring. But you have my brother's eyes and the same expression when he was bewildered."

Letting the information sink in, she switched to other important subjects. "So if I'm not on Earth, where am I?"

"Fyr." It sounded as if her aunt said the word "fewer" too fast.

"Fewer?"

"Never mind. No one speaks the old language anymore, forgetting their roots and their god and goddess. It's 'Fire' in these times."

"Fire?"

The woman rolled her eyes, annoyed, and Toury couldn't figure out why. Perhaps it was her different accent that made her aunt feel as if she were saying everything wrong. To Toury, they were both saying "fire." Her aunt got up, crossed the room, and motioned Toury to join her just as the tea cart came in. A serving girl set up the tea on the table as this woman, her aunt, pointed to a strange metal item that had a globe inside a bunch of circles. She remembered her history teacher, Mrs. Blooms, having a small version of this, a paperweight on her desk. The students would spin the circles and marvel how they never crashed into each other.

"This is—"

"The Music of the Spheres, celestial spheres." She cut her aunt off.

"You know then?"

"No, I just remember it from school. My teacher said it was the old way of understanding the universe."

"Not an old way, *the* way. It is the universe. Think of each sphere"—she pointed to each circle—"as a realm if you will."

Toury looked at Earth in the middle and the names of the spheres and spotted Fyr. She pointed at it.

"Yes, that is where we are and where you are from. Your parents were involved in many controversial things that banished all of us from the court, including myself, although the only involvement I had was sharing a surname with my brother."

Now Toury understood the cold manner toward her.

"How do I get back to Earth?"

"Do you want to go back?" she asked, astonished.

"They have medicine, electricity, plumbing, hygiene—"

"We are on Fyr, not a desolate plane." Her aunt pointed up at the ceiling, and Toury saw the chandelier above her; it had what looked like candles, but she noted it was electric with raindrop-shaped bulbs. "And there is indoor plumbing. Although adding washrooms would ruin these old buildings' structures, there are bath houses built next to most properties, for the nobles at least. The cunning folk go to public wash houses."

Toury was confused because the houses looked ancient and the clothing archaic, and yet she hadn't gone back in time. She had assumed, incorrectly, that this place was behind the times in every way since the styles were. "Sorry, this place just looks so much like an older time in Earth's history."

Her aunt made a scoffing noise at that. "I've heard Earth has been consumed by technology and is slowly killing itself. The magic there is almost dead. Could you practice any magic there?"

"No," Toury said, wanting to defend her homeland but from an outside perspective, it sounded legitimate. "But I can't here either."

"Oh, you can. You're a Hematite. You just need to learn is all. I should send you to a finishing school."

"Whoa, what?"

"It's the only type of school for a girl your age. They'll teach you how to fit in here, the laws, the court, and how to use your powers."

"But I thought if I couldn't go home, I might stay here."

Her Aunt Edwina gave her a stiff smile. "I suppose for a little while till you settle in, but one misstep, and I will send you to that school. I have no patience, and I am not an apt teacher. Don't have any expectations from me."

Toury sure didn't with this woman's attitude, but being sent off to a school in a foreign land without a friend or family member kind of freaked her out. It was a situation she was used to with her parents on Earth, but this wasn't Earth. She had no idea what this was even. "Realm" was a term only in fantasy books...until now. For the first time since she was eight, she was trying to cling onto an unloving family member.

"I don't expect anything but food and shelter...and maybe an outfit to fit in. Can you understand I'm completely overwhelmed with my situation, not being told any of this and being thrust here suddenly? I want to get home."

"Do you have an interesting life there? The family that raised you, were they kind?"

Toury opened her mouth and closed it again. She could not admit to her aunt that she had no boyfriend or real friends, or that her soon-to-be-divorced parents treated her like unwanted baggage. Worse, it was likely no one would miss her, and she felt the same about all of them.

"They weren't abusive." Toury stared at the floor.

"Damn Aschen!" The woman shook her head. "So impulsive, never thinking anything through. Not abusive? That does not endear them to me at all. Hematites deserve better than that. It does not sound like you have much to go back to. Pray, how did you even get here?"

Toury relayed the story to her aunt, knowing how far-fetched it sounded, but her aunt took it all in stride, looking pensive and nodding here and there.

"Do you have this stone, still?" Edwina asked.

Toury took it out of her pocket. Her aunt leaned in closer and peered at it through some spectacles she pulled out of the side table. She didn't touch it at first but just examined it.

"It is labradorite."

"Yes."

"Do you know what that kind of stone is capable of?"

"Not really."

"It is capable of transporting one from realm to realm—"

"Then I can go back!"

"They don't generally work that way. They're enchanted for travel to Earth, but rarely will it contain enough magic for more than a couple trips. Traveling between spheres takes great amounts of power and is not often done," her aunt said.

"But I found it on Earth, in my purse. Maybe it's from home, and I can go back."

"Earth, as I said, holds very little magic anymore. Stones only hold this kind of magic, in this intensity, on Fyr. Someone brought it there, maybe to bring you back to where you belong."

"My parents?"

"I know as little as you about their whereabouts. Let me see it." Her aunt put out her palm. "Sometimes these stones can house secrets." Hesitantly, as if knowing deep down no one should touch it aside from her, she held it out in her palm, forcing her aunt to take it from her.

As soon as Edwina's fingers touched the stone, sparks ignited, much like they had for Toury. Only the stone didn't try to transport her elsewhere. Her aunt was thrown back into the couch with a fiery blast. It was so powerful, the explosion sent the couch sliding across the floor into the wall. A resounding thud echoed throughout the room. The woman's hair frizzed on end and was smoking slightly. Her fingers were still curled as if electrified into that position. Toury dropped the stone. It clattered to the floor. She rushed over to the panting woman, asking if she was okay.

"That stone is full of exceptional magic. It has marked you as its owner. You need to transfer it into you. No one else can bear it or, as you've just witnessed, touch it." Her aunt held her deformed hand, her expression still screwed up in pain.

"Are you all right?"

"Nothing that won't heal quickly with some power stones."

Toury couldn't even ask what power stones were. Her brain was mush, and she had more significant concerns than pieces of rock.

"How do I transfer it?"

"It depends on the charm that was used upon it. There really is no telling how or when. I've heard, at times, it transfers but remains dormant until needed or until something happens to unleash it. It is mighty powerful to shock me like that. And power is important. Don't tell anyone about it, and keep it on you at all times." She paused, her face pensive. "Hmm, perhaps a brooch, yes. There is a man in the capital who can touch anything; he sets many powerful stones in jewelry. He won't be able to access the magic, but he'll be able to set it in something more portable. Tomorrow, we will get you a wardrobe, set the stone, and make inquiries at the school. For now, get some rest. I'm sure it's been an exhausting day for you."

Without further ado, her aunt rang a bell and had a servant lead Toury to a guest room, despite the fact that she hadn't eaten a single sandwich or drunk the tea yet. Although she had many questions and was anxious about her situation, she picked up the stone and followed the servant. She was led to a bedroom, where she passed out as soon as she hit the bed, still fully clothed.

6
A DRESS

Alex wished he could walk somewhere without everyone staring at him. He was even dressed down in the simplest noble jerkin, breeches, and boots he owned. All the cunning folk stopped, stared, and went down on their knees in supplication as he passed, the nobility on the streets giving slight bows or curtsies. He and Mary were walking down Palace Road to go to the shops, the best Celestia—the best the entire land—had. They left the carriage a ways back, much to the guards' dismay. He wanted a diversion from his apocalyptic worries, and his sister wanted a new gown for the Citrine Ball. He wasn't going to bother with new clothing. A new outfit might, to some, look like him wanting to impress Lady Justine. And he did not want to be linked to Justine any more than her power-hungry mother had already falsely spread. Rumors were irritating. He doubted anyone who made them up knew the real him. No one did. He had his family, his servant, and his best friend, Cobalt, but even they only knew parts of him. Alex always had to hide facets of himself for various reasons—to avoid angering his father, disappointing his mother, or being seen as vulnerable or weak. Aloof, strong, ruthless—that was what he needed to be.

When they entered the shop, he put up his hand to stop the retinue, and only David and Mary's waiting maid-bodyguard, Lucy, followed. The shop was bustling with last-minute purchases for the ball, but everyone stopped to bow and curtsy to Mary and Alex. It went completely silent, all except a flurry of activity and noise from one corner of the room.

"You expect me to wear this! Like, on a daily basis?" an exasperated female voice called out in a bizarre accent. The silence his presence evoked allowed everyone to hear the distressed girl.

He looked over to see what the fuss was about while his sister spoke to the shop owner. A girl with ink-black hair, a tan complexion, and startlingly gray eyes stood with her one hand on her hip, the other exemplifying her predicament as it moved in front of her chest as if to present it to an audience of a play. The bodice of her dress squeezed her bosom and offset it to her advantage. His gaze roamed down her body, tracing her curves. She seemed to be blessed with suppleness in the right areas, yet her arms, waist, and neck were slender. She stood tall, but not exceptionally so. She was the opposite of what the court valued, so his appreciation for what he saw seemed misplaced. According to society, he should value the pale, petite, light-haired girls—like Justine. This was no Justine, but a girl who obviously had a spine, although it seemed a bit too rugged and defiant at the moment. Maybe because she was opposite of what others deemed as beautiful, or perhaps because the sight of her made his stomach drop in nervousness for some inexplicable reason, he felt an inclination to learn her name.

"Lower your voice, and show some decorum! Ladies of nobility dress in such finery to find themselves wealthy and powerful lifemates."

"I'm only seventeen. I just got here. I'm not getting married anytime soon." She was his age with the same sentiment about marriage. Interesting. Most debutantes could not wait to land a man and leave their parents' house to run their own.

"I've explained it to you already. People marry younger here, as early as fifteen. You reach twenty-three, you'll be set on a shelf like me. No one will marry you."

"Well then, I have six years to worry about it."

The old spinster pinched the bridge of her nose in annoyance. He was enjoying this girl's sassiness, although he found it puzzling that she was clueless about social customs.

"See, this is too much cleavage. Look, he's staring!"

He looked away quickly, his cheeks blazing from discomfiture. Her insubordination and the fact she embarrassed him was enough to get her fined or jailed. No one ever showed disrespect to the royal family. It was seen as a type of heresy.

His attention was drawn back when he heard a sharp intake of breath. The spinster was down on her knees in supplication, despite being a noble who only needed to curtsy. The young vixen simply stood there, looking around in confusion. Her mouth made a cute little O shape, her eyes were open wide, and he wished to see her perpetually surprised for it was beyond adorable.

People looked away, some murmuring, but they were fully vested in listening. This gossip would make its rounds through the court. He had to say something, do something, for it was uncomfortably silent. But this little beauty, with her luscious lips, sharp tongue, and exotic accent, rendered him speechless.

"Your Royal Highness, please, my apologies. My niece, she knows not what she says," the older woman said.

He did not look at her. His eyes remained fixed on the girl who would defy the Prince of Fyr. Anger due to the insult warred with an emotion he rarely felt, a type of lusty intrigue. The angry dragon in him was competing with the man himself, and usually, the curse let the dragon win.

He did not believe her eyes could open wider, but the sooty lashes sprang open more, and her mouth sagged open as if she lost all sense. Then she fell to the ground, gracelessly kneeling as if someone kicked her feet out from under her.

She didn't recognize him.

Everyone knew him. He was the only prince in the land. His profile was even on one of the coins. He should be insulted. What girl his age would not know him?

"Shall I have the man-at-arms arrest her?" David asked quietly, for Alex still was distracted by her appearance. David's question sobered him, and he realized he had to take some kind of action.

The girl looked up slightly, giving him a full view of her spilling bosom. She was right. It was too delectable. Men would ogle her, maybe sneak a cheeky touch. He didn't like the idea of anyone's hands roaming over that caramel flesh. Except that was the very thing he wanted to do at this moment.

"No, that won't be necessary," he said quietly, and David retreated.

He walked over, his boots creaking over the floor, and he felt the gaze of every patron in the store watching to see what would happen next. He paid them no heed as he tried to focus on what he'd do with this insubordinate girl.

"Rise, ladies," he told them, for he did not recognize them enough to know their names. He knew he had never seen this gray-eyed beauty before because he would have definitely remembered her. Eye color was very telling in Fyr, but gray eyes could lead to a few noble families. He took the girl's hand and helped her up.

"I'm sorry, Your Highness," the girl said, her eyes searching his. She looked him in the eye, another sign of believing she was equal to royalty, another slight to his station. "I did not know. I've never been here before."

"Ah," he said, knowing neither what to say nor what she meant by that. She had this bewitching power over him that he didn't like. He realized he still held her hand, and the spinster with her was glaring at the poor girl. "And what is your name, my lady?"

"Toury. I mean, Tourmaline Hematite. This here is my aunt, Lady Edwina Hematite." Then she curtsied awkwardly.

The name was a red flag, a good and bad one. Just like his Tourmaline amulet, if she was from the Tourmaline family, she most likely could ward off evil. But it was her first name, not surname, which could have meant nothing. After all, his cousin Ruby had nothing to do with the power of the Ruby family. And then there was the Hematite problem. His parents never explained why, but Hematite was a blacklisted family, not allowed at court.

"Well, despite the accidental affront, it is a pleasure to meet you, Lady Tourmaline." He kissed the back of her hand on impulse, wishing he could kiss her lips instead. This got some of the mothers tittering. He realized too late that he had already treated her differently than other girls. He never showed any marked interest in a girl, lest they get the wrong idea and expect marriage. "Since you seem to be unaware of court life, let me introduce myself. I'm His Royal Highness, Prince Alexander Rowland Sapphirian of Fyr." Then he let go of her hand because he really could think of no excuse to continue the contact. This was the first time he had needed to introduce himself to someone. It felt strange.

The room was utterly silent, so he realized he had to continue this scene in front of their unwanted audience.

"Well, Lady Edwina, Lady Tourmaline has a valid point about the dress. Perhaps some lace at the top for propriety's sake?" He was crossing the line of decorum himself, but no one would dare admonish him. He waved his hand to one of the workers, and she snapped out of her staring trance, grabbing some lace and rushing over to tuck it in to show him what it would look like. He used the excuse to stare at her bosom more but then looked at the worker. "Yes, that will do. We do want her to find a *suitable* lifemate, Lady Edwina, don't we? A woman's mind is more attractive to a suitor than physical attributes alone."

"Yes, Your Highness." He could tell the woman disagreed but would never challenge him. Truly, he meant the notion deep down, despite the feelings stirring inside him, that he admired a woman's wit as much as her appearance.

He could think of nothing more to say to detain them. "Enjoy your shopping, ladies," he said, meeting Toury's gaze one more time before he turned away. He returned to his sister, who was giving him a candid look and biting her lip as she always did when she wanted to laugh. She knew him better than anyone, which meant she could tell he was fascinated. That wouldn't matter much if he had ever been intrigued before by any girl. Why she intrigued him was still a little puzzling. She was rude, ignorant of decorum, and sassy. She would never make a good queen. Thinking about her as queen, even fleetingly, told Alex he was in trouble already. And by the haughty stare and smirk his sister gave him, she agreed.

For the first time ever, he was annoyed that Mary wanted to put in her order quickly, without her typical dallying around looking at materials. While she was preoccupied, a thought crossed his mind, albeit, an impulsive and reckless one, but he would see it through.

7

SAPPHIRE

Her heart was pounding, her breath was coming quick, and she thought she might faint. And it had nothing to do with those startlingly bright blue eyes, just like sapphires when the sun sparkles through them. He was gorgeous, arrogantly so, but still, he was a guy no girl would willingly tear her eyes from. His skin was pale, his cheeks with a healthy youthful blush, his hair dark but not black like hers. It was a warm brown with hints of red and gold, rich and varied, and more disheveled than her image of a prince would have been. He stood tall and to the thin side, but his shoulders were broad, and his form seemed muscular. He exuded strength and formality, and yet that hair and those eyes gave him a devil-may-care look.

And when he smiled as he said her name, her stomach began to wobble fitfully like it was full of butterflies. He had a dazzling smile and beautiful lips that were symmetrical, the top lip as full as the bottom, and the rest of his features were chiseled and flawless. Too perfect.

She was glad when he finally stepped away so she could get ahold of herself because he did something to her—magic perhaps—to render her completely transfixed. Once he stepped away, it was gone.

The hyperventilating, however, was not stopping. It was the shock of almost telling off someone of the royal family and the corset squeezing the life out of her that made her unable to breathe. She shot back into the dressing room, begging the worker to unlace her a little. The woman tutted her for having her laces drawn too tight. Like she could control her vindictive aunt. She sure hoped the woman didn't assume Toury had it done on purpose. The worker laced her all over again, making it more bearable.

Then her aunt came in to tell her exactly what she knew was coming. "You were allowed one misstep—"

"And I jumped off a cliff," Toury said in defeat. Apparently, she was going to go to boarding school to become refined and find a lifemate as they called them here. It was a daunting future mapped out for her, but at least she could deny any suitor, and if anyone tried to force her to marry, she'd find a way back to Earth.

After the prince had left, and everyone calmed down, Toury tried on dress after dress: day dresses, evening wear, travel dresses, riding habits, and ball gowns. It was much more complex than her usual jeans and T-shirt getup. Since she needed to be measured and try on samples of each, and an entire wardrobe was required, it took forever. She was in the shop for almost two hours, and it was the third shop. They had already purchased chemises, drawers, corsets, sleepwear, and shoes and dropped off the stone to be set. After this, they were still to get shawls, hats, and snoods. Then there were cosmetics—although she tried to tell her aunt she never wore makeup—and going back to pick up her stone brooch.

They were at the counter where the dress shopkeeper was tallying up the bill aloud. She never mentioned the purple dress with the added lace. Her aunt inquired as that was her favorite for it softened her grey eyes, making them appear a little more lavender, or so her aunt had told her. She trusted her aunt in this, for her aunt had the same cloud-gray eyes as she. Just as those beautiful sapphire eyes she had gazed upon matched the eyes of the girl he was with. She peered around the store, but Prince Sapphirian and the girl were gone. Were they related? Aside from the eyes, they didn't look very much alike. The girl was petite and had much lighter hair and smoother features.

Aunt Edwina brought the missing dress to the woman's attention.

"That dress was purchased already."

"What do you mean?" Edwina crossed her arms, her face going firm. With the gray eyes and large nose, her aunt presented a formidable sight. From her aunt's countenance, Toury realized that someone may have nabbed the gown because the prince admired it.

"His Royal Highness has purchased it, my lady," the shopkeeper said in a conspiratorial whisper.

Aunt Edwina's mouth went slack, and she looked at Toury and the shopkeeper, wide-eyed. Then she pulled herself together and said, "Very well then." She settled the bill, and they left the store in a hurry.

Her aunt was silently pensive throughout the rest of the shopping trip and the carriage ride back to the Hematite Estate. But once inside, she let loose. "I do not know what that was about with His Royal Highness, but I do not like it."

"I told you I was sorry. I didn't know who he was."

"Not that, foolish girl. The fact that he bought you a dress."

"He didn't."

"Oh yes, he did, dear. As soon as that lace is added, I'm positive it will arrive here, maybe even this evening. They would deliver it promptly for him." Her aunt fretted, throwing her shawl and bonnet into the waiting servant's arms. Trying to fit into this world, she did as well, despite it feeling weird to have a servant do such a menial task for her.

"Maybe it's just to show he has no hard feelings for my ignorance," Toury said.

"No, you don't understand, Toury." Then her aunt looked at her sympathetically like one would gaze upon a bumbling puppy making a mess. She gave her a small smile. "Come, let us have some tea and a little chat."

Toury followed her aunt into her sitting room, utterly baffled by the woman's behavior. Yesterday, Toury was treated with dismay and coldness, even after she proved she was not an imposter. There was this weird stone her aunt had made her hold that lit up with bright white light which, apparently, was enough to prove she was a Hematite. The way her aunt had even described her own brother—Toury's father—was disheartening. This morning, her aunt was all about turning her into a lady and spending loads of money, which Toury learned was half hers anyway. Toury had the impression that her aunt wanted to get rid of her by pawning her off on a husband as soon as possible. Toury had been a nuisance, but now her aunt's tone had changed.

After the tea and sandwiches were served, and the servants had retreated, her aunt spoke. "I did not wish the servants to overhear what I had to say. I will not have gossip spreading from my corner, although the shopkeeper or any patrons who overheard about the dress will be sure to spread it." She paused and must have seen Toury's bemused expression. "A man does not buy a gift for a woman unless he has an interest in her. To do so and in public is almost a declaration of interest. Prince Sapphirian does not—has never—shown an interest in a lady before. You sure got his attention with your uncouthness, but you need some refining to land him. My only concern is his intentions. If your father were here, he could inquire, but as a lady, I cannot bring up the subject to the prince."

"Intentions?"

"A man who buys a woman a gift is thinking of setting her up either as a mistress or a lifemate. He is the future king of Fyr, yet to be a mistress—a lot of women would want that position, and it is lofty—it's just not worthy of a Hematite, even if our name is dying out, and we have been tossed out of court. We come from a long line of nobility dating back thousands of years. To be a mistress would be a step down, even if it is with the future king."

"I am definitely not going to be his mistress or his wife, Aunt Edwina. I think you are getting way too ahead of yourself. It could just be a gift without any strings attached, and that's if he even bought it for me. It could be going to someone else, the girl in there with him, maybe."

"Girl?" her aunt shook her head. "You must go to this school and right away. Your ineptitude will get you into even more trouble. That *girl* is Princess Mary. And the dress was measured for you. It would not fit anyone else well without alterations. Mary is a good head shorter than you. It was purchased for you, I'm sure of it." Then her aunt sighed as if anxious. "I'm dreadfully concerned he'll make you his mistress. Your behavior is so far removed from genteel, he could not possibly be thinking of you seriously. And marry soon, he must."

"Whatever," Toury deflected the insult and inwardly hoped the prince couldn't force her into any mistress role. "But a gift can just be a gift."

"We'll see," her aunt sniffed haughtily. Toury already understood that look from her aunt. Her aunt believed herself right and Toury wrong and would end the discussion promptly instead of arguing her case.

The dress did arrive that evening. With a simple, unsigned note. *For the girl who has the courage to meet me eye for eye.*

Her aunt sighed. "You met his gaze and lingered?"

"How was I to know that was brave or wrong? What makes him so godly and above anyone else, anyway?"

"Power, magical gifts, and being descended from the first men to grace Fyr, for starters," she said with frustration. "Well then, in two days, you are sure to join Madame Mage's school where you will be refined, educated about the court, and trained in your powers."

"Two days!"

"Yes, not tomorrow but the next. Your little stunt happens to coincide with the quarterly admission. New girls can enter in two days' time. Otherwise, it'll be months, and you clearly need to go as soon as possible. There is so much for you to learn, and I don't know where to begin."

For the first time, Toury did not object. She really had committed quite a few social faux pas on her first trip into the city, and she had no clue about powers. Although she was loathe to admit it, her aunt took more care of her than her Earth parents ever had. She hardly wondered about them, and she sure didn't miss them yet.

"The school will do one more thing for you better than I can. They will keep the prince in line, so to speak. If he visits, it will be chaperoned. Which reminds me. We need a waiting-maid for you."

"I don't need a personal servant."

"They are much more than that. They are bodyguards, and you will need one—don't give me that look—nobles are vanishing, starting with your parents eighteen years ago and most recently with Duchess Ruby, the prince's cousin. I have no idea what enemies your parents had or what they wanted. Not to mention Prince Sapphirian paying court, if he decides to do so, will make you many enemies of other ladies vying for the position. When the king became engaged to the queen, she was almost murdered. This is serious, Tourmaline."

Toury simply nodded. What kind of world had she entered where it was the norm for girls to kill each other over a man? Sure he was a prince, a hot one, and thinking of him made her feel warm all over, but he was still just a boy.

8

A CURTSY

At the Citrine Centennial Ball, Alex found himself oddly excited. He had completely changed his tone from the other day. He couldn't deny, nor did he want to, the fact he was looking for a pair of gray eyes in a beautiful face. Surely, she'd be there, since she had been purchasing gowns the other day. On impulse, he had bought her the dress. He could not regret it, but if it got out, which it probably would, it would appear as if he were courting her. According to Mary, he already was courting her since he had never acted interested in anyone before. He had no idea he was so transparent, but there was an instant connection, and he hardly knew what he was feeling until he reflected on it afterward. He was unable to hide it, despite always being in control of his emotions before meeting the girl. But he didn't care to. He wanted to run into Toury again and see if he felt the same in her presence—like all his worries, even the curse, didn't exist, and nothing mattered but her.

He searched but did not see Toury or her aunt anywhere. He hardly danced, which was typical of him, despite all the girls eyeing him up and trying to be near him to get the coveted chance. Both Toury's absence and Justine's covert stalking of him diminished his good mood quickly. He tried to keep up the appearance of his chipper mood, but he felt it slipping away.

"She's not here," Mary told him as they sought some refreshments. Mary's fingers went up to her crown, a simple circlet woven into her hair, and adjusted it for the umpteenth time. She was never comfortable, never accepting of her role as princess. He, on the other hand, had gotten accustomed to the hefty medallion around his neck. Responsibility had a tangible weight, he well knew.

"Who?" He feigned confusion.

Her eyes squinted at him, and her mouth curled up in a wry grin as if to say he wasn't fooling her. He looked away from her probing gaze and surveyed the room. The girls, covered in powder, their hair lightened with bleaching elixirs, faces painted, bodices pulled too tight, and bosoms spilling, all simpered and smirked and stared at the men, particularly him, as if they were prizes to be won. They swirled around in the ballroom, a swish of dresses and blasts of vibrant colors against the dark tones of the men's attire. But there were no shocking tresses of black hair, no tanned skin, and no gray eyes. He could not get Lady Tourmaline off his mind.

"Apparently, Father hates Hematites, so only a few of the nobility dare to invite them to these kinds of events," Mary said.

"You're a terrible gossip," he teased. Oh, but deep down, he wanted to hear more. He could never ask. Mary would torture him and never let it go if he dared.

"I know, but tread lightly, brother. Her father was banned from court, and no one seems to know why. I don't think our father will be accepting of her."

"I don't need his permission." Alex waved it off.

Mary was silent, and he looked over to see her mouth agog. "You're that serious about her?"

Alex realized his blunder too late to backpedal, but he'd give it a try. "No, I was just saying if I were. I hardly know the girl." He tried to look annoyed by rolling his eyes at her. Deep down, his masochistic mind was planning how to see her tomorrow and the day after that.

Mary gave him a smirk. She wasn't fooled.

"How many of these Hematites are there?" He shifted the subject from his possible amour to her family.

"Only her spinster aunt and her that I know of."

"Hardly a threat then," he mused.

"One person can be a threat, Brother," Mary chided him.

"True," he admitted. He wanted to deny it but couldn't since he knew nothing about Lady Tourmaline. The mystery was tantalizing, and yet, as Mary so candidly pointed out, it could be deadly. But, Alex didn't want to hear anything bad about Lady Tourmaline Hematite and wished he could stop thinking about her. At least he had control over the first. "Want to do a reel with me, Mary?"

She smiled, and he took his sister for a turn on the dance floor. But when the dance ended, the thoughts of Toury still hadn't left him. He had to find out more about her, talk to her again. For now, she was this enigma of intrigue that would only get more interesting until he puzzled out the real her. Maybe if he learned more about her, he'd stop feeling this way.

David entered his quarters the next morning with his breakfast, light pouring in from the window. Alex squinted at the glare and motioned for David to bring the tray to him in bed. He bit into a piece of toast, inquiring as to the time.

"Midday, Your Highness. My apologies. The ball had you up late, and you have no engagements today. I ventured out into the city to make those discreet inquiries you spoke about. Seemed like the best time since not many were about, and you would not need me."

"Of course. I obviously needed the rest. What did you discover?"

"Well, the lady and her aunt live in Ludford, but no one remembers the girl being around or the aunt ever speaking of her until recently. She also purchased an entire wardrobe and other essentials, as if she didn't have any." Alex did not like the sound of this. It explained why she didn't know him but created more mystery and danger surrounding who she really was and where she came from. "After the stunt she pulled in the dress shop, her mortified aunt enrolled her in finishing school. As a noble, obviously, she will be entering Madam Mage's this term."

"Strange," he said. The toast stuck in his throat, and he had to drink some tea to dislodge it. That clogged throat feeling stuck with him, though. Girls who attended the program usually left engaged, or with a roster of suitors so long, their mothers were proudly overwhelmed. That did not sit right with him. He wasn't sure if he wanted her, but after hearing she was heading off to the number one school for fostering marriages, no one else could have her, not until he could gauge how far this interest went. "Isn't my sister off to Mage's today?"

"Yes, I believe she leaves before supper."

"I think we should escort her there ourselves, David."

"As you wish, Prince, but..." the man stopped mid-sentence and looked as if he swallowed a bug.

"But what?"

"Nothing, Your Highness."

"Speak your mind, David. You were about to do one of those annoying speeches to chide my behavior or scold me, usually rightfully. I won't take offense."

"I wasn't going to reprimand you, Your Highness." David turned bright red. That was exactly what he was about to do. Not that Alex minded. He liked that David was honest with him. It was hard to come by as a prince and even harder to get from the help.

"Finish your sentence," Alex ordered, getting a bit annoyed now having to work so hard for a comment he probably didn't truly want to hear. Had David found out something terrible about the gray-eyed beauty who had begun to occupy almost every thought of his?

"But, why? What is this girl to you?"

"Does it matter?"

"To me, kind of. I would just like to know what is going on is all. Fawning over a girl—albeit a beautiful one—isn't like you. Neither is having me make inquiries when you never showed any interest before in a mistress or any inclination to bow down to your parents' demands of matrimony."

"I don't know how to explain what I think about her, yet."

"Sounds a bit like love, Your Highness."

"Don't be daft, David." He chuckled. "I don't know a thing about her. But I want to see her again to see if I still think she's worth getting to know. That is why I want to take Mary to school. That and I feel guilty sleeping away half of her last day." The last statement he said was in haste but the truth. He would miss his sister, having never parted with her before.

If Mary knew his hidden intentions for going with her, she neither let on nor commented. She was lamenting the end of her fun and the beginning of her "prison sentence." Her waiting maid's comment about how the girls would fawn over her and befriend her for their own gain did not improve Mary's mood in the least, according to her ever-growing scowl. It probably was true. He could imagine silly young girls thinking by befriending her, they'd get to the palace and to him. The girls were relentless, their pushy mothers worse. So why was he daring to walk into the viper's nest again?

Once he had his sister registered, there was an informal luncheon out in the gardens for the new girls and their families. When he walked outside into the courtyard, he regretted it, for every eye was upon them, mostly females and the rare fathers who doted on their daughters more than most nobles. Up in the balcony, which wrapped all the way around the courtyard, stood girls two rows thick. There must've been a hundred girls in attendance. Thankfully, he would only have to deal with their stares since the courtyard was reserved for the luncheon. Only about a couple dozen girls were new this round, such as his sister and those gray eyes set in that beautiful face.

He clutched Mary's arm that was wound in his as if to tell her not to leave him. She smiled and looked at him from the corner of her eye, smug and teasing, yet she stayed. They walked around as his sister spoke to others, meeting the girls. He acted aloof, gave his bows to all the debutantes, and acted bored. He hated acting and pretenses, but he learned when young that a dazzling smile and accidental lingering look sent the wrong message.

Some girls read so far into a simple grin that they assumed Alex must love them. When he realized he broke some hearts by merely being pleasant, he refrained from smiling or even making eye contact.

His sister made her way artfully over to Toury as if that were never their destination in the first place, a well-performed feigned meander. He really didn't give Mary enough credit. He would pay her back for her help in this by protesting any engagement with someone she did not desire.

The gray-eyed girl refused to meet his gaze and curtsied deeply. When she sank down, he could see down the plunging neck of her gown to the glorious flesh that spilled out just enough to entice him but not enough to appear wanton. Then, as he bowed his head to her acknowledgment, her eyes momentarily met his before she cast them back at the ground. All it took was that millisecond of eye contact for him to realize his curiosity had turned into a full-fledged fixation. This was not enough. He had to speak with her again, but he couldn't find an excuse. To remain longer with her and her aunt after his sister finished making pleasantries would single her out again.

As Mary tugged his arm gently to suggest they move on, something in his chest twisted violently. He had to speak to her, see her again, and not here, with all these people, but alone.

"Lady Tourmaline, I would like it very much if I could call upon you one day in the near future."

Her mouth opened, and her eyes bulged in shock, hardly a lady-like reaction, but it was so open and honest. This girl could not lie, could not hide anything. She was the complete opposite of the court's ladies and their false propriety, superficial looks, and playacting. She regained her composure and meekly said, "You honor me. I would like that very much, Your Highness." Then she curtsied again, and Mary subtly tugged him along.

Once they were away from her, Mary leaned in and whispered. "Alex, have you lost your mind?"

"I know what I'm doing."

"What, courting her?" Mary asked in a preposterous, hushed tone.

"For appearance's sake, for now, at least. There's something about her, Mary. She's not from here and not like anyone else. Why has she suddenly come to the city? I want to solve the mystery, and yes, I see you rolling your eyes. That is all true, but I will not deny I find her to be the most appealing girl I have met so far. Wouldn't you explore that possibility if you were me?"

Mary breathed out heavily. "Girls will try to trap you. Be careful."

"Oh, I plan on nagging you to play reconnaissance. You know the bad eggs from the good better than anyone." He fluffed her ego.

He stayed with Mary, talking to her for another quarter of an hour until she told him he could go. He was thankful she let him go so quickly because he was tired of everyone staring at him. As he left the gardens to head back to the palace, he threw one more fleeting look over his shoulder to find those steely gray eyes on him. She looked away too late, and her cheeks lit up with a blush that made her all the more appealing. His heart thumped a bit faster in pride and knowledge that she might feel the same level of interest as him.

9

FRIENDSHIP

After the prince and her aunt left, things changed dramatically for Toury. Dozens of people glared at her or rolled their eyes and whispered. Toury steeled herself. She could do this. She was simply the new girl again, something she was used to on Earth. It was the first normal emotion she had felt since entering this world. It was oddly comforting. She needed something familiar in this world, which seemed to be painted from the pages of a fantasy novel. She was alone, true, but she was used to that feeling as well.

"Don't mind them. The normally aloof prince spoke to you and not them. They must hate you on instinct," sounded a voice behind her.

Toury turned and saw the princess. "Princess...Your Highness," Toury fumbled over a greeting and a curtsy.

"Please, drop it to Princess Mary. I'm trying to be incognito."

Toury was astounded and then caught on that the princess was joking. "You might want to rethink that headdress then." Toury referred to the circlet Mary wore.

Mary smiled brightly and laughed. Her laughter fell as she touched her crown. "Don't tell anyone, but I absolutely detest this thing. As a child, I broke several of them on purpose. A new one was always made, so I eventually gave up." Mary looked at Toury as if inspecting her, not in a cruel, fault-finding way as most kids at new schools had done to Toury in the past, but as if she were trying to puzzle Toury out. "I think I like you already. We might very well be the best of friends, Lady Tourmaline."

"Toury. Please, call me Toury."

"Well, Toury, we will suit just fine," Mary said and looped her arm through Toury's.

Toury was stunned by the friendly gesture, but the girls were less abrasive in their stares and looked at Toury in what seemed like awe.

"This will be quite fun, I think. Look at their faces. They're now questioning who you are. You must be a princess from another sphere or a noble who lived far from the capital, a mysterious long-lost daughter of a duke. You're somehow on good terms with royalty, and they're trying to puzzle out why."

Toury smiled a little, but she did not like the limelight. And part of her wondered what this prince really wanted and hoped his sister would know. "Princess Mary, I'm puzzled too. Don't get me wrong. I could use a friend, and I understand the honor you give me."

Mary laughed, leading her inside under the huge archway of stone. Others were clustered around a large staircase with ornately carved wooden railings, so Mary turned her down the side toward the back of the building where the great hall was located. Toury could tell the princess was looking for privacy. "I'm going to make sure we are roomed near each other. To think I dreaded school, and now I have my best friend here, finally meeting you...well, properly at least."

"Finally?" Toury was utterly lost. She tried not to think of the only other time she had seen Mary, which was in the dress shop where she mortified herself.

On seeing they were alone in the hall, Princess Mary sat on a bench, and Toury sat beside her. A wall of intermittent stained glass windows depicted images of dragons, fire, and light, but she didn't understand enough of this place to know what stories they told.

"I'm sorry, Toury." The princess gasped in realization. "Do you not know what we Sapphirians can do?"

Toury shook her head, biting her lip. How could she explain it all without revealing where she came from? "I was abandoned by my parents, and I've had no real education."

"Oh, look at you, fretting so. Toury, all will be well. You are at a great school, and I will be your tutor if you'd like." They were by the main hall, watching as others hugged their families goodbye. Neither of them had anyone there since both her aunt and the prince had left earlier. Her aunt's goodbye was scolding Toury to behave.

"Toury, my family can see the future in the flames, snippets, and we have to know what to look for, so it's never exact. Let's just say, after we ran into you in the dress shop, I was curious. We will be the best of friends, and you'll have to just trust me on that."

Toury wanted to know more, so many things about the future. She was unsure about everything and wanted some kind of assurance, and yet she felt it would be rude to ask. She let the questions fade to the back of her mind.

"Honestly, I did see it, but my brother tried to order it of me." Mary laughed at the idea.

"He ordered you to be my friend?"

"No! Not literally." Mary laughed. "My brother knows if he orders me to do anything, I'll flat out defy it just to irk him. He asked me to scope you out, but I had already seen that we'd get along."

"Why would he do that?" Toury pried.

Mary gave her a pointed look, but when Toury didn't respond, she continued. "I think he wants to know more about you, Toury. Don't ask me why, because he hardly tells me anything. But he doesn't have the freedoms that other men have. He has to be careful around ladies who may have expectations."

Toury was lost and said as much.

"Marriage."

"Oh." Toury's shock was apparent. "Well, I only agreed to come here to be educated. I don't want to marry."

"I see you feel the same way I do about marriage. I am here because I refused to marry. Anyway, don't take it into account too much. I'm supposed to scope all the ladies out for my mother to facilitate a marriage for my brother while finding my own lifemate as well. He's been dodging it for two years now. Because of that, my parents have been much stricter with me. Once they catch wind of Alex actually talking to a girl, my mother will go into a frenzy."

Toury's stomach dropped at the thought. Would the queen have expectations of her? Her trepidation must've been apparent on her face, for Mary patted her hand reassuringly.

"Don't worry over it. Alex is the heir. He gets away with everything. Plus, the more she pushes Alex toward something, the more he backs away. No, she will leave him alone for the most part. But not me. I'm the spare, so my mother will redouble her efforts once she feels like Alex is on a set course. She will expect me to marry within the year, I think."

"I don't understand this custom. To force you to marry someone you hardly know or do not love and at such a young age? It's not fair."

"I'm a princess. It's not all tiaras and gowns. It's duties and facades, smoke and illusions."

"Oh, Princess Mary," Toury lamented. She didn't know what else to say.

"You cannot pity me. I'm a princess. At least I get to pick my spouse. Royal decrees over a thousand years ago banned arranged or forced marriages. I can't say the same for all the spheres."

"Do you have your eye on anyone in particular?" Toury dared to ask.

"You are bold, Lady Toury. I like that. Come, let's to our rooms and see how terribly small they are." The princess deflected the question rather than denying it.

They were shown to their rooms in the same hall. They weren't too small for Toury's standards, although Mary begged to differ. She turned about in her new room while the maid Aunt Edwina had acquired for Toury unpacked her things. The room was cold both in palette and temperature. The walls were blank gray stone as well as the floor, only interrupted by a somewhat worn red carpet. There was a sizeable ornate bed, a desk, a tiny window, a maid's pallet bed in the corner, and a bookshelf. On the shelf was a stack of textbooks. She ran her fingers along the covers: magic, geography, history, and etiquette. That last one would be a good read, she thought sarcastically. And she was right. It was an awful book that discussed how girls should act demure and weak, only speak to men when spoken to, to hide intellect and strength in order to make men feel they were superior. It made her sick with rage at what kind of world she was in. She thought it could not get worse, but the etiquette class itself that she had to go through the following morning was abysmal.

First, Mary was nowhere to be seen. She guessed a princess was exempt from such a class or that she wasn't in her class since there must be a few. Second, the professor found it a delight to use Toury as an example in front of the entire class of what not to do in every social situation. The girls who had been envious of the prince's attention now gloated in Toury's quick fall from grace. She was mortified, angry, frustrated, and overwhelmed...and now crying in her room. She had no friends in this world but the fragile new relationship with the princess, no family but her aunt, who wanted only to be rid of Toury. It started as a new opportunity and adventure, and now it was just like Earth all over again. Yet it made Earth look better than here. One thing was for sure: she wasn't going to do well in this kind of school or in this sphere. The next day, her studies would center on ways to get back to Earth.

10
A PROMISE

Alex was trying to listen to the reports, but it was really hard to pay attention when no one cared what he had to say on the subject. He sat in these meetings to learn but was chastised if he spoke his own opinion. His father never let Alex have an ounce of power or responsibility, and then privately berated him for not having a spine or initiative. The truth was, his father could be a brute, and Alex had learned in his youth to work around his father and do things underhandedly instead of directly through the king.

No, his attention was elsewhere. It was on a girl with tan skin and midnight hair. He could not get Lady Tourmaline out of his head. Never had he been so enthralled by a girl before. Her eyes were such a strange gray color, like a half-polished hematite stone, rich, dark, and sparkling. He had seen gray eyes on others, but usually a pale, cold gray or a gray-blue like a twilight evening such as Susanna Danburite, a beauty of the court who married a couple years ago. All the sons in the noble family Onyx even had almost coal-black eyes, but the eyes of the Hematite ladies were different. The old spinster and Lady Toury had the same eye color, but the way the eye color contrasted with Toury's skin and the vivacity behind her gaze made them so much more appealing than any other eyes he had gazed upon.

And then like that, he saw her in the flickering flames of the fireplace. He jerked upright in his chair, inadvertently garnering his father's attention and receiving a glare. He met his father's gaze and held steady in a challenge. His father looked away first because the general was asking him a direct question. Alex looked over to the fire and saw Toury in the flames. He focused his thoughts on her, and she came more into detail, as if she were carved of orange and black light. He saw himself dancing with her, kissing her, and...

"Alex!" his father's voice barked.

He reluctantly yanked his eyes away from a somewhat scandalous and intimate-looking scene. What did this mean? He had never seen any women in the flames and had given up hope in finding *the one* in the flames, a game he and Mary had played now and then as children to satisfy her precocious mind. She proclaimed to know who her lifemate might be but refused to tell a soul. He hadn't really believed her until now. Was Toury his lifemate?

His heart thumped wildly at the idea and also the conflicting anxiety of settling down. The scene his father interrupted was one only a man and his lifemate, or his mistress perhaps, would partake in.

"Boy! Are you even listening?" his father demanded.

"No," he said in a tone much bolder than his father probably anticipated. "I was seeing the future in the flames. My apologies, Father, gentlemen, but I have to go." Alex spoke hurriedly and then rushed from the room before his father could protest, not that he would much since he was always worried about appearances.

"Young men," he heard his father scoff as the door closed behind him.

David flanked him, Alex's eternal shadow, when all Alex wanted was to be alone. In his quarters, he entered his personal living room and lit a fire in the grate. David looked over in wonderment since Alex never had a fire in his room except to firebrand, but David went about cleaning up Alex's things. Alex tried to ignore the servant's presence and stared deeply into the flames. He did not see her. He thought of those eyes, that hair, and the svelte, long body, supple in the right areas. But when he tried to think of her smile, he couldn't remember it in detail or how her lips broke over her teeth. Did he know? Had he even seen her smile? He had to see her again. And the flames weren't cooperating. What was the point of this kind of magic when it was so fickle?

"Prince?" David asked quietly, not wanting to disrupt him, and yet his tone was concerned.

"Yes?" He turned away from the flames.

"Does something trouble you?"

"The future, David, and not knowing it irritates me."

"Most don't, Your Highness."

A tap at the door sounded, and David promptly opened it to reveal Alex's mother. Visiting him in his quarters? She must have heard he had fled from the meeting. He hoped she wasn't there to admonish him too. He was at the age where he'd dare to defy his father but felt guilty when defying his mother.

"To what do I owe this pleasure, Mother?" The ever-dutiful son stood up and greeted his mother chivalrously, leading her to the settee to sit down.

"I craved a word in private. I've been meaning to talk to you without your father or Mary around. You fleeing from the military funding meeting presented a good time to do so."

"You're not here to scold me mercilessly?"

"Alex, you're a grown man, even if you sometimes do not act like it."

That was a low blow, and he straightened his shoulders at the insult.

"You will be king before you know it. I hope you will take your responsibilities seriously."

"When am I not serious?" he countered. He never had fun, and he rarely smiled or laughed. Life was duty all the time, never his own.

His mother sighed and looked down into her hands. "I had hoped, for many reasons, that you didn't have to be so serious or always attend to your duties, that you could be free in life until you were much older. Things are not as we wish." She took a deep breath as if to gain courage. She was worrying him.

"Mother?" he asked, concerned, taking up her hand.

She squeezed it and then met his gaze. "There's a reason I'm pressing you to marry, Alex. There are the necromancers... We need the line to be secure. There's only you, Mary, and your cousin Henry now. After that..." She dramatically left the thought unfinished. "Three of you stand between order and chaos."

"Four. You're forgetting Father."

"Your father will not last long, Alex." Her voice was a ghost of a whisper. He made her repeat it, hoping he had heard her wrong. He had not.

"How much time?" He swallowed to clear his throat for his voice had wavered. The man may have been an unloving brute at times, but he was Alex's father.

"The healers said maybe half a year to a year."

Alex took a deep breath. His father was dying, and he would have to be king in less than a year's time. He knew his father's health was declining, but to be this bad without outsiders noticing showed how well his father played his part. He would have to be engaged before his father's death, or any disgruntled person would try to take his life to destroy their line. That was the reality of things.

After consoling his mother, Alex swore not to say anything to his father about knowing.

"There's one more thing, Alex," his mother said.

"I know," he stopped her. "I must be engaged before..." He could not finish the statement about his father's death. He took up her hand again. "Mother, I promise to seek out my bride. I will look in earnest, go to these suitor balls, hound Mary for information, everything. I will be engaged within six months. This I vow to you."

This simple promise seemed to lift some of the strain off her face, and her shoulders sagged just a little less. He was glad he could bestow some kind of happiness onto her during the upcoming worst days of her life. And yet he was racked with guilt for not foreseeing this, for being noncompliant when it came to matrimony.

When she left, he returned his gaze to the flames. When he saw Toury's face in the flames again, he realized how needless the guilt was. He could never have resigned himself to marriage until he met Toury. He had to see her again. If he felt the same after the visit, he would court her in earnest.

11
LIGHTNESS

Light magic, dark magic, fire magic, blood magic, and precious stone magic. It was all overwhelming, and Toury couldn't keep anything straight. She seemed to be the only one in the library studying, the only one who needed to. Toury poured over the book again, ignoring Mary's sigh of boredom. Toury gave her a leveled gaze.

"You don't have to be here, you know," Toury told her.

"What else would I do? I can't stand that lot." She nodded at the girls gossiping and laughing across the library. "All brownnosing and fake. I like how you treat me as if I were a normal person."

"Well, you are just like everyone else, except you have a better house and get to wear a crown." Toury smiled at her.

Mary touched the silver circlet on her head. "They all act like I'm some goddess and think of what they can gain by befriending me. You don't."

Half reading, half listening, Toury said, "Well, that's because I'm not looking for anything but a friend."

"I know," Mary said quietly. "I think that's what has intrigued my brother as well. You're transparent, you know, and real, but in a good way."

"Your brother?" Toury's attention snapped up.

Mary gave her a knowing grin. "You had to have noticed he treats you differently than other girls."

"But he asked to see me and hasn't come." Toury shook her head, staring down at her book. Surely, if he did like her, he'd be there visiting her. And she shouldn't care that he hadn't.

"I'm sure he has been very busy with state affairs. You realize we've only been here a week, right?"

That shocked Toury. It felt like a month with all the lessons of etiquette, dance, history, and powers. The professors had poured so much information into her overwrought brain, it felt like ages had gone by. "That's all? It feels longer."

"C'mon," Mary urged. "Let's go out for a walk in the gardens. I can't stand being cooped up too long, and you need a break."

"I have to study. I don't know any of this stuff. I wasn't educated about magic or anything. I'm completely lost," Toury couldn't hide the waver in her voice.

Mary closed the book and squeezed Toury's hand. "I'll teach you as we walk. Now come. The fresh air will do you good."

The courtyard gardens were lush and beautiful. She hadn't truly looked at them the day she arrived at school when she was nervous and distracted by the royals' attention. She hadn't been back since, and she realized she was missing out. Hedges lined the walls, and in front of them, an abundance of carefully planted flowers made beautiful patterns of varying colors and heights. She imagined if she were to look down from the above veranda, it would make a beautiful picture and noted to herself to check it out later. In the middle of the garden, there was a cluster of fir trees and a patio with some benches. The grass was a vibrant green, only interrupted by the pebbled path they walked on.

Mary and Toury walked arm in arm. Some girls glared at her, and Toury tried to ignore them but couldn't.

Mary glared at the gaggle of girls, and they scattered off, whispering furiously.

"Insufferable girls," Mary said.

"It's me they don't like," Toury reminded her.

"You can't take all the blame." She tapped her tiara. "This is like a huge marker separating me from everyone else."

"Can't you just not wear it?"

"I love your innocence, Toury. It's refreshing."

Mary bent down and plucked a flower off the rose bushes that lined the path toward the fir trees. Toury imagined if she had touched a thing in this garden, she'd be reprimanded, but a princess probably could do anything she wanted without rebuff. Mary smelled the flower with a smile.

"But your brother doesn't have to wear a crown in public..."

"Because he has a medallion, that huge round thing around his neck. Haven't you noticed it?"

Toury shook her head. How did she miss a huge medallion? She was probably fixated only on his ridiculously gorgeous eyes or his wonderfully sculpted lips. They were both dangerously distracting.

"Anyway, onto this magic," Mary began in a voice that would precipitate a lesson. Toury concentrated on her words. "I hope one day, you'll trust me enough to tell me where you came from to lack any type of knowledge, but for now, I won't push it. You know, in Fyr, the most powerful magic is through white magic—predominantly fire and light. This encompasses the firebranders and lightbearers, good people who can foresee the future in the flames, heal people, and do various other useful things. Most sorcerers fall into a mix of branders and bearers, while the cunning folk, or magicians, only have a little magic aligned with fire or light. Then there's black magic, mainly using fire and darkness for evil purposes. Dark magic is hard to control, so one pays a huge price for using it, not to mention that it's illegal. There are necromancers in our land, a secret society of seemingly powerful people who conjure the opposite of what makes Fyr what it is. Power comes from light and fire magic, but these people learn how to feed off evil and darkness. And they use the dark to damper the light or fire through such means as curses and other evils. The necromancers can even communicate with the dead, and a few historically have been known to resurrect them."

"Yes, you've made entire books seem so simple."

Mary laughed. "There is much more to it, of course, and we haven't even discussed blood magic and the stones. I wouldn't worry about the stones yet. I don't think that is your calling."

"How do you know?"

"I'm a Sapphirian, so I can tell. We are the most powerful of all the land and the last of our race."

"Race?"

"Some are light, some are dark, some elemental—meaning in tune with the stones—and some are fire. I have fire in my blood, in my powers. Take my hand," Mary instructed. Toury took up her hand and felt the warmth radiate up her arm. Mary let go and put her arm through Toury's as they walked. Toury tried to ignore the other girls who were still nearby, whispering harshly.

"I can conjure the flames, make them do my bidding. Few are left who can boast that. We are beyond firebranders, we *are* fire."

"But how are we different? It's almost talk of other species. If there were only dragons in the beginning, and your family descended from them as the first men, how did the rest of us get here?" she asked. Betty had already told her some about Fyr's version of religion, but she only seemed to be forthcoming when Toury asked her questions, and Toury never knew the right ones to ask.

"The Great Book is what you need to answer that question," Mary told her. "To sum it up, there weren't just dragons in the beginning. There were the beings made of pure light. This land is light and fire, as you know. They battled, and eventually, man and woman were born from the flames—the god and goddess. It's very symbolic—the book I mean—but what really happened was most likely immigration from other spheres. Most of Fyr is from Earth. One of my tutors once told me they found the magic in a place called Englaland.

"England." Toury corrected.

Mary's eyes flicked knowingly over Toury before the princess continued. "But Earth has lost most of its magic, they say. No one can just come here without imported magic from another sphere."

This made so much sense to Toury now. It explained how everything on Fyr seemed to follow that of Earth over time, in language, in clothing and architecture, but completely stopped. Electricity and indoor plumbing were probably the most modern things she saw in Fyr. That must've been when magic dwindled.

"Your name, Toury, sounds as if you are descended from light. Your ancestors were around from the times of the Great Book, when the people of Fyr started writing down history. Light magic will be your calling. You just need to tap into it."

"How do I do that? I don't feel magical."

"It's difficult at first, and you're at a major disadvantage. We all learned to use our magic from birth, and it seems somehow your training was neglected. It's as if you are starting as a newborn, but at least you'll learn faster. The only way to speed up the process is for you to be tutored by one of your kind. Unfortunately, your kind are dwindling as much as firebranders. For a start, you have to become one with your power. I remember I had to stare at the fire for hours as a child before I could ever conjure it. It will come to you."

"My aunt should be helping me, but she insisted I come here to learn decorum, not powers."

"Well, decorum is not my forte. It's overrated anyway." Mary laughed lightly.

"His Royal Highness, Prince Alexander is here to see you," a servant told them.

"Tell him I will be there presently," Mary instructed.

"Sorry, Your Highness. Prince Sapphirian asked for Lady Tourmaline. I can see if he wants you to join as well, Your Highness. I'm sure he was unaware you walked together," the servant rambled nervously, his face turning beet red.

"I will see you later, Toury." Mary gave her a grin and raised her brows insinuating something more than just a friendly visit on her brother's part.

"Princess Mary, please, don't leave me. I'm sure he wants to see you as well," Toury pleaded, now nervous about why the prince would want a private audience with her and how she was supposed to behave toward him.

"My brother knows his own mind and always gets his way. He would've included me in the invitation if he wanted me to join." Mary gave Toury's shoulder a soft squeeze and abandoned her.

Toury felt as if the servant were walking her toward her execution; she was that anxious. She didn't know why he had singled her out after she insulted him. The only thing she could possibly come up with was what Mary had alluded to. She didn't fawn all over him like the other silly girls at her school did. Beyond that, she had no idea what he wanted, and that bothered her. It felt like an ambush.

When she entered the golden salon, a meeting room for only the most influential suitors, the headmistress, aptly called Miss Headmistress as all cunning folk were named by profession, was making pleasantries with Prince Alexander. Toury came in and played hostess by pouring the firespice tea. In such deep concentration, Toury hardly followed their conversation, having only learned the tea service routine the day before. As she handed the tea to the prince, their gazes met, and his finger purposefully brushed hers, making her hands shake nervously. She was glad once he had the teacup in his hands for she feared she would dump it into his lap.

She sat down across from him and sipped her tea to have something to do, despite how it scalded her tongue.

"Toury is new here, Your Highness—to the area, I mean—and it seems her education has been neglected, so we must forgive her ignorance in such social situations," Miss Headmistress told him, her cheeks pink with embarrassment.

"What have I done wrong now?" Toury asked, exasperated.

Miss Headmistress closed her eyes, and Toury realized too late that her comment made the situation worse.

"I believe she expects you to lead the conversation, my lady," the prince supplied. His voice was not playful nor teasing. He was prim and serious. She was thrown off. This wasn't the prince she'd met twice before.

"How are you this fine day, Your Highness?" she asked, mustering all the proper etiquette she had in her.

Her headmistress smiled at her in approval.

But he frowned at her. The prince was not impressed. "I am quite well, and you, my lady?"

"I am well," she replied.

He looked at her, expecting more.

"Acclimating to a new society is difficult, yet I find I can rise above most challenges."

The prince's mouth quirked at this, apparently amused. He seemed to like the real Toury, but how could she unleash her true personality with the headmistress sitting there?

"I'm sure it is difficult, yet pouring tea and making conversation shouldn't be your primary concerns if your education is lacking. Your powers should be explored."

"Your Highness, our primary concern with Lady Tourmaline is to teach her some decorum, to earn the title of lady in her behavior so she can—"

"That's not acceptable. She is a Hematite. If she has light magic, she must practice it. Dark forces are threatening this world, and you are worried about a possible lightbearer's propriety? It seems a misplaced notion to me. But what would I know?"

Toury was happy, in a way, that he was defending her right to learn her magic, yet his tone was so chiding and arrogant that she pitied her flustering, apologizing headmistress. The prince gave Toury a look as if to tell her he was in charge, and she suddenly felt rebellious, so much so, she thought about proclaiming she could fight her own battles and fleeing from the room.

12
A BROOCH

Alex was being too formal, and he could see it annoyed Toury, although she'd never show it in front of the headmistress. He just couldn't afford a scandal at the moment since his interest in her was already being spread around the land. Despite wanting to avoid gossip, he needed a more private conversation, which for him, meant her maid and his valet would be the only ones present. David would buy the maid's silence if necessary, but the other ladies in the school would see them talking and walking together. There was nothing for it. He could not bear these simple civilities and her being some strange, passive creature while he was pompous and grave. He had to talk to her, and he wanted to see the real her.

"Lady Tourmaline, would you honor me with a walk in the gardens?"

"Why yes, Your Royal Highness. I would be happy to oblige you."

He sighed, relieved. The headmistress looked a bit miffed to be left out of the deal. He was sure she had been excited to have an audience with royalty, and now she would have no gossip to share with the professors.

Once they were outside, he took up her hand and placed it on the inside of his arm. She looked at him sheepishly for forgetting her decorum, and he winked at her. "Wouldn't want your headmistress scolding you after I leave."

She smiled, but it didn't reach her eyes.

"What? Are they terrible here?" he asked.

"No. They are teaching me what I lack most effectively. I smiled because you seem much different than in the sitting room," she said.

"And that is good?"

"Yes." She bit her lip. It seemed the move was done from timidity and not done coyly as some of the debutantes in this school would do. Still, those teeth on her lip evoked something inside him that coy girls' lips did not. She did not look at him. It saddened him that she would not meet his gaze as boldly as when they first met. He wanted to see those gray eyes look into his again.

She continued, "You seemed more at ease in the dress shop." Then she squeezed his arm and quickly added, "Your Highness."

"Please, no titles. Call me Alex, and let me call you Toury."

He said it before thinking, because no one, save his family, ignored his title. If she actually called him Alex in public, people would assume she was intimate with him, and that could ruin her.

"I am sure that's against decorum. I'm trying to behave and acclimate. I'll call you Prince Alexander if you allow it."

"Prince Alexander it is then." He was glad that one of them was thinking with propriety in mind.

For some reason, he wanted to pull the sassy girl out of her. He had thought she needed to be demure and tamed, but now, after a week in this school, she seemed too docile. He preferred the rugged attitude and confidence he saw in the dress shop.

"Why do you wish to fit in so badly?"

"Well, I'm not from here, and I don't know much. I only agreed to come here to learn about my powers."

"No one taught you? Where are you from, exactly?"

"That is a long story, I'm afraid."

"Then let us sit up here, and you can tell me." He pointed to the stone benches that were hidden from most people's views by a few fir trees. He never looked up, but he felt eyes on him from the balconies above as they walked. The only person watching them on the ground level was the headmistress from the entry of the courtyard. What did they all think of him arriving not to see his sister, but some new girl whom they most likely saw as a lot of work? Maybe his visit would help her and put her in the professors' good graces.

Toury sat down, and he sat down next to her, just a little closer than he probably should have. Something about her made him want to break some rules too.

"I don't know where to begin, but I guess I should start that I'm from Earth." She let out a nervous laugh.

"From Earth?" He tried not to react. Could it be...was it possible that Toury was the savior? Had she met with Ruby? His mind churned trying to think about how to get the info he needed out of her without pressing her too hard. He had to gain her trust. "Well, that explains your accent."

"Yeah. Apparently, my parents were from here but took me there. I was somehow adopted by earthlings—wow, I never thought about it until now that I was literally an alien there. You always think about aliens being those little green beings with black eyes..." she babbled and then covered her mouth, trying to regain her decorum.

"One day, you'll have to explain these green beings to me, but right now, I'm more interested in your lineage. What happened to your parents?"

"I don't know. They just abandoned me," Toury said, shrugging. She did not seem bothered by not knowing them as some orphans did. It meant she was made of sturdier stuff, and he liked that.

"Tourmaline and Hematite. You come from those lines?"

"Yes." She winced. So she had heard her family wasn't welcomed at court. He would try to remedy that after finding out why.

"Tourmaline or Hematite, either family's power is much needed in society today. If you tap into those powers, you'll not want for anything in Fyr."

"What do you mean? What do you know about my family?"

"Just that both sides of your family were extremely talented with light magic, the Tourmalines by warding off negativity and evil, the Hematites as healers. The land is having a large problem with darkness right now. You might just be what this land needs at the right time." He was hinting to the fact he suspected she was the savior, but she didn't seem to catch on. He had to know the truth. "How did you get here from Earth, then?"

Toury met his gaze before looking down quickly. He dipped his head down lower and waited until she met his gaze again. He had this overwhelming urge to kiss her then, the girl who was not afraid to meet his gaze with her beautiful gray eyes, but he refrained. Societal dictations would have them engaged if he did that. It would make his mother happy, but he needed to know more about this girl before he could take that plunge.

"You can trust me," he told her. He backed away subtly. He should not be so close to her, forcing her to meet him eye to eye, and yet it felt so natural.

"A stone." His stomach flopped, and his heart raced as she continued, "I found it in my bag, and there was pain and light, and I woke up in a field by Ludford." She downplayed it, but he heard the wavering in her voice, and he felt protective of her. He had no idea how he felt so connected to her, so aware of her emotions, and so intrigued by her, but she had somehow wormed her way into his very being. That didn't seem good, not with everything going on now. Wasn't her being the possible savior and someone he might court be a conflict of interest? Or was his future so fortuitous that it was falling magnificently in place?

"That sounds...horrible, actually." He could think of no better word for being taken from your home and thrown into a new world. "Did you have family and—"

60

"They were never nice to me nor loved me. I never really fit in anywhere." Then she covered her mouth and looked at him, mortified. "I shouldn't have interrupted you, sorry." Then she added, "Your Highness."

"A natural conversation is much more pleasant than falsity and flowery compliments. Please, don't let them change you too much, Toury." She smiled at him, and he smiled back at her. "Just enough not to get arrested by insulting royalty, maybe."

She blushed up bright but then laughed aloud. "You will never let me forget that, will you?"

"Never," he teased back. "Are you here to stay, then?" The loaded question hung in the air. It shouldn't matter, but it did to him. As the savior, he needed her to stay. But as a man, due to whatever this feeling was building up inside him, he *wanted* her to stay.

"Well, I'm not sure, really. There's not much to go back to, but there's not much here for me yet. I guess I'm at an impasse. And I don't think this stupid thing will work again, anyway." She moved her shawl aside, and all he noticed at first were her breasts, but then he saw she clutched a brooch fastened on her dress right between what he was trying not to ogle. The brooch had a large smooth, round piece of labradorite in it.

His stomach dropped, and his face must've shown the shock he felt because she looked at him, eyes full of fear, mouth slightly trembling. It was confirmation. This was Ruby's stone full of magic, power, and knowledge. He reached out to touch it, and she backed up away from him, her face aghast.

"I apologize." He put his hands up to show her he meant no harm. "Could I please see that? It's extremely important."

"Prince Alexander." His name rolling off in her Earth accent—slightly less refined than ladies of Fyr and sexily lilted—sent chills down his spine. "I know I'm not allowed to deny you anything," she began. His mind wandered to what liberties he could take with that expression. "But this can hurt you. It shocked my aunt miserably."

Alex smiled at her ignorance. He was glad she was being educated. A girl with a strong will like hers should have a strong mind to match it. She seemed intelligent, but the fact she was suddenly dropped into Fyr put her at a great disadvantage. He could imagine the woman she would become when her knowledge of this sphere caught up with her quick turn of mind. She would become the woman he could not deny and would have to marry. She could be a queen.

"I'll be fine, and I'll give it back. We Sapphirians are immune to this type of magic. Could you take it off for a moment? I'm glad you stopped me. I wasn't thinking straight. I shouldn't have tried to touch you...there especially." He stumbled over his words, feeling nervous and awkward. He never felt that way, and he didn't like it.

She was hesitant.

"I promise I will give it back. If it is what I think it is, I might be able to unlock it."

"I don't understand."

"It's classified."

"Seriously?" She looked at him, her eyes narrowing and mouth frowning, the spitfire coming out of her.

"I am serious. This is extremely classified. Not even my family knows, not even the king himself. Special princely operation here." He kept talking, he didn't know why. He shouldn't have said anything. He didn't know or trust her. But he wanted to. This was how kings and princes fell, how they became weak and got assassinated. They said the wrong thing to the wrong person.

"Well then, I won't let you see it," she said, full of spite. She even pushed her chest out, showing the brooch—and other things—off as if to tease him.

"You will be the death of me," he said as a joke at first, but it could be true. "Literally, if I tell you this, and it leaves this garden..." He motioned to David, who began a perimeter sweep to ensure there were no eavesdroppers.

"I won't tell anyone." She frowned.

He smiled and checked to see if the headmistress lingered. Not seeing her or any professors around, he moved a bit closer, drawn to her. If he just leaned in a bit more, their shoulders would touch, but she might think he was trying to kiss her. Part of him wanted to do exactly that. Instead, he hastily picked up her hand in his. "Toury..." but words failed him. When he touched her, he felt a rush of energy surge into him. He withdrew his hand quickly. Her power raced through him, and for a moment, the darkness lifted, and he felt strong, free, and happy. Then like a cloud blocking the sun, the darkness descended again over him.

"What was that?" she asked.

"It must be your Hematite powers. If you could affect me like that, I can definitely open the stone for you."

"Please, Alex, explain."

The way she said his name, stripped of his title and intimate sounding, lowered his inhibitions, making him want to tell her everything. He wanted more than that. He wanted to pull her close to him and explore her mouth with his own. He wanted to see her in that purple dress again, the one that put her body on display. He wanted her and couldn't figure out how it was so intense so fast.

David gave him the all clear that no one was in earshot. David led her maid off a few feet, still in range to protect her charge, yet unable to hear them.

"There is so much you need to know to understand it, things they aren't going to teach you here. You know by now there is white and black magic. In short, the black magic is a threat created by those who practice it, mainly the necromancers hidden among us."

"Mary told me about them."

"Did she tell you about the curse?" Alex's self-confidence wavered. The last thing he wanted was to tell a girl he fancied about his faults. Well, it was beyond a shortcoming. It was probably a major turn-off.

Toury's brow furrowed in confusion as she shook her head.

"You see, I was cursed as an infant by a talented necromancer. It is hard for me to keep the darkness at bay. Your simple touch banished all darkness from me for just a moment. It's as if...you can use the light to ward off the dark yet heal with it too. If it is so, this would be an extraordinary talent. You must keep your powers and how you can help me a secret between us. Not for my sake, but for your safety." He sighed. "Unfortunately, the entire kingdom knows of my curse."

"My touch cures you?" she asked with a small tone of pride. She grabbed his hand in hers, and he felt the power climbing up his arm. On top of the light magic emanating from her, her touch felt pleasant for other, more scandalous, reasons.

"You better stop that, Toury, or I may never let you go," he told her. It was a loaded comment, and when she sensed his tone, she let go. He had half a mind to take her away with him to cure him—and for the other reasons her touch inflamed him. He could if he wanted to, but that would ruin her.

He changed the subject, trusting her implicitly. "That stone was my cousin Ruby's. She fled to Earth through it to hide some important knowledge. What of, I don't know. But what she knew and what power that stone has could save or destroy this entire sphere. Not many people can touch it from what you say, but royalty can and a few fireproof folk. This information and all the powers cannot fall into the wrong hands. Do you trust your maid?"

Toury shrugged.

"I'll have a waiting-maid sent to you. I'll send one I trust who is faithful and well-trained to protect you."

"Prince…"

"Not negotiable. You must be protected at all times."

"You mean the stone must be?"

"No, you. Hand it over. I'm going to unlock it for you. I cannot absorb Ruby's fire, but your light will. Do not touch the stone itself until you are alone and safe under the protection of your new waiting-maid. The transfer may be overwhelming. I'm not sure how you'll see Ruby's knowledge or if you'll be able to use her powers, but at least it will be safe inside you, where no one can access it, rather than in the stone."

"My aunt explained this same thing, sort of." She unfastened the brooch and handed it to him. His heart pounded in his chest in appreciation of her trust in him.

Alex closed his eyes to concentrate and put his hand over the brooch, conjuring fire in his hand. He felt the brooch heat up under his palm, and the stone moved as if molten under his flesh. He melded with the stone and then entered within himself to find the stone's power. It was shut up tight, and Ruby had made it hard to unlock, but he twisted and turned it to pry it open, all while fighting off the darkness in him that tried to creep in. Without the curse, he could have cracked into it in a second, but his mind always had to focus on controlling the curse so it wouldn't overtake him. Finally, it gave way, and he felt the connection sever.

He opened his eyes to steel-gray ones observing him.

"It's done." He leaned over and pinned the brooch onto her dress by her shoulder for decorum sake and so she would not touch it. "And please, tell no one, not even Mary."

Toury frowned at this. "What shall I say if she asks why you came to see me? I don't like lying, and she is my friend."

"She most likely will make assumptions rather than ask, which is typical of my sister." He smiled, thinking about how Mary would view his visit. "Do tell her I'll be there to support her at the balls, for I must go. I will return to visit you again." He stood up, and she followed.

"Is that allowed?"

"No one commands me, Toury. I can do as I please."

"I meant, is it proper?"

"They'll see me as a suitor, but they'll already assume that anyway after this visit. I don't make a habit of visiting schoolgirls."

She blushed and looked away as they walked back. "And what should I see you as?" she asked.

He liked her candid attitude. He doubted there would ever be a misunderstanding between them. "My friend, I hope."

She beamed at that. Oh, how he wished he said he wanted her to be something more. But for the first time in his life, the prince was afraid of rejection. It was much too soon to speak of serious commitments, but by the god of fire, he wanted to.

As soon as Toury entered the building, he nodded to David, who knew to grab Alex's traveling cloak so he could be transported back to the castle with Alex. One of the perks of having fire magic on the Fyr sphere was his ability to bend matter around him and will himself somewhere else and simply appear there.

Today, Alex reappeared in his sitting room and ordered David to fetch a particular maid from the servant quarters. He penned a short note, sealed with wax he melted in his palm, and stamped it with his seal. When David returned with the servant, Madge, he questioned her to assure he had chosen the right servant—there were so many of them at the palace, he often forgot who had what talent—and he delivered her to the school. When he returned, he was utterly exhausted. Transporting took a lot out of him, and he felt the dark magic sludging around inside him, trying to overpower his fire. He didn't rest long before a servant knocked on the door, announcing to David that Alex had a visitor.

Lord Cobalt was waiting for him in the Prince's Room, his room in the main wing to entertain courtiers. No one was permitted in his quarters, not even best friends; it was his safe haven, the one place he could be alone and do as he wished.

"Prince Alex," Cobalt greeted him jovially. He shook his hand, but Cobalt drew him into a half hug and a hard pat on the back before he let go. David tensed. It was the man's job to look for threats, and no one dared to really touch Alex, but Cobalt was a childhood friend. He had proven himself through time. "What is this rumor I've heard about you?"

"I hardly listen to the titters about me, half false, and I'm sure there are plenty. Which one are you referring to?" He looked to the servant lingering in the doorway. "Knox, some firewhiskey and water, please."

The servant entered and began pouring the drinks as he and Cobalt settled down into armchairs by the fireplace. Cobalt nodded to the fire. Alex smiled and lit it for him simply by thinking of it. "Are you actually cold or simply marveling over my power after all these years?" Cobalt seemed to always urge Alex to do something and was amused by his fire powers every time.

"It never gets old. It's pretty cool. My powers are pathetic."

"Peace, inspiration, the muse. Every stone, every noble family, is important. Do you know how powerful it could be to walk into a room and lift everyone's mood and create peace simply by leaking power out? It is an honorable power."

"But fire is so tough. And the ladies love it."

"You have the embodiment of charisma in you, as seen by your ability to have the girls flocking around you wherever you go. You don't need more than that."

The tray of drinks was placed on the table between them, and Knox left. David went and closed the door.

"So what of this rumor?" Alex returned to the subject now that they were alone, well, as alone as he could be. David would never utter a word to other servants about him.

"Speaking of the ladies, I heard a rumor of you, a lady, and a dress?" Cobalt raised his brows, insinuating. Alex could only tell him so much. No one knew about the savior or anything other than rumors of necromancers his father fought to squash. He'd have to present half the scenario. He knew Cobalt's cavalier and philandering ways would clash with the sentiment of courting a woman for marriage. He figured Cobalt would tease him mercilessly about it, and he did not disappoint.

13

CITRINE

Once Toury was alone in her room, she looked in the mirror and went to remove the brooch. Before she could even touch it, the door opened, and a young woman walked in. She bowed and handed Toury a scroll. Then this strange woman closed the door and eyed the room. She went over to the window and checked the lock. She began feeling the walls, most likely for loose bricks like they do in the movies—not that anyone on Fyr would get that reference since there was no television—where they'd find a secret passageway.

Toury ignored her odd behavior and looked at the rolled up and sealed paper in her hand, hoping that it would have some answers. The wax seal had the stamp of a crown with the outline of flames around it. It must be from the royal family, but Prince Alexander had just left moments ago, and Mary lived at school with her. Why would someone else send her correspondence?

She cracked it open and unfolded the paper. A small message was written across it in a neat masculine hand.

Dearest Toury,

Please accept my gift of Madge, the servant before you. She is a warrior, a scholar, and trained in courtly matters. She can help you with anything, is trustworthy, and most importantly, she will protect you.

Your humble admirer,
Prince Alexander

Toury reread it. "Dearest" and "admirer"? These weren't words to a friend, which is what he had offered only minutes ago. This seemed to insinuate much more. She was flattered, excited at the prospect of him liking her.

Toury tore her eyes away from what was the first love letter—if it qualified as one—she had ever received, and examined Madge. She looked sturdy and strong yet had a feminine grace that fooled one into thinking she could be weak. She was a warrior compared to the meek Betty her aunt had hired. A feeling of unease crept over Toury. Why wasn't her maid good enough if her aunt had thought so? The prince had sent one of his servants.

"Is the prince keeping tabs on me? Are you to report to him?"

"No, Lady Tourmaline. I am your servant. My only orders have been to help you adjust, educate and inform you, and lay my life out to protect you in every way."

The last part of that comment took Toury aback. "Surely, it won't come to that."

"I am also a magician, and my powers include the ability to read people's minds, vaguely."

"Vaguely?"

"I get the sense of every thought and mood, but no one can read one's mind word for word. And my lady, there are many jealous of you, a few who hate you, and a couple who have murderous thoughts of you. The problem is there are too many minds in this building too close together to determine who—"

"Who wants me dead," Toury finished for the candid servant. This was TMI on a first meeting, but she supposed she should get used to it. It was better to be prepared than to be caught unawares. The cold decor of the room, Prince Alexander's orders, and the fact that people wanted her dead, all chilled her. Madge stoked the fire as if she noted Toury was cold, even though Toury felt chilled on the inside. This maid was good. She would have to anticipate Toury's every need because she wasn't accustomed to or comfortable with ordering people around.

"How did the prince...? He was sending you anyway, wasn't he?"

"I'm not sure what you mean, but the prince came to me just moments ago and told me of my new assignment. My things will arrive later today."

"But...how? He just left minutes ago."

"Did you not know Prince Alexander can transport? All Sapphirians can." When Toury still looked utterly lost, Madge continued, "On Earth, I believe you call it teleporting, but the prince evokes magical fire to bend the matter around him and slip through space to wherever he envisions."

"You know of Earth?"

"I had a special assignment there and had to study Earthlings and the realm itself to blend in. I was there for two years. I believe that was one of the reasons the prince saw me fit for such an esteemed position. Now, do you have any more questions? The enchanted stone on you may help you with some of them. Shall we transfer the powers?"

Toury looked at the brooch and went to touch it.

"Wait," Madge cautioned her. "Lie down first."

Once Toury was settled on the bed, she touched the brooch. Searing pain shot up her arm. Blinding light flashed in her eyes, much like when the stone had transported her here. She shook so hard all over, her teeth rattled in her mouth. Images were flittering through her mind so fast, she couldn't make sense of them. Fire, darkness, light, dragons, stones, and blood. She felt Madge pinning her down. The sensation drove the images away. Nausea rolled over her in waves. Then her eyes grew so heavy, they closed on their own accord, and she could not open them. She faded into a deep slumber.

Toury awoke in darkness and espied Madge on the cot across the room. Toury sat up, feeling weary, and her muscles were sore. It was from the transfer of magic. She knew that somehow and wasn't surmising it. Strange. She thought for a moment and realized she knew a lot of things she shouldn't and felt a tremendous amount of power within her. She wasn't sure how to use it, but she felt it inside of her, building, bubbling, wanting to be released. Somehow she knew what to do. She held out her palm and pulled just a tad of energy out. Suddenly, a glowing orb of light was in her palm, illuminating the room. This was much different than the vague sense of déjà vu she had experienced when arriving on this sphere.

"The transfer went well, it seems."

Toury jumped, not realizing Madge was awake and watching.

"Are these the prince's cousin's powers?"

"Ruby's? No." Madge got up and poured them some water as they spoke. "The transfer of power isn't giving you her powers per se. She locked up the strength of her power into the stone and her knowledge, and you have absorbed it. You were a powerful noble to start with, just unpracticed, but she has given you the power that befits a royal. You are now one of the most powerful people in all of Fyr."

The thought floored Toury. She couldn't quite comprehend that much power mentally, but she sure felt it physically.

"I can feel the energy, the magic, but I don't feel more knowledgeable."

"Transfers like these are rare, so I can only make guesswork of it. The knowledge may be more subconscious. You may know something without realizing it. We can work on bringing it forth, but the danger in doing so is that you might lose yourself and become more like a Ruby-Tourmaline combination," Madge said.

"Let's leave it in my subconscious." Toury shook at the thought. She was already lost enough in this world. The last thing she wanted was to lose herself and become someone else.

"Try to get some rest. We will work on catching you up for the ball at the week's end."

Still exhausted even after her power-transfer nap, Toury didn't protest. Surprisingly, she slept soundly through the night.

The next morning, there was a commotion outside in the hallway that sparked Toury's curiosity. There were a bunch of girls in the doorway, talking to a new girl. She was beautiful, dainty, blonde, and absolutely perfect. She made Toury feel too tall, too gangly, and too tan. She suppressed her inkling of jealousy and made her way toward the small crowd. She noted Mary against the wall, watching but not participating in the welcome party. Mary took her arm in hers and whispered, "Lady Justine Citrine. A beauty but fake and vicious. Stay clear of her. She will despise you. She has her eye on my brother, but he can't stand her. Neither can I, for that matter. Now her parents sent her here since she spurned many suitors, holding out for Alex. She's wasted two years on him." Mary rolled her eyes in annoyance.

Mary steered Toury back to Mary's own room, away from the girl. Toury felt an odd cold feeling creeping down her neck and looked over her shoulder at Lady Justine. The girl's eyes were so dark, they looked almost black, and her face was screwed into a hateful grimace. Strange, because she could've sworn the girl's eyes were light a moment ago and her face plastered with a plastic smile. They entered Mary's room as the girl's whimsical voice inquired about her.

The first few days after the girl's arrival, Toury tried to steer clear of the offending Justine, but the girl and her new followers seemed to be everywhere Toury went. She had to be doing it on purpose. There were over a hundred girls there and a dozen places to be during free time. Was Justine trying to befriend Mary? If so, Mary wasn't taking the bait. This time, Justine's clique sat at a table near her in the library, although Mary hadn't joined Toury today. Madge had books of nobility in front of Toury that she was to study so she would know how to recognize eligible suitors at the ball. She didn't have to pour over the books long, for each time she saw a crest, she "remembered" it, or really, the Ruby part of her did.

She pretended to study as she eavesdropped on the conversation at the other table.

"Did you hear? His Highness, the Prince is coming! It's the first time he's ever attended a suitor ball." One girl was squealing and chattering with excitement. Toury couldn't recognize which girl it was without turning around, and doing so would just be asking for them to verbally attack her. They hadn't mistreated her yet, most likely due to Mary, but Toury could sense a bully, having dealt with them frequently on Earth.

"I wonder why?" Lady Beatrice—Toury thought—said sarcastically. She felt eyes on the back of her head but pretended as if she couldn't hear them.

"Don't you know?" that whimsical voice said—Lady Justine. Her voice was breathy, light, like what Marilyn Monroe sounded like. It was also utterly fake, an act to appear docile and sultry.

"The prince and I are...well acquainted, you could say," Justine said with thick implications. She was trying to insinuate she and the prince were more than what they were. "He just wouldn't settle down, so I had to take drastic measures. That is why I am here. I didn't think it would work so well or so quickly."

"I don't think that's why he's coming—"

"Of course it's why he is coming!" The breathy voice cut firmly before it returned to its fabricated softness. "He can't bear to think of others trying to woo me, see?"

"But he's been here before. And he already was on the roster of gentlemen before you arrived."

Toury was beginning to like Beatrice. At least she wasn't some sad and stupid debutante blindly following Justine. Even though she was in Justine's clique, she still challenged the girl's lies.

"Of course, because he is a loving brother to Mary," Justine said, sad desperation edging into her voice. The girl might be delusional. Toury couldn't imagine Prince Alexander leading a girl on, nor could she pretend he wasn't singling Toury out. He was interested in Toury, maybe not romantically, but there was an interest. Mary said he hated Justine. She would be able to see at the ball if Justine was lying or not.

After the library, she and Madge worked on her powers in the old dungeon area, while Mary read a novel in the dim lantern light Lucy held over her. It must be nice to not have to study and work on powers all the time, Toury lamented. It was a place they would be undisturbed and out of the way. She learned quickly that being left alone was the princess's preference. Otherwise, nobody would opt to go down in the dungeon. The school had been a noble family's home once, but they had been stripped of their title and executed during the rebellion, or so Madge told her. The place was damp, dark, and musty, but it was private, and the only reason to come down there would be for one of the professors or servants to get something out of storage. The cell doors were still intact and locked, storing away valuables and goods. She and Madge practiced in the hallway between the cells, and Toury would be a liar if she denied the shadowy cells scared her.

Exhausted, they returned to her room to find the door ajar, the lock smashed. Madge made her wait in the hall with Mary and Lucy while she made sure there were no threats. When she came back to give them the all clear, she held shreds of silver fabric in her hands. Toury took a piece in her hand and examined it. It was her ball gown. She pushed into her room, where shreds of fabric littered her floor. The dress was destroyed.

"It's ruined," Toury said, exasperated, raiding her wardrobe to make sure it was the only victim in this attack. The rest of her dresses were there and intact, but none were as fancy as the gorgeous ball gown her aunt had insisted they buy. She had been fitted for two more, but they weren't to arrive for another week due to hand-embroidered patterns.

Toury plopped onto the bed. "I can't go to the ball."

"Oh no, you must. Alex is coming because of you," Mary insisted.

"It will be an affront as well," Madge added.

"Couldn't I feign an illness?" Toury asked.

"He would demand to see you," Mary said.

"No, we must make do." Madge sighed, taking out each remaining dress and frowning.

"Borrow one of mine," Mary insisted. She vanished then in a ball of fire.

Toury let out a puppy-like yelp. She had never seen someone vanish into thin air, except on TV with CGI, let alone in real life or in a ball of fire.

Then a moment later, Mary reappeared in the middle of the room, holding five gowns. "I know you're taller than me, but perhaps we can let out the hem?"

Madge took one and held it up to Toury, pulling it tight across her chest. She shook her head. "I'm afraid it won't work. Ball gowns are form-fitting, so your bust will never fit in these."

"I'm jealous," Mary muttered. Apparently, an ample chest was a male preference across the galaxy—go figure.

"I'm almost two years older than you. You'll fill out," Toury said.

Mary smiled. Then more brightly, she said, "None of these were really your color anyway."

Mary took up the gowns and vanished. Toury jumped, still not used to the idea of disappearing people. Then, before she could still her heart, Mary scared her again by reappearing.

"Stop doing that," Toury said, clutching her hand to her chest.

"Alex was right, you do want to see the inside of our dungeons."

Toury's mouth dropped.

Mary laughed whole-heartedly. "I'm teasing you! Oh, but your face!" She laughed uncontrollably.

"Stop laughing," Toury grounded out. "Your Highness." She said the title just in case.

"She is right. You must address the royals by title, Toury."

Great, now Madge was scolding her.

Madge was putting out all of Toury's gowns on the bed. Then she returned a few to the wardrobe. She examined each of the remaining and spoke as she did so. "I'm a woman of many talents, so I can make something up for you if I have some materials." Madge shifted through the dresses.

"The purple one," Mary said excitedly. She grabbed it up in her hands. "It's the perfect message to send to him and to the wretched lady who did this. After all, he bought it for you."

"Isn't it too simple?"

"I could enhance it," Madge said. "Stitch the lace to stay inside the gown, and look, the gossamer cover for your ball gown wasn't touched. It could be attached. I can repair the dress back to its original state after. It would make the soft fabric shine."

Toury sighed with relief. "You are indispensable, Madge, thank you. But please, do restore it back after." She had become suddenly sentimental of the prince's gift. She told herself it was because Alexander and Mary were her only real friends.

"And thank you, Princess Mary," Toury added.

Mary was smirking. "I better be there to see his face."

Toury had been hesitant in accepting the attention the prince gave her, but now, she would bask in it and make Justine so jealous that it would serve as the perfect revenge for destroying Toury's dress. Because it had to be Justine who'd done it.

14

A BALL

Mere weeks ago, a suitor ball was the last place Alex expected to be. First, he wished to monitor his sister to report possible suitors to his parents. Second, he was going to take the promise he made to his mother seriously. He would check all the ladies out as objectively as possible as lifemate candidates. Third, which battled with the first in its importance and was included in his secondary reason, he wanted to see Toury. This was the sole reason he did not find this evening a chore. He wished he could find an excuse to talk to Toury every day. He'd have to court her, not because she could save the world and him, and not to make his mother happy, but because he actually liked her. He could not let her get away. He had to secure her.

He arrived late, wanting to avoid the mingling time with the men and the lengthy introduction of all the ladies. He tried to sneak in, trailed by David, but all eyes were upon him. He should be used to this, but it still felt eerie seeing all the longing, giddy, hopeful faces staring at him. The men were there looking for a lifemate and probably dreaded his arrival since he would inadvertently steal the girls' attention. They simply bowed their heads in reverence and gave him their fake smiles.

He made a beeline for Mary once he saw his sister, and only then did he see the most beautiful girl in the room next to her, the most breath-taking girl he had ever laid eyes on. He almost stopped for a moment as he took her in but then hurried his pace over to the pair of them as he drank in the sight of Toury. Her black hair was twisted up in shiny braids that reflected in her dress. It was his dress, the one that he had bought for her, but the lace was gone, making it seductively elegant, and there was some flimsy piece on the outside that made her shimmer as if she were light magic dancing in a twilight sky. It contrasted with her tan skin, making her flesh glow warmly, and the purple made her eyes almost look that color. Alex, having received everything he ever wanted since birth, finally knew what want felt like.

And so did every man in the room. Alex saw shifts in posture, eyes alighting and roving over Toury, which seemed more invasive than physical contact would be. He wanted to take off his doublet and cover her, and yet he wanted to keep on staring, torn between interest and what he had to admit was protective jealousy. That was his dress that others were enjoying.

Alex pushed the feeling away and greeted his sister with a quick hug and a kiss on her cheek. Mary looked pretty in blue and all grown up. He told her as much. Then he greeted Toury, and when she smiled, he felt himself beam back at her. He couldn't school his features or hide his feelings around her, and frankly, he was beginning not to care what gossip mongers would make of it.

He whisked Mary onto the dance floor for the first dance, and he noted a couple gentlemen talking to Toury while he was dancing, one being Lord Pyrite, the son of his father's late treasurer. It annoyed him, but he should have known it would happen. Toury was gorgeous—not the courtier norm, but exotic—and his interest in her made her worthy in the eyes of other men, who normally may have questioned her family connections. Once he returned Mary to the sidelines, he noted Lord Pyrite returning to collect Toury for a dance. The man was almost a decade older than Alex and was climbing up the ranks of the Sorcerers' Guild. His asking Toury to dance irrationally made Alex want to halt the man's career. Alex quickly grabbed Toury's hand and gave it a squeeze. "Save me a dance." Then he let go.

He watched her dance. She was so graceful in dances she must've just learned. Her moves were fluid, and her height gave her an air of elegance. He needed to talk to her. He had so many questions for her since they last met. How did the power transfer go? Were they helping her learn how to use her powers? Had she thought of him? Why was she smiling at Lord Pyrite so much? She laughed in another man's arms. The fire began building up, rage flickering inside him. He had to look away.

"I didn't know you attended suitor balls?" Lady Justine's voice took him unawares. She came up from behind and stood close to him.

"I'm here for Mary. Need to keep an eye on her for my mother," Alex told a half-truth. He didn't bother to turn around but continued watching Toury twirl around. She was enjoying herself. The fact that it wasn't with him was vexing, and yet to see her happy was more important. Her happiness made her glow with an unaffected beauty no woman of the court could feign.

"I thought perhaps you were here for yourself." Justine laid it on too thickly as she always did. She touched the crook of his arm, suddenly next to him. "Are you going to dance?"

He gently removed her arm from his and took a step away from her, trying to subtly create a distance between them without embarrassing her. People were already looking, and he was sure the rumors put them together, gossip Lady Citrine and Lady Justine had invented themselves. Justine was growing desperate. She had denied three suitors already, hoping to ensnare him. No one was good enough for her except the highest royal, and even then, Alex wondered if her conceited mind thought herself above him.

"I may dance again. I may not. I'm not sure how that is a concern of yours," he said flatly. He was tired of her and felt unrestrained without his mother's presence telling him to be a gentleman.

Justine's eyes bulged at his affront. Then she glared at him but swept it away with a nauseatingly fake smile. "I thought you might ask me, seeing that we are such great friends."

"Are we friends?" he challenged. "The gentleman asks the lady, as you well know. Please, stop fishing for attention or a dance that I do not wish to bestow. I'm sorry to disappoint any hopes you or your mother may have had, but I have never given you any reason to expect anything from me. It is not my duty or fault your mother's tongue spread a web of fiction from which you can't save face. I see Lord Cobalt, and I must attend some state business. Good evening."

A few girls close by giggled, but he could not regret putting the girl in her place. He wanted nothing to do with Justine, and he didn't want false rumors to go back to Toury.

He fled over to Lord Cobalt, who was like a brother to him, the only person at court who understood him back when they were children and now. And like Toury, he was real and spoke the truth, even if Alex didn't like what he had to say at times.

"You look as if you are running away from a damsel, Prince, but I realize it is from Lady Justine, and I can sympathize. What did that viper want?" Cobalt asked him after they greeted each other.

"Fishing, and I'm not biting. She had the audacity to hint to me that I should dance with her. She's unhinged."

"I think you may be right. But who is that exquisite creature you have all eyes for? I don't blame you. She is breathtakingly delicious, but Your Highness, are you here for her or for Mary?" With Cobalt staring at Toury, Alex felt a possessive rage fill him.

"Both, perhaps," he admitted.

"The dress girl," Cobalt said knowingly and then laughed, which unnerved Alex. When he saw Alex's resentful face, his laughter fell.

"Forgive me, Your Highness, I didn't think you were serious. I misunderstood. I thought...mistress, but your face tells me otherwise. May I have an innocent turn with your lady without you calling us to blows?"

Alex was cheered up by his friend's banter. "I am only intrigued, my friend, as I told you before. You may dance with her."

"You may want to sign your name on her list, Prince Alex. She is new, unique, and popular. A lot of men have already signed."

"How do you know how many men are on her suitor list?" Alex jumped to the conclusion that Cobalt had added his name to Toury's list. It would be the only way to see it. The girls' lists were not on display but with the headmistress.

Cobalt gave him a grin. "I saw your interest, so I put my name down. I thought it would be some fun gossip for the old biddies. I admit, I thought your name might have been on there already."

"You're unbelievable." Alex laughed. "You will take it off, though, right?"

"Hmm," Cobalt examined Toury. "I think not. If you decide against her, I couldn't let that kind of beauty slip by me. I'd have to see if we'd suit."

Alex glared at him, the fire power bashing around in his brain. If he wasn't careful, he might burn his friend. When Cobalt said suit, he didn't mean an honorable engagement. The thought of his friend using his power to ensnare Toury almost drove him mad.

Cobalt shook his shoulder gently. "I mean, only if you don't want her. I'd never compete with you. There's no way I'd win."

He squelched the beast inside of him that raged at the idea of his best friend seducing Toury. If he didn't know before that he had lost his willpower and heart to the girl, he did now. And his friend was now also aware.

"I am due to dance with the lady right now, actually," Alex told him. Then he left to scoop up Toury before anyone else could steal her. As he walked over, he prioritized what needed to be said for he had only one dance to speak with her. As a prince—royalty had stricter rules of decorum—he could dance with her only once this evening, to his regret, and the number of suitors vying for her attention left little downtime to chat.

15

SUITORS

Toury was still on cloud nine as Madge helped her get ready for bed. The servant seemed to feel slighted that Toury insisted she undress herself. It was weird having someone wait on her hand and foot. She had to draw the line at dressing and bathing. She chattered away to Madge, who simply listened. According to Madge, her first ball was a success.

Toury had danced all but three dances, despite there being twice as many girls as suitors. The prince had danced with her once and Mary three times and no one else at all. It was an obvious distinction, and he seemed to be courting her, but she couldn't tell if he was serious about her. He did seem interested, all smiles, intense eyes, and flirty quips, but then again, all he wanted to discuss was the power transfer and how her studies went, as if breaking the curse were the only reason he condescended to be seen with her. Only her suitor list would tell how serious he actually was. If he merely wanted her help and friendship, he wouldn't sign her suitor list. If he was serious, he would.

Aside from the prince, whose company she was beginning to enjoy, the only other man who sparked her interest was Lord Cobalt. She enjoyed his easy-going manner, his candidness, and his witty humor. He also was quite attractive with a devil-may-care smile, dimples, wavy blond locks, and these strikingly vibrant blue eyes. They didn't sparkle with power as Prince Alexander's, nor did he have the rugged, chiseled face that the prince had, but he had a pleasing countenance. Where the prince was grave and serious, Lord Cobalt was happy and carefree. Where the prince had aristocratic looks of utter perfection, Cobalt had more universal boy-next-door looks. Which type of man would best suit her? She knew which look she preferred. Cobalt was cute, but the prince made her weak in the knees and scatterbrained, even though she was far from the swooning type.

Toury was neither a dreamer nor foolish. Both men had their drawbacks as well. Prince Alexander seemed arrogant and spoiled, which went with his station and upbringing, but it irked her. He would always try to command, get his way. She wanted to take him down a rung. Lord Cobalt seemed conceited and a terrible flirt. She could never imagine him being a devoted boyfriend. She would have to wait and see her suitor list. From there, she would see if she could resign herself to a man on it. Her comparisons could be pointless if neither guy had signed his name.

She could not sleep, her mind unsettled. For the first time since she had arrived, she had a moment to think. She had been trying so hard to learn everything about the land every moment of her day between classes that she really hadn't given in to deep thought till now. She marveled how she didn't miss Earth or her adoptive parents or her so-called friends. She tried to picture what was going on back there. Were there missing person posters of her on telephone poles? Was she the big gossip item at school? She couldn't quite picture things clearly, feeling so removed—a world away. It was as if a part of them—these earthlings—and herself realized that she was different and belonged somewhere else. Most likely, her parents would've worried initially, assumed she had run away, and called the police, filed a report and such. Her parents would feel guilty, granted, but it would give them an excuse to split like they had wanted, and she would fade from their memories soon enough. Maybe they'd think her biological parents came back for her. Maybe it was all arranged that way. Anything was possible, and she'd never know the whole truth since Ruby Sapphiarian took the information to the grave. Her neglectful adoptive parents were a sad thought, but they never loved her, and she didn't love them. She had no reason to return to Earth, so she'd give life here on Fyr a go. She fell asleep dreaming of her life with possible suitors and what the future could hold. She could finally think about and anticipate falling in love and, more importantly, being loved back.

The next morning, Madge shook her awake with excitement. Toury sat up groggily and looked at the parchment Madge had thrust in her hand. Taking a moment to process, she realized it was a list. Her list of suitors! It was fairly long, considering there had been only one ball so far. The first two entries were of the two men who asked her to dance first. Lord Pyrite, a baron; Lord Diamond, a marquess; then Lord Cobalt, a duke; Lord Pearl, who was old enough to be her grandfather but a viscount; then three other barons whom she found dull, and as her heart began to sink, she finally saw the last name signed on the list: *His Royal Highness, Alexander Rowland Sapphirian, Prince of Fyr.* Her heart fluttered, and her face went hot. All these men were interested in her when, on Earth, no boy had looked at her twice. The honor of having a royal ask for wooing rights made her smile with pride. The titles—although the history nerd in her knew what they meant—she did not care about. The men themselves were what mattered. And the only one she knew on a personal level was the prince, but even then—in Earth terms—they didn't know each other well at all.

"Normally, a girl is to return the list with check marks next to the men she is willing to entertain the idea of marrying," Madge told her, handing her a quill.

"I have to choose now?" Toury asked in horror. She wasn't ready. Such an important decision had to be weighed heavily. And marriage at seventeen? She thought she had much more time before that leap.

"You are choosing who is allowed to court you, not whom you must marry. You can always change your mind, drop suitors, or add them. You are in control, but you must choose to let some of the men down gently so they can pursue other ladies who would seriously consider them. You will probably want to limit it to about three."

"Is that the standard? Or can I do two?" she asked Madge. This was interesting. If she thought of it as weeding them out rather than picking a groom, it was easier to stomach.

"Two might cause too much competition, so put on a third that you want to know better. And be careful how you treat them. If you are speaking of the two I think you are, they're best friends," Madge forewarned as the tea woman brought in her tea and toast tray. Madge began laying out her outfit out for the day with a determined look on her face. She would try to dress Toury again. Madge was relentless. Once the tea woman was gone, Toury continued. "Lord Cobalt and Prince Alexander are best friends? Why would they both select me then?" Toury bit her lip in worry. "I don't want to cause a fight."

"Lord Cobalt was on there first. Perhaps he did not know his friend's feelings on the matter?" Madge mused. "I would not discredit him from the list just because of that. He comes from a powerful family and is in great standing with the royal family. In fact, he courted Duchess Ruby."

"What happened?"

"She vanished, as you know."

This did not sit well with Toury. Only weeks ago, Ruby had disappeared, and he was courting Toury? That did not show his steadfastness.

"Only discredit him if you are completely positive in the prince. I said standard because, in this case, you could simply choose the prince and no one else."

"I'm just not sure."

"You are not choosing a lifemate yet per se, remember that. If you choose someone, you do not have to marry them or enter an engagement. Choosing the prince would simply allow him to court you and not these other men. With each ball, suitors may add their names, and you can remove them."

Toury put a checkmark next to Prince Alexander's name and pondered over the others as she drank her tea. It tasted a bit funny to her; the tea was super sweet when she usually only had half a sugar in it. Thinking merely that the tea girl had gotten her preference mixed up with another girl's, she drank some more and ate a slice of toast while she and Madge discussed the pros and cons of other suitors.

Toury yawned, feeling exhausted. She had slept well that night, so it didn't make sense. She drank the rest of her tea, hoping it would fortify her for the day. She must have danced too much and overdone it the evening before. As she tried to rationalize it, her eyes grew heavy, and her body felt like lead. This didn't make sense.

"Madge, I'm so tired," she said groggily as she fell back into her pillow. She blinked her eyes but almost couldn't open them again. Her head felt like a balloon floating up away from her body, her voice disjointed from it. She was going to lose consciousness, and there was nothing she could do about it. She saw Madge hovering over her, slapping her cheek, but she couldn't feel it.

As her eyes closed, she saw Madge taste the last bit of tea and gasp. "Toury, stay with me. Toury! You've been poisoned!"

But as much as she tried, she couldn't stay with her. As she slipped into the darkness, she thought of the prince and Cobalt both. Then their faces faded to blackness, and she could see and sense no more.

16

A PROPOSAL

Alex was pacing. The headmistress watched him with an odd look in her eyes. She was confused and insulted, he was sure, because Alex came in like a madman, accusing the school of not protecting its students, demanding the culprit be brought to him and then demanding to see with his own eyes that Toury was alive and well. At least David's ever-calm translations of what Alex had been shouting seemed to smooth over the situation. Alex had raved, and David explained in more rational terms what answers the prince was seeking. Alex calmed down after he let the headmistress speak and realized it was not the school's fault. Poison was the culprit, most likely in her morning tea, but no one saw anyone tamper with it, and the servant was in custody, hysterical and ignorant of how it had happened.

The incident snapped something in Alex, like the dams of denial broke, and every feeling possible washed over him. He realized on the way to the school—well, during his three-second transport—that Toury had become too important. He felt too much when it came to her, and she had to be his. He had to protect her and himself because she had become his one vulnerability. And if he could admit that to himself, it was only a matter of time until people noticed, including necromancers. He knew how this conversation would end. To pretend he wasn't romantically courting her was not an option anymore.

After what seemed like an eternity of waiting in uncomfortable silence, Mary came in, supporting a pale, weak but alive Toury. They were flanked by their now overly-alert bodyguards.

He sighed, feeling all of the tension leave him. But then his stomach went sour at the thought of how close to death she had been, and it was all his fault.

"I'm so sorry," he told her, taking up her hands in his. He helped Mary settle her down on the couch but did not let go of her hands. He sat next to her, way too close, but he didn't care.

"Sorry? What have you done, Your Highness?" Toury's voice was brittle and weak. He hated seeing her this way.

"Could we be alone, please?" he asked, looking at Mary and then the headmistress.

"That is against policy, Your Highness. Servants aren't proper chaperones while behind closed doors," the headmistress said. The hesitation and weakness in her voice showed her reluctance to defy him.

"Mary will stay then, for propriety," he amended.

"As you wish," she said with irritation. The woman left her own office in a huff. Once the door clicked shut, he turned to Toury.

"I'm sorry because it is my fault. I have shown a marked interest in you, which makes some overly determined girls ruthless to out the competition," Alex said. He felt awkward admitting his interest and that girls were fighting over him.

"You can't claim all the blame, Prince Alexander. I've been warned by my aunt, Madge, and Mary how these debutantes can be. I am actually very careful, but someone must have tampered with the tea. I'm tired. Madge can explain." Toury's posture slumped slightly, showing how exhausted she really was. He wished the headmistress had ignored the rules and allowed him to visit her in her room, where she could rest, as he had asked instead of making her come to the office. On impulse, Alex pulled her head down onto his shoulder and tucked it under his chin so she could rest on him. He kissed the top of her head—instinctively, for it wasn't premeditated. He wanted to kiss much more of her.

"Alex, really, you shouldn't..." Mary started looking at the door, worried someone might walk in and see their intimate pose.

"Mary," he chided. "Read the flames before you reprimand me."

Mary looked at him, perturbed, but crossed over to the fireplace to see what he meant. Mary was mad at the double standard. As an older brother, he was always checking her behavior with the opposite sex, but he snapped at her when she tried the same. Hopefully, she would understand why.

While Mary's back was turned, he prodded Toury's pallid face up to look at him, their faces only inches apart. It would be so easy to kiss her, but princes could not go around kissing girls without consequences. He ran his thumb gently along her lips instead, and when her eyes met his, her breath hitched. Her eyes were full of fear. He could not kiss her when she looked so utterly vulnerable. He tucked her head back under his chin and wrapped his arm around her, trying to hold her together if he could.

Mary bent down and stared into the flames. Like Alex, she could read the future in the flames. He couldn't verbally tell her propriety didn't matter because he planned on proposing. But he hadn't planned this out, how he'd ask Toury, how to phrase it. He needed a moment to collect his thoughts. Thinking Toury could be dead for even a moment had sped up and exposed his feelings for her.

"Madge? What was the way of it?" he asked.

"Your Highness." Madge bowed. "The tea cart service goes as such: the cart stays out, the woman prepares a small tray and then brings it into the room. She usually makes a few trays and then hands them out. The tea girl is hysterical and seems quite innocent. She is ignorant of botany. Anyone in the hall could have switched the tea sachets. There are five girls in that hall close enough to dash out, switch the sachets, and dash back in without being seen. Anyone else farther away would have gotten caught."

During the tale, Toury's hand unfurled his fist in an unspoken exchange, her telling him to calm down.

"Who are these five ladies?" He wanted someone to punish, someone to unleash this pent-up rage upon. He took a deep breath, knowing no good would come of losing his temper.

Toury squeezed his hand, comforting him when she was the one in need of comfort.

"One to cancel out is Princess Mary, the next to cancel out is Lady Opal. She is next door and would be getting the tea as the switch had to happen, lest it go to the wrong girl. The remaining three suspects would be Lady Ariel, Lady Flora, and Lady Justine."

On hearing the last name on the list, he responded, "I can very easily guess who is guilty. Can you prove it?"

"I cannot, Your Highness." Madge bowed and retreated back against the wall.

"It was belladonna, put in a sachet," Toury said quietly in his chest. "Madge saved my life, although she kept making me drink firespice whiskey until I was a mess."

"It counteracts the poison," Mary said, coming over. "I kept telling you that. Anyway, you are clear headed now, and alive." Mary exchanged an understanding look with Alex as if to say she had seen enough of the future to withhold her protests.

"I believe it was Justine. I am going to Miss Headmistress right now to see about Toury and I getting some better-protected private rooms somewhere else in this place." Mary said.

Alex wanted to stop her because he intended to take Toury home with him if she accepted his proposal, but he wasn't sure of her answer yet, and it was a good excuse for his sister to leave them alone.

Once the door closed, Alex pulled his arm from around Toury. "I was worried about you."

"Still, you shouldn't have come. It will make it worse."

"I had to see with my own eyes that you were alive. I want to protect you, Toury. I can only think of one way to do that successfully."

She backed away from him and looked at him, lost. He felt the loss of her touch.

"We should get engaged," he said without preamble.

"What?" She leaped up with strength he did not know she had until that moment. "Are you crazy?"

"Sane actually, thank you very much." His tone came out harsher than he had intended. She was refusing him as if his proposal were offensive. Denying him! The nerve.

She covered her mouth and sat down, apologizing profusely and using his formal title.

He pressed down the fire boiling up inside him. Anger would not help him here. He needed to use another tactic. He should've planned this better, but he was nervous, and words were not coming easily; the most important ones weren't coming at all.

"You seem to really want to see my dungeons," he teased her.

Her eyes went round as saucers, and then she smiled a little, realizing he was teasing.

"Listen, Toury, please, enter an engagement with me."

"Why?"

"It will protect you. I will help you. And to break the curse, of course." Her earlier outburst was stopping him from admitting more.

"So a fake engagement?"

"A temporary alliance," he corrected. "Fake" stung a bit more than her accusation that he had lost his mind. It meant he must be feeling way more for her than she was for him. And the sting was seeping further into him than just his aching pride.

"I can't."

"Why?"

"Because I would—we would—disappoint a lot of people, including some suitors I just might be interested in," she began.

He wanted to kill said suitors.

"And your parents and the entire kingdom."

"Cobalt, you mean?" His heart thudded in his ears, and he felt the fire magic flare up in rage. He had never truly felt pure unadulterated jealousy until this moment.

"Not necessarily," she said, her nose up in the air and arms stubbornly folded across her chest.

He was right. He wanted to kill Cobalt, friend or not. Why did he have to sign as a suitor? Cobalt and his stupid head games.

"Anyway, I don't think it's a good idea, considering how being involved with you is what is putting my life on the line in the first place. Staying away from you would be the healthiest option. I can't marry you or get engaged to you. I am sorry if I disappoint you, Your Highness."

"You're not sorry," he said. He sounded like an immature brat, but he couldn't care less right now as the rejection stung.

"Had you proposed to me for real and had feelings for me, I would be sorrier, but as it stands, you have some notion I need saving when you are the very threat to me. Please, keep your distance." Then she got up and left the room, bumping into Mary, who was entering. She glanced at Toury's face, confused, then saw Alex's and seemed to understand the situation.

They departed to see their new rooms, and Alex was left stunned and denied something, perhaps for the first time in his life. He would not fulfill her request to give her space. In fact, his brain was hatching a whole new plan. He would get his way. He was the prince after all.

17
DRAGON'S TRAPDOOR

Toury was fed up. Not only did she and Mary have to stay in smaller rooms in the professors' wing with zero privacy, but she also had to use Mary's poison taster before she could eat or drink anything. Half the girls in the school mocked her for it and resented her because of Alexander. The other half were overly kind and flattering, hoping to secure favor with the possible future princess or get closer to the prince in the hope of stealing him from Toury. She wasn't sure which type of girl was worse. The blatant hatred was easier to discern but cut deeper. She was now failing her dance class because of Justine and her hideous crew. Today was the worst. Another dress ruined, this time blatantly torn by Lady Margaret as they convened for their lesson. She and Madge ran back to her room so she could change, and Toury allowed the maid to dress her without complaint. She raced back down, arriving late, and dismissed Madge, who had free time when Toury was in lessons. When Toury put her dance slippers on, she learned they were full of glass shards. Justine and Lady Rose giggled to each other. Instead of letting them win, she feigned an upset stomach to excuse herself and rushed out, biting back the stabbing pain in her toes.

As soon as she was in the hallway, she ripped off each shoe and ran barefoot back to her room. She was running away from her problems. She needed to face them head-on, but she didn't know how to fight these girls on their turf, so unaware of who the enemy was and what exactly she was fighting for.

She opened the door and slammed it behind her, growling.

"Rough day?" a male voice inquired.

She yelped and turned around to see Prince Alexander sitting at her desk as if he were at home, his one ankle resting on his knee.

"What are you doing here?" she demanded loudly and then winced, hoping no professors were in the wing at the moment.

"You mean, 'A pleasure to see you, Your Highness. To what do I owe this honor?'"

She huffed and threw a pillow at him. He deflected it and stood, scooping it up in his hand. "That will land you in my dungeon, my lady." He sauntered over to her and bopped her gently in the face with the pillow.

"Fine. To what do I owe this pleasure, Your Highness," she mocked him and gave him an overexaggerated curtsy. Alexander would never lock her up, but all the same, she wanted to make sure she didn't give him a reason to. Only she had forgotten about her feet and faltered. Alexander was there to catch her, and for a moment, he froze, his face close to hers.

"I had to see you," he said quietly, his tone serious, his eyes drinking up her face.

"I asked you to stay away." She frowned. She was happy to see him, and yet the fact he disregarded her request for distance and simply did as he pleased bristled her pride.

His hands tightened on her, and he leaned in closer. "Because the girls here were making life hard for you, I know. But no one knows I'm here. I transported."

"I can't believe you guys can actually teleport," she commented, realizing now he, thankfully, had arrived unseen.

"I don't know what that is." He looked at her as if she had two heads. Of course, he wouldn't understand an Earth term like that.

"Nothing, an Earth term." She waved it away, not wanting to get into it. "I'm supposed to be in class. Were you going to wait here all day?"

Alexander's face softened. "If that's what it would take to see you again, then yes."

At that declaration, her annoyance melted away. They stood there, staring at one another for a moment. Then, as if her lips were magnets, he drew closer and pressed his lips against hers in an innocent, all-too-short kiss. It was almost like a kiss a parent might give her child—not that her Earth parents ever showed her an ounce of affection—but it wasn't as innocent. The energy between them sizzled, and she felt a surge of heat flow from his lips into her, and a blast as sparks literally flew, tickling her flesh before he pulled away. She felt different but could not put her finger on what had changed. It was her first ever kiss, so she surmised that was the feeling of warmth and power flowing through her.

She backed away, blushing, suddenly embarrassed. He looked away with the same expression on his face.

"Is that normal?" she asked, running her hand along her lips.

"No. I dunno. I don't go around kissing girls." The prince stumbled over his words, his cheeks flushing up adorably.

She must've been his first kiss, just as he had been hers. That might have been the only kiss of any kind she had ever received. She couldn't remember a kiss from her parents, a grandparent, anyone. The thought depressed her, so she grasped at something to say to distract herself and to break the awkward silence that was forming.

"Dragon's trapdoor," she translated. How did she suddenly know that term?

"So you've heard of it? It's rare. You have to have dragon's blood in the family, which is only us Sapphirians now."

"You're descended from a dragon, a blue dragon that turned to glass. That is where the sapphire came from. How do I know this? Alexander, my mind is bursting with information like someone just downloaded a whole book of knowledge in my head at once. Ruby's knowledge has been coming back in snippets after I relearn things, but just now, something opened the floodgate, if only momentarily."

"I don't know what 'downloaded' is, but I think I get the gist of what you are trying to say. The flood is Ruby's knowledge being unlocked," he told her. It was the only reasonable explanation as to why she suddenly knew it. "Unlocked by a kiss?" he mused. He touched her cheek and was about to kiss her again.

She took a step back to avoid another kiss before her mind could process the first, and pain sliced again through her feet. "Oww." She winced, the pain finally hitting her.

Alexander's face fell, breaking the spell that had come over them momentarily. "What is it?"

"My feet. They put glass shards in my dance slippers." Just as she finished, he swept her literally off her feet into his arms. He gently placed her on the bed and sat down next to her. It was clandestine, and yet she had to admit it felt natural. Alexander then took up her feet in his warm hands. A prince was holding her grubby, cut feet in his impeccably clean hands.

"They call themselves ladies?" he asked under his breath. His tone was sardonic and resentful. "I'll have them punished."

"No!" She yanked her feet from his hands. "You'll make it worse."

"I can't permit this, Toury!"

"But you must. As you said, no one knows you are here. It'll look like I'm a tattler."

"Why are you so headstrong?"

"This is my battle to fight. I have to do this on my own. I must show them I'm strong, that they cannot break me." As she spoke, she clutched her feet in her hands, letting the light magic seep out, and her feet warmed with healing power. A moment later, she let go, her feet completely healed.

Alexander had watched her actions with interest. "Look what you've learned to do already. Imagine what you could do with personal tutors. You could have them at court, you know."

She ignored his comment.

He watched her as she rubbed her newly healed skin, sat back next to her, and propped his feet up on the bed. He folded his arms behind his head, making himself comfortable. "I can think of a way to beat them. Take their prize off the market. They'll have nothing to fight over."

"Not this again," she mumbled.

Alexander beamed with a smile and laughed. She had expected him to be angry and hurt at her comment like last time, not...this. "Oh Toury, never change. You literally and figuratively are a light in the darkness."

"You say such things to confuse me—on purpose!"

"I say what I mean, what I feel. I've always been nothing but direct."

She scoffed. "You want to be friends with me and help me, and then you kiss me. That is not direct."

He met her gaze, and it felt as if the air popped and sizzled between them. She was suddenly conscious that she was lounging on a bed with a boy, an attractive, rich, and powerful one. A boy she was finding herself drawn to, despite her survival instincts screaming at her to run away.

Alexander took a deep, shaky breath and touched her cheek. She could tell he was as affected by their closeness as she was. Toury had had thoughts of kissing Alexander from time to time, but she was still unsure what she wanted when it came to him. If life here on Fyr could be less intense, like Earth, where people could date instead of jumping into matrimony, she would kiss him back right now, a real kiss, a rough one like in the movies. The thought made her heart pick up its pace.

His eyes memorized every facet of her face, his fingers traced her features, and when their eyes met, Alexander leaned in toward her. She closed her eyes, anticipating a real kiss. But it didn't come. Shaky lips touched her forehead instead. Then he pulled away. "You're right, but I assure you I normally am direct, though apparently, I'm having trouble being so around you. Maybe I should have stayed away," he whispered.

She met his gaze. And Alexander's grip tightened on the back of her neck, drawing her closer so her face nestled into the hollow of his shoulder. He was so warm, she thought she could melt into him, and he smelled pleasant but unique. Soot was the smell that set him apart. There was a hint of a coal-type smell to him that was barely present under the scent of the musky and woody soap and cologne he must use.

"Why?" She murmured into his collarbone.

"Because. We can't do this. It's all or nothing, Toury, and you know what I want."

"But I don't. Not exactly."

Alexander pulled her back and glanced at her. "How can you not?"

"You proposed an engagement of convenience! If you feel something more than that, you are so not direct."

"I proposed. That should have been enough," Alexander said with a smirk. "I didn't think you were the type of woman who needed poetry and gifts and overtures."

"I'm the type of girl who wants to know the truth, Your Highness. What do you honestly want from me?"

"Call me Alex, please."

"What do you want from me, Prince Alex?" What he was asking her to call him was improper, so she met him halfway.

Alex said nothing but pressed his lips to hers roughly, a body-tingling, bone-wobbling, movie kiss. Taken aback and frankly not knowing what to do, she froze. He deepened the kiss, and then she pressed back. Alex's hands wandered down her neck and her back, and she didn't know how to stop this kiss nor whether she wanted to.

Then he broke away abruptly and kissed her forehead again. "I want everything, Toury. Everything you're willing to give me."

Toury felt torn. Her emotions came to the surface, and her throat tightened, and her eyes prickled with tears. She was moved by his declaration, and yet her heart was hesitant. She was scared.

"Prince Alex," she tugged his collar, wanting to touch him but not wanting to lose control in each other's kisses. "What am I to do? They will literally kill me if I'm with you."

"I'll protect you."

"They will never accept me as a princess—"

"Toury..." he growled.

"Please, let me finish. They won't until I beat them at their own game, without your interference."

"Toury, as much as I respect your desire to show your strength to defeat your adversaries, time is of the essence."

"You want me to break the curse, right? You want me to learn my powers. You want all this to stay secret, and you want to see me without causing me harm, right?"

"Ye-es," Alex hesitated as if he realized he was walking into a trap.

"Then keep coming to see me when you can—secretly that is—and tutor me."

Alex grinned and leaned in to peck her lips again. "Deal."

The door opening made them jump apart, but the surprised Madge shut the door quickly and kept her composure in a curtsy. Toury felt her face go afire, but Alex kept a haughty, controlled demeanor. Madge apologized, but Alex told her he was leaving anyway. Toury wanted him to stay, but it was wrong.

"Till next time, my lady." He punctuated with a kiss on the back of her hand and vanished in a ball of flames.

Madge made no comment, as if Alex had never been there in the first place, but proceeded to clean up her room.

"Speak," Toury commanded.

"Of what, my lady?"

"Madge, I know you have an opinion about the prince being here."

"It isn't my place to say, my lady."

"I'm asking you to say. I want your honest opinion. You're supposed to help me acclimate."

"Well, you could be the future queen of this land if he asks again for your hand. No lady in this land would've denied him as you did. If you're not careful—from what I just saw—you may end up his mistress instead."

Toury gasped. "Madge!"

"My lady, Prince Sapphirian cannot dally with ladies unless he's looking for one or the other. If anyone saw you kiss, you'd be engaged or ruined."

"I see," Toury said quietly.

"Do you, my lady?"

"Of course. I must marry him or put a stop to this." And Toury knew deep down what she had to do, although she loathed the idea.

And yet, she couldn't do the right thing. The next evening, Prince Alex showed up after dinner, and she found herself drawn to him. They were kissing madly after a short greeting and didn't pull apart until Madge entered with her laundered dresses.

Toury felt her face warming from embarrassment. She was weak. She was a hypocrite. And she knew Madge must be thinking the same thing.

Alex cleared his throat, pink-cheeked and adorably embarrassed. "Right, so what subject do you need to work on most?"

It took her a moment to register that he was referring to what they were supposed to be doing: tutoring. She should say etiquette, but Alex would laugh at that, and it might be awkward for him to explain proprietary to her, considering she was sure he must be breaking every rule in her textbook by being here. She settled for the next hardest subject for her.

"Geology."

"Ah," Alex said knowingly. "Makes sense. It's all new to you, and my cousin was atrocious at the subject." He started off in a lighthearted tone but became solemn by the end. He must miss his cousin terribly. She wondered if they had been close but didn't dare ask. "So." He sat up, clapping his hands together. "Let me think. We need to start with the basics. Fyr is one massive continent that covers more than half the sphere and is surrounded by a vast ocean. It's smaller than Earth, and its osmium core is surrounded by eternal fire. I pull my magic from that very fire. It is part of the Celestial Spheres, so we're caught in Earth's orbit."

"Why can't we see the moon then, or Earth itself?"

"We'll get ahold of a telescope, and I'll show you. We can see Earth, but without magic, they cannot see us. Our inability to see the moon is a theory, never proven, but we might be in the same orbit, revolving at the same speed on different sides of the Earth." He shrugged and made himself comfortable on her bed. Madge seemed to purposely take her time putting things away to chaperone.

She was trying to keep up and got it to a point. Being part of Earth's orbit, it had the same relation to the sun, so days and years were the same scientifically, but the months and weeks must've carried over from Earthlings who came to Fyr.

"But what about seasons?"

He stared at her for a moment, a bit lost, before he seemed to understand. "No, Earth has a tilted axis, right? Fyr does not. It's the same temperature all year round, but the temperature is geographic, by mantle thickness. The mantle in places like the south is extremely thin, so the fire and molten rock come through; the north exceptional thick, so the fire doesn't come through at all."

Madge cleared her throat, interrupting their lesson. "My lady, this is usually when we work on etiquette for an hour before you're ready for bed. Do you wish me to come back later or to study?" Her penetrating gaze told Toury the maid was not asking but asserting that she should send Alex away.

She looked to the reclined prince, who was at home on her bed. "I am far from a lady. You should go."

He sat up with a wounded look on his face, his eyes mournful and his lips pulled tight in displeasure. He was not used to being told to go away. He took her face in his palms and whispered, "Don't let them change you," before kissing her gently and vanishing in a ball of magical flames.

Toury threw herself back on the bed with a huff. Why was it so hard to tell him to stop coming? She'd do it tomorrow, maybe.

18

A BREAK

Alex was livid. He felt the power and the fire simmering under his skin. How could she? After a half dozen amazing nights transporting to Toury's room and stealing time and kisses while tutoring her about geology, necromancers, and curses, she put it to a halt. She asked him—the prince of their world—to stop seeing her. *In. A. Letter.* She didn't even have the audacity to say it to his face! He burned the note to cinders in his palm and let the ashes fall from his hand. And he wanted to burn more, the curse pooling over his rage and intensifying it. He tried to push it away. Rationalize.

She was afraid. Afraid of her classmates, of him, or whatever responsibilities came from being with him, he wasn't sure. It was all of them most likely, but his pride was wounded and heart pulverized. She had strung him along, given him false hope under the pretense that she "tried many times" to tell him. Well, she didn't try hard enough. She wanted distance yet again as some attempt to defeat simpering but vicious debutantes who wanted the crown. Worse, she was putting off what he so desperately wanted: her to be his and his alone.

He would not give her distance. He would make her say these things to his face.

"You have that look on your face again, Your Highness," David said.

"What look?" he asked, suddenly coming out of his reverie.

"You're going to transport somewhere again and come back disheveled and smelling of perfume."

Alex laughed, despite how the fire and darkness together screamed for someone to take his wrath out on. "You sound like a jealous lover, David." The servant was ridiculously devoted to him, and Alex had a feeling it extended beyond the devotion that came with the man's job. Cruel to tease him so, but David was overstepping his bounds, so Alex wanted to make David squirm for his amusement.

David turned beet red and stammered out a response, "Y-y-you j-just don't seem yourself, Your Highness. You know your energy gets used up transporting so often. Then you're vulnerable—to the curse, I mean. And, frankly, I'm disappointed you're taking on a mistress at this time, or one at all for that matter."

"I'm not taking on a mistress, but taking on love, David," he said for effect, then transported to Toury's room. Little did David know, whatever energy he expended in the transport, Toury's healing touch rejuvenated.

She wasn't there, but she would come back soon after supper to retire. So he waited. Per usual, she entered in a huff. And when her eyes met his, her anger turned into a glower.

"I asked you to stay away!" Toury whined, throwing her hands up in frustration.

She was beautiful in every mood. Her stormy gray eyes met his, and like that first day he met her, he knew she had to be his lifemate.

"I can't," he told her.

"You *won't*, you mean."

"That too," he told her and crossed over to her, throwing all caution to the wind, and grabbed her and kissed her senseless. This kiss wasn't like any kiss before. He was not gentle nor tender, but unleashed his bottled up anger and attraction. He was quite aware that he might bruise her lips, but he didn't care. He couldn't hold back. His tongue slipped into her mouth as if on instinct, and he marveled at how much closer they were and how the feeling between them intensified more than he believed it could.

Finally, before he could back her onto the bed, she pushed him away, her eyes wild and lips swollen. He wanted her more than ever at that moment.

"Stop, Prince Alex!" she gasped. Her chest rose and fell with her struggling breaths, which distracted him terribly. "They know."

"Know what? Who?" He could not form a sentence, all his brain power busy trying to keep his body in control of itself and his mind off her heaving bosom.

"One of the professors heard us talking, a male in my room. Madge has suppressed it there, so Miss Headmistress hasn't heard, or I'd be ruined."

"Then all is well."

"No, that's not the half of it. I got an undercut threat by Justine. It was clear she knew somehow, but I denied it."

"I'm sure she bribed a servant to get information on you. Don't worry about Lady Justine."

"I have to! She is constantly after me in one way or another. Given the chance, she'll ruin me."

"She can't. Stop, and think, Toury. If her goal is the crown, what will she gain if she exposes that we are in here, unchaperoned, together?" As he spoke, he pulled her closer and held her to him, just marveling in the idea that her touch made him feel complete, and it wasn't just her ability to banish the dark.

"She could ruin me! I'm not used to this! On Earth, a girl caught kissing a boy in her bedroom gets grounded. Her life wouldn't be over."

"I don't know what grounded means, but it matters not. If she were to expose us, I would marry you. If she tried to say it was another man in here, I'd step in and admit it was me. I was raised to be nothing but honorable."

"You call sneaking into a girl's room and kissing her until her brains are mush honorable?"

"Mush, huh?"

"Don't get cocky."

"Like a rooster?"

Her brow furrowed, and then she laughed. "Precisely."

"And I am honorable. You should be my engagee right now, and we could kiss as much as we pleased. If we were engaged—"

He could not go on to say what he wanted to for she attacked his lips with her own. She was kissing him back, and whatever thoughts he had about engagements left him.

When they came up for air, she was rightfully disheveled, and he was sure he'd upset David with his rumpled appearance again. And when he looked her over, he noticed the bed was only a foot away. When he saw her dilated eyes, as full of passion as his were, he realized how this could easily spin out of control on them.

"You're right," he admitted, although it felt like paste in his mouth.

"What?" She shook her head as if trying to shake some sense into it.

"I should give you distance."

"What?" She gaped before she collected her thoughts. "I've been asking and asking, but what made you change your mind? What have I done?"

"Nothing, dearest Toury, nothing wrong at all. That is the problem."

"I don't understand." She looked so vulnerable, and her sad eyes exposed she was insecure about why he wanted space.

"I...I want so much more than kisses, Toury. And that is not very honorable, is it? I will leave you to fight your battle and won't return until you give me a sign."

"What kind of sign?"

"Now that would be cheating, wouldn't it? Let fate decide," he said. He wanted to laugh at her expression, knowing how she would fret over the perfect sign of what would call his attention when, in reality, he'd turn anything he could into said sign. Once Toury felt she had won this debutante battle, he'd come back. In the meantime, he would ponder on how he would get a yes from her next time he asked for her hand. He was determined to keep asking until she gave in, hang his pride.

"Where have you been!" Cobalt greeted him. "When I got the summons, I was surprised beyond belief."

His mind with Toury, as it always seemed to distractingly be, Alex shrugged off his comment and gave him excuses. He was a terrible friend for putting him off to work on courting Toury publicly and behind the scenes. There was no way he could tell Cobalt about his visits to Toury's bedroom without Cobalt egging him on to do more. And Alex might listen. Never before had he kept secrets from his friend, but as soon as Ruby vanished, the secrets began. Toury was now this wedge between them, and not just because of the savior business. Alex didn't want to share what he and Toury had with anyone. It was their own private world in her room, a place where he was happy, and the major concerns that usually smothered him fell away.

Cobalt eyed him up, not believing the excuses. "You attending the next ball?"

"Of course," Alex stalled. "I've got to for Mary."

"And because of Lady Tourmaline, I presume. Will she be our next queen? Are felicitations in order?" Cobalt teased him. If only he knew how much that comment bothered him at this moment, but no one would ever assume a lady would deny a prince.

"You're way ahead of yourself, Cobalt," he murmured as he stared into the fire, an excuse not to look him in the eye.

"I wish I could be there to observe you and your lady, but I am away for a month. My father is sending me east, per your father's request to lighten up the mood, it seems."

"The drought and famine." Another concern of the kingdom he should help figure out rather than kissing and dancing with Toury. Perhaps this separation was good. He could focus on what he should be doing, learning to rule a kingdom that might be his sooner than expected.

"Yeah, but why me? I'm the spare. My brother should get the distinction."

"Always avoiding politics," Alex chided. "My father probably wants you to get your feet wet. He knows you are my best friend. He realizes that I will depend on you when I rule. He's priming you, starting off easy."

"But why? It'll be ages before you take over."

Alex sighed. The number of secrets he was keeping from Cobalt was frustrating, but this was one he could trust his friend with. It would be noticeable soon to all the courtiers anyway that his father was dying.

And because he couldn't share everything with his friend, he decided to unload this burden onto him. Cobalt needed to know that within a year, he would need to grow up and be the friend a king could count on.

19
SAVIOR

Toury was nervous before the ball. She was confident in her new ball gown Madge had kept under lock and key for her, and she knew she looked lovely. She wasn't even scared, despite it being her first ball since being poisoned. No, what made her nervous most of all was Alex. Would he be there? Or would he respect her wishes to stay away? Worse, would he be there and ignore her? The gossip his sudden abandonment of her would create made her regret her decision to ask him to stop courting her. Would his feelings have lessened after the two weeks of no contact? She wished she could talk to him again. She really did like him, but being with him would be so dangerous and intense that it frightened her. And yet, she was equally terrified that her pushing him away would make him forsake her indefinitely.

A week prior, she was presented with her suitor list to make any alterations before this ball. She had left the prince on there. Him, alone. It was her sign. After all, she didn't want to lose him forever, and no one else interested her. Nor did any of these lords truly care about her. Lord Cobalt did not inquire at all about her, even after the attempted poisoning spread throughout the capital. Her aunt had even come days after to check on her and gave Madge an apothecary kit of hers full of antidotes for common poisons.

Toury had a feeling something profound would happen this night, but whether it would be good or bad was unknown. It made her anxious. Toury fortified herself with some tea Madge had made and tasted first, then joined the ladies waiting in line to enter the ballroom. Miss Headmistress went down her list, rearranging girls. She moved Toury from her place at a quarter from the end of the line and placed her in between Lady Emily and Princess Mary, who stood at the very end. Justine, a few places up, was upset by it. When Justine turned back to look over her shoulder, she glared. "Don't get used to the back of my head. Before long, I will be the one in front of Princess Mary."

Toury rolled her eyes and realized the line was a ranking system. The girls were ranked according to the import and wealth of their houses or their highest suitor's house from least significant to the most. Toury turned to look at Mary, who winked at her with a small smile as if to affirm Toury was, in fact, single lady number two in the entire sphere—all because of Alex's attentions. She took a deep breath, realizing how this would eventually end up, or how everyone in the entire sphere expected it to. Part of her wanted to revolt against society, but the other part wanted Alex.

It took an eternity for the line to progress, more so than the last ball. What made it worse was Mary teasing her about her brother in whispers. Toury laughed at first, then blushed, and then begged her to stop. Finally, she was able to get away from Mary when it was Toury's turn to descend the stairs. It was horrifying to see all the suitors in the back of the room, all the other ladies staring up at her. She trembled and tried to hide it by placing her hand on the railing as she descended, her other hand clamped on her dress so she wouldn't trip. She was in such deep concentration, staring at the steps—willing herself to not make a fool of herself—that she was clueless as to why the crowd was murmuring and gasping until she saw two polished boots in front of her dance slippers at the bottom.

Alex stood in front of her, impeccably dressed in dark breeches and an ornately patterned doublet that hugged his broad shoulders. A large golden medallion hung around his neck with a circular dragon etched into it. How had she always overlooked it before? He hadn't worn it the times he snuck out to see her, but he wore it every public time she saw him, just like Mary wore her circlet. She never saw it because of those eyes. His sparkling sapphire eyes met hers, and he quirked a smile.

"My lady." He grasped her hand and kissed her knuckles. And she curtsied just a second late and hoped no one noticed. The crowd gasped and tittered, and she took his offered arm. From the tone of their whispers, Alex was doing something out of the norm, but Toury was unsure what it was. Despite the professors trying to teach her rules of propriety, not much stuck.

"What are you doing?" she whispered as he turned her toward the stairs. He said nothing as Mary was announced and descended in her beautiful silver dress, the simple crown in her hair shining in the light. Mary gave Alex a look that could kill and took his offered arm. Then he led them to the other ladies and returned to where the other gentlemen were standing.

"What was that?" she whispered to Mary.

Mary looked at Toury without any of the teasing mirth she had earlier. "I think my brother just announced to all of Fyr that he's courting you in earnest." Toury's face must've given away her feelings because Mary took her hand in hers and squeezed it. "I've never seen him like this. He cares for you deeply."

So deeply that as soon as the music began, he swept her onto the dance floor. She had no idea what to say or do. She felt like the wheels were in motion, her fate set, and there would be no way to slow this down or control it. Things seemed so intense now between them and completely on display for all to see. Despite being so comfortable with him in her room, she was rigid and distant, not knowing how to act in public.

"You are quiet this evening, Lady Toury," the prince said to her as he whirled her across the dance floor. Even her dancing had improved due to that stone and, she guessed, Ruby's knowledge that Toury gained when Alex unlocked it with his kiss. She didn't want to think about kisses while in his arms. She was a little annoyed with him for making her feel so much that it rendered her powerless. It also didn't help when he said things like "That's an oddity, don't you think?" in reference to her being quiet.

She did not laugh.

"Are you angry with me?" Alex pressed when she didn't answer. "I thought when you selected me as your only suitor, it was your signal that I was forgiven for any and every infraction you could think of."

She couldn't forgive him for the way he had proposed. Didn't she deserve a real proposal, down on bended knee with a ring and words of love? Excuses of her needing to help him with some state matter and for her protection were hardly romantic notions. Fair play, he had said he wanted everything, but what really did that mean? He said it when he was kissing her, full of lust and desire, not love. No, Toury seemed doomed to never experience that emotion.

"Any and every? No. I can't let you off for every prior insult."

"It cannot be an insult for the prince to single you out or for him to admit his weakness that he needs to see you. I won't allow you to tell me that."

Her heart began to pick up in rhythm, and she misstepped. His strong arms tightened around her to allow her to find her balance again without any outward sign that she tripped. He was infuriating! Weak how? Need how? Just to save his kingdom? Or more?

"Any attention from you, I am to understand, is a compliment, Your Highness." And then she felt bad for treating him so curtly when he was

102

opening up to her. "I did send you the sign. I missed you. I'm just tired of the gossip. And staring over my shoulder every moment of every day."

"Well, there's a simple way to remedy that." He gave her a charming smile that made her pulse quicken. He was alluding to her accepting his engagement.

She rolled her eyes, and his mouth twisted as if he suppressed a laugh.

He met her gaze, and she thought she saw something there in his eyes—not quite love-struck and not the hungry stares when he kissed her—but smitten. Maybe it truly was more. That would explain how he seemed genuinely hurt by her refusal and not just his pride. It would explain his erratic behavior when she was poisoned. At first, she thought it only had to do with possibly losing the person who could heal him, but it was more now. Enough for an engagement or marriage, now *that* she still questioned.

Then he laughed. And she had the distinct feeling that he was laughing at her. She tried to pull away, but he pulled her closer, a little too close. She looked out of the corner of her eye to the professors on the sidelines. They were watching intently.

"I'm sorry. I laughed because I just thought of something. You know how I tutored you about things you didn't know of? There are topics we steered clear of that we probably should've discussed. Has anyone explained engagements to you, Toury?"

"No. It's an easy concept to understand, so why would anyone have to explain it? I'm not a simpleton you can laugh at Alex—Prince Alexander, I mean," she corrected herself. She had to be careful what she said. If anyone overheard her familiar use of his name, or how she was berating him, she'd be in deep trouble. For the life of her, she could not act like one of these simpering, weak misses she attended classes with. Alex may have been a prince, but he was still just a person.

"I'm not laughing *at* you. I'd never. I'm laughing at the situation because it just dawned on me that Earth and Fyr, although we all speak the same language, we have different traditions. What is an engagement on Earth?"

Now she felt bad. And nervous. Was Alex right, and an engagement here was different? How foolish of her to dismiss his proposal without asking him first what it meant. He would have told her the truth. She swallowed the guilt creeping over her. She told him, "An engagement is an agreement to get married at some point. It used to be a binding contract, but now it really is like a pledge of faith, a step toward marriage."

His brow furrowed for a moment, and he was adorable. It was such a natural expression that his public persona never wore. He was Alex with her right now, not the Prince of Fyr.

"Here, an engagement is an agreement as well, but it doesn't always lead to marriage. Oftentimes, it leads to other things or is broken off. Some people are engaged several times before a marriage contract is drawn. It is simply an agreement of intrigue, a pledge to one suitor alone, that one only gives attention to that person and shows no interest in another. In a sense, you have done just that by cutting your suitor list down to me, but you could still take on other suitors at the moment." Alex told her. It sounded a lot like dating. He spun her around the dance floor. "Engagements can last up to two years, and then they must be broken or fulfilled."

"Are they usually always romantic in nature?" she asked, trying not to be embarrassed. This was something she had to know because she was still unsure what Alex wanted from her. Of course, he was attracted to her, that was obvious enough. He also needed her to save him; most of their conversations in her room between kisses were about curses and the necromancers. And yet, there was more between them than just lust and power, but he never said the words she needed to hear. When she realized how it wasn't enough, that being offered a crown, wealth, and a handsome, kind, powerful lifemate didn't persuade her, she knew only one thing could. Love. That elusive feeling that she was never privy to.

"Not always," he allowed. "Some marriages are about status and progenies' power; there isn't always love." He paused. "Look Toury, I can sense your concerns. I'm only commanding your friendship, help, and loyalty." It wasn't what she wanted to hear, she realized, nor did she like his word choice. She was not used to being dictated to.

And then, as if to belie his own words, he pulled her in much too close, so close her chest pressed against his. She started to pull away since the professors had drilled into her head there must be a length of a handspan between them, but he spoke quietly in her ear. "I demand those things, but I have wants too. These and other things I have to say cannot be overheard. Please, think about the engagement. It is a way to protect you from black magic as there's no safer place than by my side. And I need you, Toury." His voice was strained.

She backed up a little to see his face. Alex looked vulnerable, the pompous and confident façade gone. He was no prince at that moment, but simply a boy asking for help. "This curse may cost me my kingdom unless it is removed. You can remove this curse. You can save our sphere. You are the savior of this land. I cannot let anything happen to you, can't let you fall into the wrong hands."

"I'm not that. I can't. I don't even know how to do any of that," Toury spouted out denials as her mind raced with confusion. Savior?

"My cousin did this to you. She chose you. You will need to learn, and you will need protection. At court, you can have both."

"Why an engagement? Can't I go to court any other way?"

"I thought about that and about getting you to go with me as soon as I saw the stone, but the only way I could think of would be as an advisor, a mistress, or an engagee. You don't appear powerful enough to be an advisor—not yet, at least—so others would look into why, and we can't have anyone knowing how important you are. As a mistress—"

"You don't even need to explain that one. I have a feeling that term translates the same."

Alex gave her a smirk, his vibrant blue eyes boring into hers. "That option does have its own appeal." His eyes roamed down to her lips. "But it might prove a bit distracting."

Toury wanted to hit him upside his head but bit back the notion. She'd probably end up arrested. Instead, she gave him an incredulous look. And he laughed, lightly squeezing her hand. He looked so carefree and happy for a moment that she realized the magic she felt flowing between them was truly lifting the curse for him. It was a glimpse of the unaffected Alex underneath, who was all lightness, fire, and strength, the way he would be if she could lift the curse permanently. This Alex she liked more than the pompous prince oppressed by the curse.

"So will you help me? Will you accept my proposal?" he asked. She felt for him and realized that it took a lot of humility to ask her for help. For a man of his station, power, and looks to have to beg a girl to align herself with him took a lot of guts and pride-swallowing. And he had done it twice now.

"I will think about it, Prince Alexander. I'm sorry I cannot answer right now," she said. His face fell, and she realized he was dumbfounded by her second denial. "I just can't unless..."

"Unless what?" he asked, hiding the bitterness in his voice poorly. "What do you want? Whatever it is, I'll give it to you."

"I...I don't know if you can give me this." She trembled, afraid of what he might say in response. "I think the only thing that could persuade me to get engaged is love."

Alex's eyes went large, and he stepped on her foot by accident before he fell back into the rhythm of the dance.

She continued to fill the uncomfortable silence. "I will help you with the curse, of course, and anything you need, Your Highness. But whatever this is between us must stop unless it can be love."

Toury was of two minds, torn between wanting him to love her and to slow everything down. She hoped he would confess he loved her, for then she could let herself fall in love. Never being loved by anyone made her hesitant. If she could not attract family or any boy to care for her on Earth, how could she possibly capture a prince? At the same time, things were moving too fast, an uncontrollable inertia pushing her towards Alex, to the role of being a savior, maybe even a princess one day. Although it was where she wanted to be, denying him allowed her to assert control over the situation. Nothing made sense or was within her power ever since she arrived here. The only thing she could master was whether she would enter an engagement or not. And an engagement felt like letting go of the tiniest sliver of autonomy she had in this world. She could not let it go for anything but the deepest love.

She awaited some kind of response to her terms. Instead of promising her it could be more one day, he was silent. The song ended a moment later, and he walked away so quickly, people were staring. She worried she angered him again, or worse, hurt him. If only they could talk alone and sort things out. The damn propriety of this realm prevented any of that. She worried she had pushed him away for the last time.

Toury tried to put Alex out of her mind and paid attention to other men in the room who sought introductions to her. And then she was wrapped up into the night, dancing with other potential suitors. Alex's interest had sparked a few other men's, and the night was flying by. Alex seemed just as busy. He danced almost every dance with numerous girls with silly besotted faces. She supposed it was an honor to be asked since he rarely danced with anyone, but it rubbed her the wrong way. It wasn't jealousy, she told herself. It was because they all wanted Alex for his crown, and for his looks possibly, but they didn't want Alex for the person he was. They wanted some version of him they invented in their heads. None of them knew the real Alex like she did, and none of them were entrusted with realm secrets. At the last suitor ball, he had only danced with Mary and her. He only had eyes for her that day, and this time, he might be looking for a real engagee, the woman he'd marry after he got his world-saving from Toury.

Her good nature and her desire to make him happy flew out the window when he danced with Lady Justine. It was a stab through the heart, a breach in their relationship—friendship—whatever it was. Justine had tried to kill her, and he had believed it. And the worst part of it was not the feeling of betrayal, but of jealousy. She wanted to deny the feeling, but it was there. She turned away from the dancing couple who looked so perfect together, like Prince Charming and Cinderella, and went outside for some fresh air before she broke down crying in front of everyone.

20

A TRAP

Alex couldn't find Toury anywhere. He was about to panic when he espied Madge standing by the doorway to the balcony. Toury was outside with a few other people but off to the side by herself. A professor sat outside, bored, watching the students and suitors. Head inclined, Toury looked at the starry night sky. He stopped behind her.

He had no idea what to do or say. He had been angry and insulted at her second denial; then he distracted himself by dancing with other girls. He half-wanted one of them to turn his head away from Toury, the other half doing it to avoid singling any girl out. Yet none of them compared. They were simple flickering flames when Toury was an inferno consuming him.

"What are you thinking?" he asked her.

"I miss seeing the moon. It had a pretty glow that took away the darkness."

He wondered what the moon looked like from the Earth sphere, but time was of the essence. There were only a few more dances left, and he fully intended to get her on the dance floor again.

"Why are you out here alone?"

"Why are you out here at all?" Her tone was a bit snarky, putting him on alert. She turned around with—he had to admit—a pretty intimidating glare.

He was confused. "What do you mean, Toury?" He sensed her anger, and her tone showed it was directed at him, but he had no idea of what he had done. He was the one who should be mad at her for denying what was going on between them. She had said she'd only get engaged for love, and she'd said no to him twice. She didn't care for him as much as he did her, for why else would she second-guess whether his intentions were born of love? He should be angry and hurt, not her.

"Why aren't you with Lady Justine?" Her voice was thick with anger, but also, there was a little pain. She had every right to hate Justine, but why was she sad?

He prodded her chin so she had to look at him, and he saw the film of tears she was blinking back. He wanted to comfort her, to draw her into his arms with assurances, to kiss her lips. Instead, he rubbed her shoulder gently. "You sound jealous, Toury."

"I'm not, Your *Highness*." She hissed the salutation. "I thought we were friends, or even more, I dunno. You said you wanted to protect me, and then you go and dance with the very girl who tried to kill me."

"I danced with her, and a dozen other girls so as not to single her out, because these private conversations away from others are frowned upon. Lady Justine would take full advantage of having me alone and try to force me into an engagement. The only way I could accuse her of murder, and threaten to burn her at the stake if she laid a finger on you again, was to dance with her."

"I don't believe you."

"What? That I said that to her or that we burn people at the stake? Both are true, I assure you," he told her, trying to tease her. "In fact, the professor looks mighty displeased right now at us for this intimate conversation but is afraid to say anything to me. Why don't we put her at ease and dance the last dance of the evening together, and we can talk some more about you not being jealous." His heart pounded, knowing well that what he was about to do was wrong, yet he hoped Toury would be ignorant of the rules. He had set the trap, and now he hoped she'd walk right into it.

She scowled at him but took up his arm to go inside. All he had to do was get her on the dance floor, and she would be his. He would force her hand because she didn't realize she needed saving nor how much he truly cared for her. His people needed her, he reminded himself. It was for the greater good. It was for her protection. Justine did not seem intimidated enough to leave Toury alone. And Alex needed her. And by the god and goddess, that was in more ways than just the curse. He just hoped she wouldn't make too embarrassing of a scene once she figured it all out.

As they danced, the whispers began, and everyone was looking at them. He tried to keep a conversation going to distract her, hoping she wouldn't notice until the dance was over that they weren't supposed to be dancing at all. He pulled her too close again, so her chest distractingly brushed his.

"So, obviously, Justine is out. Any other ladies you believe unworthy of my attention?" he asked.

She scoffed. "You're a prince. Is anyone worthy?"

"A savior might be. A Tourmaline is. Even the Hematites are from an ancient family of high nobility. You will be one of the most powerful people in the entire sphere."

"No more of that, please. I'm still wrapping my head around it."

He wanted to protest, to shock her. He wanted to say nobles disappeared and died now on almost a weekly basis, and the necromancers seemed to be stealing his father's control over the kingdom. She did not have time to digest her role. She needed to save them all and as quickly as possible. And she had to be his and his alone. He could not afford being distracted by all these suitors drooling over her. But he could not say these things to her, especially after what he was doing right now and her previous reactions to his logical proposals.

"What about you? You think it escaped my notice that you danced with every gentleman in the room? The Baron Ruby twice, and Lord Opal as well?"

"I didn't..." then she stopped herself and smiled. "Who's jealous now, Alex?"

He was jealous he had to admit, but when Toury used his name stripped of the title, it was all too much for him. It was intimate and teasing, and something snapped in him. Fire burned through him, and the light magic pulsating from her into him ignited his feelings even more, and he was no longer in possession of his faculties. He leaned in and kissed her lips, a kiss that no one would call chaste, but one full of his unquenchable desire. She pulled away from him too quickly for it to become too scandalous, making him realize he had displayed his feelings for all to see, something he never did. He hadn't meant to do it. He had ensured her engagement with the dance alone. He was the one who was now causing a scene.

Toury stared at him in horror, the musicians stopped playing, and there was nothing for it. He couldn't take it back, so he leaned his forehead against hers and whispered, "I'm so sorry."

Everyone was talking and staring, and Toury looked around, his forehead shifting to her temple. He could not face the crowd in his shame but looked out of the corner of his eye. The headmistress glowered at them, and professors were closing in. Justine—her eyes dark and glaring—stared at them, along with everyone one else in the room. Then it went utterly silent. No one said anything. No one moved.

Toury looked back at him, her eyes wide and glassy with forming tears. "Get me out of here, Alex," Toury said quietly in a shaky voice. His hands involuntarily cradled her face, but he stopped himself from kissing her again. She had to stop using his first name. She had been overheard this time, and many people gasped at her intimate usage of his name. Poor

Toury, in her ignorance, was thrice engaged to him, three rules of decorum broken, all because of him.

Alex wanted to get out of there as well, so he let the power out of his feet, the flames spreading around them, and envisioned them in the headmistress's office. He could not legally take her away until the headmistress released her. Taking her from school without permission would mean eloping straight to marriage, or Toury's reputation would be ruined. He had to go through these steps to give Toury the option to drop the engagement later if she wished, although the idea of her doing that made him feel sick.

As soon as they arrived, Toury flew at him like a wild dragon. "Why did you do that?" she screeched. Then she hit his shoulders and chest repeatedly with the heels of her hands. She wasn't trying to hurt him but get her frustration out. Still, it would not look good since less violence against a prince would get someone thrown into the dungeons.

"Please stop, Toury, *stop!*" When he raised his voice in command, she stopped and looked at him through teary eyes. "I'll let you throttle me later, but you cannot do so in front of anyone, and the headmistress will be here any moment."

She looked around, finally realizing where they were.

"Alex, what happens now?" she pleaded.

He swallowed the guilt and pulled her into his arms. "You need to stop calling me that. It's what got us in this predicament."

"You can't blame me!" She struggled out of his arms. "You told me to call you that once."

"It's my fault, of course, but—"

Then the door burst open, and the headmistress walked in, flanked by two professors and his sister. They all looked livid. Despite being the prince, his confidence momentarily fell. He let go of Toury, straightened his posture, and tried to look more commanding and regal than he felt. But gauging the look in their eyes, particularly his sister's, he was in for it.

21
ENGAGED

Toury was scared of how much trouble she was in and what this meant. Kissing suitors was prohibited, and if made public, meant an instant engagement or ruination. Headmistress had a stern look on her face, but upon seeing Toury's tears, it softened a little.

"Well, you two sure put on a show," she commented, hands on hips. "And Your Highness, if I am in trouble for speaking the truth, so be it, but I expected better from you."

"I give you a pardon Headmistress, but allow me." His sister stepped forward. "How could you, Alex?" Mary demanded as she thwacked him soundly. He pushed his sister away several times as she went off on him, giving him a beating that put Toury's to shame. Apparently, royalty could beat royalty just fine. Did that extend to engagees? Because that might be a perk to the situation. "You asked her to dance twice! What were you thinking? To force a girl into an engagement. Why? Then you go and kiss her...publicly?" Mary screeched. She crossed her arms in literally heated anger, steam rising off of her and her cheeks flushing.

"Dancing twice is allowed," Toury said, confused.

Her headmistress looked away, cheeks flushing with shame. "Not with royalty. I should've told you the rule, Lady Tourmaline, and for not doing so, I apologize. If royalty dances twice in the same evening with someone who isn't his relation, he is proclaiming his choice, just like a gentleman dancing a third time does, the same as you were taught. It was overlooked, and I should've informed you since the prince did show interest in courting you. It just never occured to me that he would dare to break the rules."

"No one told you, Toury, because we never could fathom Alex would stoop so low as to trap a girl into marriage." Mary's heated stare was still fixated on Alex, even as she spoke to Toury. "Had I known he would be so stupid—"

"His Royal Highness would prefer it if the people in the room would stop talking about him as if he were not here," Alex had the audacity to counter.

"I so wish we were alone because I would blast you across the room right now. I'm that mad," Mary continued.

"I had my reasons, Mary. Stay out of it!"

"Reasons?" she scoffed.

"She denied me...twice!"

"That still doesn't—"

"He proposed?" The headmistress ceased their argument.

Toury froze. The rules she had never grasped ahold of hauntingly came back: the headmistress must be notified of any proposals and the lady's response; the headmistress must be informed of any improper behavior performed by a suitor; once denied, a suitor must be taken off the list but could retry at a later date. Toury hadn't followed these rules.

"I forgot the rules," Toury said sheepishly. But it rankled her. "It doesn't matter. He still shouldn't have tricked me!"

"No, you're right in that Toury," her headmistress said. "But knowing it had become that serious, we could've better prepared you."

Not likely. They were more interested in teaching Toury how to make tea and walk elegantly than work on powers or look out for her best interests, but she held her tongue. As much as she wanted to fight against the engagement, it had to be better than this place—being treated like a hopeless case, berated, denied the knowledge she wanted, and being blamed for all they did wrong. She was over this place.

So she was engaged. Even though it was better than ruination, it hit her hard. And Alex had forced her into it with a second dance, and a kiss. Why would he force her? She was so close to giving in, especially knowing it didn't have to end in marriage. And why had he publicly kissed her? Especially after he had her secured? Despite this trap, she was angriest that he wouldn't tell her how he really felt. If he loved her, she might be able to overlook his actions.

She asked him these same questions when they were alone, in a carriage, on the way to the palace. All her things and her maid were with his manservant in a second carriage. There were a dozen or so soldiers on horseback flanking them. She finally understood what he meant by her being safe by his side. But safety was not much of a comfort at the moment.

"I can only explain the dance, which you know was premeditated. Toury, I'm an impatient man, and every week, at least one noble goes missing. We are losing control, and I'm getting weaker."

"I'm not going to feel bad for you."

"I don't want you to," he said. "Trust me, I hate myself right now as much as you hate me."

"Doubt it," she muttered.

"I care about my people, my kingdom. I needed your help, and I commanded it of you. As a subject of this sphere, you should oblige and help fellow citizens. Honestly, you're the only woman in all of Fyr who would deny an engagement to the prince...twice."

She wanted to retort but schooled her feelings. "I truly do understand the distinction, but as I told you, I could not enter an engagement without being in love. Why must you frame it as me helping you with some mission?"

"Because it's the truth," he countered. "Do you want me to profess feelings prematurely that might not last between us? You know I care. You have to know I desire you. How is that not enough?"

"It's not love!"

"I don't have the luxury of time to fall in love!" Alex shouted back, shocking her. Then he took a deep breath before he continued more calmly, "As for the very public kiss, Toury, I can't explain it. I lost control. I was jealous, and the way you said my name, and the fact I knew we'd be engaged anyway, I don't know. I wanted to kiss you, and impulsively, I did. I wasn't thinking of where we were. I don't recall thinking at all."

"Do you always take what you want?" She challenged him with a glare.

His dashing blue eyes met hers. "Always. I'm the prince. I can by right."

She was so appalled and angry at this comment, she couldn't even form a sentence. She launched herself at him and started hitting him again, knowing it was wrong, but it felt right. He batted her arms away, disabling her by pinning them to the sides of her body. He pressed her into the cushion and restrained her body with his own. His eyes were wild in surprise, and he panted, his breath tickling her face. She tried to break free by moving back and forth, her chest rubbing against his in the process.

"I'd stop that if I were you," he said quietly, his eyes on her lips. She stopped and waited, thinking he'd kiss her. If he did, she'd bite him. He let her go and backed away from her, yet his eyes studied her with interest.

She stared out the window and ignored him the rest of the way, which felt like an eternity. She couldn't understand his loaded comments. It was oppressive in the small carriage, and over large bumps, their knees knocked together when the last thing she wanted was to acknowledge his presence.

Finally, the carriage slowed, and she could not help but gaze out the window to view what would apparently be her new home until this sham of an engagement ended. She wanted to hate it. She wanted to tell Alex it was old fashioned, ugly, and she had hoped it was a crumbling heap she could complain about. But it was magnificent. Two large ornate stone dragons loomed over the road, their jaws almost touching to make an arch. Their tails disappeared into a large stone wall that most likely surrounded the property. Despite being in the heart of the city, the drive was long and sandwiched by trees and grassy fields. Ahead loomed a massive castle, the kind Toury had dreamed about living in when she thought one could be a princess if she willed it. The child Toury would love this place and adventure, but this older Toury saw it as a gilded prison.

As they got closer, she saw the massive stone front, with two large turrets that were the size of houses on Earth by themselves, like tower houses. She examined the architecture, and like the rest of this land, it was medieval yet Victorian. The stone was gray but still looked pristine. There were bay windows on the upper floors of the towers, cone-shaped turrets atop them just like the Earth's Victorian homes, yet the entire exterior was made up of stone—unlike her aunt's house—with arrow loops and a barbican, which gave it a medieval feel. Spreading out above the barbican, a long balcony overlooked the entire drive and lands. It was enormous, with four towers across the front and too many windows to count while the carriage jostled. It looked to be four stories high, but the towers stretched a little higher.

"It's been around so long, no one knows when it was built," Alex finally broke the silence. "Back when the first Sapphirians claimed the throne. There were many of us then, so the palace can sleep about 150 people. These days, the front towers are empty—we stay in the four in the back, and pretty much only the first two floors are used. Courtiers used to live here later on, the most elite nobles, but after the curse, my father cast them all out. There is a covered courtyard for sparring and athletics, and beyond the castle, there are gardens, a stable, a swimming pond, and orchard. I think if you get over hating me, you could enjoy yourself here. There's everything you need or could want."

"Except freedom," she mumbled.

"I'm not keeping you under lock and key, Toury. I'm not putting you in a dungeon."

"You took away my choices, Alex. It's about the same."

His eyes grew darker, and then he closed them, wincing as if it caused him pain. "Do not say my name like that," he muttered.

"Why? Why should I give you the distinction of your title after what you've done?"

His eyes shot open, and he suddenly darted forward, leaning over her, his arms pressed against the cushions beside her head, trapping her in a way-too-personal prison. His face was mere inches from her, his eyes dilated. "It has nothing to do with pride or distinction," he hissed. His anger and power rippled with such intensity that she could see how he could be likened to a dragon. "I'm not used to beautiful women saying my name with such familiarity. It makes me... I am a man, Toury, flesh and blood. I can only take so much." His squinting, angry eyes transformed into an open, helpless defeat, and his mouth covered hers. She could hardly bat him away, but she was saved by the carriage coming to a halt, the inertia making Alex fall back into his seat away from her.

The carriage door opened, and he hopped out the door onto the cobblestones below. Toury was staggered by his anger, confused by his admittance, and she couldn't even fathom how she felt about the kiss. But when he helped her down from the carriage, his hands on her waist, and she saw that look still in his eyes, it clicked. He couldn't stand being called Alex because it made him want to kiss her. Interesting. She had a power over him she hadn't counted on.

"Thank you, Your Highness," she said formally.

He offered his arm, but she did not take it. They walked through the barbican, and she saw the tell-tale spikes sticking out above: a portcullis. Upon seeing the grate which would close down to keep out enemies, it did feel very much like a prison locking her in. The main entrance was right there: a pair of large wooden double doors that looked indestructible. It wasn't a true barbican, then, but she knew no other way to describe it. When they entered, there was no fuss, no servants but the two trailing them, no reception, no family to meet them. Only impassive soldiers who reminded her of Beefeaters but dressed closer to knights with lightweight sculpted armor. She didn't know why she expected it. Although Alex had planned it, it wasn't something he'd tell his parents about. They would hardly be ready there to congratulate them.

She was led to the rear of the castle and up to the second floor. Alex wordlessly and quickly led the way, veering to the left side, down a long hall, to a tower house. There was a large door that looked thick and heavy, like a smaller version of the large front doors of the entire castle. On the door, an ornate A was engraved in the wood, a dragon wrapping around it. She understood at once that this was Alex's quarters, a house within a castle. Her stomach dropped in realization that she might be living with him, and technically alone.

"My lady." He gestured her to enter. She could not move.

After a moment, he spoke: "Is there a problem?"

"Am I going to live with you?"

"That's how an engagement works, for royals at least."

"And for nobles?"

He sighed. "They don't live together until a date is set. If it bothers you, I could have you placed somewhere else in the castle. It just makes the most sense to live together as it won't arouse suspicion, I will know you are safe, and we'll be able to talk freely of top-secret things that could be overheard elsewhere in the castle."

"I meant Fyr is so strict. We weren't allowed to dance twice, and now I'm allowed to live with you...unchaperoned?"

Alex's gaze flickered to hers, and he looked away quickly, his cheeks flushing. "Oh, um. You see, when entering marriage one day, they...uh...measure a girl's virtue by—"

"I don't think I need to know," she cut him off.

She looked at him, and his mouth quirked, although he turned redder. "No, they, um, measure her virtue by placing a stone...on her stomach."

Weird. What a weird world.

"But it doesn't deter other things from happening between two engagees, everything but...you know."

"Too bad *you'll* never know." She fired the barb at him and then entered the room. Her false bravado faded right away when she took in the room and quickly fell into an overwhelmed silence.

He sighed impatiently, flipped a switch, and lights flickered on in an ornate chandelier above what looked like a rather large and inviting sitting room. He flicked his hand, and a fire leaped up in the grate. She had never seen Mary use her fire magic like that before, so his little trick surprised her. The room was cold. She rubbed her arms to warm herself.

"David, Madge, you will keep a fire always going for Lady Tourmaline. She is to have whatever she needs and wants. That is all for now. Come back in an hour's time to help her to bed, Madge."

"I'd rather manage on my own tonight." Toury felt the need to assert some power. She would not be dictated to like he did his servants.

"You heard her, you're dismissed for the evening," Alex said.

Now alone, she suddenly felt shy and nervous. She had no clue what to say, and her anger at him momentarily faded to unease and fear of the unknown. She was at his mercy. He took a blanket off the couch and wrapped it around her shoulders. He rubbed her arms.

"I'm sorry. The castle is quite drafty. You'll need to tell me when you're cold and remind me to keep it warm for you."

"Don't you get cold?" She looked at him in a new light. He removed the medallion and dropped it with a thud on the table. He unbuttoned the collar of his doublet and seemed completely content, despite the chill in the air. She tried not to stare at the bare skin of his neck and the top of his chest. On Earth, it was equivalent to a V-neck T-shirt, but on Fyr, it was a bit inappropriate. How had she become so used to this rigid propriety?

"Never," he said quietly. "Dragon's blood runs warmer than a human's, so I'm never cold," he said nonchalantly.

Mary felt warmer to the touch, but dragon- and human-blooded? She thought of Alex as human, not some dragon-human hybrid. It was yet another weird thing to wrap her mind around.

"Weird," she looked around, uncomfortable.

"So this is the sitting room we will uh...share. There are two more floors above us that are part of our apartment. You can do as you wish with them since I've never used them. Below us is the bathing room, a safe room, and a walk-in closet that you probably could never fill up. My room is through here,"—he pointed to a door—"and yours is through here." He opened the door, switched on a light, and flicked his wrist to light a fire for her. The bedroom put her dorm to shame. It was three times the size and had a desk by a window, a small table by the bedside, a chaise, and a larger table with two chairs. One wall had an empty bookshelf. She ran her finger along the shelf to find it dusty. The bed was massive.

"I will have it cleaned, and you can have it decorated to your liking. If you'd rather sleep in my room for tonight—"

"No," she cut him off, unnerved by his suggestion.

He turned bright red. "I meant you could have my room, and I would sleep on the settee." He pointed to the sofa. "Or we could call back Madge to fix it up for you now?"

"Why did you let me send her off?" Toury moaned, now realizing she would, in fact, need her help for several things. She wasn't used to not having her servant sleeping in her room. It seemed servants were dismissed for the night while in the safety of the palace, which was more like a guarded fortress.

"I didn't wish to challenge you in front of servants. I can summon her. There are quarters for personal servants directly across the hall from us. Frankly, it slipped my mind that it may be dusty and the bed unmade. I was more worried about how you'd get out of that dress by yourself." After realizing what he said, he became even redder.

"No. I will manage on my own, thank you very much," she clipped. "I would like to rest, and the dust won't bother me at all. Good night."

He took up her hand and kissed the back of it, his mouth warm and soft on her flesh, sending chills up her traitorous spine. Then he gave her a wistful look and headed for another door she had not noticed. He paused in the doorway and said, "I'm not...my family won't bother you. I want you to be comfortable, happy if you can be." Then he entered the room next to hers—his bedroom, she realized—and closed the adjoining door.

All that stood between them was a wooden door. She crept over and clicked the lock on it to feel safer. The sound echoed throughout the room, so he probably heard it. Then she locked the other door that led to the sitting room, just in case. She didn't want to see him, and she was quite frightened by his aggressive behavior in the carriage.

Realizing she could not manage on her own because she could not get the laces of her dress undone, she gave up and threw herself onto the dusty bed, fully clothed, and tried to get comfortable. Although she was exhausted, she was more overwhelmed than anything. Not caring and partially wanting him to hear, she gave in to her emotions and cried.

22

A REGRET

Alex couldn't sleep. Aside from the guilt overwhelming him, he was well aware of Toury next door due to her crying. It varied from loud sobs to ones she tried to muffle in her pillow, but after an hour, it could not be healthy. Should he summon the stone healer or the apothecary to ease her? Or would she be better off left alone to let her emotions out?

He told himself at every outburst that he had to do this. He had done the right thing. A few uncomfortable nights for her versus saving all of Fyr was a small price to pay. His duty came first. His people came first. He was one of the last Sapphirians and had to keep the line going. Why did that enter his mind? The girl evoked an unquenchable desire in him. Obviously, Toury was far from ever wanting to marry him at the moment, and he wasn't ready for that anyway. But he had her secure. She could not entertain anyone else's affections while engaged to him. Whenever this mess was over with, and she saved his people and him, they could marry. They had a couple years until the engagement would have to be broken or satisfied. And he realized he wanted it to happen. He had fulfilled his promise to his mother. He had chosen his bride and was engaged while his father was still in command. He couldn't give Toury love yet, but no other woman would do. He had to make it work.

He rolled over, fluffing his pillow, but a new outburst of sobs prevented his comfort. Giving up, he got out of bed. He didn't know what he could say, but he had to try. He slipped into a robe, but feeling too scantily clad, he pulled on some pantaloons underneath too. He should probably stop sleeping in the nude now that Toury was here. Having not worn nightshirts since he was a child, he'd have to send a servant to buy some.

Alex knocked on the door. The crying ceased. "Toury?" he asked.

"Leave me alone!" She wailed, her voice sounding gravelly.

His heart lurched, and his stomach felt sour. He was awful for making her feel this way. It was as if her pain were his pain.

Alex tried the knob, but it was locked; so was the door in their common room. He returned to his bedroom and shoved the door and pleaded with her, but she was stubborn to the bone and would not relent. Nor would she stop bawling.

Despite the fact she would see this as another abuse of his position and power, he conjured flames over the door and walked through them and entered her room. She was staring at the spectacle, and he momentarily could see her tear-streaked face and free-flowing hair before the flames behind him went out, and then they were in darkness, only the embers of the dying fire in the grate casting a small glow.

"Leave me alone."

"I can't. I can't sleep," he said.

"I'll try to be quieter," she said, venom dripping in her voice.

"I didn't mean the noise." He crept closer to the bed but was still afraid to comfort her.

"Oh, His *Highness* has a conscience after all?" she mocked him.

He sat on the side of her bed. "I know you think it is all selfishness—and I will not insult you by saying none of it is—but my people, this sphere needs you. I need you, Toury, and to be honest, I don't even know what I mean by that. I know it is more than just the curse. I can't stand knowing you are out there unprotected, vulnerable, and admired by others. I know what I've done to you, but know that when it comes to you and me, I will not hold you to any expectations. Once you are safe, once this curse is lifted, I will let you out of this engagement if that is what you want."

She made no response. The oppressive silence stretched throughout the room.

"Please say something," he pleaded.

Whatever she'd say would be filled with anger, and rightfully so. Alex braced himself.

"You trapped me," she said quietly. "I was thinking of saying yes to you. I really liked you, and then you do this, and now, Alex, I can never forgive you. You robbed me of choice, of my autonomy. You took me like a possession. Where I'm from, women are equal to men. Decorum doesn't really matter, and if someone was a friend or really cared about her, he'd never force her into a situation like this." She never raised her voice, but it wavered with a sadness and a sound of defeat that consumed him. He loathed himself.

Alex had no words that could remedy the situation except for a sorry she wouldn't believe. Actions were needed. He relit the fire, which cast some light in the room, then lifted her up and put her on the chaise. Wordlessly, he took sheets and a quilt out of the wardrobe and awkwardly made the bed in a way that would make David cringe. Toury didn't say a thing, but her sniffling and sobbing ceased. He went over to her, pulled her up by her hands, and turned her around. When he began to undo her laces, she tried to pull away.

"Toury," he said, his voice embarrassingly cracking. He cleared his throat. "I mean no harm, but it's a miracle you haven't fainted, being laced up so tight and crying so long."

She stopped struggling and sighed, able to breathe. He let go, not trusting himself to unlace her all the way. He led her to the bed, tucked her in, and she closed her eyes.

He turned to leave but couldn't. His guilt and the intensity of his feelings for her prevented him. Instead, he found himself lifting up the quilt and slipping under the covers with her. She made to move away from him, but he wrapped his arms around her and pulled her close to him, burying his face in her wild dark hair. She tried to move away, but he shushed her in a soothing whisper, "I'm not trying anything. Just let me hold you. It will make both of us feel better if we comfort each other."

She relaxed slightly in his arms. She scoffed. "What comfort do you need?"

"I sacrificed my principles, my public image, and my family's opinion, all for my people, and none of them know they need saving. And despite what you believe, you need protection. No one knows you are the savior, no one, not even my family. I can't trust anyone but you. We're in this together, just you and me, Toury."

She stayed silent. The magic pulsing between them not only made him feel strong, but it comforted him as well. He hoped his touch did the same to her. Toury didn't say a word, but he could tell from her breathing she wasn't sleeping yet.

"You won't believe me, but I'm deeply sorry, and someday, somehow, I will make it up to you."

"Well, that will take forever," she mumbled.

"I hope it takes a lifetime," he whispered. It was all he could give her. He could not express his feelings in words nor show her in caresses. He had been denied twice and feared it would happen a third time.

She didn't speak but didn't kick him out of bed either. He was so comfortable, he did not want to leave. Exhausted from the long evening and emotional turmoil, he fell asleep quickly. Before he lost himself to sleep, Toury's breathing grew deep, finally giving in to the sleep she so desperately needed.

23
AMULET

Toury woke to a brightly lit room. The sun blazed in on her from a large window behind the bed. She turned to ask Alex what time it was, but he was gone. She wasn't sure what to think about how he had trapped her or his apology. Despite wanting to stay mad, she had found comfort and sleep in his arms. Toury wanted to hate him, and yet a piece of her longed for him. If he loved her, truly showed he loved her, she could simply let herself feel. She rolled over to the pillow he had slept on and inhaled. His enticing scent was still there—a manly, musky scent with a hint of acrid charcoal. Her stomach flopped, and she hid her smile in that pillow.

She wouldn't forgive him easily. She was still furious with him, but she would make the best of the situation. After all, it wasn't permanent, and it sounded as if she would be allowed more freedom here than at school. Toury would practice her powers and learn as much as possible about this world, all while giving Alex hell. If Alex were true to his word, that was, which was a problem right now. How could she trust him after what he had done?

She sat up and stretched, her body feeling more relaxed than ever. The bed was a dream of silky softness, like sleeping on a cloud. Yes, she could get used to luxuries such as this. She pondered how lavish the bathing room would be. The ones at school had been like Earth locker rooms, but surely, the palace would be a vast improvement.

She climbed out of bed, peeled off her crushed ball gown, and slipped on a robe that was left for her on the foot of the bed. It was silky and smooth and felt like a caress around the skin that wasn't covered by her chemise. It was warm to the touch as well, as if enchanted with fire, which meant it was high quality and not the kind of item sold in even the best shops.

There was a small wrapped box on the table by the window, and when she approached, she saw a note next to it.

My dearest Toury,

Please accept the robe and this present as the beginning of many gifts for my atonement. Breakfast awaits you in our sitting

So there was a lot of freedom. And presents. She could get used to this. She unwrapped the box. Inside was an exquisite silver bracelet loaded all the way around with blue beads. She picked it up and realized from the size and weight it was actually an anklet, and the beads were polished pure sapphires. It was extremely expensive since the sapphire was the most sought after stone in the land. In Earth terms, it was like holding about twelve or more carats worth of diamonds. She sat down, opened the clasp, and fastened it around her left ankle. It fit perfectly, not too tight, not too much slack. Why had he spent so much money on something no one would see, since it would be hidden under her skirts?

Feeling nosey, since she had free rein and he had referred to the connected suites as "our" rooms, she tried the handle to his bedroom door. It was unlocked. He really did trust her. For a moment, she did not want to breach that trust, but with her ire at him still simmering under the surface, she gave in to her eavesdropping impulse. After all, he'd simply waltzed into her room. It would serve him right.

His room smelled pleasantly of him, overwhelmingly so. It was immaculate, with the bed made and nothing out of place. It wasn't cluttered with junk as her Earth room had been. She snooped around, but there was nothing much to see: some books about dark magic, protection stones, and history on his bedside table; a decanter of water and a glass on a sideboard; some unused scroll ink and a pen on the desk. She looked through most of the drawers but found nothing to shed light into his character, except a few choice childhood trinkets hidden away. His desk held important missives, but she grew bored after reading two. They mostly spoke of things he had already shared with her: famines, necromancers, missing nobles.

Then she felt around one desk drawer that was too shallow, looking for a spring to open what must be a hidden compartment. After she removed the paper and quills, she saw a small scorch mark in one of the corners and realized only his magic would open it. Thinking it might be worth trying, she looked around for a candle. This land had electricity, but it was only really used for overhead lighting, not electronics or lamps, so plugs and sockets didn't exist. Candles were used for everything else. Something to do with interference with magic, Madge told her when she had complained about practicing light magic in the dark dungeons. She supposed that was why her aunt accused Earth of losing its magic, although Toury wasn't sure she believed Earth housed magic as Fyr did.

She found a candle by his bedside, but there seemed to be no flint lying around to light it. Of course, there wouldn't be. Alex had fire magic and wouldn't need flint. She returned to her room, found some in her nightstand drawer, and then lit the candle. She dipped the flame down in the corner of the drawer by the scorch mark, hoping she would not burn the entire desk down.

The wood vanished before her eyes, and she placed the candle down to inspect what was inside. There were tons of sapphires and other stones, most smooth and rounded into little balls. She also ran her hands across strips and bars of silver, and some clasps. She picked up a small knife, not sure of its use, and placed it back down. Out of her subconscious, some knowledge floated up from the abyss and told her the knife was probably used for blood magic, that one could fuse their blood to a stone to enhance some kind of power. The fact that she knew this without ever actually learning it unnerved her. It was Ruby knowledge.

Then the board suddenly reappeared. Interesting.

She realized then that Alex had made her the anklet with his own two hands. That he probably fused his magic to the anklet. What it did, she didn't know, but she felt an odd feeling like he was claiming her with it. She went to take it off, but the clasp was no longer a clasp; it was fused as if someone had welded it shut. It had been enchanted to only clasp once.

She hurried back to her room and then the sitting room. Again, there wasn't much there to shed a lot of light on Alex's character, and it also had a dominant masculine air to it. She was positive she must be the first woman to grace these rooms. She had never asked Alex if he had been engaged before or had a mistress. The thought of either being a possibility unnerved her, but Madge had said Alex never dallied with girls before. She hoped it was true.

She tried to banish Alex from her mind and sat down to eat her huge breakfast, kept warm by a fireplate, another luxury that kept food perpetually hot for extended periods of time. Despite the massive quantities of toast, eggs, bacon, and fruit, she was so famished, she finished all of it. A couple of the fruits she could not identify, but they tasted delicious.

When she was finished, she pulled the bell, and Madge arrived a minute later, followed by another servant. The other servant cleared away her breakfast and left.

"What time is it, Madge?"

"Past the first hour of the noon."

It always took Toury a moment to figure out what they all meant when speaking of the time in Fyr, despite it having the same twenty-four hour cycle Earth had. Past one o'clock, she surmised.

"I never thought you'd wake, but you did have a trying evening."

"Yes, no thanks to any of you. Why didn't you tell me I couldn't dance with Alex twice? Why didn't you protect me in every way? Why did you lie to me?"

"I didn't lie, but I did omit. If you did not ask, I didn't tell. I was the prince's servant. Also, I was after your best interests. This is the best match you could make. This is the safest place for someone like you." The insinuation in her voice made it sound as if Alex had told her about her being the savior, and yet Madge had never said anything. "Please believe I was in a hard place. I had to do what I could for you without defying his wishes as well."

"But you said you weren't reporting to him."

"I was not, but I couldn't treat him like an ordinary suitor and keep my job. When he was in your room, had he not been my employer and my future king, I would've run him from there to preserve your innocence. I have...people depending on me."'

"Who?"

Madge looked at her pleadingly.

"Why should I trust you now, ever again, unless you answer everything I ask?"

"I now serve you and you alone. You will be given an allowance and will pay me out of that. I am your only employee and the only person you should trust. The maids see everything, and they tend to gossip, so be wary. The prince cannot fire me."

"But I could?" Toury said.

Madge's gaze darted up to meet hers, panic in her eyes.

"Tell me why you felt beholden to obey a spoiled prince who was willing to take everything from me, and you can keep your job." She meant it as a snide remark with the confidence that Madge couldn't possibly have an excuse to forsake her charge, but Madge surprised her by getting down on bended knee. She was bowing, and it made Toury feel like an imposter.

"Only time will allow me to regain your trust if you keep me on. The prince didn't have a hold over me, but the salary of this esteemed position did. I have a bedridden mother, deceased father, and ten siblings, only half of us able to work, but most of their pay goes to our mother's care, and mine puts food in their bellies."

Toury had no idea what to say to that. She understood now, and yet she felt insignificant. Would no one ever put her first? And as the thought came out, it felt selfish. Her conflicted feelings would have to wait. She had so many questions but decided to start with the more innocuous ones after such a heavy discussion.

"What is my agenda for the day? What is that exquisite blue fruit I ate, and what kind of blood magic has the prince trapped me in?"

Madge seemed stunned at the sudden change in subject, but Toury wanted to end that conversation without awkward apologies and feigned forgiveness. She wouldn't get rid of Madge. The waiting-maid was all Toury had here in this intimidating castle.

"One step at a time, Princess-to-Be, and let us get you dressed."

Madge walked toward the bedroom, so Toury had to follow. "Princess-to-Be?"

"That is your new title. All people must refer to you as Lady Tourmaline, Princess-to-Be. The 'Highness' comes after marriage."

Princess-to-Be. That was a bit overwhelming. She pushed it to the back of her mind to think about later. Madge went into the wardrobe and pulled out some garments. She had no clue where the clothes came from or when they were put in there, most likely while she was sleeping, which felt a bit weird. Her dresses were there, but there were at least half a dozen more she didn't recognize.

"Whose clothes are these?"

"Yours."

"But how?"

"I purchased some ready-made dresses for everyday use this morning. The palace seamstress altered a couple of them already. She wishes to schedule a fitting for other necessities, but at some point, you'll want to go to the shops in town for formal wear."

"I have formal gowns."

"They are fit for a lady but not a princess."

"Fine. But I would rather go to the shops than be pampered like this."

"I knew you'd say that." Madge laughed to herself, but she did not proceed to tell her that they would head to town. "You'll only be able to wear these dresses around the palace. In public, you'll need much finer gowns. Considering how the prince only takes up the tiniest area of that massive closet downstairs, you can shop your heart out."

Toury was about to ask for a bath and demand to go to town to start bleeding the prince's wallet dry in revenge, but Madge continued, "That blue fruit's common name is dragon's eggs, but its official name is a dracaberry. It has beneficial nutritional properties. As for your agenda, it is not set, but there are a few things Prince Sapphirian requires of you today."

"Of course," Toury said, the derision not lost on Madge, but the servant held her tongue.

"He'd like you to go to the combat rooms to train in self-defense. I will be your trainer. He wishes for us to do so every day. The same for a tutoring session for powers. He has sent for a powerful magician with light magic like yours to do so. The times for these are at your leisure, though, of course." Madge pointed to the trousers and simple white shirt on the bed. "I figured combat before bathing would be most efficient." Madge started undressing Toury.

"I can get dressed myself," Toury said.

"You are a princess-to-be, my lady. You will do nothing of the sort. I have indulged you long enough with this odd Earth custom," Madge quipped and proceeded to undress her. Toury gave in.

"After my lessons, what am I to do?"

"Whatever you like. I could give you a tour of the palace. You could have lunch with the queen if you'd like or go horseback riding?"

Toury's stomach sank. She was nervous about meeting his family. This was going to be a disaster. She was not princess-to-be material, and they would hate her.

As if noticing Toury's unease, Madge continued. "Usually, the prince dines with the king and queen every evening for supper and has his other meals elsewhere. However, I believe the prince doesn't want to overwhelm you. He has ordered supper in your sitting room, where he hopes you will join him later," Madge told her.

Toury relaxed slightly. She could not handle a king and queen right now. Alex was considerate, thinking of everything.

Madge began brushing Toury's thick hair. "And what was your last question? Ah, blood magic? You're referencing the amulet on your ankle? Sapphires alone will protect you from harm, help you find favor with others, and bring good luck. Adding Prince Sapphirian's blood to it will enhance that ten-fold and most likely includes his fire-power. Smashing one of these most likely will result in a huge fiery blast, like a weapon for you."

"Is that all?" Toury challenged. There must be some controlling factor involved, for she was beginning to understand Alex well. With all this freedom, there had to be a catch.

"He can trace you as well, your whereabouts." Madge reluctantly met her gaze, cringing in anticipation of Toury's reaction. "He can find his kin, his blood; most sorcerers can. Your tutor will show you how. Using his blood on the amulet makes it traceable to him, to any other Sapphirian."

"Let's go train then. I need to blow off steam." Toury kept her voice neutral. Inside, she was furious. He was going to keep tabs on her. Madge led the way. "Um. Madge? Shoes?" Toury wiggled her bare feet.

"Where we are headed, we don't need shoes."

Pants, corset free, no shoes? Toury thought she might like training after all. It had been so long since she had worn pants.

24

A BLOOD BOND

Alex was losing his strength and stamina. The amulet around his wrist could not keep his powers up. The crystal ceiling did nothing to assist in healing him or fortifying his powers as it should. The dark magic in him always got in the way. It was as if his body was fighting it, constantly draining him. Not to mention David was relentlessly bashing him with powers. David was a conjurer of energy. He could blast him with what felt like a huge hammer made up of air, or more correctly, the energy around them. He also could block Alex's fire with it, just as Alex used fire to block the energy.

"Enough." He put up his hand to stop him. Sweat trickled down his back.

"Onto swords, Your Highness?"

Alex nodded, went over and wiped his face on a towel, and drank some water. David knew him well, particularly when Alex hit his limits. He hoped he had chosen wisely for Toury with Madge and the tutor. He was still second-guessing himself with giving Toury full power over her allowance and Madge's trust. He had instructed the woman to never report to him again and to be faithful to Toury alone, even if the king or Alex himself demanded information. But it was the right thing to do. Toury needed someone to be her champion, someone after her best interests. His own judgment was compromised. David pointed that out, and although Alex tried to deny having a bias, he knew when it came to Toury, he could not be trusted. Whether it was the love Toury hoped to hold out for was another story. He wasn't sure what love was supposed to feel like. He trusted Madge to do what was best for Toury despite the consequences. If breaking the engagement and freeing herself from Alex was best for Toury, then he expected Madge to urge Toury to do it. Toury needed guidance, yet she was used to autonomy. Madge was the perfect solution.

He was hot, and the room was stifling, which his dragon blood usually welcomed, but on occasion, the curse threw off his ability to regulate his temperature. Rarely did he sweat, so the curse was clearly wreaking havoc on his system. The heat became oppressive, so he slipped off his shirt. David looked relieved and stripped his off as well. Then David picked up a broadsword and a parrying dagger, so Alex followed suit, and before he knew it, David attacked. He parried it off and swung at his man. David ducked and gave him a look as if to protest how close it was. Alex smirked, and then they were off swinging, parrying, tumbling, and ducking. From practicing combat together since they were children, they knew each other's next move, so they rarely injured each other. The weapons were blunted but could still cut or bruise soundly.

They exchanged blows until they were dripping with sweat and out of breath. When David called it, Alex was glad. He was physically exhausted as well. He had missed a few sparring matches and workouts due to courting Toury and visiting Tobias. That reminded him... "Any word on Tobias and my men?"

"They have not returned yet, Your Highness."

"It's been almost two months."

"They'd have to trace the stone to find out if it has returned. They will not want to come back empty-handed as well," David informed him. "And I'm sure they will end those who murdered your cousin."

Alex nodded. He would've liked to have seen those men suffer, but there wasn't a way to bring them all back without labradorite charged with power from Fyr. He would have to settle for an account when the firebrander returned. It was frustrating, though, that he had unknowingly sent the man on a fool's errand and needed him back. He needed help speeding up Toury's abilities and learning how she could cure the curse. He could trust no one with Toury's abilities but Tobias.

"Perhaps we should go? I did not want to distract you, but we've had company for a few minutes. I think they are waiting for the arena." David looked up and on the balcony, and Alex's gaze followed. Toury and Madge sat watching.

His eyes met those thunderous gray ones, which told him she had not forgiven him. However, he took satisfaction in the fact that Toury's eyes raked over his half-naked form. From her lingering gaze, it seemed she liked what she saw. So he did get under her skin. Good to know.

She and Madge descended the stairs, and David took the time to put his shirt on. Alex, enjoying this thoroughly, did not clothe himself as propriety demanded, but simply dried off some of the soot-smelling sweat.

When Toury stood in front of him, he realized it was not one-sided. He could not help but look at her in her form-fitting boy's clothing, with her slender naked calves and bare feet. Her arms were bare to the elbow, and she had such thin wrists, he wondered if she could actually wield a sword.

Her hair fought to free itself from a ponytail, which he found actually more attractive than the intricate twist updos that were in fashion.

"You're angry," he said, assessing her demeanor.

"Why wouldn't I be?" she challenged.

"About something new?" He scrutinized her, trying to figure out what offended her now. From how defeated she had been last night, he surmised something had set off her ire again. Rather than guess and, in doing so, point out to the room how much of a scoundrel he was, he thought he'd just ask her out flat. Toury was a fascinating woman, so much so it probably would take his lifetime to figure her out.

She shook her beautifully bare ankle, and he saw the amulet he had made for her in the wee hours of the morning while he watched her sleep, not that he'd ever admit that to her. Luckily for him, she slept like the dead; nothing seemed to wake her, even when he had caressed her bare ankle with the excuse of measuring it for the anklet. Funny how seductive that innocuous flesh was when uncovered.

"That is for your protection," he told her. Madge must have told her all of the qualities of it then, such as blood tracking.

"Hardly fair that you can know where I am at all times, but you get to gallivant around as you please without me knowing where you are." She crossed her arms. Goodness, she was a pain, but at least this would never get boring. It wasn't as if she could transport to him if she found him. It would only help her track him. He, on the other hand, could transport right to her wherever she was on Fyr. He was figuring her out, though. It was the idea of it not being fair, or equal, that upset her. He was going to suggest doing this anyway since it would strengthen his protection against dark magic even more.

He shook his wrist to bring attention to the black tourmaline amulet Tobias had given him. Then without warning, he picked up her hand and pricked the point of his dagger into her pinky. She drew in a shocked breath and pulled her hand away. He yanked it back and rubbed the blood pooling from her finger onto each bead, and the stones sucked it up. Then he let her hand go.

"Happy?"

When the realization that now she could find him as well crossed her features, she nodded. "Yes."

"I'll leave you to it then. See you at supper?" he asked.

She nodded, which made him happy. She wasn't angry enough to take meals in her room then.

He grabbed his shirt and walked out, David following.

"This might just work out, David."

"If you say so, Your Highness. I think you have a ways to go before you're in her good graces, and you can't ignore your father forever. Remember, he is not a fan of Hematites."

Curse David for ruining his high moment. Alex decided maybe it would be best to keep Toury away from his family even longer. After the way his parents had berated him about the scandal earlier that morning, he would make sure to keep Toury away from them as long as possible.

25

LIGHTBEARER

Madge was trying to kill her, Toury believed, through excessive training. They would run in the early hours of the morning, followed by horseback riding, then weapon sparring. She'd get to indulge in a bath in bathing quarters fit to be a commercial spa, sometimes have her lunch with Alex when he was free; then Toury would overload her brain in the library, learning everything possible about stones, history, politics, necromancers, and curses—everything the future Queen of Fyr would need to know.

After a fifth day of wanting to kill Madge, Toury's power tutor arrived. She met him in the crystal courtyard. He was a middle-aged man with brown hair graying around his temples and a tall, thin build. When she approached him, she stopped short in confusion. His eyes were gray, steel gray, exactly like hers.

He bowed and addressed her as the princess-to-be. "My name is Gareth Lightbearer, and I'm to be your tutor."

"Lightbearer? I understand only magicians or baseborns take on the name of their power. I didn't think the prince would bring a magician to train me." She gathered all the austere authority she could muster. But it rang false. She just couldn't be arrogant like Alex or commanding like Mary. "Not that I mind," she added, which felt more 'Toury.'

"You are right, Princess-to-Be, and I saw your reaction to my eyes, so you can surmise that I am a relation. Illegitimate, of course."

"But who are you to me?"

"No one, unless you recognize it as so."

"And no one has recognized you?"

"Edwina is the only one left, aside from you, so no, I was not recognized. It is rare."

"I was told my grandparents were the last Hematites, aside from my father and aunt, correct? Then you'd have to be my uncle," she concluded.

Gareth seemed surprised at her saying this. "I am the illegitimate son of your grandfather Ambrose Hematite, according to my mother."

Why did he differentiate it that way? He was technically her uncle. She didn't understand why she couldn't call him that or legitimize him but would ask Madge later.

"Shall we get started?" she prompted.

"Yes. First, I need to see what kind of light power you have. I can simply do it through our hands." Gareth took up her hand and placed his palm against hers. He closed his eyes as if concentrating deeply and then pulled away. "Interesting. Your powers combined, which is rare but not unheard of. Your father had light magic and your mother, healing. Combined, I think you could heal the worst magical wounds and curses. I see now why the prince brought you here."

"He thought as much. Do you think I can cure him?"

"You are strong enough to, yes, but magic curses are a fickle thing. Sometimes it takes more than magic to break a curse. Getting you to use these powers effectively will improve your chances of success. I was unable to break the curse myself. As a lightbearer, I can break many curses, but the one bestowed upon the prince is the darkest and most complex I've ever seen."

"Did you know my parents?"

Gareth was taken aback, startled by her boldness. "Only of them. Princess-to-Be, we must get started. If you have questions about the past, ask your aunt. I am not privy to the information you most likely seek."

"I just want to know about them, who they were."

"I don't think you will like what you hear, Princess-to-Be. Now please, do not press me. If I tell you anything, they very well may punish me. The king does not like things spoken of that he has banned from court." Gareth was so serious that she feared to press anymore. Why weren't her parents even allowed to be mentioned in the castle?

She realized something in that moment. She had to watch what she said or asked of people, lest she say the wrong thing and get innocent people punished or maybe even executed. It was strange having the power to do so, and she marveled over the idea. If this worked out, she could be the Queen of Fyr one day, and everything she said would be listened to, every order followed. That amount of power scared her, yet she would be a liar if she didn't admit that it was equally exciting. There were so many things she could do to help people with the influence the royals had.

She left it at that and allowed the lightbearer to proceed with her lesson.

Every night after dinner, she regaled Alex with her day's events, so this night's topic was her first session with the lightbearer.

"He showed me how to focus my power and control it so I can direct it."

Alex raised his brows. "Can you project balls of light?"

She shrugged. "Gareth's making me take it slow, but I think I could. I draw the light in my hand and mentally knead it like you would with dough. When it's small enough, I can control it and push it onto something. I managed to knock some books over and unlock a door."

Alex smiled. "Sounds like the inverse of my power. The fire starts small, and I mentally feed the flame."

"Small? You flick your wrist to start a roaring fire. You transport places in a ball of flames. How is that small?"

Alex laughed lightly. "It started out small, but I gained power and speed as I grew up. I've been using my fire power for sixteen years."

"You played with fire as a baby?" Toury asked. The idea astonished her.

"Toddler. It was very interesting for my nannies, or so I'm told. Mary's started at about five. It varies, I suppose, but it's good he's starting you small. I can imagine how your potential power could backfire if unleashed all at once."

"Could I hurt someone?" Toury peered down at her hands with mixed feelings of awe and fright at what she possibly could do.

"Yes," he said quietly. "Stone magic and blood magic are more innocuous. But light and fire magic can do great and terrible things."

Toury shook at the thought. Alex flared the fire higher as if she were cold. "You are all that is good, Toury. You have no worries."

Night after night, he asked about her powers but patiently never asked if she was any closer to curse breaking. She learned how to sense the light in others and, inversely, the darkness. Gareth and Toury continued using her light and blasting things as Madge had instructed her during her training in the school's dungeon. As Alex foresaw, the light became stronger. She informed Alex each evening, and he responded with what seemed like pride. Each time, after they exhausted the topic of her training, the conversation lagged. They ended up talking of weather, tomorrow's plans—which were always the same—and he'd tell her goodnight, kissing her hand before retreating to his room, although she saw the light on in his room for at least an hour afterward. Things were more than awkward, and she had no idea how to fix it. She was still a bit angry at him for all of this, but she was tired of being angry.

"What is the matter, Princess-to-Be?" Madge asked her as she brushed Toury's hair out before bed.

"Nothing."

"You've sighed in that way three times in a span of a few minutes. Something is bothering you."

Toury didn't want to say anything at first, for she still didn't trust Madge, but who else could she speak to? She didn't have anyone but Alex, but she was still angry with him. And even if she could write to Mary, her brother's lack of intimacy or effort in courting Toury was no subject for the princess's eyes.

"It's just...well, the prince has been distant. I've been rightfully angry at him over this, but to see him so cool and not giving much effort after trying so hard in the past and being so...passionate...I don't know what to think. I'm beginning to think he never really cared. He's got me trapped now, so he doesn't have to pretend anymore."

"I don't think the prince faked anything. I believe, Princess-to-Be, he might just be giving you some space. A man denied twice most likely won't make another attempt at wooing unless he is sure the lady will receive his attentions. In these cases, I believe, the lady must make a move or officially forgive him."

"Madge, I cannot forgive him, not yet."

"Then kiss him."

She turned to look at her servant, shocked. Madge gave her an impish grin. Toury had never seen the woman smile before.

"Kiss him?"

"Yes, men rarely deny a kiss."

She found this advice most likely to be true, but to her, kissing was like forgiving, and yet she wanted peace. She wanted the Alex from before. Still, forgiving him was a lot to ask.

"I will give it some thought," Toury mused. But how could she pull it off? She just wasn't the type to make a move.

26
A SUPPER

Alex waited for her in their common room. They were going to be late if she didn't hurry, and his father was strict about punctuality. He didn't want to rush her because he wanted her to look her best and feel confident; she needed to win over his parents, and a first impression meant everything. He had only kept his parents at bay for over a week, but this morning, his father demanded they attend supper, refusing any more of his excuses. He was out of excuses anyway, after craftily lying his way out of their meeting Toury for days on end. And there was that troublesome little bit. His father had hated and banished all Hematites from court, and now his son had suddenly brought one home, surrounded by scandal and engaged. He had also brought another one—although baseborn—into the castle as well. This would have to go well. He expected his father to be a little snide, his mother accepting. Hopefully, his father took out all his negativity on Alex. Every time he had seen his father, the king reprimanded Alex as if he were four years old again and caught stealing pastries from the kitchen.

His mother was different. While she was upset by the scandal and how Toury had come to be his engagee, she was excited he was engaged and could read Alex's emotions as if he were a book. If he dared to tell her it was an engagement of convenience, she would see through him. A whole other problem would be slowing down his mother's eagerness to marry them. She was probably planning the wedding right now. He still needed some time to win Toury over and save a kingdom that didn't know it needed saving.

Toury came out wearing that purple dress with lace, making his heart swell with pride and honor. No matter how mad she was at him, she was still honoring him, and he deeply appreciated her effort. She took his breath away with her beauty. To him, this engagement was real, but he feared if he pushed things too fast, he would lose her forever. And he had no idea how to go about it. He wasn't ready for a third beating from her.

"My dear, you look amazing," he told her and offered his arm.

"You have to say that."

"No, I don't." He frowned.

"Pouts don't suit you," she said in a cold tone.

He drew back as if she had slapped him.

She responded, "Don't worry, I'll behave at dinner. Sing your graces, tell your parents how infatuated I am with their darling prince." She was mocking him.

"You'll do nothing of the sort. You will be honest and be yourself. Toury, don't worry. No matter what they think, it will not influence me. Whether we fulfill the engagement or not is our decision and not theirs. My parents have no say in my choice of a lifemate."

Tory blushed and looked away, seemingly unprepared for his honesty. He was telling her the truth. He needed to be more open with her, but trust did not come easily to someone who was cursed before he was old enough to know what betrayal meant. He wouldn't fully pursue her, yet he couldn't lie to her as if a true marriage weren't an option.

"I've been warned your father will hate me regardless. Shall I prepare for war?"

"Perhaps, or at least have a shield up. Most likely, he'll attack me instead for my seemingly rash actions again."

"Seemingly, because your nefarious plan was to trap me the entire time."

It was a low blow, but he deserved it. Part of him could not let it go, however. They neared the dining hall, so he'd have the last word. "It wasn't my entire plan. I wasn't plotting to do things this way. Yes, I trapped you, as you so aptly put it, after you denied me—twice, may I add. Although, when I met you in that dress shop, I admit I was intrigued. Had you not been the savior, I still would have courted you, but much later down the line. I do not have that luxury of time, though. Perhaps one day, I will still properly court you."

She looked as if she'd speak, but they approached the servants who opened the double doors, and she shut her mouth, a blush lighting up her cheeks, making her all the more attractive. They entered the dining room and were announced, during which he bowed as she curtsied. Surprisingly, his mother rose, came to him, and hugged him, kissing his cheek, and did the same to Toury. His mother took Toury's hand and led her to her seat. Although his mother was overbearing at times, moments like this made him truly appreciate her. The welcoming reception from her would bolster Toury, he was sure, and make his father a tad softer.

The watered firespice whiskey was served, along with the first course. His mother made a few pleasantries and questioned Toury about her comfort, and Toury responded politely.

His father glared at Toury and gruffly asked, "Where did you two meet?"

Toury looked to Alex for the answer, but the question had been directed toward her, so he nodded for her to respond. Toury met his father's gaze. Thankfully, as a royal engagee, she was now allowed that privilege, something she had been ignorant of when they had first met.

"In a dress shop, Your Majesty," Toury said, leaving it simple.

"And then he simply decided to visit you at your school?" he asked, seeming not to believe her.

"That, sir, is a question to direct toward your son, for I know not why he courted me in the first place," Toury responded with her characteristic wit. Although he feared his father's wrath, he loved seeing Toury's strength and sass, even when under pressure.

His father was surprised at her answer but schooled his features not to give away his feelings, which were most likely centered on anger. He turned to Alex for a better explanation.

"She insulted me by calling me out for ogling her, of which I was fully guilty."

No one said a word, but Toury looked at him in shock, and then his mother held back a giggle, and his father started laughing, a full belly laughter that ended in a short coughing fit. Once his father caught his breath, he wanted to hear more.

"I did not know who he was, Your Majesty. I came from..."

Alex squeezed her hand to signal her to stop. The servants entered with the next course. She paused as they took away the first course and laid down the soup. Toury took a sip of her drink. She swallowed and grimaced. Alex could not help but smile at her reaction. He was sure she had hated firespice whiskey ever since the poisoning.

"...Ludford," Toury continued, cleverly changing the direction of her discourse, "to buy some dresses. This very dress was at fault for your son's ogling. The addition of the lace was his idea."

"Never. Alex!" his mother playfully scolded him.

"Then I discreetly bought it for her and decided to visit her."

"Alex, how improper! And all this time I thought you were visiting your sister—"

His mother was interrupted by the slam of the goblet on the table. All attention went to his father.

With a baleful glower, his father spoke: "Seeing that you did not recognize royalty and are not used to firespice whiskey, you are from another sphere. Which one?"

Toury paused and gave Alex a questioning look. Although he wanted it to remain a secret, there was no way to avoid a direct question from his father. Alex sighed but nodded subtly.

"Earth, Your Majesty."

"So that is where that blasted Hematite vanished to," his father said more to himself than them. "And where, pray, is your father, child?"

"I don't know, Your Majesty. I must have been abandoned. I was adopted and raised by Earth people. My adoptive parents knew nothing of spheres, nor did I until I appeared here."

"And, how, exactly, did that occur?" his father asked next.

Alex did not know how to signal to Toury, without others noticing, to withhold the truth. Sadly, he could not trust his father. He hoped she remembered what details to hide from others.

"I was at this Renaissance Faire. Ironically, it was unknowingly staged to look like this sphere. I bought a bag of gemstones from a market stand, and when I touched one of them, I ended up here."

He could kiss her, really. She managed to lie and tell the basic truth all at once. He reached under the table and entwined his fingers with hers.

His father's eyes narrowed. "A bit coincidental. Sorry if I don't believe that. Smells more like your daddy sent you back to cause more trouble."

"My *daddy*," she retorted, "I know nothing about, being abandoned as I said. And I agree with you. It was obviously not a coincidence. Someone made sure I got that stone, but I don't know why."

"Also, is it not ironic how you ended up infiltrating the very place your father was cast out from?" his father continued.

His mother opened her mouth to say something, but there was no need. Toury rose to the occasion. "Infiltrated?" Toury raised her voice. "I am here because your son tricked me into this engagement! Being from Earth, I didn't know your laws of propriety! And being a stranger to this world, I don't yet have an appreciation for the so-called status I've risen to. Not knowing the prince very well, I haven't formed a solid opinion of him either."

That hurt a bit, but she was careful about their secrets while defending herself.

"Father, please. She's not some Hematite spy!" Alex cut in. "I did this, and I have my reasons for it, of a personal nature." He was hoping it sounded as if he were only attracted to Toury.

"I don't like it," his father said gruffly.

"You have no say in it, Father."

"I could state you unfit to rule and put your sister on the throne," he challenged.

Alex's stomach flopped uneasily, and he was embarrassed to be taken down a rung in front of Toury.

"You know I could with the curse on you."

"He is not unfit, Your Majesty. He fights off the dark just like you are at the moment," Toury challenged. "I thought you might be able to sympathize with him since you're in a similar situation."

Alex looked from Toury to his father and back again. What did she mean? Was his father cursed as well, the same darkness? His mother grew pale and watched his father cautiously, her back rigid and lips clamped together. So she had known about the curse and now was worried his father might lash out.

His gaze darted over to his father, who glared at Toury. The king's face turned red and trembled, fighting the fire blazing with rage inside of him. His mother gasped and gave Alex a look of horror. Alex knew what would happen next and stood up so abruptly, his chair fell back and crashed onto the floor. As Alex felt the fire surging toward them, he dove on top of Toury, tackling her to the ground, chair and all, and covered her from the flames that scorched his back.

He enclosed the two of them in a ring of protective fire and then stood up slowly to meet his father's gaze. All the while, his own fire and rage roiled inside him, wanting to attack back.

"You have attacked the princess-to-be, Father. You do so again, and I will retaliate, so help me!" Alex shouted, patting out flames on his clothes.

"Craig! How could you?" his mother exclaimed. Her brow furrowed, and her mouth went agog in one of those mixed expressions she had mastered, somewhere between disappointment and disbelief.

Alex helped the shaky Toury up. The poor girl was frightened out of her wits, her eyes round and hands trembling. He pulled her into his arms, and she fell into him.

"How'd you know about my malady?" his father growled at her. And then Alex saw his father's face contort in pain before he began a coughing fit that didn't seem to end. Alex had thought the illness physical, but now, in light of what Toury must have seen and how the outburst of power weakened his father, it all made sense. He and his father had the same problem, and now Alex wondered where the curse really came from. Why had his father hidden it from him, from everyone? He felt betrayed and bitter that his father used Alex's curse as leverage to keep him down or threaten him while the man went through precisely the same thing. Yet Alex was relieved he was keeping his own secrets too instead of relying on his father for help.

Toury pushed herself out of his arms. Alex wanted to reclaim her, protect her, but at the same time, he marveled at her strength and ability to bounce back after a fright. He dropped his fire ring to free her. She walked a bit unsteadily toward his father, speaking quietly. "I have a healing light in me. A trait of my family, I've been told. My tutor taught me how to sense darkness, like these curses. I will now show you what probably attracted your son to me, although he may not even realize it."

The king could not protest since he could not breathe and was turning blue. Alex stood transfixed by his conflicting emotions while Toury approached his father. His mother had run to his father's side, trying to thwack his back to get him breathing, but it didn't seem to work. His father simply couldn't die, not like this, not now, and yet he was just as terrified his father would attack Toury again.

Then Toury knelt down in front of his father and grabbed his hand. Although he tried to withdraw, she clamped on his hand. The king relaxed, and the coughing stopped. Alex could imagine what his father physically felt because Toury had done the same to Alex. He could envision the dark magic overwhelming his father's body recede and return to where it came from as his father's color returned. Alex's mother marveled over how Toury could do what no healer had done before.

"Welcome to the family," his father gasped, and then he threw her hand away. "Save your strength."

Alex felt relieved Toury was accepted, but he was also wary of part of her gift being revealed, worried that his father would exploit her power for his own benefit. It angered Alex and yet shamed him. Alex essentially demanded Toury help the kingdom and hoped she could cure him, but he cared about her well-being foremost. His father, Alex could imagine, might physically drain Toury just to keep himself alive. No matter what, as long as Toury could fight the darkness in any capacity, his father would not condemn her as he had her parents. Alex wondered what Toury's father had done to create such animosity that the king would attack Toury.

27

DRACABERRY

They were silent the entire way back to their quarters, and she feared Alex was angry with her. How could she not defend herself? How could she let his father suffer? He could have died. Since Alex said nothing, she figured he had nothing good to say.

Then, after they reached their quarters, he asked her to meet him in the sitting room after Madge helped her change. What did he want? Why couldn't he speak in front of the servants? She wasn't looking forward to any admonishment, but she complied. Madge helped her get out of the dress and corset and get into her nightgown and robe. She observed herself in the mirror as Madge undid the pins from her hair, and looked as she felt, too little fabric between her body and the world outside. She had grown so used to the layers of clothes that two thin layers now seemed almost nude.

As Madge brushed out her hair, Toury fidgeted nervously. She wasn't afraid of Alex or worried he'd try to reprimand her. If he did, she'd give him a piece of her mind. She didn't know why things suddenly felt different, but they were. Alex had protected her, defying his father, the King of Fyr. She had seen Alex as an arrogant boy taking what he wanted, but tonight, he was a man, one whose strength she could not deny made her feel secure and a little warm and flustered.

When Madge left, Toury could not stall any longer and went into the sitting room. Alex was stoking the fire with his bare hands, and she marveled at his ability to not burn or even feel the heat. Alex stood up when he heard her enter. He was wearing a robe as well, and it seemed so clandestine to her, especially since he had dismissed the servants.

"Would you like a drink?" he asked, pointing over to two decanters, one looking like water, the other of that horrid firespice whiskey.

"Of that stuff?" She crinkled her nose.

"You get used to it. When mixed with water equally, it would take many drinks to affect you. The amount you had to counteract the poison was excessive. If you drink it sparingly, it's actually beneficial to your health," he explained. He did not seem mad at her, but that made her unsure of why he wanted to talk to her.

As he poured one for himself with a lot of water, she told him she would have one too. Maybe it would steady her nerves for whatever he was about to say.

Unable to handle the suspense any longer, she blurted out, "I know you're probably furious with me for how badly supper went, but really, what was I to do?"

His face was calm and collected when he turned around and handed her the drink. He didn't speak for a moment but motioned for her to sit in a chair by the fire. He sat in one next to her.

"Angry?" He looked at her perplexed. "You were magnificent. My father, on the other hand, was wretched. I expect him to spoil you rotten with gifts of apology. I'm sorry you even had to go through that. I have no clue what altercation occurred between him and your father, so I hadn't expected such an outburst. Can you forgive me?"

"That depends." She raised her brows, giving him a playfully leery look which matched her mood: she wanted to forgive him but didn't want to end up hurt again. "What am I forgiving you for?"

"I knew you would not forgive so easily. I'm terrible for putting you through all this. But I need you here, and I want you here, Toury." He drank his firespice whiskey with water and stared into the flames. She wasn't sure exactly what he meant or what he was saying. He pensively watched the fire, his eyes animated and scanning as if reading a book, and she realized then it must be true that he could read the future in them. She could not stop seeing him differently. He looked masculine and brooding. She realized how much pressure he must be under on a daily basis, seeing and knowing more than he should, holding secrets in and attempting to solve them alone.

"What do you see in the flames?"

"What has my sister told you about our abilities?" He looked at her over the rim of his glass as he took a sip. She couldn't help but look at his lips and think of how long it had been since they kissed.

"That you see the future. She's never told me anything but did say knowing can destroy it."

"Time changes as much as the flame flickers," he murmured.

"What do you mean?"

"It's an expression," he looked over at her. "It means even though I see the future, it changes as much as flames in a fire move."

"I never thought of the weight knowing things must have on you." She felt for him. How exhausting it must be to see a future you cannot change, or one that changes when you don't want it to. How futile it must seem to have that gift.

"How is your training going?"

"Well. Why didn't you tell me I had an uncle?"

"Well, baseborns aren't recognized for one, unless you want to decree it. As queen one day, you could do whatever you wish. Second, I hadn't known until I found him. I was seeking the best lightbearer in the land. Coincidentally, he has the same blood in his veins as you. Is he teaching you things? I was impressed you could sense the curse in my father. He kept that one from me my entire life."

"I'm sorry, Alex. As strict as your father seems, he is better than my Earth parents. At least, he cares in his own way."

Alex looked at her with a furrowed brow. "Was your Earth family that bad?"

Toury looked at the flickering flames to avoid his poignant stare. She didn't want his pity. "They didn't abuse me, but they saw me as more of a burden than a blessing."

Alex blew out a shaky breath. "They were idiots and completely blind then, but their loss is our gain. I'm glad that you are here with us. Ruby chose well, for maybe you needed us as much as we needed you."

He said "us" meaning the realm, not himself, but she supposed it was a start to him admitting his feelings again. She wished there was a reset button or, at least, a pause so they could return to how things were when he'd sneak in her room and they'd simply talk and kiss.

"I think you may be right. I haven't thought of returning to Earth in a while."

Alex smiled, one of those broad, unaffected smiles that banished the normal strain his face wore due to the stress of his position and self-appointed quest to save his people. "That's good, because before I even found out about the brooch or your role in all this, I was already determined I couldn't let you leave."

His tone was teasing, so she didn't want to take offense and fight with him again, but he had to know that if they one day married, she would not allow him to dictate her life. "Let me?" She lifted her brow in challenge.

His smile did not fall, and his intense gaze pierced hers, and she knew in that moment that despite how things seemed, he loved her strength and vivacity. He liked her the way she was, which was breaking most of the rules in her etiquette textbook.

"To word it more properly, I would've pulled out all the stops to convince you to stay."

"Why?" she pressed, hoping to get something out of him.

He scanned her face, eyes dancing across her features, and looked away into the fire. Whatever he read in her face made him close her off.

"It's been a long day. I'm going to bed," he announced as he finished the last of his drink. He stood and took her hand up, placing a kiss on the back of her hand. Then he went into his room.

Toury sighed with frustration. He was so close to admitting his feelings, but of course, he stopped himself. Why would he say anything if she hurt him by denying him twice? Madge was right: Toury had to make a move somehow. She downed her drink and went to her room, feeling unsettled and dissatisfied. She had slept so well in Alex's arms the first night here. She craved that feeling of security and affection that she had received there and hoped he wouldn't mind if she snuck into those arms again. She needed rest, her body weary from combat training and horseback riding, her mind from her power training and then helping the king, yet her thoughts of Alex fed her insomnia. After about a half hour of tossing and turning, she got out of bed and crept over to knock on the adjoining door, but it suddenly opened, and Alex stood there. They stared at each other, stunned.

"I...uh...I couldn't sleep," she said.

"Me neither." He smiled. "I confess, I was about to ask if I could join you in hopes to rest well like your first night here."

"I was doing the same." She tried not to laugh.

"I wanted to suggest it earlier but was afraid you'd get mad, and I'd ruin whatever peace has formed between us."

She backed away from the door awkwardly and let him in. She didn't say anything because if he had asked earlier, she probably would've been offended, refused, and then regretted the denial.

Then she crawled back in bed, her feet feeling cold, and he slipped in next her, his eyes dark, his expression serious in the firelight. Something felt different—she wasn't sure what it was—but when he pulled her body into the crook of his, she became nervous almost. She heard him smell her hair and give a little moan of satisfaction. This was vastly different than that first night. That night, she had been angry, emotionally spent, and scared of the unknown; tonight, she felt happy and empowered. She could be a queen if she chose to be, and it would be her decision. That first night, Alex had been in control, and she hated herself for finding solace in his arms; tonight, she was finding mutual security and comfort. Oh, there would always be a struggle over who was in charge of their relationship if she became queen. He would be the one to rule the land, but she wouldn't let him lord over her.

"See, there's nothing better in this sphere than this," he whispered. She didn't have the guts to comment or respond to his admission. It took a lot for him to say it, and her brain tried to formulate a response. Before she could muster up the courage or a fitting response, he was breathing the deep pattern of sleep.

The next morning, she woke up to an empty bed and a note that simply said, *Best sleep of my life!* Another gift came with it. Surely, he'd run out of things to give her one day, or she'd be the most spoiled girl in Fyr. This one was a book about geography. She already had three books in total that were solely hers, but the library on the first floor was so massive, there was no way to read even half of them in her lifetime.

Breakfast was there for her, but this time, two plates were warming, so she decided to wait. A gift basket drew her attention, and she pulled out its contents: everything dracaberry. There were all forms—dried, fresh, candied, twisted licorice sticks, lollipops, and taffies. She had no clue there were so many forms of the delicious food. The note proved it was from the king.

"There you are, sleepyhead," Alex said as he entered from the bathing chamber, drying his hair with a towel. He was dressed, but barely, just in his pants and a loose white shirt open at the neck. "I was waiting to join you for breakfast."

They had breakfast and lunch together, and dinner with his parents that day and the rest of the week. Despite their busy schedules, Alex made time to see her, and each night, they chatted by the fire and slept in each other's arms. It was a comfortable pattern she easily embraced, although she would be lying if she denied a hope growing in her that it would shift more toward the romantic side soon. Things were stilted, platonic. Alex didn't overtly flirt, admit any feelings, or try to cross lines by doing more than hold her. Then, after about two weeks of this bliss, the pattern was disrupted. She woke to an empty bed and sitting room. There was no note or present on the table either. Alex was an early riser, but he wasn't in the bathing quarters, nor did he show up for breakfast. As she polished off her plate, it dawned on her that he wasn't coming.

Feeling dejected, she summoned Madge. When asked, the servant told her he had left with David in a carriage early that morning, but she didn't know where they were headed.

Why hadn't Alex told her? Toury was frustrated.

Madge dressed her for horseback riding and picked up the rumpled sheets that had fallen onto the floor. Something clattered onto the cobblestones. Madge picked it up. It was a pair of silver decorative hair combs encrusted with amethysts, the ones stylish women wore that Toury had called hair jewelry, much to Alex's delight for he loved her "Earth terms." There was a note after all too. The contents explained that Alex had gone into town to pick up his sister, who was being "asked to leave school" for fighting and to meet with a man who might be able to help them with the curse.

The note, however, did not relieve her despondent mood. He hadn't asked her to join him. This bothered her. She'd rather have their conversations and breakfast together than hair combs in Alex's stead. And this funk followed her throughout her day. She was utterly bored without Alex and hated herself for becoming so dependent on him.

What could she do? Her only friend was Mary, who had been away at school. Toury hadn't left the palace since she had arrived. She didn't fully understand this world yet, and the only people who were helping her acclimate were Alex, Madge, and "Uncle" Gareth. It made perfect sense for Alex to become the epicenter of her world, but it didn't mean she had to like it or herself for being so dependent.

A summons from the queen was just the distraction she needed after her lessons with Gareth. She met the queen on the back veranda and found her holding two baskets.

"Dragon egg picking? I've heard you're fond of them."

Toury smiled and nodded. The queen walked her out through the gardens and toward the orchards, the only place she had yet to explore on the palace grounds. The queen wasted no time starting a conversation.

"I apologize if it seems I am being distant, but Alex has refused to share you, except at dinner. When he offered to accompany me to retrieve Mary, I told him to go in my stead so I could steal some time with you."

"Alex has forbidden you to talk to me?" Toury asked, confused.

"He insisted we leave you be, let you acclimate, to paraphrase his sentiment. I can't blame him with that disastrous first meeting and our uncomfortable dinners. We can be an overwhelming bunch, especially the king. But now Mary is coming home, and as much as I'm disappointed in her conduct, it will be nice to have her back. Things will be livelier, I hope. Mary and you, I understand, were friends at school?"

"Yes, I'm looking forward to seeing her again."

"I was hoping you could help me with her."

"I'm not sure what I could possibly do."

"She must enter an engagement and do so soon."

"Your Majesty? Can I ask you something?"

"Anything, my dear. You are to be my daughter soon." The queen beamed at this comment.

Toury looked away, feeling like an imposter. She and Alex would disappoint this woman when she found out it started as a temporary alliance, especially if it never became more. Toury wasn't sure what it was now.

"Why do people in this sphere wish to marry so young and push their children into doing so? I'm not judging. It's just, Earth was entirely different. At least in the century I lived in," Toury tried to explain.

"It is true people marry early. We marry early to stop children out of wedlock. Of course, it does happen still, but not too often. And then there are those who are baseborn from infidelity. But this is not why I push my children. My children are different. Lately, we lost Ruby, so there are only three Sapphirians left in their generation. I expect my children to marry young and soon and give me numerous grandchildren to help save their race. There used to be hundreds of Sapphirians, and they are the most powerful of all people on Fyr. Without Sapphirian power over the land, there will be a scramble over who would rule, wars and chaos, and the dragons could revolt. The fire and magic may all go out, and there will be no saving anyone from the darkness. My children must marry and have many children. You see, I always wanted a large family, and we planned on having a lot of children, but after the curse, the king became ill, and his body began a slow decline. No more children came after Mary."

Could Alex have children, or would her removing the curse fix that? Why was she even worried about Alex having children? Wait, there were actual dragons on Fyr? Toury pushed aside her questions, not wanting to sound ignorant. Her curiosity gave way to guilt. She did not want to be an imposter. She did not want to lie to the queen and pretend as if she would be the one to help Alex continue his lineage soon. That thought made her feel overheated, and her stomach flopped.

"I'm not sure... Things are..." After two false starts trying to tell Queen Sapphirian the truth—whatever it actually was and without mentioning "savior"—she gave up.

"I know what Alex has done, and I won't pretend to understand why he did it. He was adamant about never settling down just days before meeting you. I'd been harping on him for two years to wed. You may think it is only because the lightness in you chases away his darkness, but there's more to it than that. I see the way he looks at you, and my son is in love. A mother knows these things. And you, if you give him a chance, will learn to love him. But then again, I am biased. I think the world of him."

They arrived at the dragon egg fruit trees, and Toury tried to digest what she had just heard. Alex didn't love her. It was much too soon, and he had never said the words. She guessed in Earth standards, it was true they were "together," but now he never kissed her. If he loved her, he'd kiss her as he had before. At school, he couldn't resist her, but now it was like she was merely his friend and cuddle buddy.

His mother did not talk anymore about marriage or grandchildren but shared stories of her youth and asked Toury loads of questions about Earth. She decided she liked the queen as much as she liked Mary and that life at the palace was less like a prison than it had been.

Alex and Mary did not show in time for supper as he had promised, which made it all the worse, having to face his father alone. The queen carried the conversation, and the king behaved. He even managed not to glare at Toury. She politely declined the invitation to join the king and queen in their quarters, which she was sure relieved the king, who seemed tired all the time.

Toury wasn't sure what was worse: facing the king longer or what she was doing now, fretting as she waited up for Alex. It was past their normal bedtime, and he still had not come. She paced in their sitting room, worrying herself sick, wondering what she should do. Ring Madge, who was probably sleeping, and make her ask the queen? But she didn't want to trouble anyone or seem like she was overreacting.

If something happened to him, she didn't know what she would do. And at that moment, she realized how important Alex had become to her.

28

A KISS

Alex walked into the well-lit sitting room, surprised to see Toury still awake. She looked stricken and terrified, and he worried something was terribly wrong, and someone had died. But he had just seen his parents and his sister. They had returned a little while ago and gotten wrapped up in discussing Mary's conduct, and he had figured Toury was asleep. He should've known better. She probably couldn't sleep without him, just as he probably couldn't sleep without her either.

"What is it?" he asked, hating the suspense.

"Where have you been? I was worried sick!" Her eyes filmed over with unshed tears.

"I thought you were asleep! I was with my family downstairs, trying to buffer my parents' anger at poor Mary. My mother said you had retired ages ago. Had I known you were waiting on me, I would've come straight up." He was at a loss. She was emotional and distressed, and he had no idea why. Sometimes, he really didn't understand women nor why they just didn't say what they were thinking upfront. It would simplify everything instead of him trying to guess and usually being wrong.

He pulled her into his arms and held her, not knowing what else to do aside from comfort her. She broke down crying onto his shoulder. He hated when girls cried, and Toury even more so. He suddenly became a pot of boiling emotions. He wasn't sure what was going on, but he was falling hard for her, and to hear her cry and to know he somehow hurt her ripped him to shreds. And his mind started hoping for too much too soon. Although he dreaded rejection—since she'd already shown him twice how it stung—he had to see how she felt about him.

"What is it, Toury?"

"I dunno!" She wailed. "I thought something happened to you. I thought I'd be left here alone or be thrown out, and I'd never see you again, and I know I'm being childish and silly and..." Then she fell into a blubbering mess again, and he could no longer understand what she was trying to say.

He assured her he was fine, apologized again for whatever it was that he supposedly did, then scooped her up in his arms, carried her into her bedroom, and placed her gently down onto the bed. He didn't bother to change, but kicked off his boots and unbuttoned his doublet, slipping it off. Then he slipped into bed with her and pulled her close to him.

Then she did something she hadn't done before over the past few weeks while sleeping in the same bed. She rolled over to face him. His pulse quickened at the close proximity of her face. Those eyes, those lips. They were much too close. He seemed to be able to cool his ardor when comforting her and hugging and cuddling her, but this he was unsure about. He focused on her face and tried to banish the fantasies that were beginning to crowd his mind.

"I missed you," she admitted, and she bit her lip, not realizing how seductive it was.

"And I missed you," he told her. "I'll bring you next time, I promise." He kissed her forehead, wanting to kiss her lips but afraid of her rebuff, afraid even more of her accepting his kiss. He knew he should take this slow like they had been. He couldn't simply return to those stolen nights they had in the school, but by the god of fire, he wanted it to. It was difficult lying in bed next to a girl he was attracted to. It would be easy to claim her lips again like he had longed to do every day for the past month.

"By the way, Mary was expelled for punching Justine in the face. Gave her a black eye."

"What?" Toury gasped and covered her mouth to hide her guilty smile.

"She was defending your honor, and mine, I suppose." Toury appeared confused, so he had to elaborate. "Justine was spreading rumors that you were my mistress and that she and I have a secret engagement." Alex left off the worst of it, which asserted Toury was with child, and Justine parading around fake gifts from him. He doubted such rumors would leave the school or be believed outside of it, but they'd go away regardless in a couple months when no pregnancy was noticed nor the engagement broken.

"She's..." Toury began, but her mouth just hung open, lost for words.

"Delusional, yes."

Toury shook her head and then changed the subject. "Did this firebrander tell you anything to help us break your curse?"

"Yes and no. I don't want to talk about it right now. I want to know what you did with your day." He tried to divert her thoughts. He could not discuss what Tobias had told him. If he did, he could ruin everything—the future, their relationship, and his chance to rid himself of the curse. Only time could help them, and he hoped that was enough. In the back of his mind, he worried it would be impossible.

Toury told him of her day, and he felt a bit guilty for secluding her from the rest of the world. He promised to present her to the courtiers, the nobles, so that she could have friends, a life outside of him. Part of him wanted to keep her to himself, to keep her safe, but that wasn't fair to her. He could see the toll it was taking on her and wanted to smack himself for not realizing she needed more than him. Just like he sat in on meetings, learning from his father, and saw Cobalt weekly, she needed people and something to do.

"Alex, your mother has hopes for us, and I feel so guilty misleading her."

"My mother always has hopes," he said vaguely. He felt as if she kicked him in the gut. It seemed as if she were working her way to breaking off the engagement. And his mind panicked. Their relationship had developed enough that she would help him with the curse no matter what, and he knew that. She would not forsake him as a friend, but he wanted more, so much more, and it had nothing to do with what Tobias had told him.

"But I don't want to disappoint anyone." She frowned, her brow furrowing.

"What about me?" He couldn't help but touch her, finding an excuse by tucking her hair behind her ear. He let his hand linger on her cheek.

"You most of all," she whispered.

Before he even thought about possible rebuff, he pulled her flush against him and kissed her hard on the mouth. She squealed in surprise, but the sound drowned inside his mouth. At first, Toury did nothing, but then her free arm wrapped around his neck, and her fingers curled in his hair as she kissed him back. Goddess of light, he found heaven in her lips.

Her touch and kiss did something to him then, and the fire in him raged but in a pleasing way, and he lost all restraint, pressing her down into the bed as his tongue plunged into her mouth. A month of withholding his feelings for her was bursting out of him all at once. She held him close and tried to match his ardor, and he felt his body respond to hers in ways he never before imagined. He never had wanted someone so much, loved someone so completely, and he felt as if he were losing himself in her. Worse, he was losing control. He had to stop the fire burning within him that told his lust to do unspeakable things.

He pushed himself off her and flung himself onto his back. They were both panting for breath, and he made the mistake of peeking at her from the corner of his eyes to see the same fire in her smitten eyes. He closed his eyes to suppress his lascivious thoughts and then said, "I'm sorry. I got a little carried away."

"Me too," she said quietly as she snuggled up innocuously by his side. Except nothing was innocent anymore. His mind, at least, was spinning off into fantasies that he seemed unable to quell.

"I think I'll have to sleep in my own room from now on," he said.

"Why?" she cried out. She propped up on her elbow, leaning over him, frowning as if he offended and wounded her.

"Don't be upset. I didn't expect us to pick up where we left off. After that, I don't think I can control myself around you anymore."

"Oh," she said. She blushed a little and looked away. His fingers traced the blush and lingered on her lips. Then he leaned up and kissed her lips as chastely as he could muster.

"We have to wait until we're married to be...more physical," he awkwardly stumbled over his words. He sat up, leaning against the headboard.

She laughed at this, then crawled up to sit next to him, her beautiful black hair tumbling over her shoulders. She kissed him gently on the lips.

"I'm serious," he protested. To him right now, celibacy was not a laughing matter.

"I know you are," she said. "It was a happy laugh. You just admitted you want something more without even realizing it. Are you saying the engagement is real now?"

He stalled for a moment, not wanting to confess feelings she might not reciprocate. He pulled her legs across his lap and draped his arm around her waist to buy some time before he met her gaze.

"Yes, Toury. I think, for me at least, it was always real. I want you to be my lifemate," he said. Heart hammering in his chest, part of him was afraid she'd refuse him a third time, but he could tell she was becoming attached to him. The sad thing was, she wasn't in love with him as much as he was with her. If she were, the curse would have lifted. But this he could not tell her. She couldn't force or fake her feelings for him to end the curse. It had to happen on its own. This was what Tobias told him. Fire and light magic could only do so much, but the true magic that could defeat all darkness must be born of love.

"Well, since your ruse had proper intentions, I forgive you...for everything," she teased.

"Finally," he said. Tension left his body, and he couldn't help but grin like a fool. "Maybe I should've kissed you sooner."

"Maybe you should have," she quipped.

This banter had him kissing her again and again, and he could hardly restrain his thoughts when she was half perched in his lap. Going into this relationship too fast could ruin everything between them, and it was not just about them anymore. Unknowingly, the entire realm depended on this relationship to work out. No pressure, Alex sardonically thought to himself. He only had to make a girl fall in love with him.

29

DARKNESS

It was the first gathering she attended among the courtiers, and they were all staring.

"Fortify yourself," Mary said, handing her a glass of what looked like watered firespice whiskey, without much water. "You are entering the vipers' nest."

"Mary," the queen censured lightly. "Don't scare the princess-to-be. Toury is capable of sniffing out the rats, which is another important duty. Take note of the darkness if you see it in any of the courtiers. Only you can pinpoint it." Toury understood. Since her light magic could ferret out the darkness in the curses, she should sense a large amount of it in necromancers. She should be able to sense who was against her family and who their true friends were. Her family? When did she start thinking of Alex's family as hers? Her stomach flopped uneasily, for whenever she thought of Alex now, it was of kissing him in her bed. She wished he was by her side, but the men and women met separately and joined together later at these types of gatherings, she was told.

They mingled. She touched no one, keeping her hands enclosed in gloves as Alex had warned her, lest anyone feel her light magic trying to conquer their dark. Alex believed there were enemies among them, and she wanted to discover them without them knowing she could actually do that very trick. She put the watered firespice whiskey down after one sip told her she had thought right. Perhaps Mary did need to settle down some. She was wild and carefree and almost finished with her drink already, not to mention the expulsion from school and what had caused it.

Everyone was kind to her face, but each person had a seething repressed annoyance with her. Firmly pressed lips, gazes scanning her body, eye rolling, catty whispers, and fake smiles all tipped her off that she was not well liked. She tried not to take it personally since they didn't really know her well enough to actually judge. She had taken the most eligible bachelor off the market in their eyes. And Toury realized for the first time that the notion was officially true.

She lost Mary and the queen in the crowd right when she needed them most. Justine and a few of her followers sauntered up to Toury, most likely waiting for her to be alone before they attacked. Justine appeared ready to verbally spar, her eyes glaring, her mouth drawn in a self-appreciating sneer, her haughty head held high. The airs the girl gave herself when she was losing the battle over Alex made Toury wonder if the girl had a trick up her sleeve or if she were simply as delusional as Alex professed.

Toury properly greeted them all with a curtsy that would make Miss Headmistress proud, but they returned an improper address. They called her simply Lady Tourmaline, and Justine even let off the noble distinction of "lady." Although Toury was not one hung up on correcting others, she needed to put up a strong front and not take any flak. Alex had told her she needed to act the part in public, no matter how nice or normal she wanted to be. If she showed weakness, the queen had warned her, they would pounce and forever dominate her.

Here went nothing.

"You mean Lady Tourmaline, *Princess-to-Be*."

The other girls quickly added the title with looks of surprise at Toury's rebuff and, hopefully, realization that Justine was taking them down a dangerous road by insulting future royalty, not a mistress. Justine, however, stared at Toury, her face turning red with suppressed rage. Toury could see how she tried to hide the black eye with a lot of cosmetics. Why was Justine even there if she and Mary had a fight? She glanced over to see the queen in deep conversation with a few ladies, and one of them looked much like an older, heavier Justine. Toury guessed her mother was friends with the queen. Great.

Part of Toury wanted to egg her on until she exploded, but a direct insult to Toury would get Justine in trouble, and Alex's comment about threatening to burn her at the stake came to mind. Toury disliked Justine but could never wish someone dead, even if she had tried to kill her.

When Justine's heavy glare met Toury's, she saw something odd. The lovely amber eyes were darkened, black, almost as if her pupil had dilated so much it swallowed up the iris. A chill crept over Toury, raising goose bumps across her flesh, as Justine grounded out the proper salutation. Toury held the girl's gaze a moment longer, and the chill turned into a realization. She was seeing the darkness, the evil in the girl. She examined the girls' eyes who stood with her, but they were all normal. She had seen the darkness before in Justine's eyes and in some others but had thought the lighting cast a shadow or that her eyes were playing tricks on her. Now that she was more in tune with her powers, she understood what she was seeing. Understanding the trick to weed out the enemy, she was going to go on a mission to look everyone else in the eye whom she could and to draw out the darkness. Emotion seemed to let the façade crumble away for her to see inside their true natures. But for right now, she had to escape Justine.

"How is palace life?" Justine asked awkwardly. It was as if Justine's only plan had been to snub Toury, and now she was awkwardly trying to backpedal since it did not go as planned.

"Wonderful, actually," Toury said, trying to leave it short. She didn't want to gossip or gloat. Justine's friends waited on edge for more. "The royal family are so accepting and kind. It's beginning to feel like home."

"I wouldn't get too comfortable. It is my understanding that the prince does not want to settle down. He's probably grooming you to be his whore." Justine gave her a wicked smile.

"According to your delusional rumors, I already am." Toury laughed lightly. "Do you think the queen herself would allow me at such functions if that were true?"

Her friends looked at each other, the seed of doubt spreading.

"Well, he plans on making you one. Sorry to give you ill tidings," Justine said.

"My, how you understand such things when he doesn't even talk to you is astounding," Toury shot coolly back. Her desire not to gloat vanished with such a saucy comment. She was sure calling the princess-to-be a whore was a punishable offense.

"I have it on good authority—"

"Yes, but I have it on the *best* authority," Toury cut her off. "From his own lips, which—" Toury paused for a melodramatic sigh "—are absolutely divine."

Justine's entourage giggled and smiled as if they hoped they could hear more or that they could vicariously live through Toury, but the blackness of jealousy and dark magic consumed Justine. Her face distorted into a grimace that turned her beautiful visage into that of a crone. Hideous and cruel in her darkness, she looked as if she were about to attack Toury in some way, magically or physically, when Justine's gaze shot to the doorway behind her. Toury stared her down and did not turn around, even after she heard the doors open. Justine fled the scene without a proper curtsy, and her friends stood transfixed, unsure if they wanted to follow her or try to wheedle info out of her about Alex.

Suddenly, two arms encircled Toury's waist from behind, and lips gently brushed her neck in a subtle kiss which traced upward, pulling away slightly when they reached her ear. All the tension from Justine's confrontation left her at his touch.

"I've missed you," Alex said only for her ears.

There were gasps and tittering by the women at this public display of affection, making Toury blush. The girls from school sighed dreamily and stared at them with doe eyes. Then men scattered into the room after Alex. Toury looked at the people around them and noted several dilated eyes of mothers and other girls. The worst were the Citrines. The mother—she had guessed right—Justine, a sister, from the looks of it, and three men all had the blackest eyes she had ever seen. The man she assumed was the father was turned away from her, talking to another gentleman who had clear, ordinary, brown eyes. She turned away from them toward Alex, but he didn't unclasp his hands, keeping her wrapped in his arms. He was all lightness and happiness, his eyes a vibrant blue.

"Can we escape?"

He smirked at her. "Not fun?"

She shrugged.

"Are they not being kind to you?" Alex's eyes narrowed at the girls by them, then over at Justine. The girls scattered as if afraid. To be afraid of Alex, she could never imagine. Their reaction, though, warned her to tread lightly. She realized whatever she had to say should be carefully done. She fully believed he would punish, maybe even execute, anyone who hurt her.

"No, it's...I can see the darkness in people's eyes, Alex. It's very unsettling."

Alex looked around as if he were trying to see what she was seeing; then he let her go out of his embrace, took her hand and placed it in the crook of his arm and led her toward his mother, thankfully, away from the Citrines.

"Just a few more minutes, my dear, and I will take you back to our rooms myself, but Mother will want us to linger a bit longer. Okay?" He kissed her temple. Then before he pulled away, he whispered, "Take a mental note of who is a threat as I introduce you to people."

After the social gathering, she and Alex made a list of everyone she remembered, having to describe a few by appearance since their names escaped her. Then they had family dinner, where the topic of politics was usually barred from the conversation at the queen's request.

During after-dinner drinks was where the king caught them up to speed with the happenings of the sphere. The servant handed her a firespice whiskey with water that was too strong for her liking. When Toury tried to refuse, the king gave her a look of censure. Despite being a strong woman, the man was too intimidating, and she took a hearty sip, cringing after.

"Drink, my daughter-to-be, for we will talk politics, and you are not used to it yet."

Alex sighed. "He's being melodramatic, or he undervalues your strength."

"Not the latter, I assure you," King Sapphirian said. "You have made a good choice in queen on that front, Alex. She won't wilt in the face of troubles." Then he directed to Toury, "You remind me of your mother in that regard, a great woman until she lost her mind and ran off with your father."

"Inconveniently fell in love with him, you mean," the queen amended. Toury wanted to press and hear more about her parents, but she was afraid to. Not many intimidated her, but the king was someone whom you did not provoke.

The king drank. "What is it you needed to tell me?" He directed his question to Alex.

"Father, we made a discovery. In short, Toury can see evil, the darkness in others. I think she could figure out who the necromancers are without them knowing."

The king perked up at this and looked at Toury anew. He motioned her to come closer. Then he patted the seat across from him. Not wanting to be so close to this man, she was hesitant, but Alex was there taking her arm, leading her and depositing her in the chair. Then he sat on the arm of her chair as close as possible to her. It gave her the comfort and strength she needed. To have this one-on-one with the king was unnerving, to say the least.

"Explain, child," the king prompted.

Toury sipped some firespice whiskey to fortify herself and then began, "I'm not sure how to describe it. It seems like when someone 'evil,' for lack of a better word, shows some emotion—anger maybe—I can see it in their eyes."

"As in, you sense it?" Mary interjected. "Alex said you could sense the curse."

Toury shook her head. The horror of their liquid black eyes haunted her.

"No. She can actually see it. I think her light can see the dark," Alex supplied.

She sighed, mustering her strength. "I'll explain it the best I can. I first noticed it at school when I met a girl who hated me. Her eyes turned black as if they had dilated until everything else was gone."

"And this you saw today, someone in court?" Queen Sapphirian pressed.

"Who is the fiend?" the king demanded.

"We made a list for you, Father." Alex fished into his pocket and took out the folded list. He handed the king the small piece of parchment, and the queen sat down, clutching her hand to her stomach as if feeling unwell.

"An entire list?" the queen breathed out. "And in our home today?"

"Why are you even surprised?" Mary muttered. "They're all grappling for the power teat and looking for ways to destroy us. We're idly sitting here, waiting for them to attack."

"Hardly helpful, Mary," the queen chided her.

"Fourteen people?" the king remarked skeptically. "A lot, don't you think?"

"Father, I told you I believed the evil ran deep. I don't think the rumors of the necromancers hiding in the north are quite true. I have a bad feeling they're everywhere, including at the court among us."

His father's face drained, and his hand crumbled the list.

"He's right, Father," Mary interjected, trying to prevent their father from lashing out at Alex. "Not all courtiers were present, nor half the Sorcerers' Guild."

"You cannot accuse the very people we call friends of secretly being enemies! I mean, the Citrines are faithful to me in everything. I cannot believe this. The Magicians' Guild is what we need to worry about. They will be the necromancers. They are the ones after power."

"No!" Toury heard herself object before she thought about it. Then all eyes were on her. "Sorry, Your Majesty, but I must say that accusing a group of people merely by their inferior birth is downright preposterous, not to mention completely illogical and prejudiced."

"Toury," Alex hissed her to halt. He squeezed her hand, his eyes wide in fright, and shook his head a fraction. The queen was rigid but staring at the floor, feigning disinterest, and Mary's mouth was agog, her gaze darting between the king and Toury repeatedly.

Toury knew taking this any further could have terrible repercussions, but wouldn't the consequences of allowing the king to blame the wrong people be worse? Then the king's very friends could usurp him. Alex's warning was telling her even family couldn't object to the king, at least so candidly. But she would be heard. "No, I won't be hushed, Alex. We are among family—at least, one day we'll be. If family cannot express their opinions to each other, then who can we rely on for true advice? Surely, not many magicians—due to their inferior birth—would have the power to raise the dead or evoke the darkness. That is what I mean by illogical."

The king frowned but relaxed in his seat. "All right, Princess-to-Be, you have a point. Inferior birth usually means inferior power. What do you suggest we do?"

She was taken aback by his lack of censure and took a moment to formulate her thoughts. Alex let out a breath he must've been holding. It was hard for Alex to go against his father's wishes, but his half-hearted attempt to stop her showed he agreed with her. She was glad he didn't back her up. This had to be done by Toury alone to show the king she was strong, that she had what it took to be Alex's equal. "Simply observe them, and be cautious around them. Calling anyone out without evidence could spark a rebellion. In the meantime, I would like to meet as many courtiers as possible. I could add to this list," Toury continued, fearing any moment King Sapphirian would cut her off.

"Too dangerous. Anyone who has physical contact with you, Toury, will feel your power and see you as a threat," Alex interjected.

"At least let her interview the staff," Mary said. "If they're in the palace daily, we might as well just off ourselves!"

"Mary!" the queen scolded and shook her head at the girl.

"No, I should do it," Toury insisted. "We need to check all the people who are with us daily."

"This cannot be," the king persisted.

"Your Majesty, I only know what I see, not what it means. I may just see the propensity for evil, a darkness that maybe a lot of people have but may not act on. Or I may be seeing necromancers. I don't know. I know you won't like the idea, but we could see if my aunt or my...tutor have the same ability. They wouldn't be as much of a target as me."

The king cringed. "Hematites." Then he sighed and concluded, "I will mull it over."

Alex's hand gripped hers as if he were anxious about something. She looked to him and saw some guarded fear in his eyes. He looked away. She understood, suddenly, why her comment bothered him. "I haven't seen the darkness in any of you. It doesn't seem to be the curse. I sense the curse. Evil is more tangible, visible." The tension eased out of Alex.

"Thank you, Lady Toury. Your loyalty is an asset it seems we need desperately," the king said quietly. Seeing how tired he was, they excused themselves.

30

A COURT

Once they were alone in their private living room, Alex sighed and took off his medallion, then undid his cuffs and collar. He loathed the restricting garments and couldn't care less about propriety around Toury. He met her gaze and noted the smirk on her lips and her playful eyes.

"What?" he questioned, a bit afraid of what she might say. Toury surprised him at every turn; she was utterly unpredictable, strong, and beautiful. She was everything he could've ever wanted in a woman, and he wished he could tell her that. The words never came easily to him, though.

"You remind me of those men on Earth who wear ties to the office but cannot stand them. The moment they leave work, they undo them."

"Ties?" he asked. The rest of her sentiment translated, but he was curious about the tie thing. It did feel like work being presentable all the time, wearing these restricting collars and shirt cuffs. He wished he could walk around in a shirt and trousers, his feet bare.

"A type of cloth that goes around the neck and hangs down, like a sash almost."

"A neck sash?"

"Sort of."

"How strange," he commented, kicking off his boots. "Did you find that these ties made men attractive?"

"Well, some women do, but mostly older men wear them, rarely guys our age. And before you ask, no, I don't admire older men."

"What kind of men do you admire?" he asked.

Her eyes shot up to meet his and were round as saucers as she took in his tone and his less-than-formally-clad appearance. He shirked off his doublet, feeling so free in his shirt. She turned a shade of pink and looked away.

"Boys never really noticed me, so I dunno. I don't have a type."

"First off,"—he moved toward her—"boys not noticing you must be some lie stemming from your modesty, and two, you can admire and not act on it."

"Are you asking what I look for in a man?"

"Yes, I am."

"Well, then you must tell me what you look for in a woman."

"Seems fair enough."

"I like guys who are confident, but not so much that they ignore everyone else."

"I like confidence in a woman, too. I like some sass, a backbone. As you know well, it's the fashion to hide that."

"I don't hide it."

"Precisely," he said with such a serious tone that she blushed, knowing he was talking about her.

"I've always preferred tall men because I like when they're taller than me."

"I like a woman on my level," he said. He reached out to touch her hair. "Dark hair and tan skin, as if kissed by the sun, everything against what the court dictates, but not intentionally."

"Alex," Toury began nervously.

He didn't want questions or denials or anything she'd say to ruin the moment. He leaned in and kissed her. She kissed him back, and he took full advantage, kissing her more deeply and pulling her body against his till every inch of her pressed against him, showing her how convenient it could be that they were almost the same height.

"I like light eyes," Toury gasped between kisses.

"Gray," he breathed into her mouth, and he started backing her toward her bedroom. He wanted her on the bed and in his arms, and his mind wanted much more than he could possibly have without a signed marriage license. He knew then, at the threshold of the door, that he couldn't go in there, not only because she deserved much more than to become his mistress, but because he wanted her to be much more.

He pulled away from her.

"What's wrong?" Toury asked, running the back of her fingers down his cheek.

"I was finding the willpower to walk away."

"What if you didn't?" she asked, biting her lip.

"Toury," he moaned, pushing his way into her room and kissing her eagerly.

He backed away to take in her vibrant features, so full of attraction for him. He wanted to tell her, wanted her to know the truth. He loved her. The words were tripping up on his tongue.

"I don't want to wait two years. I don't think I can," was what came out of his confused and aroused mind instead.

Her brow furrowed, and then when recognition dawned on her, her features lit up with a smile. "You want to get married?" But her reaction was not what he expected, nor was her tone. They both seemed accepting of the idea and dare he hope—desiring it.

"Well, if you're asking, then yes," he teased her.

"Alex, I'm serious. What of the curse and saving the sphere and all that?"

"Truth be told, you've made me forget about the curse almost entirely," he admitted before stealing a kiss. "And if we're married, well, you'd have to help me save the world because it wouldn't be mine anymore but ours."

For the first time, he felt as if he wouldn't be denied.

"I will marry you, Alex, but I want us to be in love first," she said quietly.

The air whooshed out of his lungs, and he felt a palpable pain inside him at her comment. He loved her. There was no use in denying it, but her comment meant she didn't love him. He was hurt, but the feeling of uselessness clouded his mind. He was at a loss about how to make her love him back.

He looked away, but she pulled his chin back so he met her gaze. "Don't think I don't care. I prefer you over all other men. I want to be with you, and I love everything about you. Each day we grow closer, a bond between us grows stronger, and obviously, there's this attraction. We cannot wait two years, but just a bit longer. However long it takes for us to know we're in love."

He held her close, their breath mixing. "I want to give you everything. Just ask for it, and it's yours." After it was out, he realized how desperate he had become. She was his one true weakness, and he hated feeling soft.

"Well, I've been thinking. I do want one thing," she ventured nervously.

"What is it?" No matter what she asked for, he—quite pathetically—couldn't deny her anything.

"I would like some friends to occupy my time, holding court as you call it."

Alex smiled at this and pulled her flush against him. He kissed her, not wanting it to stop, wanting to walk her onto the bed and fulfill the wicked thoughts in his head.

Toury pulled away too soon. "So, that's a yes?"

"Toury." He sighed, feeling extremely conflicted. "Do you know when royalty holds court?"

"When a princess turns eighteen or marries, and when one marries into royalty after the marriage. I know, Alex, but when I looked at the decrees in all my hours of studying, no actual rule or law that prohibits me from doing it now."

"It would mean you are serious about this marriage, Toury," he ventured, hoping she would actually admit something to him. "At least, to the outside world," he added. He had no confidence when it came to her. He was confident in almost everything he did, and when it came to women, he could have any one of them. No one would deny him but her, and it killed him when he cared for her so much.

"Outside and inside, Alex," Toury told him.

His stomach turned in nervous anticipation.

She giggled. "Don't look at me like that."

"Like what?" He had no clue what expression crossed his face at that moment.

"Surprised. Why? You know I care about you. We admitted this engagement was real. You said yourself we can't wait two years..."

"Toury, I'm happy beyond what words can express, but we don't have to rush this. I don't think you're ready." He tried to think sensibly, although his hormones screamed otherwise.

"Can you honestly say you're ready to get married?" She asked him while her fingers toyed with the open collar of his shirt.

"If you asked me three months ago, before I met you, absolutely not. I was trying to escape matrimony as if it were the plague. But now...now, I'm absolutely positive that you are the one for me. And although marriage is still daunting and kind of scary, I can think of many perks." And he started to show her what perks by kissing her neck and unlacing her gown.

"Alex," she protested half-heartedly as her skin goose-pimpled under his touch. "I have a secondary motive for this court aside from much-needed friends."

Alex froze and pulled away, looking at her.

"Oh, Alex, I wouldn't have my own courtiers if I had a shred of doubt about us. I want to marry you, please believe that. But like you say, the curse. There's another thing I need to do before we marry. I need to feel as though the people of Fyr accept me for me, not because they have to."

"And having a court will help that along." He was following her logic. He subdued the desires that seemed to addle his brain. "You'll have wealthy noble families' support. Ingenious, Toury."

"And I can exclude those who have the darkness..."

"Creating a larger divide for us to know who is on our side and against us..." He marveled at her brilliant mind. And it was wrapped up in this beautiful body.

"We make a good team," she said.

He kissed her, intending to get most of her clothes off and to get her onto that bed that taunted him from the very moment he walked in. She did not object when he continued to kiss her and untie her laces. He should tell her the truth that royalty was different, that consummating their relationship would void her ability to marry him, but his selfish desires were stronger, and he told himself he wouldn't let it get that far. He just hoped his willpower was strong enough.

Willpower wasn't putting up much of a fight, he realized minutes later, nor did it seem like Toury's was present either, for she shed him of his upper clothes and was marveling over the planes of his chest. The dragon was purring, urging him on. It was strange that the fire power in him, which he had always connected to his temper, flared in this other instance.

Before he let the dragon win, he grappled for any shred of logic. He loved her. He wanted to marry her.

He slowed the intensity of their kissing and pecked away from her lips, moving his hands off her onto the pillows under her head. He slowed his breathing, staring at the fire instead of her. He could not look at her right now as his principles were barely existent.

"We can't..." Alex forced himself to say, "do anything...physical."

"Such a saint, aren't you? You make me feel wanton."

He tried to focus on the moment and pushed the idea of her being wanton out of his mind.

"You are wanton, but so am I. But what is this saint thing, my little earthling?"

She tried to tell him, but he couldn't help himself, and he cut her off constantly with kisses. She had to repeat her definition of a saint to him.

"Well then, I am no saint. I've done wrong, and I'm not swearing to any celibacy clause. Well, that is I do swear until I marry you. Then, celibacy won't be a word in my vocabulary. But now, we cannot. You must be pure when we marry."

"Why does it matter so much? I don't understand this obsession with women's purity when men can frolic as much as they want."

He smiled at her and smoothed her hair back. "Toury, please never change. You will be a champion of women that this world sorely needs. It is not me who is obsessed with your purity, but old edicts for royalty that are unchangeable. There's another set of rules for me. I cannot marry an impure woman, even if I were the one to...you know. If you were impure, you could never be my lifemate, no matter how much I wanted it. You could only be my mistress, and our children, they'd be...bastards..." He cringed at the thought. Admitting that aloud doused the fire of his desire instantly. "I cannot bear to continue, but it needed to be said. I can't ruin you. I want you, need you, to be my queen."

After a round of kissing, instigated by Toury, he spooned her and behaved, and they spoke of inconsequential things until they were drowsy with sleep.

31
FUTURE

Toury woke up in Alex's arms, a first. She had missed him. She could see how marriage would suit them well, and she realized last night that they should marry soon. This strange propriety and rules of the land actually suited her, oddly enough. She had never even kissed a boy before Alex, and yet they were becoming hot and heavy. She was glad Alex had stopped, even though part of her wanted to see and feel things she could only vaguely imagine.

Alex stirred, and his groggy eyes opened. His eyes alighted on her, and a small smile crept upon his face. His hair was adorably askew, and the way he looked at her sent chills down her spine. To wake like this every morning would be a blessing.

"You, awake at this hour?" he taunted.

"You stayed."

"I shouldn't have." And then his easygoing expression faded.

"Always a gentleman." She pecked his lips when he searched for a kiss.

"Born and bred that way." He chuckled. "I'll let you go back to sleep."

"No." She sat up. "We talked. We need this curse broken, so I'm going to write my invitations for a luncheon where I'll select my ladies in waiting. How soon can I do that, by the way?"

"You're the princess-to-be, one day, the queen. You can demand they be here tomorrow, and they will be here."

"Seriously?"

"Seriously." Then he tickled her sides, making her flail about in that uncontrollably euphoric way only tickles could elicit. He stopped and kissed her hard on the mouth and then got up out of bed. He was only wearing his breeches but slipped his discarded shirt back on before she could fully enjoy a look at his sculpted arms and chest. He looked over his shoulder at her, catching her ogling, and grinned. It made his morning, she could tell, and she realized she ought to be more forthcoming in the future with her feelings. Last night, he had seemed completely taken by surprise when she admitted she wanted to marry him.

"When will I see you today?" she called as he entered his room to dress.

He turned on the threshold. "When do you want to see me?"

"All day?"

He smiled broadly, his features all displayed to their advantage. She never realized she held this power over his happiness. A few kind and truthful words would push the curse away and make him himself again, even if it was just for a moment.

And then uncharacteristically of him, he ran over and leaped into bed. She squealed at his newfound level of spontaneity. He rolled over onto her, the pressure of him crushing her but in a pleasing way. He pressed his forearms into the bed to lessen the weight on her and gazed at her.

"If only we could have all day," he murmured, kissing her forehead.

"But there is a kingdom to run."

"Yes. Do you want to help me run it?"

"What do you mean?" she asked, perplexed.

"I want...I want to know what you want. What do you see in our future?"

"I dunno. To be honest, ever since I came to Fyr, it's been so overwhelming that I keep thinking about now. To think I could be a queen one day is still surreal."

"Will be one day, Toury. You will be."

"Okay, passing into overwhelming territory."

"Then politics can wait, and that is if you ever want to get involved. I thought, knowing you," he said, a youthful blush creeping onto his cheeks, "you'd want to be partners in everything."

And just like that, Toury realized she was falling deeply in love with Alex. He knew her so well, and despite it being such a patriarchal sphere, he wanted her to be his equal, to share every endeavor. She wanted to tell him how deeply she cared for him and how she would marry him tomorrow if they set the date, but she could not. She was scared. She relied so much on Alex for everything, and becoming his wife would mean losing more of herself. She would become a wife and a queen, but what would become of Toury?

"The fact you just said that, Alex, shows how well you know me and value me. I'm the luckiest woman alive. I want to be your partner in everything, but you are right. I might need to learn my duties in doses."

He kissed her eagerly, but when things began to get a little hot, he rolled off her with a disappointed sigh. He pulled her into his arms, though, and they lay there together snuggling.

"What did you want to be when you were on Earth? Before all this?" he asked.

"That's like asking what you'd be if you weren't the prince, an impossibility." She laughed.

"I would have ended up a firebrander most likely, reading people their futures off the flames. I like to see the joy on people's faces when a firebrander tells them something good will befall them, but then there's the bad part of the job where you must tell them bad tidings and then watch it play out. Because no matter what they do, they cannot escape the path that is set."

"I thought you said the visions change like the flame flickers?" she mused.

He smiled sheepishly at her. "You miss nothing. I was purposefully evasive then because you weren't ready to hear what I saw..."

"Which was?"

"You and me, Toury, together as we are now. But it technically can change, not saying we will, just in general. There are variations of future events when fate is determined by someone's choices."

"So you knew all along, we'd end up together?" Too late she realized her voice was accusatory when she really wasn't that mad. Shocked was the correct emotion.

"Yes, if you did not deter from my vision, but I had no idea how to make it happen."

What must it be like to live that way, to know it will happen but not know exactly how to bring it about?

"They're simply snippets of what could be. The only things that will happen are things determined by the god of fire and the goddess of light... One cannot escape death, for example."

"That sounds awful." She shivered in his arms. "That won't do. Pick something else."

He chuckled breathily and played with her hair, winding it around his finger. "I would be a glassmaker, I think. I used to do it all the time as a kid, turning my sandcastles into glass ones. I think my mother kept one somewhere. It was fun, easy, a stress reliever to do something with my hands."

"You should start again. That sounds like a great hobby. And the people would buy it like crazy because it's made by you."

"Toury, you know we'll never want for money, right?"

"I was thinking a charity, for the poor."

"You are thinking politics already, I see." They were silent for a moment, just him twisting her hair in his fingers idly. "You never answered me. What would you have been on Earth?"

"I wanted to go into social services, but I was still unsure." His puzzled look told her she had to expand. "Social services help people..."

"Of course, nothing else would do for your giving heart."

"...and I wanted to work with orphans or children of parents who won't or can't care for them properly. I wanted to give them love most of all. I never was...as I told you already, I didn't exactly have the best parents on Earth. I wasn't theirs, and they weren't equipped to love a child who wasn't theirs."

"You can still help orphans here if you wish. Charity is sorely lacking. My father is...he's a good king, but he does not have the same priorities as I do, the same line of thinking when it comes to those beneath us in station."

How diplomatic of him. Alex really could turn a good phrase. He meant his father was entitled and did nothing for the poor.

"And, my lady, you have a loving family now—except my father, who sees love as a weakness. One day, we will have our own family, and we will make sure they have more love than we received."

Then he turned her chin to face him and sealed what felt like a vow with a kiss.

"Your mother loves you," Toury pointed out. He was right about his cold father, though.

"It was a strange childhood, I'll admit. My mother had to sneak love in. My father would never allow her or himself to show any public displays of affection or doting attention, not even in front of servants. She would sneak in and wake us just to put us back to bed at night. Those were the best memories of my childhood. Her reading us stories and hugging us, tickles and laughter, kisses all over our faces until we begged her to stop. Those were probably the only happy moments of my childhood. Everything else was always a presentation, to act regal, to behave, to be quiet, to be cooped up with books rather than playing. I won't do that to you or our children..."

She had been listening to him intently, soaking up the words he was bleeding straight from his heart, but on the mention of their kids, her stomach flopped nervously. Their kids. What a thought.

"You will be yourself Toury, not some role someone expects you to play. Our kids will be hugged and kissed and loved by us, publicly even."

174

Then he stopped. He looked at her hesitantly from the corner of his eyes. "I've gone and said too much now, haven't I?"

"No!" She realized she said it too quickly. "I forgot about motherhood as being part of the deal. I never thought of marriage either on Earth. Things are truly different here, but I think I can say after acclimating that it is better here. I think a large part of that is due to you."

He kissed her then, again and again, and it seemed as if nothing would break them apart until a knock sounded on her bedroom door.

"Your Highness?" There was censure in the man's voice, as if he were afraid to enter and see why Alex was in her room.

"I'll be in my room in a moment, David," he said reluctantly. He kissed her forehead and slipped out of bed.

"Madge won't be far behind," she told him.

"Hmm. Duty does literally come to call, and you have your invitations to write. I want to see much more of you today than I have so far this week. How about lunch...in the city?"

"Truly?" she squealed. She leaped up out of bed, not realizing how excited she was to see Celestia.

"I've kept you cooped up long enough, no?" Then he added, "I think you're ready."

"For what?"

"You'll see," he said, a mischievous glint in his eyes. Then he darted into his room and left the question looming.

32

AN OUTING

It really was cruel not to warn her. She was so excited to go out into the city, but the anticipation probably wouldn't last. He knew Toury's disposition well enough to know how she'd react. It was the very reason he didn't want to take her out until now. There was no putting it off any longer. He couldn't keep her tucked away forever, nor should he. Plus she hardly had much in the way of clothes worthy of her status. Going into public was a good test to see how she'd handle things.

As soon as they left the castle, people stopped to look at the carriage as it went by. Then when they hit the city center, and the carriage stopped, so did the people. And when they alighted out of the carriage, people rushed over to see them, calling out to them in hopes to gain their notice. It started with a dozen or so, but then more appeared, coming out of shops and alleyways. Kids were running up, weaving their way to the front to get a look at the royals.

Toury was overwhelmed instantly. He could see it in her eyes. But as soon as the fright came to her, it was gone, and in its place was a fierce, determined look and a genuine smile as she waved to his people, soon to be her people.

"I see," she said quietly, the smile not fading. She looped her arm through his, and the people were ensorcelled by them as his retinue gently parted the crowd so they could walk through.

"Do you? You're handling it quite well."

"You were right."

"Where are the scribes? I need to get this phrase recorded for it has never escaped your lips, nor is it likely to ever again," he teased her.

She gave him a beaming grin and beheld him as if no one else were there. He thought of the other ladies whom his mother had tried to push on him, especially Justine. How Justine would have pandered to the crowd while spitting in their faces. She wouldn't have noticed him at all, seeing only how the crowd reacted to her. But Toury, she only had eyes for him, and her posture showed she knew they were being watched. She acknowledged the crowd but then went on her merry way. In short, she was perfection.

"Alex," she gasped. "I don't act like you're wrong all the time!"

He gave her a pointed look.

Then she shrugged as they walked on. "You love it. You're tired of everyone simpering and bowing down to your every whim. They let you get away with everything, and I hold you accountable."

She was partially right, so he said nothing.

"But as much as I criticize you, I must applaud when you are right. It's only fair. I see why you kept delaying this outing. I don't think I would've handled it very well a month ago. Back then, it would have felt oppressive."

"But now?"

"Now it's just one thing I must learn to deal with if I want you."

"Really, Toury?" he asked. He could not withhold the surprise from his voice.

"I want you, not the crown, to be honest. But if the crown comes with you, I'll learn to wear it. I'm sure I could do some good in this world with such influence. When I think about it in those terms, it becomes easier to accept." Her face was genuine, and he couldn't believe that Ruby had found, out of all the spheres, probably the only girl in the universe who would choose him over his crown. He was damn lucky.

Despite the people around, he took his arm from hers and wrapped it around her shoulder, pulling her to his side. He kissed her forehead, and the crowd was erupting with noise, eating it up, most likely loving that they were the first to see the royal engagees together in public.

The crowd thinned, and some street urchins stepped out onto the path, begging. Guilt always racked him when he saw kids out on the street, but his father had taught him to ignore their existence and keep walking. His father never allowed him or Mary to give them a coin, but what was the point of having more money than you could spend if you couldn't help your people? He slipped out his coin purse and took out a few sapphirians. To him, it was a pittance, but to the four boys he saw, it would keep their bellies full for a week. Something better had to be done about the magician orphans. In the meantime, he gave them each a coin. Three of them ran off excited and most likely scared of his guards who had been pushing them back. The last boy stood frozen, looking at Toury, and she stopped, peering at him.

"Duric?" Toury questioned.

"Lady Tourmaline, Princess-to-Be." The dirty little boy bowed, his impeccable manners clashing with his grubby appearance.

"Duric, what are you doing in Celestia? Does your mother know you're this far from home?" Toury asked, concerned. She obviously knew this boy, and Alex realized he didn't know anything about her short time in Ludford.

The boy bit his lip, his eyes welled up, and he looked down. He was an orphan as Alex thought. His guards shifted uncomfortably, not liking how they were stopped in the middle of the road, surrounded by what now looked like almost a hundred people.

"Toury." He tugged her arm a little. "We can't stay in the open like this long. We need to get moving."

Toury looked away from the boy, who was wiping away his tears. When she looked at Alex, her eyes were glistening.

Oh god of fire, he could not see her cry. He couldn't handle that. "Just over here, on the sidewalk," he urged her. He led her away, but her eyes went back to the boy, who clutched onto the coin with all his might, trying not to weep about his deceased mother. Once safely out of the middle of the crowd, he asked her about the boy.

"He's the one who found me when I transported, the first person I met in Fyr. He was picking mushrooms for his mother to sell. He took me to my aunt's house. I can't leave him on the street like this, Alex."

"Then we won't. You'll be a princess, Toury. You can command anything you see fit at any time. There are perks to this station you seem to overlook." He motioned to one of the guards and handed him an ample amount of coin. "See to it that that boy there is taken to the bathhouse and properly washed. Then get him a wardrobe for a foraging servant. He is your charge. See to it you get him back to the castle and arrange some accommodations."

He looked back to Toury, who was smiling. "Thank you."

"Just don't adopt all of the urchins, or we'll have more servants than work for them to do," he playfully chided.

"What does a foraging servant actually do?"

"For one, pick mushrooms. I don't know how they grow on Earth, but in Fyr, there are many poisonous ones, medicinal ones, and edible ones. To be able to tell the difference at his age is to his credit. But most likely, he'll work the orchard, picking your dracaberry."

"I love that stuff."

"I know." He kissed her hand.

At last satisfied, she left the little servant and resumed walking with Alex.

He led the way into one of the shops, and once they were safely inside with just David and Madge, he let go of Toury. Madge eyed up the patrons, overly cautious with her hand on the hilt of her saber, which was not-so-hidden in her skirts. When Toury took in where they were, her hand went to her chest, and her eyes lit up. She turned and regarded him with a look so much like love, it unhinged him.

"Where we met..." she said breathlessly.

And he couldn't form a coherent thought but found himself kissing her. The gasps of the few patrons were enough to pull them apart, although he longed to sneak her into a dressing room and create a real scandal.

The proprietor came over instantly and began to cater to them, showing Toury all of her materials and styles. Toury listened patiently, but then finally said, "I will only be purchasing one dress."

"No, my lady," Alex cut in. "You'll be purchasing an entire trousseau."

And with that, the proprietor announced the store would be closing for the next hour, and the patrons were rushed through their purchases and sent out of the store.

"Alex, I only want a dress for my luncheon, not a wardrobe."

"First, you must look the part. The princess will set the standard of fashion for the entire sphere, so choose what you like, and the world will follow. You must dress well, though, befitting your station." He added the last part so she wouldn't take this too far. Knowing her, she'd have women wearing pants like he heard they did on Earth. Change had to come slowly.

"But you dress plainly for your station." She frowned.

"I choose simple patterns, true, but the materials and quality are the best. You can choose simple, Toury, but it must be the best fabrics. To be taken seriously, you must look your station. Don't give girls like Justine any room to criticize. Second, buy your wardrobe, or you'll have to make this trip every time you need a dress for every occasion."

"True," she allowed.

"And Toury," he leaned in so no one could hear him whisper, "You might want to pick out your plans for *the dress*. The detail alone on wedding dresses can take over a month from what I hear."

She blushed a becoming red as the proprietor returned to them with apologies and assurances that the store was theirs.

"You may want to return in an hour, Your Highness."

"I'll do nothing of the sort," he insisted and sat down in one of the chairs. "I'd like to see what my lady will pick out."

"Strange, indeed, with all due respect," she murmured. Then she seemed to collect herself and went into her sales mode.

He took Toury to shop after shop, and she began to enjoy the shopping and how they catered to her, making it easy. She accepted the owners' pampering a bit more than he expected. Most girls loved to spend like crazy, and yet he had to urge Toury to get more at each place.

They dined at a café, Toury's humble choice, and then returned to the castle, with hardly room in the carriage for themselves, which didn't account for all the clothing that still had to be made and delivered.

There was hardly time to change for dinner. His father was moody and his mother excited about Toury's luncheon. After dinner was over, Toury began interviewing servants with Mary under the pretense that they were looking to promote for their future household staff. He, meanwhile, was stuck listening to his father and advisors debate over laws Alex found to be outdated. He was distracted, wondering the entire time which of these men were necromancers.

As soon as they both returned to their sitting room, and the door closed behind them, she loosened her top laces as this gown had them in the front. He was stunned.

She laughed. "You can undo your cuffs and doublet, but I'm not allowed to breathe?"

He pulled her to him. "Not unless you want me to keep untying them."

"Alex!" She playfully hit him.

"Can I sleep in your bed tonight?" he begged, kissing her.

"That's dangerous, and I do have a big day tomorrow."

"The more reason for me to help you sleep." He tried to persuade her in every way possible to let him sleep by her side but to no avail.

33

FRIENDS

Toury was nervous, but Mary would be by her side the entire time. Alex reminded Toury she was in charge, and Mary said she'd step in if Toury couldn't handle herself. All Toury had to do was give her a sign. The queen was to drop in too. Toury should have felt secure and protected. She was in charge. And yet, with the way some of the girls at school had treated her, she was dreading this. She was nervous that her plan to deal with Justine might go awry as well.

She steeled herself and opened the double doors fashionably late as instructed. She watched as the room full of young ladies bowed to her and Mary in acquiescence, and then she greeted them.

"Good day, my ladies. I am glad you could join me. The prince and I decided my ladies in waiting should be established to help me acclimate to court life and to later prepare for the wedding, even if it's against tradition. Being new to Fyr, I beg of you ladies for help, guidance, and most importantly, friendship." She continued to the table the queen had set up to be higher than the rest to remind them Toury was now their better. Mary followed, allowing Toury to outrank her for the occasion. The idea of her being above any of them felt odd and wrong.

As Toury stood behind her chair, she announced the day's events. "As you can see, there are seven tables of ladies. For each of the seven courses, a group will join Mary and me for polite conversation, and those whom I find...compatible with my own interests will join me for an exclusive dance with the gentlemen my betrothed is entertaining."

This last part was Mary's addition to the day, and the tittering of the girls showed it was a sound plan. They'd enjoy a suitor-type ball without professors chaperoning. Mary said it was important, from her own experience, to see who was after Alex or who genuinely wished to be her friend. Alex was not looking forward to dancing with these girls, but Mary pointed out it was to get rid of those who might use Toury. He agreed after that without more fuss.

After her little speech, Toury sat and casually waved her hand at the head servant, aptly named George Servant like most commoners who served. He signaled the other servants to bring the first course, and the ladies sat down now that the royals had. George then asked the first table to join them. Toury looked around before the girls obstructed her view. She saw Justine and her friends from school together, some looking around haughtily, insinuating this day was beneath their notice, but Justine glowered at her, then venomously whispered in another girl's ear. Toury had put her with her comrades in hopes her confidence would be high and anger even worse so she might make a scene. Toury was counting on it. The key to cracking into Fyr's female elite was taking Justine down a few rungs.

The first group of girls was unremarkable, to say the least, half of them in awe, the other half being so nice that it rang fake. Each introduced herself as Madge loomed over Toury's shoulder, whispering her connections and public opinion of her in Madge's wonderfully brief way. No one stuck out to her in that group to be sent home or to remain. Toury lingered over her salad, trying to garner what she could from the conversation, and Mary pried too, but they gleaned nothing.

She motioned for George to serve the next course, and the girls were taken back to their table, a few looking nervous or put out. They knew they had not made an impression.

"What a load of bore," Mary mumbled.

"How many of these girls must I bring into my confidence?"

"However many you wish, but you don't have to invite them over all the time unless Alex decides to invite the court back to actually live here. You control it all. And you want quite a few, for most will marry and no longer be able to be at your beck and call after that."

The conversation halted as the next group sat down across from them. Before they even introduced themselves, a bubbly, voluptuous girl spoke to her. "Princess-to-Be, this is such good fun. Even if you don't choose me as a friend, I say this is such a fun affair. What a way to meet as many people as possible. Goodness, excuse me for rattling on. My name is Lady Delphine Opal." She was large, well past the point of the court's desirable thin physique, which Toury thought a ridiculous standard to live up to in any realm.

Toury nodded and smiled at her. Madge whispered what she already knew; the girl's father had tried to court Toury, and the poor girl did not have much hope of an advantageous marriage due to her figure and her chattiness. Eyeing the girl over once more before she gave her attention to the others, Toury decided she liked Delphine. Another girl in this group who seemed full of sarcasm and energy sparked her interest too, a Lady Julia Garnet.

And so it went on: each group, she mentally selected anyone whom she thought she could help through her influence, who seemed fun and entertaining, and who seemed genuine. In a pack of girls raised to be superficial and pleasing, the latter was quite challenging to find. Luckily, there weren't any black eyes staring at her yet, and most girls were nervous, which was a heightened emotion. If they were evil, she'd have seen it, but this sphere left a lot of ladies out of politics, so finding a ton of necromancers among her gender was not likely.

She saved the worst table for last because she was almost positive a scene would ensue, which would have ruined the luncheon and the other girls' disposition. Justine and her crew marched up as dessert was laid out. In the group of fifteen girls, only four were not a part of Justine's clique. This would be rough. Mary had wanted them separated, but considering she wouldn't select any of them, and she wanted them to feel powerful enough to show their true colors, Toury insisted they sit together.

The girls introduced themselves, and Justine started immediately with a snide remark. "Such a waste of extravagance, this whole idea. Seven meals for lunch?" It was under her breath to her friend, who tried not to smile.

"And what do you suggest, Lady Justine? That I hold the typical ten luncheons of the past with smaller groups? Because that would cost more time and money, no?" Toury fired back, ready for this battle.

Justine turned red, and her eyes dilated the full eerie black Toury had espied before. Her nostrils flared, and Justine's body went rigid as if she could hardly control her temper.

"It's quite ingenious, really," Mary fawned, "and Mother loved it."

"Well, what I would've done was visit each girl in her own home," Justine said with an air of importance.

"Yes, personal," another girl said. "Typical of you to think of others' comfort before your own." The girl to her left, one she had not met at school, had the black eyes too, but her countenance was more controlled. Toury scoped the rest of them out. Four of them, counting Justine. She had hit the mother lode of daughter necromancers.

Mary snorted over her cake at the idea of Justine thinking of anyone but herself.

"Yes, very personal, but that would take over a hundred visits and a lot of manpower away from the palace. Plus, Alex would never hear of it. He's highly protective, and *someone* did try to kill me." Toury ended the sentence by staring Justine down. A couple girls gasped, and out of the corner of her eye, she could see them look away. When it came down to offending royalty, Justine's troops would never be so bold.

"*Prince* Alexander, Toury," Justine corrected her through a clenched jaw.

"'Prince Alexander, Lady Tourmaline, Princess-to-Be,' you mean to say," Toury corrected her, keeping her cool.

"Not if I can help it," she spat.

"Is that a threat to the prince's engagee?" Mary challenged loudly. The entire room went silent.

"*Alex* gave me leave to call him whatever I want." Toury made sure the comment sounded as if there were an intimacy behind it, which there was, but not as far as Justine might take it.

Justine surprised her by laughing loudly. "You think you're going to marry him? Sounds more like you're simply his whore!"

The room collectively gasped.

"That's enough!" Mary shouted, even though Toury hadn't given her the sign to intervene.

Toury kept calm and rose, steadying herself by resting her hands on the table. The entire room slowly followed due to the rules of decorum. Justine did not rise, but one of her friends pulled her up to standing, begging her in whispers to desist. It was one of the black-eyed girls, but she seemed scared rather than angry.

"Lady Justine of the Citrine family. I hereby banish you from court. If found on the palace grounds at any time, you will be arrested on sight," Toury commanded in her most austere voice, glad she'd practiced the line in front of her mirror in case she'd have to say it.

Justine trembled and faltered, but only for a second. She shook her friend's hand off and stood solid, glaring at Toury. "You don't have the power. You're not royalty. You're no better than the dirt on my boots! You won't marry him. I won't let you!"

"And how, please do tell, will you stop me?" Toury asked, feigning her calm. Hating confrontation, she was only held together by Madge's, Mary's, and George's presence, not to mention the two footmen crossing to them.

"I'll succeed this time," she hissed.

"In what?" Toury paused to allow the ladies to realize Justine was about to incriminate herself. "You wouldn't dare," she egged her on. "And you can't. You'll never step back in court ever again. Alex will do whatever I wish. All he has to do is second my decision. And once we marry, I'll make sure it is a lasting ban."

Then, before Toury could even react, Justine snapped. Her face grimaced into the eerie crone. Knife in hand, she launched herself across the table toward Toury. Madge nudged Toury back and stopped Justine's dinner knife with her sword. It was inches from Toury's face before Madge parried it away. Then another girl at the table, hazel-eyed Beth, grabbed Justine's hair and tugged it hard. Justine toppled backward into the guards, who grabbed her. They had to restrain her as she thrashed. Beth squeaked as Justine's hair seemed to come off in her hand, but it had only been a hairpiece. Regardless, she threw it to the floor, wiping her hands off as if it were tainted.

Toury's heart was in her throat. She had been hoping Justine would admit to poisoning her or say something about the necromancers, not dare to attack her in front of everyone. She felt faint, dizzy. Mary took up Toury's arm after she pushed her own bodyguard Lucy back and urged Toury to leave.

"I can't show any weakness," she whispered, steeling herself. Then louder to the guards, she said, "Take her to the dungeons until the king decides if she lives or dies."

Justine tried to shake off the guards and bellowed and pleaded with all the ladies to help her, which rang false. No one moved to help her, so she shifted to threatening everyone with her family's connections before she was out of earshot.

The room was silent, and Toury felt as if she'd fall. So instead of leaving, she sat down. Mary followed, and all the other ladies sat down, still staring at Toury, agape.

"I believe we may all need a drink after that episode." Mary flicked her hand to command the servants to supply drinks. Then she asked the shocked girls in front of them to kindly return to their table.

A few servants scurried around, not having decanters on hand, but soon, small glasses of the amber liquid were being passed around the room. That was when Queen Sapphirian entered in a hurry, masking the concern in her expression, but she couldn't hide the emotion in her eyes. Everyone stood and then sat again after the queen sat on Toury's other side.

The queen addressed her quietly. "I was told everything was going quite well, but my dear, she attacked you? I should have been here."

"No, Your Majesty." Toury shook her head. "I'm shaken up, but I had to do this. It was the only way for everyone to see what darkness we face. She was not herself, but almost possessed by the dark power inside her. The king would never trust me in this unless he saw her true colors."

"Toury, you will be an amazing queen one day. You already understand politics and how to handle the king. I did not understand how to persuade him to listen to my opinions until about a decade into our marriage. Please, drink quickly, dear, and head back to your rooms. Alex is beside himself with worry. I wouldn't let him come."

"He knows?" Toury groaned.

"The men's hunting party returned to see Justine carted toward the dungeon. Among them were her brothers, demanding to know what happened."

"She won't be freed?"

"No. An attack on any royal or royal-to-be is punishable by death, banishment from the sphere, or life in the dungeon if the king permits. With any of those punishments, her powers will be stripped from her. There's no way she should be freed or pardoned at this point. Too many witnesses."

Toury felt a little guilty that the girl could die, so she hoped she could speak with the king to avoid the girl's death, despite everything. When she realized everyone was waiting on her to drink or make an address, she looked to Mary. Toury's fortitude was waning, and her mind was blank.

Mary stood. "To Princess Tourmaline, who looks death in the face with fortitude and looks to her real friends with kindness." They all saluted her as princess, leaving the "to-be" off.

Toury was touched. For the first time, she gladly took a large sip from the firespice whiskey. The queen quickly drank hers, then stood, half lifting Toury out of her seat, and announced the girls would remain, the lucky few would be called to retire to the Princess Salon, a room for Mary and now Toury to entertain their friends in, so the girls could rest and prepare for the ball. Hardly aware of what was going on, Toury was led outside the back door, down a hall, and upstairs by Madge. As soon as she entered their living area, a disheveled Alex anxiously looked at her.

34

A ROW

Alex almost fell to pieces when he saw the ashen face of Toury as she entered, leaning on Madge. It was the day of the poisoning all over again. He wrapped her up in his arms, the thoughts in his mind centering on love and not being able to live without her, and yet he could not form these thoughts into words. He kissed her until she almost collapsed, and then scooped her up and placed her onto the settee. Then he knelt by her side, holding her hands.

"I will see her burn at the stake," he vowed to her. "I will do it myself."

"No, no," Toury insisted. "Not death. I provoked her on purpose."

"What!" He wanted to throttle her and hold her simultaneously. She was infuriating.

"It was the only way for everyone to see what she is, your father especially, and to expose the necromancers. We must stop them, Alex."

"Not at the expense of your life!" He stood up and paced rather than shaking sense into her like he wanted to. He tore at his hair instead of screaming at her. Didn't she realize how important she was to him? How he needed her? "Toury, you'll be the future Queen of Fyr. You cannot risk yourself, even for the good of the kingdom."

"I am not queen yet, not even a princess, so risks were taken, Alex. I didn't know she'd try to attack me!"

"She tried with a *knife* Toury." He paused for dramatic effect. "What course were you on?"

"Dessert, why?"

"Did a servant not clear the dinner dishes?"

He watched her face to see the recognition flitter across it. "It was premeditated?"

"She tried to poison you, so she most likely hid her dinner knife on her person. But that matters not, Toury. You cannot endanger yourself. Do you understand? All I want is you. If something happens to you, I want no other. It'll be the end of my line."

She blushed and looked away at his reference to their descendants. "I understand the importance of one of my future jobs," she muttered, completely ignoring his admittance, his weakness for her, and homing in on the one thing she found to be negative.

"Stop it!" he shouted.

She looked at him, her eyes welling.

"It's not our possible future children I worry about. Damn it, Toury! I need *you*. Just you."

She said nothing but stared at him, dumbfounded. He decided he had to go for it. He would tell her he loved her. She apparently needed the words because those dastardly earthlings had treated Toury as if she were insignificant when she was so much more than she could ever realize. "Toury, I—"

The door burst open.

Mary stood in the doorway, their mother behind her. They froze on the threshold, realizing too late that they had walked into the middle of an argument.

"Can't you knock? We were in the middle of a discussion," he growled, trying and failing to keep his cool.

"No," his mother pushed her way in. "Toury has one hundred and three girls, to be precise, awaiting her verdict."

"Cancel this nonsense. She needs to rest," Alex protested.

"Cancel your comment. I know what I need. I have two lists I must write down right now before I forget everything: one of the potential necromancers and one of my future friends so most these girls can go home. Madge," Toury called. The servant came out of the corner of the room. "I'll need some firespice tea, some parchment, and a quill."

As soon Madge left to gather the items, Mary sat down, making herself comfortable next to Toury. "I'll write for you. You dictate. I know how you struggle with your quill still."

Toury gave her a smile and squeezed her hand in thanks. His mother sat in another chair, completely calm, waiting for the list so the rejected girls could be sent home and the lucky ones could get ready for the ball.

"Are we not going to talk about this?" Alex demanded, looking at them all incredulously.

"Duty always comes first," his mother said, her lips firm, her eyes daring him to object. He knew better than to challenge her. It was his father's motto, and he also knew it could not be ignored.

"Alex," Toury's frustrated voice pleaded, but she reached out, seeking his hand off the couch behind her. She looked up at him, and he could see the worry in her face and the fatigue. "I will do my duty, and then I promise I will rest before the ball. We will dance and talk and be merry, and after that, we can continue our conversation."

He, the Prince of Fyr, was being commanded by her. It felt wrong, and yet it sounded exactly like something he would say—rational, duty before personal preference. When he saw Mary hiding a smile by pinching her lips together, he felt he had to save face. But commanding Toury never worked out well.

"You get those lists completed, and *then* we finish our conversation before you rest. Then I will be as merry as you command, my lady." It was a compromise, but at least he wasn't allowing her to fully command him.

Toury looked at him, a bit perplexed, but nodded in agreement.

He told them, "I'm going to talk to Cobalt about upping security in the ballroom tonight."

And then he escaped the oppressive room.

Cobalt didn't greet him jovially as he always did. "My, you've been busy." It was an accusation. "I leave for a month, and you get engaged. If I had been here, I'd have talked you out of it. You're insane. This is the end of your life as you know it."

"You know my father is dying. I have to marry soon. Secure the crown with progeny. I don't have the luxury you have as a second son to do as I please." Alex was still angry with Toury taking such risks, but as soon as it was out of his mouth, he regretted it. He watered down his strong feelings for Toury as a duty. He was taking out his anger at Justine on Cobalt.

"I'm sorry, Your Highness..." Cobalt was flabbergasted at his mood. "I didn't get back in time for the hunt, but did something happen?"

"It is I who should be sorry for many things, Cobalt. You did miss much, and I'm taking it out on you. Necromancers are among us, and Justine Citrine is one of them. She just made an assassination attempt on Toury, unsuccessfully, thank the god and goddess."

Cobalt's eyes bulged, and his mouth dropped open awkwardly.

"There's more." Alex paused to think about how to phrase this properly. "I need you on security detail for this ridiculous ball the ladies insist must go forward. And Cobalt, you must ensure my men keep her safe. She's the one, my future queen. I'll have no other."

Cobalt's mouth closed, but he still was in shock. He shook his head slightly as if to take it all in, and then stood up straighter, looking more serious and grave than Alex had ever seen him. He bowed his head and then said, "It would be an honor to take on this endeavor. I will have this place secure. I will protect her at all costs, Prince Alex. You can depend upon me."

On hearing that, and knowing that his friend would take this duty seriously, he felt a bit lighter. Cobalt would see the captain of the palace guards and set up a plan. If there was anything Cobalt excelled at, other than the seduction of the fairer sex, it was military strategy. They worked out some details, but his friend soon took over with ideas. He let him go to the guards to coordinate. Alex felt better. Now there was a plan in place, and he could delegate that duty, he returned to find Toury. She wasn't in the living room nor in her bedroom. He was about to ring for David to locate her whereabouts but thought to check his room first. And there she was, snuggled up in his bed, fast asleep, looking so peaceful and beautiful. Unable to resist, he partially disrobed and slipped into bed with her, pulling her to him.

She gave a little happy moan that almost unhinged him. She didn't know the power she had over him, and he was thankful for that. "Hi," she murmured.

"What are you doing in here?" he asked her.

"The bed, it smells of you, and it made me feel safe."

"You could have summoned me if you were scared."

"You were increasing security. It wouldn't be prudent to interrupt." Then she rolled over to face him. "Alex, I'm sorry. I will not willingly put myself at risk again, but I needed to do this and to do it without your influence. Without showing the ladies of the sphere who was in charge, without defeating Justine, I wouldn't gain support. Just as you have to act a certain way in public, so must I."

"I know, Toury. And I am sorry for overreacting. Reverse the roles. How would you respond to me being attacked inside the palace and finding out I provoked the person on purpose?"

She bit her lip and looked away.

"I know you may not love me yet, but you have to care enough to be a little upset," he pried.

Her eyes shot up to his in shock. "Of course I care! I'd be furious with the attacker and with you. I never said your reaction was wrong, just that you need to see it from my perspective too." Then she paused, moving a lock of hair off his forehead. "All I want and need is you too."

He ravaged her lips upon hearing that. It wasn't an admittance of love, but the intensity of the power transferring between them told him it was damn close to it. He should say the words, really, but the curse was still there. It meant he loved her, and she did not yet love him. Suddenly insecure and afraid his admittance might foil all his curse-breaking plans, he held his tongue.

At the ball, Alex was at first bewildered by Toury's choices of female companions, wondering why in all of Fyr she chose this ragamuffin crew. They were an eclectic group and not many of the fashionable norm. After he noticed that the first three girls he danced with were unattractive or a bit annoying, he wondered if Toury had a lack of trust when it came to him and that she didn't want anyone pretty or pleasing by her side. But then he dismissed the thought. Toury was not prone to self-conscious bouts of doubt, and he had never given her reason to distrust him. He had never looked at a girl twice until Toury entered the sphere.

No, it clicked when a particularly rotund, chatty girl nervously slaughtered his ear that this was a sort of charity Toury was running. As the companion of a princess or future queen, any friend of hers would marry well. His heart warmed at the thought. If he had ever questioned her ability to be a queen, this maneuver of hers would have set him straight. And he knew Toury would find real friends in a crew who saw her goodness. Disregarding his initial superficial judgment on their appearance and feeling awful for thinking badly of them, these girls seemed to be the most honest, sweet, and unaffected girls the kingdom had to offer. Not one spoiled, conceited debutante was in the room. He and Toury would change this world for the better, starting with the court, their innermost friends. Toury, in this instance, was the person he wanted to become once he could fully shed his father's influence.

Finally, for the last dance of the night—he had to order the musicians to play an extra song just for him—he took his future wife into his arms. After dealing with twenty awestruck girls and watching her dance with all the gentlemen in the room—he refused to admit there was any jealousy on his part—it was heaven to have her in his arms. Per usual, he pulled her a bit too close and whispered, "I approve of your friends."

"Really?" She looked at him, amazed.

"Even without being able to see the darkness in people as you do, I can tell they are all kind and wholesome girls full of light who will unknowingly benefit from your patronage."

"I was hoping you'd help me weed some out."

"You can keep them all as friends if you'd like, but official waiting maids who are in the palace daily are usually limited to five. How would I help you limit them?"

"Were any of them horrid flirts?" She chewed her lip, concerned.

He could not help but laugh loudly at this.

"Don't laugh." She frowned. "Mary said to watch out for the girls who would be after you. Some may think they can stop the wedding. Others may be happy to be a mistress."

Alex could not think of one girl of the bunch he'd look at for more than a cursory glance. Sure, a couple were tolerably pretty by the court's standards, but his standards didn't seem to be the same. He chose his words carefully. "I'm not the one to ask about the flirting. I hardly take notice of that since most girls will grovel and simper in my presence. This medallion sets me apart from the rest."

"Just the medallion?"

"No, honestly, ask Cobalt about the flirts and light-skirts. He'd know."

Her mouth went agape. "Shocking you are, Alex."

"I can think of better ways to shock you," he insinuated, nuzzling her ear. The whispers and dreamy sighs of the women in the room were drowned out by Toury's giggles.

35

LIGHT AND DARK

Toury felt weightless, on cloud nine. She had never imagined in all her dreams that she'd find this much happiness and feel loved and part of a family. It only took going to another sphere to find it, but at least she did. The palace was home, no longer a prison. Her engagement was real now, and she was on her way to having some real friends while weeding out her enemies. She was ecstatic. She had no clue how much happiness one could bear, but it kept coming to her, making her feel as if she might burst.

It was late, but the king wanted their weekly nightcap. Although Toury was still intimidated by him, King Sapphirian had these family moments so they could be themselves and discuss things privately.

This evening, he was slumped by the fire, looking tired. Mary was at his side, trying to restore him with a peppy regaling of the ball since he stayed to his rooms these days. His skin was gray, his lips blue as if cold. Even without in-depth knowledge of curses or biology, Toury knew he was dying. As the embodiment of fire, his flame was dwindling.

"Lady Toury." He greeted her with a weak but genuine smile. "I've been briefed on the day's events and about Lady Justine's actions. I would like you to know that Lady Justine will be burned at the stake for her crimes, and all Citrines, except Lord Citrine, will be banished from court. Lord Citrine assures me his daughter has acted alone and has quite lost her mind. He deeply apologizes but did not realize she was so bad off. He's at a loss and agrees that we should banish all his children to be safe."

Toury found this last part odd and was irritated that the king trusted any Citrine. Then the words clicked in her head that Justine would die.

"Your Majesty." She hurried over and curtsied. She took up his hands in hers, channeling her light healing magic into him. "Do not kill her. It is too awful, burning someone. I can't bear the thought."

He shook her hands off gently. "You will learn this role comes with weight. I do not want to kill the daughter of my best friend, but even he understands that no one attempts to murder a royal and lives. You may have a heart, Toury, but you must only have it privately. Otherwise, you are doomed to weaken the crown."

She didn't care about the crown. She wanted Alex, but she couldn't say that to him. She noted the other three Sapphirians were talking in the corner privately. "Yes, Your Majesty."

"Your heart shows you're your mother's child. Before she met your father, she loved everything and everyone. She was to be my sister. She brought such light and happiness to all. That would've been a blessing. But now we have you. That, I hope to see, will be the better blessing."

She was dumbstruck. He had rarely been kind to her, never nice like this. And her mother was to be his sister? She dared to ask him.

"Yes, she was engaged to my brother before she fled with your father."

She dared to continue, "And this banished them from court?" He seemed weak and kind, so she was hoping it meant he wouldn't attack her. The concerned looks from Alex, Mary, and the queen put her on alert. He really must be dying.

"I suppose you should know." He sighed. "Your father outwardly disliked my younger brother Alfred. Everyone knew. And your father was an extremely talented lightbearer. Anyone who has a light that is powerful enough to break curses could do the opposite and create them if they went dark." Toury could guess where this was headed. "The night your parents ran away, I was cursed in my sleep, as was Alex, a mere helpless infant at the time. Alfred was found dead, cursed so strongly that his heart ceased beating. There were no other suspects. Your father had a strong motive because your mother was engaged to my brother, and your father turned her head. " The king continued, "Plus, it is very interesting how old you are, Toury, since your parents weren't married when they left court. It gave them the ultimate motive: to get rid of my brother so they could marry because you were on the way. But you know nothing of that."

Toury's mouth dropped as she wondered what the implications of being baseborn meant.

"A lot of the details were covered up, as was necessary to hide weaknesses. We proclaimed they married secretly, betraying the crown and killing Alfred. We found out later that they actually had married. A lightbearer brought in to help Alex leaked out the curse information. She was silenced but too late. The land knew about Alex, which made hiding my affliction all the more necessary."

Toury had an inkling that silence involved a stake and fire, and that this probably had been some distant relative of hers.

"I tell you all this so you know why I suspected he sent you here and why I didn't trust you," the king said. She noted his use of past tense.

"But you trust me now?"

"Yes," he said without hesitation. "You've proven yourself and your influence"—his eyes flickered over to Alex momentarily—"has been beneficial."

Toury couldn't form a sentence, her disbelief was so great.

"You're shocked that I can be nice. I like that. Never trust anyone but yourself, not even Alex."

"Alex would never—"

King Sapphirian cut her off with sudden energy, "You cannot trust him as long as there is darkness in him."

"There is darkness, Your Highness, but I see more light in him, the fire that burns the dark away. But I understand your meaning."

She grabbed up his hand again and pushed energy into him.

"No," he told her, trying to shake her off. "Save your strength."

"No, you need it."

"Desist. That's a command," he growled.

"Your fire's sputtering out, and soon, nothing will be left but ashes."

"That is the cycle of life, is it not?"

"Alex is not ready," she whispered. There was curse-breaking and necromancer-ousting to do first. How could he rule over every facet of this land on top of his top secret mission?

"He'll have to be, and he will be fine with you by his side."

She was not ready for this at all. Becoming a queen suddenly seemed impossible. "No, I hardly know down from up just yet. I'm more of a burden than help when it comes to this kingdom. You've let him learn all his life but never allowed him any control. You must delegate to him, let him take over piece by piece, and then soon enough, he'll realize he's doing it all on his own."

"You know him so well after so little time, and yet I know him not, after all these years. His mother suggested the exact same thing." The man rubbed his hand down his face, distressed. "I pushed him down, suppressed his defiance, and I didn't let him become the leader he will suddenly need to be. I thought I'd have more time. But as much as I wish I could fight off death, it's impossible."

"Not if I can help it," she told him, pushing energy into him with all her might. "I will give you time to right this. He is strong. He is a leader and has opinions that he simply doesn't voice. Let him voice them, let him take over. I, in turn, will learn how to help him."

He sighed as if giving in, and she could feel the dark battling her light, much stronger than it ever was in Alex. The king moaned. Would it all be too much for him to bear? But soon enough, his lips were gaining color, his flesh becoming tan and pink again, his eyes becoming more aware every second. Then she felt drained, weak, and dizzy. She let go and tried to get up but fell down onto her bottom. Alex was instantly there, scooping her up in his arms and insisting she'd had too trying of a day and had to go to bed. For once, she did not protest.

Somewhere from the king and queen's tower to their own, she fell fast asleep in Alex's arms. The steady rhythm of his boots clicking on the floor and the beat of his heart in her ear were like a somnolent metronome lulling her under.

She was pulled out of her deep sleep when she was placed down but was too drained to open her eyes. She felt Alex pulling away from her, so she clung on. His breathy laugh danced across her cheek. "Toury, let go, my love." She did only because she felt too weak to protest. Did he really just call her "his love?" She was too exhausted to respond. Warm, trembling hands untied her laces, which were at the front of her dress. He slipped her arms out of the cuffs and gently placed them down. She felt him tug her dress downward, his breathing becoming a bit rapid. Then suddenly, she felt wide awake when his lips pressed on hers. His hands touched her face and then slid down her shoulders, skimming her bare arms, creating goosebumps in their wake.

She opened her eyes to see his full of desire. He backed away, regret in his eyes. "I should go." His voice did not carry the sentiment of his words.

"No," she said.

He breathed in a deep, unsteady breath. "I'll come back, I promise. Sleep, my love."

The moniker made her smile.

Then he stood up and away from her. "There are a couple things I need to attend to, including an ice bath, before I can sleep by your side."

She smiled, closed her eyes, and rolled onto her side. "You're wicked." It came out as a mumble.

"I wish I could be," he said, his voice soft and gravelly. Then she heard him leave.

Another pair of lighter footsteps came in, and she felt Madge continue to undress her, slip her nightgown onto her, and pull the quilt over her. Then she pulled the pins out of Toury's hair and began gently brushing.

The soothing and repetitive motion of her hair being brushed sent her right back into a deep slumber.

Hours later, or maybe moments, she wasn't sure how long, she woke up. She looked around, confused, but realized she was in her bedroom, and it was still dark. She reached over, but Alex wasn't there. Something had woken her, so she strained to hear what it could be while her eyes tried to discern shapes in the darkness. Her bedroom door from the sitting room was ajar. That was odd because Alex always entered through their adjoined doors after he changed into his bedclothes. She heard footsteps. She sat up a little to see a person come in and instantly noted something was amiss. The figure was too short and slender, and the footsteps too light, to be Alex.

By the time she realized this was an unwanted intruder and tried to scream, it was too late, and the person had her mouth covered. Cold, sharp steel was pressing into her throat.

"You make a sound or one wrong move, and I will have my accomplice murder the prince while he bathes," the voice said in a whisper. Although she was trying to disguise her voice, Toury recognized Justine. She wasn't scared of Justine, but what made her comply with being gagged and bound was the massive form of a man in the doorway, with a machete in his hand. Alex could not be harmed. He was safe the floor below her in their bathing chambers. Alex had an army that could recover her, but if he alone tried to save her, his heart could cloud his head, and he might be rash and get them both killed.

She stayed silent, knowing Alex could find her anywhere in Fyr due to the amulet on her ankle. She just had to figure out what was going on, stay strong, and wait it out.

36

A PLAN

Alex was going crazy. Toury was missing. He had come up from his bath to her empty room. He had just laid her down there an hour ago and summoned Madge to do what he could not trust himself to do: get her into her nightgown. She was not in their quarters at all, and Madge hadn't seen her since she had readied her for bed. He could not transport to her anklet either, opening his eyes to find himself where he started. He could not read her whereabouts in the flames nor see what would happen to her in the near future. And after a second scouring of the entire castle and lands—even the closed floors and towers—there was no sign of her. He was panicking inside, so much so that David and Cobalt were running the search. He was useless, and Madge wasn't much better. She blamed herself, he knew without her saying the words. She was Toury's protector and had failed her. But Alex himself hadn't heard a word above him while he was in the bath, so how could Madge or David hear anything across the hall from his and Toury's rooms?

He searched, he paced, and he upturned her entire bedroom, looking for clues. Nothing. Not one item of clothing was missing. Wherever she was, she wore only her robe and nightgown. This clue proved beyond a doubt that she had been taken and had not left of her own accord.

Mary said nothing when he apprised his family of the situation. His father grew grave and worried, and his mother demanded more be done to find her.

"Have you called the courtiers to assembly?" Mary asked.

They stared at her. Annoyed they weren't catching on, she said hurriedly, "You'll see who's missing—not that it matters, for we know who's behind this—but calling them to court will make everyone else know as well."

"Who do you think is behind this, know-it-all daughter?" his father demanded.

"The Citrines!" Mary shouted and met Alex's gaze.

How had he forgotten the girl in his panic? They should make sure she was still imprisoned. She had tried to kill Toury twice now and was a necromancer.

"That's preposterous! How could she? She's in the dungeon!" His father shook it off. "The Citrines are an exemplary noble family and cannot help that the daughter lost her mind from not being able to ensnare the prince."

"I'll admit, she's lost her mind, but it doesn't make sense," his mother mused.

"You, man!" Alex shouted at the nearest servant. "To the dungeons at once, and check on the prisoners." The man ran off in a hurry.

"How could she possibly escape?" his father insisted.

Alex mused for a moment. "There was one person of that family you didn't banish from court, Father. One who can enter and exit this castle as he pleases. It's time to question our very friendships."

"Jasper Citrine is my best—" his father began petulantly.

"I won't hear it! Everyone will be questioned until I get to the root of this!" Alex shouted at his father.

King Sapphirian was taken aback, and Alex awaited the return of the temper, but instead, he saw something strange in his father's eyes: a gleaming shine and a grim smile. If Alex didn't know better, it could have been pride.

His mother squeezed his shoulder. "It will be fine. We will find her."

"You don't know that. None of us can see it in the flames. Don't you understand? I won't marry another. Mary's line will rule after me. Toury is my princess. No one else will ever do."

"Alex, stop," Mary insisted. "Think rationally right now. Fret about the future of the sphere later."

His father's shaky hand went to his forehead. Alex wanted to help his father here, but he needed to see Tobias and find Toury. He was needed here and yet there. This was most likely a move to separate him from his father, two Sapphirians in different places to divide the strength of their power. Together, their power was unstoppable, but apart...even a lone Sapphirian could be taken down by enough men. His family was in just as much danger as Toury, but they had protection, troops, and Toury was alone. If anything happened to Toury, he couldn't live with himself. He was torn between familial duty and love.

The servant returned, huffing and puffing, "The Citrine girl is missing. The guards are dead. Two other prisoners were freed as well. All other prisoners in that block were murdered. The rest of the dungeon was untouched, prisoners alive, and the other guards heard nothing."

So they only freed certain people: necromancers.

Mary gripped his hand. "I've got this, Alex. Go get my sister, and bring her back to us."

He squeezed her hand back. "Trust only the Cobalts, Mary."

"Can we trust anyone?"

"No," he reluctantly admitted. "But you need someone on your side, and Toury has checked them. We have no choice."

She nodded in understanding. Alex needed help, and although he should trust no one, he couldn't believe his best friend could backstab him, and Cobalt's father was a man of integrity and influence. Aside from Tobias, who had no power in the court, Alex had no one else. How had it come to this?

Alex fled the room, and David flanked him to inform him Tobias had arrived and was waiting in the foyer. When they reached Tobias, a few courtiers were loitering, one of them being Lord Citrine, most likely eavesdropping. Alex plastered on a smile he did not feel and shook Tobias's hand as if all were well. Tobias looked at him oddly, but when Alex asked what the man was doing there—even though Alex had summoned him—Tobias caught on. He walked the man out into the gardens and then to the orchards, talking nonsense, although he was desperate for answers and assistance.

Once he felt safe, he stopped and apprised him of everything. Tobias rubbed his chin in thought, and his mind churned. "I need to summon the Magicians' Guild to guard the palace gates. I don't want to start a war, but you have no idea how many necromancers are among you, do you?"

"Toury saw the darkness in them and said there were a lot. She gave my mother a list, and we've been adding to it, maybe thirty names now. David, go make a copy of the list the queen has, and deliver it to the head magician."

"Your Highness, I cannot leave—"

"The kingdom depends on you, David. The king's life depends on you. And it is an order. Do not deny me right now," he threatened.

After a moment's hesitation, David stalked inside. Alex needed to get away from David, for he had a feeling what would ensue, and he would not want David's blood on his hands.

"Tobias, I need to get to Toury, and I need your help."

Tobias sighed. "You know it is most likely a trap, Your Highness."

Alex wanted to shake the man for his defeatist tone. Didn't the man realize it didn't matter? "I don't care."

"Your Highness, they will most likely turn you dark, ignite the curse. You'll need to let them," Tobias told him. "You will not be strong enough to fight it off, to fight them. The only way is to become one of them and pray Toury comes through to destroy it."

"I can't go dark. Toury is the greatest threat to the curse. If I let it take over control, then I may hurt her, kill her even."

"Do you trust she will be able to defeat the curse?" Tobias challenged.

"She is capable. I think she is strong enough."

"You know what I mean," Tobias said.

Alex only hesitated a moment, "Yes, yes. She has everything she needs to break it." He hoped he was right.

"Good, let us go inside, and you send your troops ahead of us, and I will gather the Magicians' Guild. At nightfall, you and I will go save your princess."

"Nightfall!" Was the man insane? It was dawn, and he was suggesting they wait half a day.

"Prince, they took her because they want you. They will wait for you. You can transport us but not your army. At least give your men a chance to get halfway there."

"To where exactly? We don't know where they've taken her, and—"

"They are headed up north, Prince Sapphirian."

"But how? They cannot transport!" He was equally full of angry flames and anxiety over how far they had gotten her in mere hours. If they had the power to travel as he did, he'd never catch them if they kept relocating.

"Not much is known about the necromancers, but I've come across them during my translations." Tobias was a translator of ancient books as well as a firebrander. "There are a few books I do not translate for a reason: ones written by necromancers back when your ancestors formed the throne to evoke peace among the chaos." Tobias referred to the beginnings of their land. "But I've read them. In these books, there are sinister spells such as reanimating the dead, curses like your own…"

"That's how you figured out how to break it," Alex murmured to himself.

"…and there is one about increasing one's speed or agility," Tobias told him.

Alex was confused. He was trying to imagine Justine running at super speed.

Tobias concluded for him, "Your Highness, I think they raised dead horses and imbued them with speed. I have sent a magician from the guild to check the horse graveyard to see."

Alex sighed. Humans were sent on to the Ultimate Realm through a pyre, but animals, particularly heroic warhorses, had their own place of burial. The largest cemetery was not far from Ludford. Mary was right. They had been sitting ducks, waiting for an attack, and the necromancers had had plenty of time to plan this.

"You're sure north?" Alex asked. "Can they be there already?"

"Most likely not, but they'd be moving too fast for you to transport to her, and once there...it's the only place they could possibly take her since blood magic doesn't work in such conditions."

"And neither does fire," Alex mused aloud. The north was not a good place for him. He would be vulnerable to black magic. They definitely would take her to the place he'd be weakest.

"But light magic does. I think they took your princess to get to you. They have no clue who she is or what she is capable of."

Alex nodded. They didn't know they were holding the greatest weapon against them, and that was keeping Toury alive.

"The troops must stay here to protect my family and fight the necromancers already in Celestia. Like you, they will expect me to take my most trusted and powerful troops housed here, which would make the castle vulnerable. Instead, I will send my southernmost troops to the north by sea, which will take them roughly a day and a half—too late, but they can surprise the necromancers from behind no matter how far south toward Celestia they reach. My troops from Aberdane up north can arrive at nightfall, give or take, so will be there to support us," Alex started planning aloud. All his hours of geography and military combat study were paying off. "I will go and warn each fort from the north to Celestia to be on alert. I will make sure the necromancers don't reach the capital." He had to get his father to write these commands and sign them. He'd have to deliver them each personally by transporting, but also warn them not to follow any commands he would make in the future. He would have to tell them what was going on and hope he could trust the commanders.

"What if the commanders are necromancers?" Alex wondered. "I'll have to have the Hematite baseborn go with me to ensure they are on our side."

"Prince, with this curse, you'll be using up a lot of your energy."

"Well, I better get this done quickly and ask the lightbearer to give me energy. He's not as powerful as Toury, but it should help. There's nothing for it. It must be done. I have to command everything in advance to defeat not only the necromancers, but also the future dark version of myself."

They ironed out a few more details about how the Magicians' Guild could help, and then he sent the man on his way. Alex knew he might never come back from this, but at least, there was a plan. He sought out Mary and Cobalt first, the only other people he trusted. It was time to take others in the fold. After all, if he never came back from this, Mary would have to take control over the realm after his father passed, and Cobalt would need to weed out friend from foe among the court. He had to let Mary know Toury was the savior, and he had to tell her to imprison him if he came back not as himself. He could not rule when dark, or the necromancers would win, and if they ruled the land, all would be lost. Fire, light, dragons, hope, and happiness would be blighted out forever. More than this apocalyptic doom, the idea of losing Toury weighed heavily. This might be a suicide mission, but that didn't matter. He simply could not live in a world where Toury wasn't his or was gone from him forever.

37
NECROMANCY

Toury woke up shivering, beyond the chill she should have anywhere near the temperate Celestia. She looked around. She was in what looked like a cargo carriage, the canvas sides flapping in the hissing icy wind. They'd had her in an ordinary carriage when they had left the castle. Justine had said some weird nonsense in another language that made her sleepy. Who knew how much later, she woke up here, obviously far away from the capital. She tried to sit up but fell off balance due to her hands and ankles being bound.

Before she completely pieced together last night's memories, the carriage halted to a stop. Her stomach lurched at the change of speed, like when an airplane lands and pulls on the breaks. Voices called to each other, and the back tarp was flung open, pouring bright light inside. She squinted and couldn't make out her captor's shadow, the face of the person being blotted out by the excessive light from behind him. It was daylight, so the entire night had gone by and dawn, at least. Why hadn't Alex found her yet?

She screamed when the form lurched into the wagon and yanked her out by the rope on her wrist. It bit into her flesh, tearing away a layer with it. Thrust out into the sunlight and glare, it took a moment for her eyes to adjust to the people in front of her. It was Justine and the machete-wielding man.

Toury shivered in the cold air, despite the enchanted silky nightgown Alex had given her. It was still trying to warm her with magic heat but hardly worked in the freezing wind. Her feet were bare and going numb, as well as her nose and fingers. She wouldn't last long here before she'd die of exposure or hypothermia. Her hair whipped around her. Looking around, she saw snow everywhere, which made the glare of the sun even more intense on her eyes.

Justine stood, her face inches from Toury's. She had a smug look on her haughty face, and her amber eyes had turned black, just as Toury had seen them at court. She looked worse for wear, her fine hair barely making a pile on her head, the fake curly yellow hairpiece gone. She had changed out of her prison garb into a fancy dress, but it seemed as if her nefarious plans were more important than wearing makeup. She looked utterly different without the layers of makeup caked on, not necessarily bad, but more average. "You had no idea who you were messing with, but you will soon," Justine said with venom.

"I know," Toury said quietly. She had to keep her talking, prolong whatever plans Justine had for her. "You would say you're a powerful necromancer, but I see you just as a vapid, evil, spoiled brat who is jealous of me."

"Jealous!" Justine snapped and slapped Toury across the face.

Her head whipped back from the action, but she did not cry out and give Justine the satisfaction. It stung miserably, making her eyes water, but she met the girl's nasty black eyes and did not waver. "Alex will never be with you, black magic or not. You will never defeat his army, and you know he'll send them for me."

"I won't have to fight his army long to overtake the kingdom. None of us will have to." She smiled eerily.

Toury looked around to see she was in a camp. There was a handful of black-eyed nobles whom she recognized from court, but mostly there were servants and soldiers. It didn't look like enough people to last five seconds against any army, no matter the size. She imagined the king had legions of men to fight.

"The prince will come willingly to save his *true love*," Justine mocked her. "And we will turn him against his own people and family. The curse will be a tool for us to control the entire kingdom. It's been the purpose of the curse from the beginning. The spineless cowards never found a good time to use it until you came along."

"Me?" Toury's heart sank. Did they know she was the savior? God, they would kill her before she ever saw Alex again, before she could at least say goodbye.

Justine rolled her eyes at her. "You're engaged. If it is allowed to continue, you will marry and have children. The necromancers lose their power then unless they can curse your spawn too, like starting over again. They failed to overtake the king, but at least the curse is finally killing him."

They didn't know about Toury being the savior after all. Toury understood their plans now, but she had to stall the girl and play dumb. "Wait, what do you mean?"

Justine laughed and rolled her eyes. "And this was to be our princess."

A couple of the men laughed, but most simply ignored Justine.

"The necromancers have been around since the beginning of time. There were times long ago when it wasn't frowned upon to have a gift for darkness. Things changed, but they will change again. We will snuff out the light and reign with darkness. The king, as you obviously know, is dying but, somehow, is still clinging on."

Toury realized they had no idea she was full of such powerful light magic, that she could heal, or that she was the one keeping the king alive. They saw her as a weak pawn, someone to dispose of after they got Alex, not a savior, not an enemy. This might be the only thing that would get her through this alive—them underestimating her.

Justine prattled on, and Toury observed her surroundings as she half listened to the girl speak. "He was cursed; only, it didn't work as quickly as they intended, but since Prince Alexander was a baby, the curse seemed to grow with him. Plans were foiled, and no one could place a curse on the princess. She had protection. They learned their lesson. But they can't stop us. Mary will be eliminated as well as the king, and Alex will become our puppet."

"You seriously underestimate Alex's strength," Toury told her. "Curse or no curse, he will not bow to your commands, and he will still want me." Toury thought she was just faking bravado, trying to anger the girl, but deep down, she knew it was true. She loved Alex, and he loved her, and nothing could ever come between that, not even the strongest darkness. She wished she had told him she loved him. What if she died, and he'd never know?

"He won't marry you once he realizes there are better options out there." She smiled smugly and touched her throat as if to demurely refer to herself.

Toury took a deep breath and reached inside herself for strength. "He still won't want you. No curse can squash how someone feels. No curse can banish love. It's the strongest magic of them all," Toury said without thinking. It seemed as if it were a quote from a text she could not recall, so it must have been from her Ruby fact-bank.

A couple of the nobles looked at each other a little wary; the man closest shifted his weight nervously, so she knew she had struck a nerve. The way the noble necromancers reacted to her statement proved that love could conquer all. She racked her brain on how to use love as magic. She hoped Ruby's knowledge would come to her, but the connection no longer seemed to be working, or Ruby had never known.

"Love?" Justine laughed. "You're a fool to think Prince Alexander could love you. You're such a...dark-looking and dull thing, so weird and out of place. It matters not. I never wanted Alex for love, or even for himself. He is boring and grave. True, he is stunningly handsome. I'll give him that, and our babies will be utterly beautiful, but that is hardly the point." Every word Justine spoke stabbed her, and the snarky grin showed she knew the pain she was inflicting on Toury. "The point is, I'll be queen, and I'll be in charge, controlling and training Alex like a little king pet."

Why was Toury still alive then? They must have needed her for something other than bait. "And what happens to me?" she asked boldly, showing no fear.

"That depends on how forthcoming you are." Justine smirked. "I will take much pleasure in watching you be tortured, I won't lie."

"Forthcoming about what?"

"How is the prince fighting off the curse?" she demanded outright. "How does the king still live?"

They really had no clue. Toury would have to destroy the curse once and for all. This would be her only chance for her to get out of this alive and for Alex to keep his autonomy. She concentrated, thinking of everything her uncle had shown her in their lessons. She prayed to the goddess of light and the god of fire—although she really didn't understand the religion of this land—for them to release the Ruby intel locked up in her brain.

"I have no idea," Toury lied.

"I was hoping you'd say that." Justine laughed, her musical, breathy voice eerie. Then she chanted something in some strange language, and the ground began to quake beneath them. The earth crumbled, and the snow split, dirt rising up from under. Hands were clawing their way up, out of the earth. Boney hands of the undead, half-covered in rotting flesh, were followed by matted, sparsely haired heads and eyeless, fleshless faces. Toury retched and almost fell down. The buffoon who had "helped" her from the carriage caught her and held her tight, and she realized he was scared as well and was planning to use her as a human shield. Toury hoped to wake from a nightmare as she gazed upon these monstrosities rising up until hundreds of the undead stood before them. It was an army for the deranged Justine to command. When one ambled toward Toury, she let out a scream.

"Silence her," Justine commanded. Then she told the creature to halt, and it froze in place. Toury heard tearing and felt a tug on her nightgown.

The beefy henchman put the bottom of her nightgown into her mouth and pulled it, pinching the corner of her lips. He tied it too tight, but it did make her unable to speak, even though she had gone quiet already.

"I wonder if the necromancers knew they'd one day fulfill their purpose." Justine waved her arms as if presenting someone with a surprise. Then she glared at Toury. "That's right, little ignoramus. You don't know anything about history, do you? These northern grounds were selected as the battlefront because Alex would be weak, yes, but more because it is the unmarked graveyard of the necromancers. They went into hiding up here when King Rowland Sapphirian—Alex's great-grandfather if you're too stupid to follow Alex's lineage—outlawed dark magic, and his army pushed them up north. He butchered all these people because he was scared of the power we have and how it could be used to dethrone him. Today, they will get their revenge!"

A few of the men whooped and hollered at this speech—the alive ones. The undead just stood there, utterly immobile after her command.

"Put her in the cavern over there, in the back. There's only one way in and out, so stand guard right inside," Justine commanded.

"Now what?" one noble challenged her.

"We wait for the prince and turn him. Once my father sends word the palace is under his control, and the royal family is dead, we march on Celestia. Take half my army and meet the prince's army. Do not let them reach here, and capture the prince, but do not harm him."

The man bowed and walked away, issuing orders. Toury was unceremoniously shoved toward a dark-looking cave. She had never been so scared in her life—or for her new family. Until this moment, she did not realize how much she loved them. Mary was her best friend, like her sister, while the queen was the only woman to ever care about her as a mother would. Even the king. His domineering ways at least showed he cared. It was much more than she had gotten from her Earth family, and now she might never see her new family again.

38

A SACRIFICE

As soon as the sun hit the horizon at sunset, Alex could wait no longer. He transported Tobias and himself to the northernmost point. Never having been there before, he could only imagine the location he wanted from a map of the land. He landed them right where he wanted, between the mountain range that separated most of the northernmost area from the rest of Fyr and the rock edifice that marked the northernmost point. Luckily, they were in the shadows and were not noticed right away, for there were tents—a dozen or so—but around those tents were hundreds of soldiers. They stood immobile, and an eerie feeling crept over him as he didn't even see their chest rise and fall nor any steamy breath exiting their mouths.

"What are they?" Alex asked, but deep down, he knew the answer.

"The undead," Tobias whispered. A look of dread passed across the man's face. "Thousands of people died up here over a hundred years ago. They must've sent the rest toward Celestia already."

"I cannot do this, Tobias. I cannot hurt her. I should be leading my men against this army," Alex lamented.

"They will keep returning, keep fighting. The dead are endless, and they will keep raising them. The more people they kill, the more they have on their side, your people, your men. It has to stop today. I will find your princess. Go to the necromancers, let them change you. Make them think you're alone, and convince them the curse is overtaking you."

"How?"

"Simply stop fighting it, Prince Sapphirian."

Alex cringed at the idea. Fighting the curse was innate now, like breathing. He would have to quell the dragon, his strength. It was the only way for the curse to take over.

"Will it all end well? What have the flames said?" Alex asked, on edge. He was a bundle of nerves.

"A great many things, both good and bad. Let's hope for at least getting an in-between," Tobias told him. "I will protect her with my life. Now, go."

Alex left the man in there, looping around before he exited the mountains' shadows. As he walked, he thought of Toury's beautiful gray eyes and told himself the only way to see her again would be to finally rid himself of the darkness by letting it consume him. Then, after she banished the curse for good, they could come together and marry, with him no longer tarnished by evil; instead, he'd be the embodiment of pure fire. Toury deserved a better, stronger lifemate, and he would do this for her and his people.

By the time he reached the front of the camp, the thick black magic had stolen over him, weighing him down, and he felt as if he were drowning in it. When it felt overwhelming to the point he wanted to push it back to its hiding place, he closed his eyes and breathed deeply. Instead of drowning, he felt a burst of strength and an ire rise in him so strong, he wanted blood. He wanted to inflict pain and misery.

The first soldier stepped forward and thrust his sword at Alex. It was a mechanical type of gesture, the limbs of the undead soldier stiff from disuse. Alex unsheathed his sword and swung, lopping off the head of the already dead creature. The body fell to the ground, lifeless once more. So they could die again.

Another soldier stepped forward, but a female voice rang out, "Halt at once! This is your prince, you brainless monsters!"

The creature lowered its sword, but Alex lopped its head off regardless. It was a monster, its eyes empty and lifeless. He pitied the disturbed peace that the creatures' spirits were going through since the necromancers reanimated their bodies. It made him sick, and he wanted to burn them all, but he couldn't. Not only was he playing a part here, but the fire magic in him was so subdued, he didn't know if he could even conjure it. It felt cold and sluggish in his veins.

Seeing Justine there suddenly rushing up to him, he thought of snapping her dainty neck. He saw the blackness in her eyes—what Toury must have seen—and knew from Justine's pleased expression that his must be black too. Part of him swelled with pride while the other half of him shrank in disgust. He felt the duality of his power, fire and blackness inside of him, like two different people in the same mold.

"Prince Alexander," Justine bowed deeply, showing off her bosom to him. "Have you come for that lightbearer?" She scoffed at the idea. She looked plain and hardly had much in the way of hair, which he found odd, but she didn't look so fake or meek anymore.

"I'm not sure. I was, but now..." His mind was working slowly because the curse and dragon were warring over control of him. Inside he was screaming, "Yes, where is she?" but it wasn't coming out. He felt trapped inside and not in control of his body.

"If you don't know, Your Highness, the dragon is not fully quelled yet. I can feel the dark power in you already, though." Justine ran her hands seductively down her body as if the idea of dark magic were arousing. "Let me help you." She leaned into him, her body pressing into his.

Even with the curse taking over his body, he was still repulsed by her. She tried to kiss him, but he backed away.

"You will want me. The black magic in you will call out to the black magic in me. Give me your hands."

Alex handed them over, feeling heavy and weak inside. He wasn't fighting the dark, but as Justine understood, the dragon in him was still fighting, raging against suppression. He had to give in, give up the dragon's hold. It would be a sacrifice, one he might never come back from, but the sacrifice had to be made for Toury, for his family, and for his people. Toury—he hoped he still loved her when the curse took control. As for Justine, he really hoped the darkness in him didn't want her, not like how his fire wanted Toury's light. He cringed at the thought of Justine and him together.

Justine quickly drew her hand back and scowled as if something had burned her. She yanked up his sleeve to see the tourmaline amulet and made a face. "There's the problem, Your Highness."

She pulled a small dagger out a pocket hidden among the folds of her dress and slid it under the bracelet. She sliced it and let go. The beaded stones fell into the snow, scattering, and he felt the last bits of resistance in him fade away like dispersing smoke in the breeze. It pained him, and the dragon in him roared with sorrow, as if Toury and her light were slipping away forever.

Justine's hands latched back onto his, and she began to pour her power into him, which felt vastly different from Toury's light magic. He felt the icy power surge through his arms, up into his body, the pain excruciating, the fire and warmth of his body and soul dying out. When the ice hit his heart and mind, Alex was gone, his consciousness simply vanished, and something very dark and sinister replaced it.

39

BLACK MAGIC

Toury heard the crashing of steel, screams, battle cries, and the soft swishes of magic being thrown, quietly at first, but then it grew louder. The fact she could hear it in the cavern told her the battle must be right outside now. This was a good thing. She could be saved. She cried out for help, but the sounds merely echoed throughout, hurting her own ears. She stopped. Hearing the battle was more comfortable than screaming or the silence that had tortured her all day. It had been a long day of various, tedious attempts that didn't lead her any closer to freedom.

Earlier, Toury had been dragged by the machete-wielding brute into a cave, kicking and trying to scream through the gag. He dumped her onto the ice cold stone floor, and she thought her tailbone broke in the process. The cavern was shallow and small, so the guard retreated just out of sight into the mouth of the cavern. There were no tunnels to escape through, nothing that could be used as a weapon, the stone walls all smooth, loose stone almost non-existent, pebbles really. Light shone through a tiny fissure high above her, too small to fit through. It seemed hopeless.

The first thing she had done when left alone was ungag herself, which gave her some relief. At some point, her guard came in with a lantern and a loaf of bread and left it on the middle of the ground, which gave her enough light to see what was going on. She scarfed half the bread down and tried to ration the rest, but her growling stomach demanded more a couple hours later—she guessed—and she ate the rest. The guard checked on her frequently until her sad attempt to throw pebbles in his eyes, her bound hands throwing off her aim, landed her a slap across the face and the threat of cutting her toes off with his beloved machete. At least her attempt counted for something; he didn't check on her after that. She crept forward once to confirm he was still there, but he was accompanied by three other men, blocking her only escape by two men thick. That's when she realized, she'd have to wait for Alex. That was a terrible plan, but she couldn't figure a way out of this.

Frustrated with being idle and trapped, Toury looked for any way to improve her situation. If she could get free of her binds, she would have a fighting chance of escape. She spent the interval between her "meals" to check out the lantern. The fissure above told her it was night. It was an oil lamp, but there was hardly any oil in it. She'd rather not use it as a weapon if it meant she'd be unable to see her way out. The clamp atop was bolted shut too, so she couldn't get her ropes close enough to the flames. Still, she rested her hands over it to try to get some warmth.

The ropes had not frayed either during the half hour she rubbed them on the rocks, not that anywhere in this glacier-carved cavern was very sharp. Instead, her arms were rubbed raw. After shifts of rubbing till she bled and wasting energy to heal herself only to get some of the outer strands fraying, she gave up and slept for a little before starting afresh. She was also able to conjure light into her hands but could not direct it toward the binds on her wrists, and decided it best to save her magic's strength. Like her body's strength, all of her was waning, powers included. Then, when the battle came close enough to hear, she shouted for ages until her voice was raw. She needed an idea, and she was inwardly cursing Ruby for letting her down.

And just as she was cursing the girl, an image of fire burst forward in her mind. But fire magic didn't work here, and Toury couldn't conjure it anyway. As she attempted to untie the intricate knot on the rope around her ankles, she felt it. Her anklet. She concentrated her light magic into her palm and made a ball. She molded it, pressed it, and pulled some back inside until it was small but strong as her uncle had taught her, like kneading dough... Once she had it ready, she pushed it onto the anklet's clasp and let go. A small spark emitted, and a pop sizzled in the air. The anklet was open, and she had managed not to blow up her leg. She carefully weaved the anklet out to the rope and held in tight in her hand. She had a weapon and her light magic. Should she take on the guards? To what end? There was a literal battle outside, it was dark, and it was freezing. If she blasted the men with the anklet and escaped the cave, she could find one of the king's soldiers. They could help her, give her a weapon. With a saber and her light magic, she could defend herself, could help them defeat the necromancers.

Before she gained the conviction to follow through with her plan, Alex suddenly rushed into the cavern with another man and, oddly, Justine. Toury leaped up so quickly, so relieved to see him that she almost fell over. That's when she realized something was off. The man was tied up, his head bleeding, and Justine looked pleased. She took the torch she held and propped it against the wall, then possessively grabbed Alex's arm in hers. Alex didn't shirk her off as he normally would; he didn't seem to notice her touch at all.

"Stay here, Tobias," Alex commanded, shoving the man to the ground. "The necromancers aren't close enough to Celestia, and we are outnumbered here. You said the Sapphirian army couldn't reach here until at least dawn," Alex said to Justine, but his tone was angry and laced with worry as if his army winning was a bad thing. Toury thought he might be pretending for some purpose and waited for him to acknowledge her and give her a conspiratorial wink, but he didn't notice her. She was afraid to draw attention to herself due to his gruff behavior and the bitter expression on his face like he was smelling something offensive.

"You, when you weren't embracing your true power, must've sent them right away in haste. You weren't supposed to notice the wretched girl was gone until morning, but you must've tried to join her in bed that night, you naughty boy. And then somehow you figured out where we were almost right away. The only explanation is you sent other, closer armies. You are clever, Your Highness, but the darker you is smarter. Don't worry, my love, the dark you will trump the dragon's plans. Things are simply a day ahead of schedule," Justine crooned, touching his cheek.

Jealousy raged inside Toury. She wanted to attack Justine but needed to think this through. She couldn't leave Alex, who seemed almost possessed.

"I'm not worried about a bloody timetable, damn it! They are here instead of us meeting them in Aberdane. That means we have to battle our whole way there instead of surprising them closer to home."

"Stop worrying. I can reanimate all who fall, as long as their heads stay attached. Each city we conquer, we'll add the dead men to our ranks. Plus, my father will send reinforcements once all the sorcerers of the court who are against the Black Order are dead. And when the king succumbs, you will rule this sphere with power, darkness, and fear. And I will be your queen."

"Perhaps," he shook her hand off. "When the king falls, I will rule, and I will not be challenged by anyone. I may want a docile creature to be my lifemate, one stripped of magic and powerless," he mused.

Toury's blood ran cold at the lighthearted talk of his father's demise, and when his gaze finally found her, she whimpered. Where Alex's eyes should be were empty-looking black sockets. The evil she had seen in others' eyes had consumed his lovely blue eyes until there was nothing left but inky blackness.

"This one." Alex cocked his head sideways to examine her. The effect of his empty-looking eyes in the dim light of the cave was chilling, and she

214

cringed. "This one is beautiful." One, not even referred to as a person, as if her life didn't matter. Alex was a necromancer? No, no, she would've seen it in his eyes before now. Nothing made sense anymore. How? Why? Alex was stronger than Justine, the darkness, but the proof in front of her showed otherwise. She was stupid to think he could save her. She believed in him, thought he could conquer the darkness in himself, that fire consumes the shadows, but now...

"No!" Justine screeched, losing her cool. Her eyes were just as black as Alex's. "No! You cannot want her after all this. I've blackened you. I freed the curse for you and made you this powerful! You cannot pick her after all this!"

Alex grabbed Justine by the throat and picked her up. She struggled for air, and he growled at her, a feral-sounding growl that frightened Toury to her core. She slipped the anklet into her robe pocket and tried to build the light in her hands. Her nerves and fear were making it quite difficult.

Tobias, seeing that he was being ignored, crept closer to Toury. She shook her head at him, trying to motion for him to flee, to save himself, but of course, the kindhearted man would not leave her. Alex had said Tobias was a firebrander who knew how to break the curse. She wished Alex had given her particulars. She needed to talk to Tobias and get those particulars.

What do I do? She mouthed to the man.

He mouthed something in return, but she couldn't make sense of it and was distracted by the shouting.

"I am in charge! Is that clear?" Alex condescendingly thundered only inches from Justine's face.

She nodded. Then he threw her to the ground as she gasped for air.

"It's just," Justine panted for air. "She is light magic and will ruin you."

"No, we will destroy the magic in her and keep the vessel. It's far too beautiful to destroy." And if Alex's eyes had been their normal hue, he'd be leering. Toury wanted to vomit at the thought of what this version of Alex would do to her. Make her powerless, submit to him, be his slave of pleasure—she had to do something.

Justine gave Toury a look of fright, her eyes their gorgeous amber hue again, and then they rolled into her head. Justine lost consciousness—Toury hoped—because even if she hated Justine, she didn't want Alex to be a murderer, even in this state.

Then Alex noticed Tobias making motions at Toury. He was making a kissy face and nodding his head toward Alex.

"Old man, what do you think you're doing?" Alex ground out.

"I...I was simply going to comfort her. She's frightened," Tobias said.

"You will do more than that. You will consume her magic, firebrander."

"I can't. It would be too much for me to handle."

"And you will be remembered for your sacrifice." Alex's face screwed up into a sneering grin. The expression wasn't his.

"I won't do it."

"Well then, I'll have to get persuasive." Alex laughed haughtily. And then he kicked the man in the face. "I may not be able to make my own fire in this place, so it's a good thing they supplied some lighting."

Alex snatched the torch from the rocks it was propped against and, without hesitation, held the torch to Tobias's face until the man screamed in agony and then pulled it away. The process was repeated, and there didn't seem to be an end in sight.

Toury could not believe this was happening. The old man lay immobile on the ground, his clothes scorched, his skin puckering in third-degree burns, and Alex didn't seem as if he'd stop. The darkness was making Alex someone so completely different than the Alex she knew, the Alex who held her in bed, who kissed her and loved her and talked to her into the wee hours of the night. This monster wasn't him. This monster torturing Tobias, the man who was helping them, the man Alex said was the smartest man in existence, and with such reverence that she'd assumed they were great friends. Or had been. Toury fought with herself, knowing she must stop Alex somehow, save the poor man, but she was afraid to turn his attention onto herself. She didn't know how to conquer this Alex. She was afraid she'd do more than hurt Alex. If he was fully dark, would her ball of light kill him? Why hadn't she asked her uncle more questions?

Then it all clicked in her mind. Ruby making her say love was the strongest magic. Tobias making kissy faces. She must get through to Alex, use love and light to find him inside this dark beast. Kissing must be a magic channel. After all, it had unlocked Ruby's knowledge and pressed the curse back before.

Toury steeled herself with a deep breath while she reached into her pocket, grabbing the anklet. She threw it at Alex with all her might, knowing fire wouldn't harm him but hoping it might snap him out of this or, at least, distract him. And she got it. The blast threw her back into the wall so hard, the wind was knocked out of her, and she fell forward hard, scraping her hands on the rocks. Alex was on the ground on the other side of the cavern. Tobias lay where he had been before the blast, and Justine was now waking. Tobias grabbed Justine, despite his wounds, and she was fighting to get away. When she looked back at him, Alex was storming at her. Before she could scramble away, he lifted her up by her throat and pinned her against the wall. His face was contorted by dark magic, and she hardly recognized him.

"How dare you attack me?" he spat.

She desperately flung her bound hands at him and kicked her feet out. "I had to get your attention," she gasped as his fingers squeezed on her throat. "I know you're in there, Alex, please. It's Toury. You love me, and I love you..."

"Love?" The maniac in front of her laughed.

She refused to think it was him. Alex would never hurt her. It was the curse doing this, not him. All she could think about, as the black dots formed in the corners of her eyes, was how he'd cope, knowing he had killed her. That was, if the real Alex ever returned.

No, it could not end this way. She would not let it. The situation had been hopeless, but now she could do something. She did have to wait for Alex, but not for him to save her. She had to do the saving. Anger, hope, desperation roiled up inside her, and she let the light magic burst out of her. The ropes binding her arms and legs crumbled off her as if made of ash, and Alex let go of her, the blackness shrinking back into his pupils. He peered around with confused blue eyes. But as soon as Alex was back, he was gone again, eyes inky black. That one second her light blast had withheld the curse gave her enough time to wind her arms around his waist, placing her arms around him to channel all her healing light magic into him. She stared up into his eyes and saw the battle within raging, the curse and Alex's goodness, his fire, fighting. His pupils alternated, dilating and shrinking, and his face struggled through an array of expressions.

"C'mon, Alex," she whispered, pressing up against him. "Fight it. Fight the dark; join my light."

Ignoring the crushing grip he had on her, as if he wanted to hug her and crush her to death simultaneously, she tried to kiss him, but he turned his head away, still fighting. She grabbed his wrist to place his hand on her cheek, a move he always performed when he kissed her. Alex went rigid in her arms but looked at her with one confused blue iris, the other eye a bitter black. She leaned in and pressed her lips against his, her thoughts purely about her love for him and her need for him to return it. She thought about when they had first met, kissed, slept in each other's arms, when he had admitted he did truly want to marry her, every happy moment they had had together.

Alex's head whipped back as if he were ripped away from her by some invisible being behind him. Having no more tricks up her sleeve, she rested her head on the crook of his neck, continuously saying she loved him, holding him close in her arms so every inch of them touched. She was feeling her light magic dwindle as her stock of energy began to run low. Even though his body suddenly lost some of its rigidity, she feared she wasn't powerful enough. If only she knew what else she needed to do to break this curse.

Alex pried her off himself, roughly shoving her shoulders back, but she clung tight, not letting him go. His hands moved to cradle her face, but his grip was still bitingly firm. She kept her eyes tightly shut and head down, not wanting her last sight of him, before she died, to be the monster. She would die with those memories of prior happiness flittering through her mind.

40

A MELD

As if awoken by someone dousing him with a bucket of ice water, Alex suddenly and painfully became aware of his surroundings: a freezing cold cavern, darkness, and Toury in his arms crying "I love you" over and over again, her light magic pouring into him. He tried to get her to loosen her crushing grip, but she was rigid. He forced her away a bit roughly, feeling the dark curse lash out, but he pushed it back, and it receded easily with Toury's healing light. A bit more gently, he tilted her chin up, and she finally opened her eyes a crack to look at him. Her cheeks were smudged with tears and dirt, and her hair was everywhere, but she was beauty itself. His heart swelled at the sight of her, and he felt the curse lashing out against her attack. He pushed it back again with all his might and kissed Toury, gently at first. Then he devoured her mouth, unable to get enough of her. She kissed him back with equal vigor.

That's when he sensed something profound happening. The light magic met the fire magic, and he and Toury melded into one burning and powerful energy. The two strongest forces of the land were together inside him—inside her—he wasn't sure. As he was lost in her lips, it was unclear where he ended and she began. They were one.

The white fire burned through him until the blackness was gone and not back into the place it had hidden all his life. He could see it, sense it wither and burn into nothingness. Then it was gone. He felt lighter and freer than he had ever felt before. He felt completely different, as if he were a new person, extraordinarily powerful, happier, and then the magic ended when Toury pushed him away.

She almost fell, but he caught her, and the way she fought to get away made him realize he must've not been himself, although he couldn't remember anything after he had started talking to Justine. Toury was terrified and fighting for her life.

"It's me," he pleaded with her. "Look at me. It's me. It's gone. I don't know what just happened, but you did it. I don't feel the curse there anymore. You did it. You broke the curse." He tried to kiss her, but she pushed away and fell to the ground sobbing. He crouched down, afraid to touch her and scare her more. "Toury," he begged.

She finally looked at him with frightened eyes. "Let me see your eyes," she said, her voice hoarse.

He lit up a fireball in his palm, a weak one due to the lack of power up north, but it was enough for her to see his eyes. She seemed to relax at the sight of them and then lay back on the ground, exhausted but smiling. That's when he saw the red marks on her neck. He studied them and, in that moment, realized they were fingerprints, his fingerprints, as if he had choked her, and he felt sick.

"Oh, Toury, what did I do?" His voice cracked.

From the ground, she looked over at him, "It wasn't you, not really." It didn't make him feel any better.

"I'm sorry," he said, even though the words would never be enough to assuage his guilt. "I had to let the dark overtake me. Tobias said the only way to destroy the curse was to coax it out in the open." He did not finish, for he knew she probably would know the rest. "I should have never put you in such danger. I'll never expect you to forgive me, but I am sorry." The apology felt empty.

"It wasn't you," she whispered again softly as her eyes closed shut, and her quickened pants fell back down to even breaths. He scooped her up into his arms and carried her toward the entrance, where he saw Tobias on the ground, looking close to death's door, and a motionless Justine. He hoped there was enough fire energy up north for him to conjure to make it back with both of them, but it was so hard to use his magic in this icy cold place. He touched Tobias's leg with his foot and let his fire magic flare up, imagining himself in his quarters at the palace.

He opened his eyes to see himself in a field on the outskirts of a battle. His soldiers and the undead clashing swords. He had to let them continue fighting to stop the corpse army from reaching the castle gates. He could see his uncle's keep in the skyline of Ludford. Making it this far in one transport from the northernmost point meant his magic must be much more powerful without the curse. Alex closed his eyes again and thought of his bedroom, knowing he was south enough now to clutch onto some fire magic.

He opened his eyes to see astonished servants running about. He hadn't made it far enough, but at least he made it to the great foyer of the palace. Someone took Tobias from him, but when they tried to take Toury, Alex fought them off. Then he saw his mother's face and then Mary's, and came back to himself. "Take Toury to our quarters."

"The guest quarters are closest," his mother commanded.

"No!" he boomed at her, and everyone stopped. "Transport Toury to my quarters, Mary. We can't trust anyone right now."

Mary examined him for a moment and must've decided he was himself and did as instructed. With Toury taken care of, he scanned the room, seeing a few of his father's advisors in the hall, watching. His mother gave him a sympathetic but relieved look and touched his shoulder. He shook her off, not wanting to appear weak. He looked around at the advisors and noted Lord Citrine was there.

"Prince Sapphirian, we have kept the magicians at bay and believe we have won this round," Lord Citrine had the audacity to say. He was sweating profusely, and his hands were shaking. Alex knew right then and there the man had expected a different and compliant prince to return.

"Where are the Cobalts!" Alex demanded, glaring at the man.

"They were resisting authority! Lord Cobalt was trying to say he was in charge," another lord said, his face self-satisfied and eyes glaring.

"He was named temporary Lord of the Castle by myself and Princess Mary," Alex said, using his diaphragm to sound stronger than he felt. "The Magicians' Guild was asked to protect the castle! They weren't attacking. Use your heads, for god and goddess's sake! Who convinced you they were attacking?"

Alex grabbed Lord Diamond's doublet in his rage and pulled the man closer. The man's eyes widen in surprise. "You are the Head General. Unless you want to burn at the stake for disobeying my orders—no, let me just do it for fun right here, make an example out—"

"Lord Citrine said he had overriding orders from the king. The queen and princess protested, but Lord Citrine presented you—Your Highness, forgive me—as a reckless, lovesick fool, running after the magicians who kidnapped your princess-to-be." The normally stoic man was terrified, and Alex realized for the first time the power he had outside the shadow of his father. He let the man go.

"Guards, seize Lord Citrine and throw him in the dungeons. Seal the doors. Enclose all the sorcerers in the ballroom," Alex commanded.

There was a murmur of discord among them and protests, but the guards, all magician born, readily complied.

"The sorcerers? We were defending the castle!" Lord Crystal protested.

"No, you're fighting the very people trying to protect my family. The traitors among us know this, and the rest of you were unknowingly partaking in a coup attempt. No one goes anywhere until we weed out who is part of this Black Order of necromancers. If you're innocent, you have nothing to fear. If you're guilty, you will feel the wrath of the *draca*," Alex spat at them.

Having never shown power, never given them a cross word before, they were stunned into silence. His reference to the ancient name of his race, the draca or "dragons," made some of the men tremble. That had been his intention.

"You heard the king proxy," his mother shouted. The title disconcerted him, but it meant his father was still hanging on although unable to rule. "There are traitors among us. Time to get to the bottom of this."

"Bring me the Cobalts!" Alex shouted.

Out of the throng of the nobility being pushed back into the ballroom by the foot soldiers, Cobalt came forward, his eyes full of worry, his hands bound together, and one eye bruised and swollen. His friend had put up a good fight, it seemed. As did his father and older brother, from the looks of them. Cobalt approached Alex hesitantly.

"Outside of my family, you're all I can trust. You did well, friends, but I have to see to Toury and my father. Let the magicians in. We'll need the added protection." He used his fire magic to burn away the binds around each of their wrists. "And, Cobalt." Alex took him aside. The other two Cobalts were helping push the angry lords back. "I need you to lead the investigation to see which lords are necromancers. Get Toury's power tutor, the Hematite lightbearer. Send someone for Lady Edwina Hematite. I fear for her safety, and we need her. They both should be able to seek out the evil in the necromancers' eyes when they're emotional and get you the guilty parties. Mother, get Cobalt the list Toury made." Then he said to Cobalt quietly, "Have your father immediately round up all Citrines and imprison them. I have a desire to wipe their name out of the sphere for good, but hopefully, he will be more lenient than I. Also have him imprison any man in that room who vehemently defied my orders. The rest can wait in the comfort of the ballroom until the lightbearer clears or condemns them."

"I will do my best, Your Highness, and with pleasure." Cobalt formally bowed. Alex knew his friend would do his duty well. Alex just sent him from paperwork pusher to a head inquisitor at the snap of his fingers.

"Lord Stephen Cobalt is the temporary Lord of the Castle. Anyone who challenges that will burn!" Alex shouted. This made some of the men fighting to get away calm down and give up.

Cobalt gave him a huge grin. At the moment, Cobalt was like a king; even his father had to listen to his commands. Then Cobalt grabbed his father and brother and began imparting duties.

"Go to her, Alex," his mother said. "I will send the healers. Your father is stable and resting."

He didn't have to be told twice. He transported into Toury's room, scaring the maids and Madge, who tried to shoo him out since Toury wasn't dressed under the sheets, but he refused and took his place in a chair by her bedside, holding her hand. The healers came and put stones and crystals all over her, and yet he remained. They tried to place stones on him, but he refused. Then David entered, fussing over him, and he let David clean his cuts just to shut the valet up.

The entire time Alex sat there, all he could do was stare at the blotches around Toury's neck as they turned from red to purple to black tinged with yellow, hating himself and wondering how much she would loathe him when she woke up. He knew the right thing to do would be to let her go, but he wasn't quite sure he could do that. He longed for her to wake but dreaded it at the same time.

41

GILDED CAGE

Toury woke up feeling stiff all over, and her throat was killing her. She swallowed, and a tight band of pain followed the motion. Her hand went up to her throat, and she heard a ragged sigh next to her. She opened her eyes to see Alex sitting next to the bed, his elbows resting on the edge, his one hand tangled in hers. The sweat between their palms, his disheveled hair, and his stubble-covered face told her he had been there for a while. She met his gaze and saw his gorgeous azure eyes shining back. It was over. She smiled a little and stared into those eyes. Instead of joy in them, she saw sadness, pain, and guilt.

"Alex," she tried to speak, but it felt like someone had crushed her voice box. Then she remembered it all and why Alex was racked with guilt. She withdrew her hand from his on instinct, fear and panic welling up inside her. Pain flashed in his eyes. He had done this to her, and without asking, she could see his eyes follow what must have been the trail of ugly bruises around her neck. Something hurt more than the physical pain of what he inflicted. She had trusted him, had faith in him and what she thought was love. It was all a mistake. She never should've trusted him, relied on him, believed in him. He was weaker than she had presumed. The hurt gave way to disappointment as she processed the night's events.

"Water," she managed. She heard Madge bustle about.

"David," Alex said, still looking at her neck. "Tell my mother and the healers that Toury is awake."

Despite her disappointment in him, her feelings were still there, tearing her apart. She wanted to tell him she still loved him. She wanted to tell him that she knew it wasn't he who had hurt her, but the curse. Toury wanted him to climb into the bed, hold her, and tell her it was all over, that they could lie about in the mornings and pick dragon eggs and not worry about anything dark or evil ever again. She wanted to tell him she loved him no matter what and to hear that he loved her, even now after he didn't need her as a curse breaker. But she couldn't speak the words because to say these things would be lying. When she looked at him, she saw the prince she had fallen in love with, but she also saw the monster who tried to kill her. Her mind grappled over how to come to terms with that.

"Tobias?" she rasped.

"Alive and healing," Alex said quietly, staring at the floor as if it were the most interesting thing in all the world.

"Justine?"

His eyes shot up to Toury's. "You actually care?" He was thunderstruck. "After all Justine did?"

"No," Toury said and laughed, which turned into a painful cough. She drank more water. "I want justice."

"Well, you got it. Tobias tried to destroy the dark magic in her, but she fought it, and when he ripped the darkness out of her, she died. There was no light, energy, or fire magic left in her to sustain her life. She was completely dark," Alex finished.

"That's justice." She frowned. She'd rather see the girl rot in jail and rub it in. Maybe force her to watch Toury's wedding to Alex, but the girl was gone, and Toury couldn't feel bad about it. "I'm just glad you didn't have to do it."

Alex scoffed at this. "I did enough damage, don't you think?"

"Alex," she began.

"No, I don't want you to try to downplay what I've done to you and Tobias or make excuses for me. That would be too much for me to bear. Toury, I went dark on purpose. I let Justine release the curse. Tobias said it was the only way to kill it. It had to be fully in control for you to destroy it. I chose to break the curse once and for all, to save myself so I could rule my people. I did this, knowing I might hurt you. I did this, knowing if it all went wrong, I might kill you and stay that monster forever. It was a chance I took that I shouldn't have."

Toury wanted to protest but let him finish. The way he described his actions, he saw them as selfish, and she had to admit they were. But without doing what he had done, without taking that gamble, the curse would always have been a wedge between them. She should have been mad at him for his willingness to sacrifice her life for his people, but she couldn't find the rage inside her. She felt empty, and she still loved him despite everything. She still needed him and wanted him, and she was annoyed with herself for that. Alex deserved her rage; he expected it and wanted it, but she could not deliver.

His eyes met hers, and it was as if he understood what she was thinking, although she couldn't utter the words. He looked down at her hand and snatched it up in his. "I release you from this engagement. You no longer have to be bound to me." Then he kissed her hand with shaking lips and fled the room before she had time to react. Hearing him say those words shattered her heart into a million pieces.

The healers came in with the queen, and they put all sorts of crystals on her body to measure things, heal things, and such. She really wanted to be alone to wallow over her broken heart, first betrayed and then forsaken. After all, Alex had technically just broken up with her.

As if the queen sensed something amiss, she visited every day, and on the third day, she forced Toury out of bed and into the bathing quarters. The bath refreshed her, the purple bruises were fading to yellow, and Queen Sapphirian gave her a beautiful scarf to hide them from gossipy servants as they walked in the gardens. The fresh air fortified her and made her feel strong again—emotionally—that is. The physical and magical power had returned to her that first day. In fact, she felt more powerful than ever.

They ran into Cobalt and Tobias walking the gardens, the latter with a small limp and some bandages on his face and arms covering his burns. Toury hurried to the man and took up his hand, squeezing it affectionately. They made pleasantries, but she was so happy to see he was well. The queen and Cobalt walked off in their own private conversation, leaving her with Tobias.

"How are you so healed?" she asked.

"Droughts and healing stones do wonders."

She gave him a critical look, not buying into that excuse. They had done the same to her, and the bruises were barely healed.

The man sighed reluctantly. "I'm a firebrander. Most of us are distantly related somehow to the Sapphirians. They cannot burn, so although diluted in my blood, the ability is still there, a little. I burn as you have seen, but I heal quickly from them." The man motioned for her to lead the way. "More importantly, how are you feeling?"

"Different. Powerful."

"I've wanted an audience with you to explain—"

"You don't have to. Alex explained how the curse had to be broken."

"Did he?" Tobias asked, confused. "Then why do you both mope around as if you have broken hearts?"

"What do you mean?" She didn't think to deny it, nor did she want to talk about her personal life with a man who, by outside standards, was a stranger, despite the series of events they had gone through together.

"I don't think the prince told you everything about that curse, but it isn't my place to explain that part of it. Talk to him."

"Tobias, tell me!" She said, exasperated.

"Queen Proxy-to-Be, please don't put me in a place that could get me in trouble. I cannot betray His Majesty's confidence. I slipped because you said you knew everything. Please." Tobias was afraid, and yet again, Toury realized the power the prince had over lives, a power she was beginning to wield. It was a frightening power, indeed. And the title made her drop the issue. Queen Proxy would mean the king was dying, and Alex was acting as king. Second, it meant Alex hadn't told anyone they weren't engaged anymore.

"You feel powerful for a reason." Tobias treaded back into safer waters of conversation. "The merging of your powers fully unlocked Ruby's power and knowledge. You should have full access to it all. If we work at it, you may even be able to dabble a little into Sapphirian powers. There's no telling how much Ruby imparted into that stone and into you."

Toury inwardly cringed at the thought that someone was inside her in spirit and memory. She did feel different and wanted to feel like just Toury again. The idea of someone inside her, controlling her, brought back images of the evil Alex.

"I want to be myself. I want to find myself," Toury mumbled. She left the last part silent—that she needed to get out of here and away from court to do that.

"With all due respect, Queen Proxy-to-Be, you are the savior, the only one aside from two relatives who can wipe out black magic, and they cannot do half of what you can. The necromancers' numbers have dwindled, and they have scattered, their undead armies destroyed, but they are still out there. They need to be found, the black magic stripped from them, curses broken. If you are one of only three who can do that—and they know that now since you saved the king proxy—you will be targeted—"

"My aunt!"

"His Highness has invited her back to court. She arrives tomorrow, I believe, but he sent a retinue to protect her as soon as he got back. Queen Proxy-to-Be, the world needs you, and they need you here, safe in the palace. You are the savior. There's no hiding or running from yourself."

Toury felt the prison closing in on her again. She was in her gilded cage, trapped with Alex, who wanted to be free of her, in a role she had only accepted to be with him. She could see the future spread out in front of her as a dream come true for most girls, but instead, it felt hollow. Her entire life, she would have to act a part and say goodbye to the real Toury inside.

42

AN ARGUMENT

Alex was busy, partly because he wanted to be, and partly because he had a kingdom to tend. His father, with the curse, his ailing health, and the stress from the battle between the guilds, was unable to rule and bedridden. As soon as Alex saw him, his father officially crowned Alex king proxy. The kingdom was Alex's now, but he wasn't at all happy about it. Although his father's health made him sad, he couldn't pretend the real problem wasn't the princess-to-be. Only she was the queen-to-be now, or was she just Lady Toury Hematite? He had released her, but she never said whether she wanted to be released or not.

He managed to avoid Toury, only returning to their quarters to bathe and sleep in his own room. There was so much to do, so much he was suddenly responsible for. His father had never let him have control, and now, he was asked to command everything. In the mornings, there were the courtier trials and hearing of grievances; in the afternoons, he had to negotiate peace meetings between the Magicians' Guild and what remained of the Sorcerers' Guild, then review legislature. Evenings consisted of him communicating with the head general about war tactics on hunting down the scattered necromancers, redistributing resources to ease the drought and famine in the east, and reports of other minor problems that needed future attention. Unfortunately, some of this consisted of him learning there was a lot of unrest in the kingdom his father had hidden from him. The people were unhappy.

He'd be a liar if he said his responsibilities were the only things keeping him from Toury. He couldn't handle the guilt when he saw her. She was a frailer, quieter version of herself. A damaged shell of who she had once been. And he had done that to her. Worse, he had chosen to do that to her. It was too much guilt to bear, and yet on top of the guilt was her fear of him. Outwardly, she acted distant but pleasant. At times, however, he saw flickers of fear in her eyes when she met his gaze. He imagined she saw the black-eyed monster in those moments. He also pretended to be ignorant of the fact she woke up screaming each night from nightmares, but every time, her pain sliced through him as if it were a real knife. She didn't talk to him about them, and he didn't ask. He was too afraid to hear what she saw. He, thankfully, had no memories of what he had done. Knowing was hard enough. He hated himself more than she could imagine.

On the fifth night after Toury awoke, he returned to their quarters, exhausted and mentally drained. This night, the sitting room was not empty, and there was no backpedaling out of the room without looking like a coward.

"Where have you been?" Toury asked as soon as Alex entered the room. She seemed angry, which he would take over her melancholy any day, but he was weary.

"Nice to see you too," he muttered. He flopped down into the chair and started undoing the restraining clothing around his neck and wrists. He tossed the even heavier King Medallion onto the sofa. He felt as if he were suffocating under the pressure of it all, including the last few days of drama. He needed Toury to be his rock, his partner, to help him right now, but since they had gotten back, things were...strange. He didn't know how to right things between them. He wanted her, craved her so badly, but he thought after what he had done, how he had hurt her, what she must think of him now—he was sure she couldn't possibly love him.

"Alex, what's going on?" Toury asked. Her lips pressed in a bitter and angry frown, but her eyes were so sad. He felt sick to his stomach. It was his fault for making her feel this way.

"I'm sorry. I know it looks like I've been avoiding you, but there's so much going on, so much to do." He wished that she didn't hate him, that he didn't feel guilty. He wished he could take it all back, undo that last week's events and make her his queen right now. Then he could share everything with her, including these stately burdens.

"And you couldn't send a message?"

"I guess it slipped my mind."

"Ever since I cured you, everything to do with me seems to slip your mind. It's like I don't even exist!" she accused.

He looked up at her, astounded. Why would she ever think he'd forget her? "I never stop thinking about you, Toury!" he said, sounding as he felt. Tortured.

Her face melted briefly into softness, but her eyes went hard again. "You have a terrible way of showing it."

He grabbed her hand and pulled her closer in front of him. He buried his face in the stomach of her soft, warm robe. Her arms wrapped around his head, and she held him. It made every stress, every fear, fade away. He no longer needed the light energy to burn away the dark, but he needed her.

What passed between them now wasn't healing light, but a pleasant warming energy, fire being flamed by light.

"What's wrong?" she asked softly.

He pulled her into his lap and swept her hair off her shoulder. She was beauty itself, but he couldn't peer into those gray eyes. He placed his fingers gently on her fading bruises to show one of the many things wrong. She smacked his hands away. It was a silent exchange, but she was telling him to stop beating himself up about it. He didn't want to stop, though. He was sickened every time he saw how he had hurt her, and he knew she was just as hurt mentally as she was physically.

"I meant other than that," she prodded after he didn't answer.

"My father is not doing well. He has named me King Proxy."

"I know. I found out when Tobias called me Queen Proxy-to-Be. Congratulations," she said, pushing up out of his arms. She turned her back on him. He reached for her, but then pulled his hand back. How could she say something so hurtful?

"I'm not happy about this Toury! I'm not ready. I don't want this. I want my father to live, to be healthy. I want to go shopping in the city, eat dragon egg fruit in the orchard, and lie about in bed all night talking to you, not listening to grievances, overseeing the trials, and planning military missions."

"You were bred for this. You'll be fine. You don't need me or anyone else. What is next Alex? What of our agreement?" She was acting bitter, but her voice wavered.

He watched her in the fading firelight. "I am a man of my word, and I already told you, I free you from this engagement if that is what you want."

"Is that what you want? No one knows you broke it off." She spun around, glaring at him, her hands on her hips.

Broke it off? She had wanted freedom, and now he was giving her a choice. "Oh, no," he threw his hand up flippantly. "This is your decision, and yours alone."

"Mine alone? It would greatly affect both of our lives, no matter which choice is made."

"I trapped you before. I won't do it again. I didn't 'break it off' as you put it, which is why I didn't go around announcing to all of Fyr that we aren't engaged. I'm allowing you an out if that is what you want," he insisted. He desperately wanted her to say that she still loved him, that she wanted to stay. They loved each other. The curse couldn't have been broken if that weren't the case, but he needed this to be her decision. He needed to know if she still felt that way despite seeing the darkness in him, despite how he had hurt her.

"What has changed between us?" she asked.

He got up. "Nothing. Everything. I don't know. Toury, I care about you—you know I do—but I don't want you to feel trapped. Don't lie. I know you do."

"You care about me?" she asked. "Or did you conveniently care about me to save yourself?"

"What does that mean? It doesn't even make sense!"

"Don't shout at me! And you're right. This has been one giant gilded cage from the start! Why did you have to trick me, force me into this? Because on my own, I probably would have gotten engaged to you and loved you and married you. But I was forced."

"But you aren't being forced now! That's my point. You need to decide what you want." He took a deep breath to call his boiling emotions. "I hear you every night, Toury. The nightmares. And what I've done to you haunts me, but it haunts you more. Do you still..." he was so afraid to ask, but it had to be done. "Do you still care for me at all? I know I don't deserve you, but all the same, we cannot be engaged if your feelings have changed."

"I still care about you, Alex, of course I do. But every time I look at you..." She didn't need to finish the thought. She saw him as a monster.

"That wasn't me," he said weakly, for he knew it was futile.

"But I can't forget it, Alex! How? How can I forget that?" She was lashing out with well-earned fury.

"You forgive. You forget. You try to move on!" He was losing his cool, not in anger, but in desperation for her to be wrong, even though he knew she was right. He was watching her slip away from him, and he could do nothing about it.

"I don't want to argue," she pleaded.

"Neither do I."

"Good. I'm done."

"Yeah, me too. Maybe we should get some sleep. We can finish this discussion tomorrow. You don't have to decide now."

"No, Alex, I mean I'm leaving. In the morning, I'll talk to my aunt about going back to her estate. Don't worry. She and I will accept your protection. I know I'll never be safe, no matter where I live. Alex, I just can't think here. I don't know. I want to feel free. I want to see if I'll miss you. I want to figure out who I want to be, what I want to do. I want to forget, move on. I can't do that as...queen proxy to-be."

His heart squeezed in his chest, and he couldn't breathe. His head spun. He didn't want her to leave. He needed her, but he couldn't say that and force her hand again. He tried to form a coherent thought, say something convincing without sounding forceful. "You can do anything you want to do in this sphere, be anyone you want to be, whether you are Toury Sapphirian or Toury Hematite. Under either name, I will give you the world, and you can do with it as you please."

Then, to cheat the situation and fearing it might be the last time he could do so, he kissed her and kissed her soundly, making her moan into his mouth. Then he parted from her and fled to his room, hoping his ardor would cool and his heart would not burst from want of her.

Neither occurred, nor did sleep.

43
LIFEMATE

Toury packed the last of her things, mostly gifts from Alex. She left a lot of the dresses that were fit for royalty since she would not need them anymore, but she couldn't give back the gifts Alex had given her without offending him. All these things would haunt her, and Alex's presence would still dominate a life away from him. Her heart was heavy, her head pounding, and her stomach sour. She didn't know what to do except that she had already made the motion to leave, so she had to see it through. Part of her wanted to leave, truly leave by going back to Earth, and never come back, and part of her wanted Alex to chase her across Fyr to win her back. Somehow, she felt as if she were on the losing end. The king proxy would never have to beg any woman to be his. She would lose him, but surely, not losing herself was more important.

Alex suddenly appeared via a ball of flames in her bedroom, making her jump.

"You're actually leaving?" His mouth was drawn in a bitter frown, his face flushed with anger and eyes drowning in agony.

"I said I was last night. I am a woman of my word," she mocked him. She had no idea where the bitterness came from, but she was defensive. She needed to push him away to make leaving easier.

"I thought...I thought you'd second guess it, give me a chance to convince you to stay, mull it over, not leave right away. Don't go like this. Stay, stay one more day, and let us go into the city, visit the orchards, lie in each other's arms." The anger faded, and his face looked youthful and vulnerable. "Whatever you want, we'll do."

It was the first time she looked into his eyes without seeing a flash of the black-eyed monster. She was cracking under his candid weakness for her, and she needed to stay firm on this decision. He had hurt her again and again, and she could not go through it anymore, especially since she was more than willing to forgive him and allow it to happen again. She hated love when it made her so weak. "It's not that simple."

"It is!" he shouted in exasperation. "If not as my engagee, then at least, stay as my advisor. There is dark magic still in court. You're needed. I can order you to stay if I have to!"

"What about you wanting to give me a choice? Now you go and take that away because it's not the choice you prefer?" She put her hands on her hips, exuding the anger she felt, but she also was quivering inside, wanting to break down crying. She was losing herself, bit by bit, like sand slipping down an hourglass.

"Prefer? No, it's more than that. You need to stay. I need you here, and you need to be here, even if you don't want to be with me. This is where you belong."

She hesitated, torn, but it just wasn't enough. Alex was groveling, but he wasn't explaining why. He simply wanted her around for his kingdom. It was his engagement of convenience all over again. "Why should I stay here, Alex? Why? Don't feed me any more nonsense about necromancers. I can help you with that out there as well."

He looked as if he were about to say something but, instead, closed the gap between them, pulled her in by the waist, and kissed her hard on the mouth. She placed her hands on his shoulders, wanting to push him away but rendered senseless when his tongue entered her mouth. They kissed madly for a moment, his hand winding through her hair, his body pressing against every inch of hers. Every part of her body was aware of his. Oh, how could she give this up? Finally, she broke away from him.

"That is sort of an answer but...I'm confused." After those kisses, she hardly could make sense. He wanted her, and her body responded to him, but lust was not a basis for a future. She loved him, and she said so to save him, but it was clear he didn't feel the same. Why else wouldn't he say it?

"I need you. I need you, Toury. Please, stay," he asked softly. He leaned his forehead against hers.

"In what capacity?"

He didn't hesitate to say, "Queen Proxy-to-Be."

"That's not exactly an answer," she told him. "That puts us where we just were."

He sighed, looked away, and loosened his hold on her but kept her wrapped in his arms. Then his gaze shot up to meet hers.

"Toury, when you asked me what Tobias had said about breaking the curse—you know, back when we said the engagement was real—I couldn't tell you. I deflected because it had to happen on its own. The curse could only be broken by powerful white magic meeting powerful fire magic, which you obviously know, but there was more to it. Putting your life on the line to save my people and me was the hardest decision I ever had to make. It is the only decision in my life so far that I regret. I never want to hurt you again."

"You did it because you had faith that I could break the curse, that I would save you," Toury mused quietly. "You did it to save your people." They would always come first, as they should, but she selfishly wanted to matter more. She wanted to be the most important thing in Alex's life.

"Yes, that was only part of the solution to the curse, though. Our magic couldn't fuse on its own, and it wouldn't be strong enough to defeat such a curse. It could only be banished by..."

"Love," Toury finished for him. "I know. I think Ruby helped me realize that love could defeat the darkness."

He stood rigid and stared at her, his mouth agog and eyes crinkled in bewilderment. His hands fell off of her in shock, and he took a step back. "Then why in the name of the god and goddess are you leaving?" He ran his hands through his hair in agitation.

"Because..." Toury began, hesitating as she searched for the right words. How does one explain the fact that they aren't loved back by the person they are mad for?

His gaze penetratingly searched hers for answers.

"Because I don't think we feel the same about each other."

Alex's shoulders sank. He looked down as if ashamed. "I understand if your feelings have changed. I cannot blame you."

"No!" Toury shouted.

His stare shot up to meet hers in shock.

"God, will you make me say it?"

"Toury, you must. I'm utterly lost."

She growled and then looked away from him. "You know I love you, but you don't love me, okay? You feel like you have to go through with this to make amends for using me to stop the curse, for trying to kill me, or you're just too damn honorable to go back on your word. I dunno why!" Admitting her innermost thoughts and fears to him broke the dam holding in her emotions. Tears sprang to her eyes, her throat went tight, and she could hardly breathe.

Toury was staring at the fire through blinding tears, so she was taken aback when his warm hands turned her face toward his. "Are you that daft, my silly little queen," he chided in a soft whisper. He drew her face to his and kissed her softly. Then he pulled back, wiping away her tears with the pads of his thumbs. "The love that sparked *between* us is what destroyed the curse, not just your love for me. It worked, so you know what that means, don't you? You love me, and I love you. There's no way the curse would have been lifted if that weren't true."

Toury looked into his azure eyes and saw the truth in them. He loved her, and the thought of her leaving was tearing him apart. He must have hidden it to try to give her a choice, but in the end, he loved her too much to let her go.

"But you never said it."

"It didn't mean I didn't feel it."

"But why didn't you tell me?"

"Because you refused me twice, remember? Then you told me you could only marry me for love, even though I already loved you. Thrice you broke this heart in my chest. And when I found out the curse could only be broken if you loved me back, how could I simply just tell you?" He wrapped her up in his warm, strong arms. "But I said it many times in my own way. You were just too modest, just too hurt by others, by myself, to see it, to accept it. My darling, those earthlings have wounded you through their neglect, but if you allow me to, I will show you for the rest of our lives what love truly is. I love you, Toury. And you still love me?"

"I do," she said. "But I don't know, Alex. What if I cannot forget what happened?"

"We will make new, happier memories to banish the dark."

"It will be a wedge between us."

"But time can pull us together. Just give it a chance, Toury. Stay," he pleaded, "as my lifemate, my queen, as my everything."

"What if it takes a lifetime?"

"I hope it does." He reiterated what he had said her very first night in the castle. He had been trying to tell her then he loved her, but she refused to see it. "Marry me? I cannot imagine anyone else by my side but you."

She nodded, unable to speak or see through her tears. But she could feel. She could feel the smiling kiss he gave her and the warmth of fiery happiness he exuded. He had told her what she needed to hear. He needed her and loved her as much as she did him. They could conquer this, just as they conquered the necromancers and the curse. Figuring out her calling and purpose in life could happen without him, but it still could happen with him. She realized that it all had to happen this way for her to come to this profound realization: he was part of her now but did not, nor would he try to, define her. Queen Sapphirian could simply be one of the many roles she'd live in her life. Alex said he'd give her the world, and she meant to take it and set it ablaze.

ACKNOWLEDGMENTS

They say it takes a village to raise a child. Well, the same goes for a novel.

First, I'd like to thank my husband, without whom, this book would not be possible, especially the cover. Credit must be given to my son for being that wild, intelligent boy with such a zeal for life, who gives me the drive to succeed. I'd like to acknowledge my parents and brother for fostering my imagination through watching and making movies, creating bedtime stories, and urging us to devour books. Thank you Uncle Chuck and Grandmom for all the support.

I deeply appreciate the teachers, professors, and all my friends who inspired my love of reading and writing throughout life—shout out to the lifeguards at Hatboro Memorial Pool and fellow Card Club geeks for acting out my first manuscripts. Thank you to my best friend crew, who are more like family than friends. This book also wouldn't be possible without Ms. Kate, who is the best beta and first editor an author could ask for. Thanks Tiff for all the amazing photos. I'm indebted to my colleagues who are so invested and proud of my work, especially Ray for all his help with Old English.

A big thanks must be given to readers, fellow authors, and my students who inspire me to keep creating. Most importantly, thank you, Authors 4 Authors Publishing, for taking a chance on *Fyr* and being so enthusiastic, personable, and detail-oriented to not only make the experience a pleasure, but to also bring forth the best book it possibly could be.

ABOUT THE AUTHOR

Lisa Borne Graves is a YA author, English Lecturer, wife, and supermom of one wild child. Originally from the Philadelphia area, she relocated to the Deep South and found her true place of inspiration. Her love for all literature led her to branch out from the academic arena to spin her own tales. Lisa has a voracious appetite for books, British television, and pizza. Her inability to sit still makes her enjoy life to its fullest, and she can be found at the beach, pool, or on some crazy adventure.

Follow her online:

lisabornegraves.com
Twitter: @lisabornegraves
Facebook: @lisabornegravesauthor
Instagram: @lisabornegraves

ALSO BY LISA BORNE GRAVES

THE IMMORTAL TRANSCRIPTS I

QUIVER

What would you do if you could live forever? Could you hide it from the one you truly loved, especially if her life depended on it?

Thanks to his dysfunctional Olympian family, Archer Ambrose finds out firsthand how difficult this can be. He never falls in love but bestows it on others—until he meets Callie.

When Callie Syches moves to the Upper East Side to prepare for her father's impending death, she doesn't expect to meet the boy of her dreams. She also never believed her father's harebrained theory about myths, but her uncanny ability to "see" uncovers godly secrets Callie can hardly fathom.

With an immortal family demanding absolute obedience, how far will Archer go to protect his love from the storm the gods will unleash upon them?

In this reinvention of Cupid and Psyche, experience an electrifying series where familial and romantic bonds are at war, and knowledge could mean the end of everything...or a new beginning.

books2read.com/quiver

Authors 4 Authors Publishing

A publishing company for authors, run by authors, blending the best of traditional and independent publishing

We specialize in speculative fiction: science fiction, fantasy, paranormal, and romance. Get lost in another world!

Check out our collection at https://books2read.com/rl/a4a
or visit Authors4AuthorsPublishing.com/books

For updates, scan the QR code or visit our website to join our semi-monthly newsletter!

Want more romantic fantasy? We recommend:

KISS OF TREASON
by Brandi Spencer

Two forbidden lovers share the rare gift to heal others with a kiss—but at a cost. Odelia's life has been a lie. When the queen tries to remove her from the palace, Odelia uncovers the truth. Now she must decide whether to forsake her people or embrace a destiny that would pit her against the current heir to the throne...her best friend. Though her only hope of avoiding a civil war lies in winning his heart, revealing her secrets too soon could cost both their lives. And a kiss might not be strong enough to save them...

books2read.com/kisstreason